ONE BOY'S SHADOW

Ross A. McCoubrey

iUniverse, Inc.
Bloomington

One Boy's Shadow

This is a work of fiction. All of the characters, names, incidents, organizations, and dialogue in this novel are either the products of the author's imagination or are used fictitiously.

iUniverse books may be ordered through booksellers or by contacting:

iUniverse
1663 Liberty Drive
Bloomington, IN 47403
www.iuniverse.com
1-800-Authors (1-800-288-4677)

ISBN: 978-1-4759-0356-0 (sc)
ISBN: 978-1-4759-0357-7 (hc)
ISBN: 978-1-4759-0358-4 (e)

Library of Congress Control Number: 2012904939

Printed in the United States of America

iUniverse rev. date: 4/5/2012

Artist Name: Danik Tomyn
www.daniktomyn.com

Acknowledgments

It is with great appreciation that I would like to extend my heart-felt thanks to my parents, David and Margaret McCoubrey, and my sister, Katharine, for their un-ending support, love, and encouragement.

I am also fortunate enough to have some truly amazing friends: Rick and Daphne Debouver, John Dulong, Brandon Illsley, Jonathan "Richie" MacNeil, Odessa Taylor, Karen and Philip Townsend, and Michelle and Ryan White, who are always there for me with a kind word and a coffee when I need them most. Thanks to you all.

I would be remiss in failing to thank the teachers who believed in me even when I didn't believe in myself: Mr. Don Aker, Mr. Dave Stewart, Mr. David Ritchie, and Mr. Bill Hines. Thanks for reading all those essays, poems, short stories, and book reports. You have no idea how much your feedback meant to me.

I would like to offer special thanks to Cody White, for modeling for the book's cover, and to Danik Tomyn, a gifted artist and true friend, who designed and drew the original artwork for the cover of this novel. I can never thank you enough. Here's hoping this is just the first of our collaborations.

For Lukas

You are forever in my heart.

Where Claribel low-lieth
The breezes pause and die,
Letting the rose-leaves fall.
But the solemn oak-tree sigheth,
Thick-leaved, ambrosial,
With an ancient melody
Of an inward agony,
Where Claribel low-lieth.

—Alfred Lord Tennyson,
"Claribel: A Melody"

Prologue

I was fifteen when it happened—the life-changing event people talk about that helps define who you are. I didn't believe anything like that existed before then. But there were a lot of things I didn't believe in before that summer.

My name is Caleb Lincoln Mackenzie. I'm not good at describing myself, but I'll try to give you an idea of what I look like. Here are the facts: I'm about five feet six inches tall and 135 pounds. I've got green eyes, light brown hair (that looks blond in the sunlight), and a small scar on my right eyebrow from where a skipping rope slapped me when I was six. I'm a bit farsighted, so when reading things close up, I sometimes wear glasses. I've got an earring in my left ear (almost always a small black hoop), I'm kind of pale, and I've got size-nine feet.

I hope that gives you a rough idea of what to picture. If you'd prefer to picture some Hollywood heartthrob in my place, by all means do so—I promise not to be offended. Just remember, I'm a real person like you and what you're going to read really happened to me. I'm going to do my best to not leave anything out. It wouldn't be fair to you—or to the truth.

Chapter One

Two days after my fifteenth birthday (April 3, 2010, in case you were wondering, which makes me an Aries, if you're interested in my Zodiac sign), my parents sat me down at the kitchen table, along with my older brother, Blake, for a family meeting. Rain splashed against the panes of the small window above the sink on that dark Monday night. The old harvest-gold General Electric refrigerator made an annoying whirring sound as it attempted to keep the vanilla ice cream in the freezer hard. My dad wrapped his large-knuckled hands around his favourite blue pottery mug, with the slightest chip out of the handle. The steam from his cup of Red Rose was making ringlets in the air until they dissipated. My mother fussed with a shell-shaped plate she had put out with various kinds of store-bought cookies on it. Everyone was silent for what seemed an eternity. Dad took a sip of his tea and then, without taking his eyes from the table, said, "Boys, we're moving."

A lengthy conversation ensued. There were no dramatic screaming fits or cries of "I'm not going!" No one stormed from the table in an angry refusal to have any part of the move. There were no complaints from any of us. Everything was very clear. My father, Frey (in his early forties but looking older from years of hard, physical work and long hours), had taken a transfer from his job at the shipping warehouse. Instead of working on the floor of a warehouse, he'd be in an office. His

1

pay would be a bit better but his hours likely longer. The major incentive was that it kept him from having to be on his feet all day. Dad had hurt his left knee about five years back when he put our old brown Taurus in the ditch on an icy road (having been called in to work the late shift because some newly hired guy didn't show up for work). There were nights when his knee caused him so much pain, all he could do was sit up in the living room for the entire night and attempt to soothe it with ice packs or heat. The doctors had told him they could do different surgeries on the knee, but there were no guarantees that any of them would be successful and he would be laid up for six months while he healed. The idea of not working for six months was not an option to my father. Dad was the kind of guy who always liked to be busy. So, weighing his options, he got up every morning and went to work. Most days he found the pain bearable, but even if it wasn't a particularly good day, he never complained. Knowing what he did every day to provide for us and still come home with a smile on his face, how could any of us even think to argue about his new job and our having to move? Blake and I congratulated Dad on the news, and we all remained seated at the table for some time, discussing what was going to happen.

Dad was to start his new job on the following Monday, which only gave us a week to figure out a plethora of details. We would have to put our modest storey-and-a-half house on the market and find a new home in or near the place where Dad would be working, a small town called Stapeton. It was about a two-hour drive from where we were living on the outskirts of Halifax, Nova Scotia, and didn't have much to offer in the way of excitement, according to my father. Stapeton did, he pointed out, offer us all a fresh start in a scenic little area where it was still actually dark enough at night to see the stars. It sounded good to me. I felt ready for a change.

When everyone had gone to bed, I walked down the hallway to my brother's room and tapped on the door. I heard him mumble that I could come in. I opened the door and strolled over to sit on the end of his bed.

"So, pretty big news, huh?"

"Yep."

"Whattaya think? Really?"

He sat up in his bed and leaned on his right arm. Even late at night, with bed head and dark stubble, anyone could see how attractive my brother was. He was nearly six feet tall, with dark hair and broad shoulders. He was active in volleyball and soccer, and he swam a lot too, all of which were good things because he could cook up a storm and eat like a horse. He weighed about one-eighty and was well-toned. He was into sports like I was into cars—or anything with an engine for that matter—so he got six-pack abs and I got grease-stained hands.

"Well, I'm glad Dad won't be doing the manual labour anymore, so any complaints I might have about moving are pretty petty in comparison to his health. I mean, it kinda sucks that I won't get to graduate with all my friends next year, but that's about all that I'll miss about this place. How about you? You doing okay?"

I took a moment to respond to Blake's question "Yeah, I'm doing all right. Guess I'm actually kinda lookin' forward to moving. Be cool to have a new house—maybe make some friends. But I'm a little nervous, too. I mean, it's not like I love it here or anything, but it's familiar."

"True." Blake paused for a moment, contemplating. "Change is always a little nerve-racking at first, but you'll be fine. We're both gonna make new friends, and besides, even if we don't, I was on the computer earlier and I looked up Stapeton—turns out there's a lake really close by, so no matter what, you and I can go fishing and canoeing and stuff. Sound good?" Blake tried to show enthusiasm as he spoke.

"Yeah, that'd rock." I loved doing outdoor things with Blake. When he got his driver's licence, he borrowed Dad's half-ton (an Oxford white, 1995 Ford F-150 XLT) and picked me up from school, taking me for a surprise fishing trip. Dad had wanted to go too, but couldn't, due to work. And, selfishly, I was glad it was just Blake and me. Don't get me wrong—my father and I get along pretty well and everything, but it was easier with Blake. I could talk to Blake about anything, and I never felt stupid or embarrassed. There were lots of times growing up I'd wake my brother at night or find a chance to talk to him privately when I'd ask him all the pressing questions on my mind. Everything from: *"Blake, is Santa Claus real?"* to: *"Blake, how come my dick is hard every morning?"*

"Anything else on your mind, Caleb?"

"Hmm?" I had to snap back to reality, having let my mind wander.

"Anything else you wanna talk about?"

"Oh … umm … nah, I guess not. Not tonight anyway. I'm pretty tired, to tell you the truth. I just wanted to find out what you were thinking about everything."

"We're gonna be fine. Count on it."

"Yeah. I'm sure you're right." I got up from the bed and smiled. "Night, Blake."

"Night, bud. Get a good sleep."

I closed the door behind me and headed to the washroom before going back to my own room and to bed.

I looked over the walls of my small room. I'd be taking down my posters soon, carefully rolling up Sidney Crosby, the black Mustang GT, and *Bullitt* (the best car-chase scene ever filmed is in that movie, in case you haven't seen it), and packing them in cardboard tubes so they wouldn't get crushed on the way to the new house. I began to wonder what the new house would look like and where it was going to be. I got all keyed up thinking about it, and I couldn't wait for the weekend to arrive.

Mom had told us that we were going to look through the real estate papers on the weekend and work on finding a place. Everything felt so sudden and rushed, but that was what made it exciting. Our family normally plotted everything out so carefully. My parents were methodical and meticulous when it came to any significant event or purchase; for them to do something so hurriedly and unexpectedly was a surprise. I think we were all feeling a positive rush of adrenaline. I noticed my parents' light was still on when I went downstairs to the kitchen for something to drink at two o'clock. I could hear the mumbled sound of voices from beyond their door. I pulled out a chair at the round kitchen table and sat down with my glass of Graves apple juice. The sodium-vapour streetlamp spilled some luminance into the room and showed me the water still gently tapping against the window as the rain continued to fall. I finished my juice and went back upstairs to bed. It took me awhile, but eventually I fell asleep that night.

On Sunday afternoon, my father left for Stapeton. He had to start work the next morning and wanted to be sure to get a decent rest beforehand. He'd call when he arrived at his motel to let us know how the town looked and if he had seen anything of interest along the way.

After he had gone, I sat down in the living room with my mother and went through some real estate papers with her. My mother, Karen (who stood five feet four inches in height and weighed about the same as me, though, naturally, she carried it differently), kept running a hand through her shoulder-length dirty-blonde hair, which had just a bit of natural curl to it. She'd sigh every time she put aside another paper or saw the price of a house she liked that was out of our league. Whenever we'd find something we liked, whether feasible or not, we'd read aloud the description. Unfortunately, most were well out of our price range, but it was fun to imagine all the same: like winning the lottery or being the last person on earth—the things you could do. The places we could afford never sounded very appealing, so we needed some fun intermixed with our reality. We were still going through the pages when Blake came home from a friend's house.

"Hi, sweetie. Have a nice time at Mark's?" Mom asked as Blake hung his brown leather jacket up on the coat hook inside the door.

"Yeah, I guess. It's kinda weird knowing you won't be going back, though. Everyone was kinda awkward once I dropped the news. What have you two been up to?" Blake grabbed a Coke from the fridge and came across the hall into the living room with us. He cracked the can open and sat down on the faux-suede brown recliner.

"We've just been checking out the different places for sale in Stapeton and the surrounding communities. Your dad said that anything within a ten-minute drive to work is best. We don't want to live farther than that if we can avoid it," she explained.

"Want me to go online and see what I can find?" he offered.

"Maybe we can try that later on. Right now we're kinda swamped as it is," Mom explained as she picked up a pile of papers to emphasize her point. "But thanks for the offer."

"Finding anything good?"

Mom and I both sighed. "Well, this is the pile of possibilities," I said, pointing to a thin stack of three sheets to my left. "And this is a pile of the ones we like." I pointed to a much thicker stack on my right.

Blake laughed. "It can't be that bad. Let's see the possibilities pile."

I handed him the sheets, and he quietly looked them over. I watched his facial expressions as he flipped through the pages. He scrunched his nose at the first one, stuck his tongue out at the second, and rubbed his forehead at the third. "Okay, are there any of the other pile I can look at? I'm not too keen on any of these." That was Blake's polite way of saying he hated the short list and wanted desperately to find something better.

"Here I was thinking this was going to be fun." Mom chuckled in her anxious way.

"No worries, Mom. We'll find something great. I bet Dad will call and tell us about something he saw on his drive out today, or maybe we'll still find one in this pile," I suggested hopefully.

"That pile isn't any good to us; it's all places too far from the town," Mom said to Blake as he picked up some papers from the centre of the long, rectangular coffee table.

"Mind if I look at them anyway?" he asked.

"Feel free," Mom replied, getting up from the sofa. "I'm getting a coffee. You boys want one?"

"Nah, I'm good, thanks," Blake answered, holding up his can of Coke.

"No thanks," I said.

Mom went out to the kitchen and returned with her coffee to see Blake scrutinizing one of the data sheets. I could tell he liked what he was reading. Mom sat back down on the sofa, the cushion covered with newspapers separating where she and I sat.

"Find something?" I asked my brother.

"Listen to this: Well-maintained two-storey farmhouse on fifty acres of land. Three bedrooms, two and a half bathrooms, partially finished basement, screened-in porch, and large outbuilding. Situated near a stream at the end of a gravel road."

"That sounds awesome," I said, trying not to get too excited.

"Yeah, and very expensive," Mom added. "How much do they want for it?"

"One forty nine, nine."

"That can't be right. It must be two forty nine, nine," Mom stated. She put down her coffee and looked over at Blake, a faint hope in her eyes.

"See for yourself," he offered, handing her the page.

Mom studied it for a moment before saying, "Must be something wrong with it. There's no picture. I bet it's dilapidated or at least needs a great deal of work." She peered closely at the write-up.

"That doesn't necessarily mean it's bad, Mom," Blake said. "And it sure as hell sounds better than the others we can afford."

"Oh wait, there's the real problem." Mom placed the page on the table in a disappointed grumble. "This place is a good fifteen-minute drive from Stapeton. It's out in the boonies. That'd be one long bus ride to school every day. Not to mention the winter. Think of it—the end of a dirt road, we'd be forever and a day to get plowed out."

"Well, couldn't Dad get a plow attachment for the truck? He could plow us out himself. Or I could do it, and when Caleb gets his licence next year, so could he. This place sounds too good to give up on just because it's a little less convenient."

Sensing Blake's uncommon desire for something (Blake's a pretty laid-back, easygoing guy when he's not playing a sport), Mom picked the paper back up again. "It does sound nice." She paused, imagining the possibilities. "Tell you what: when your father calls, I'll ask him to take a drive out and look at the place. If it looks at all decent, we'll go and have a proper viewing of it. We're not going to rush into anything, though. And besides, even if it is great, it'll be up to your father whether we consider it or not. He's the one who has to drive back and forth to work every day. If he thinks it will be too much extra, then that's that. So don't get your hopes up, okay? I don't want either of you to be disappointed."

The page with the farmhouse was put on the top of the possibilities list, and we continued going through the remaining papers. I don't think our hearts were in it after that, though. We all had our minds on the house by the stream, the peaceful country home with land and trees and lots of privacy. I don't know how I knew we would be getting that house for sure, but I did all the same. I think we all did, almost as if it were calling us to it. It just felt meant to be. I knew we were all thinking the same thing, as no one spoke of the house all through dinner. We didn't talk about anything at all to do with the move until the phone rang as we were clearing the table. Dad had reached Stapeton safely and was telling Mom all about the town. Mom had a smile on her face the entire time. That was a good sign. Blake and I awaited the moment when she told Dad about the house. It took about five minutes before the conversation got to that point. Shortly afterward, Mom hung up the receiver and sat down at the kitchen table with us.

"So, what did he say?" Blake asked immediately.

"Well, he's there safely, and the motel seems half decent. There's a coffee shop just down the street, so he grabbed a sandwich for his supper and he was going to go for a walk to see what else was around. He sounded tired but happy."

"What about the house?" I wanted to know.

"He said he'd go take a look tomorrow after work. He didn't sound very enthused about the distance from the town, so I think we'd better really start to look more seriously at the other houses." Mom's voice was somewhat dejected. She tried her best to force a smile, but we all knew how predictable Dad was. Convenience was much more important to him than any aesthetic quality. He'd go look at the house to humour my mother (well, all of us), but he'd find something about it that he didn't like and that would be enough to cross it off the list. Blake and Mom seemed to abandon hope at that moment. For some reason, I believed that, for once in my father's life, he'd do the impractical thing. I was certainly hoping, anyway.

The next day seemed to drag on forever. Classes were painfully slow, and the hands of the clock didn't appear to move at all. Finally the bell rang signalling the end of the last period, and everybody thundered into the halls, heading for lockers or buses or girlfriends or boyfriends. I simply headed for the door.

I had gotten used to the kilometre-and-a-half walk home after school by myself. It could be lonely at times, but other days it was a welcome relief from the constant noise that I had been subjected to at school. Blake and I walked together most mornings, which had given us many chances to talk over the years, but coming home I was alone because he was involved in so many school activities. I went to all his games and meets, but on that day, it was just a practice for the track team.

As I walked home that Monday afternoon, I wondered if I would make any friends at my new school. Maybe I'd have to take the bus. Maybe Blake wouldn't get on the teams there. Maybe he'd be the star player. Maybe. Maybe. Maybe. There were so many maybes to think about, it made my head hurt. For the first time I began to get nervous about moving. I thought about the chance that maybe I wouldn't get along well at the new school and I'd have to deal with all sorts of bullying and garbage like that. At least at the school I was going to, I simply went unnoticed. I wasn't different enough to be picked on for just standing out, and I wasn't similar enough to just blend in with a group. I was, have been, and always will be, just me. I don't know how to be anything else. I like what I like, and I don't like what I don't like. The only people I wanted to please were my family members. That's all there was to it. I never understood what made other people my own age tick. Hell, I barely even knew myself or what made *me* tick. If nothing else, moving away would be a learning experience. And from everything I've ever read about it, as an Aries, I'm supposed to have a *tendency to like change in my home that stems from a desire to progress in life.* Who am I to argue with fate?

I spent the next three days waiting and worrying. Dad had called each night but hadn't mentioned anything about the house. We all read that as a sign that we should drop the idea and face reality. We sat around the kitchen table eating the tuna casserole that Blake had made. Mom was dragging her fork back and forth over a rotini noodle, which prompted Blake to ask, "Isn't it okay?"

"Hmm? Oh, yes. It's fine, hon. I was just thinking. Sorry." Mom smiled at him and put her fork down. "It's a lovely casserole. Thank you for making it." She took a sip of her water. "I'm just getting a little overwhelmed by everything. I think I'm going to call your father and tell him I'm going to Stapeton tomorrow. We talked about it the other night, and he said he'd like it if we could go around together to look at houses and things like that. Do you boys think you can manage okay for a day or two?"

"Yeah, you don't need to worry about us," I said.

"Couldn't we go with you? I mean, there's hardly any point to going to school here anyway. Once people know you're going, they almost look pissed that you're still around. I had one guy say to me today, 'What are you still doing here?'" Blake chuckled to himself. "Guess we're overstaying our welcome."

Mom rolled her eyes. "Well, normally I would say yes, but I really would like some time alone with your dad to discuss things."

"Is everything okay?" I asked. I always tended to read too much into everything.

"Oh yes, everything's fine. We just need to crunch some numbers, and we don't want to talk about finances in front of you guys. My parents did that all the time—well, actually, they fought about money all the time—and I swore I'd never do that in front of my kids. Not that your father and I fight," she added quickly on the end.

"Well, is there anything we can do to help while you're gone?" Blake wanted to know.

"Just look out for each other and keep the place tidy. You guys always do those things anyway."

It was true; Blake and I were both inclined toward neatness. We also knew that with the house going on the market, we had to make sure everything was presentable for viewings. We promised Mom that we'd be sure to take care of everything.

"You guys are going to love the house!" were the first words we heard from Mom the next evening. She was calling from the motel room while Dad was still at work. She talked so excitedly that I had to ask her to slow down. She was loud enough that Blake could hear every word from where he was sitting in the living room. He got up and grabbed an extension to listen in more clearly. Turned out Mom had even more good news. When she had gotten to the room, she found a note that Dad had left for her that informed her that he had made arrangements to view the house the following morning. Mom hadn't been able to resist the urge to go and have a look beforehand, though, and was telling us all about it.

When we got off the phone, Blake and I discussed Mom's enthusiasm. Both of us knew that Dad's one weakness was Mom when she had her heart set on something. We agreed that it was a foregone conclusion that the house would be ours, barring that it didn't need a tremendous amount of repairs. We both figured with our luck, the entire thing would need to be renovated, winterized, have all its pipes replaced, you name it. Still, we held out hope.

At quarter past three the next afternoon, both of us began to worry. We hadn't heard from Mom or Dad that day, and we thought they must be looking at other houses as the one we all liked wasn't going to work out. We had expected a call to let us know one way or the other. So you can imagine our surprise when we heard Mom's 2005 black Ford Focus SES ZX4 come up the driveway. We went to the back door and watched her run up to the house.

"Hey, Mom. We weren't expecting to see you back tonight," Blake stated, giving her a hug at the doorway.

She was grinning from ear to ear as she gave Blake a peck on the cheek. She turned to hug me, saying, "Hi, sweetheart," as she kissed my cheek, too. She sounded a bit out of breath but appeared really happy. She closed the door and said, "Okay—no time to talk. Go and pack some things for overnight."

Blake and I both smiled. "What's going on?" I needed to know.

"The house is just awesome. You guys are gonna love it. The rooms are big and airy. The lot is gorgeous. And the peacefulness of it all. Ohhh, it's heavenly."

"What does Dad think?" Blake asked Mom as she poured herself a cold drink of water from the Brita filter in the fridge.

"He didn't say too much at first, just got that little smirk on his face." We all knew that smirk well. It meant, no matter if it wasn't the most practical thing in the world to do, he just kind of wanted it all the same. He didn't get that look very often. "We agreed that if we both really liked it, we'd get you boys out to have a look before making an offer. We want everyone to be happy. It's a big step and the place will definitely require more upkeep than a house in town would, but we both thought it would be well worth it."

"What about Dad's commute to work?" I asked.

"He said he didn't mind the extra drive if he got to come home to a place that nice. He also said he'd look to get some sort of plow or plow attachment for the truck, which would likely mean some early mornings for you guys come winter."

Blake snickered. "Only for one year in my case. After that, it's all Caleb's job."

"Hey, I won't mind. If it means getting to drive, I'm in."

Mom looked at us both standing around the kitchen. "Well, come on now, go throw some things together." She clapped her hands to speed us up. "I told your dad we'd be there by seven. We're going out for dinner, and tomorrow morning we'll go see the house."

I don't recall ever packing so fast in my entire life. I threw in the first things that I saw in my chest of drawers. I grabbed my toothbrush and bolted down the stairs for the kitchen. Mom walked over to me and gave me another hug. "I think this is going to be the best thing to ever happen to this family," she said softly.

"Will you be happy there?"

"Oh, I think I'll be very happy there. There's a library in town I can volunteer at, and hopefully I can pick up a part-time job at one of the stores. I really want to get to know the community and take part in it. But that's only after we all get settled. Perhaps by the start of summer vacation." Mom let out a deep sigh. "Summer in the country on a dirt road. Just think of it." She looked genuinely pleased with the thought of her country home. On the way to Stapeton, we pulled every detail from her that we could.

Stapeton didn't have much to choose from for restaurants, so we went to a pizza place called Sam's. Dad sounded a bit tired, it having been a long week at work, but was otherwise in good spirits. As the meal progressed, the talk became solely about the house. Dad was never one to go on and on about anything, regardless of how much he liked it, so it was sort of like pulling teeth to get any kind of reaction from him beyond his basic statement, "It seems about right."

Blake and I shared a room back at the Kelly Street Motel, two doors down from our parents. It was one of those side-of-the-road, drive-up-to-your-door motels that seem to only exist in small towns and movies. The rooms had been recently painted taupe, with large framed prints of sailing ships over the beds. There was relatively new burgundy carpeting in the main room, and the fixtures were all decent, modern, and functioning. It was basic, but it was clean and smoke-free—it could have been a lot worse. There was nothing at all on television, so Blake and I played some hands of crazy eights before calling it a night.

When I came out of the bathroom after brushing my teeth, Blake was standing by his bed (the one closer to the door) stretching in his bright yellow Joe Boxers. My brother looked so strong and healthy. He had defined pecs where I had flat skin with nipples on either side. "I wish I had a better build," I said as he turned to face me.

"You look fine, Caleb. Don't be one of those assholes who's obsessed with body image."

"I'm not; I'd just like to feel better about myself, that's all. Not for anyone else, just me. I don't wanna be all ripped or anything, just, I dunno …" I wasn't really sure what I meant. Whenever I get that way, I trail off. I put my toothbrush back in my bag and climbed into my bed. The sheets were crisp and smelled faintly of fabric softener.

Blake crawled under his own covers. "Well, maybe you'll get involved with something that will help you put on some muscle. Sports are good for that, but so are things like canoeing, splitting wood, and shovelling snow. They can all help you bulk up a bit. Just be careful not to overdo it, cuz, like I said, you're fine the way you are. Lottsa people are attracted to skinnier guys anyway," Blake added.

"I guess."

I'm sure Blake could tell by the tone of my response that I wasn't convinced. He threw a pillow at me and turned out the light. It surprised me and I laughed.

"Jerk," I said, whipping it back.

The pillow smacked his head. "Oomph. See? You're plenty strong."

I was still chuckling as I said, "Night, Blake."

"Night, bud."

I awoke to the sounds of the shower running. Blake was already up and getting ready for the day. I glanced at the digital clock radio on the nightstand between the two beds. The large red numbers informed me it was ten minutes after seven. I yawned and rubbed my eyes, clicking on the radio. I squinted out the thin rays of sunlight that pierced through the space between the heavy curtains. The radio station was crackly so I tried to tune it in, but then gave up and shut the thing off. I swung my legs over the side of the bed and stood up. I stretched and scratched myself before going over to the window and pulling back the drapes enough so I could see out. The sky was a beautiful pale blue, and there wasn't a cloud in sight. I looked both up and down the street. From my vantage point, there wasn't a soul to be seen. All was silent, but peacefully so. The faintest hint of green was starting to show on the hardwood trees, and I hoped that there would be no more snow.

Out of the corner of my eye, I saw a young boy biking along the street, his silver BMX kicking up water from the puddles and spraying a thin line up his back as he pedalled away from me. There was a fair amount of moisture on the ground, and I knew the lawns everywhere would be muddy and soft. I didn't much care for the weather of spring, always raining and never really warm, but it meant that eventually summer would arrive and all would be dry and firm and ready for fun. Autumn, I must say, despite the fact that it leads to winter, is truly my favourite season of all. The world becomes so much more colourful and subdued. People actually notice nature and take time to appreciate it. I visualized long walks down wooded trails.

The shower stopped running, and my mind snapped back to reality. I was still standing by the window in my grey boxer briefs, holding back the curtain. The bathroom door creaked open and Blake stepped out, a white towel wrapped around his waist, his wet hair dripping over his chest and back.

"Hey, Caleb. Sorry if I woke you."

"No worries, you didn't." I let the curtain fall back into place as I made my way toward the bathroom.

"You were pretty out of it. I was afraid I was going to wake you when I slipped out."

"You went out?"

"Yeah. Went for a run."

"You shoulda woken me up. I woulda gone with you."

"I thought about it, but it looked as though you could really use the rest."

I must have been visibly disappointed because Blake quickly added, "Next time, though, I promise." He ruffled my hair and grinned. "Say, I forgot to pack my hair gel. Can I swipe some of yours?"

"Yeah, sure. It's in my bag. Help yourself."

"Thanks."

I went to have my first pee of the day, and as always, it seemed to go on and on. I had that odd, but not unpleasant, piss-shiver halfway through. When I came out of the bathroom, Blake headed back in, leaving the door open as he played with his hair.

"Think you'll meet someone special today or something?" I teased as he fussed with his hair (which was so short that it really wouldn't look a lot different if he didn't try to style it at all).

"You never know, do you?" He smirked.

I laughed. "I gotta admit, I'm kinda surprised at how well you're taking this whole thing. I don't know that I would be as willing to go if I had your life."

"Whattaya mean?" He finished playing with his hair and looked at me.

"Well, I mean, you're popular, and you've got lots of friends. You've almost always got someone you're dating, and now, for graduation year, you're gonna be with nothing but strangers."

"They'll only be strangers until I get to know them, and I plan to get to know people over the summer as much as I can—and during the last two months of this school year. We gotta make the most of our time here." He stretched his arms high over his head. "And about being popular, I don't give a rat's ass. I just want to be liked by people who like me for me. The friends I have now, well, most of them haven't turned out to be very loyal. Only people I'm really gonna miss are Randy, Simon, and Lucy."

"You must be almost glad you don't have a serious girlfriend right now."

"Sorta. It sure makes it easier to move without having to deal with a breakup or an attempt at a long-distance relationship—especially since I bet there are a lot of really nice, hot girls here too. And you know what always happens in the movies when a new boy moves to town—all the girls swoon over him." Blake grinned and flexed his biceps in a mock display of narcissism.

I chuckled. "God, you're such a schmuck."

He laughed.

I continued talking with Blake as he got ready. When he was finished with the washroom, I took a shower and got dressed. I headed down to my parents' room, where Blake had already gone. The four of us got in the car and journeyed into town for breakfast.

We pulled into the parking lot of a small restaurant just past the post office. The place was called the Black Cherry Barn, and true to its name, it looked like a barn painted with black cherry paint (complete with a white outlined long-stemmed cherry on the side wall, looking like a crime scene in a police photograph). We went in the side door and headed directly over to the booths at the far side of the eating area. I slid in next to the wall, and Blake sat next to me, across from our parents.

"This seems like a decent place," my mother said in her cheery first-thing-in-the-morning-I-wish-I-were-still-in-bed-but-I-am-too-excited-to-sleep voice.

"The food here is really good. I had three meals here last week," Dad told us.

A waitress approached our booth and slid paper placemats with historical facts on them in front of us, along with four sets of utensils, each set wrapped in a napkin. She seemed a bit surprised to see unfamiliar faces and caught me watching her expression closely. She laughed and said, "Don't mind me, I'm just not used to seeing faces I don't recognize—'specially so early on a Sunday morning. Usually we get the before-church crowd or the hangover crowd at this hour of the day."

We all smiled somewhat awkwardly.

"You folks visiting the area?"

"No, actually we're moving here. I just transferred to the warehouse," Dad informed her.

"Oh hey, that's great. My boyfriend works over there. Hell, half the town works there." She chuckled. I couldn't help but like her instantly. "My name's Doris. It's nice to meet you folks."

"Thanks. Nice to meet you as well," my mother replied. "We're the Mackenzies. I'm Karen, and this is my husband, Frey. These are our sons, Blake and Caleb," Mom said, pointing lightly to each of us as she said our names.

"Mmmm, mmm." Doris shook her head from side to side. "There are going to be some very happy girls in this town when they see you boys."

I blushed, and Blake laughed.

"Can I get you folks anything to drink? Coffee? Tea?"

"Coffee sounds good," my father answered.

We all agreed, and Doris said, "Four coffees, comin' up. I'll be right back with them and your menus."

"She seems friendly." Dad chuckled.

Doris returned some time later with a tray of mugs and a pot of hot coffee. She handed out the menus and proceeded to pour the steaming beverage into each of our white ironstone mugs.

"I'm sorry I kept you people waiting like that. I hope I haven't held you up from anything. I just can't help but talk whenever I see somebody I know. And when I see somebody I don't know, well I'm likely to never shut up till I do know 'em."

"It's no problem at all. We're actually putting in a little time before we meet up with the realtor anyway," Mom said.

"May I ask, what places you folks lookin' at? I know most of the people who've moved in and out of this town and might be able to give you background info. And if you don't believe that, maybe I'll admit that I'm just a little bit curious."

Dad replied, "Well, to tell you the truth, there aren't that many places right here in town we really took an interest in, so we've mainly focused on things in the surrounding areas."

Doris good-naturedly slapped Dad on the shoulder. "I don't blame you at all. Everything in town is rather plain, and the taxes are higher too." She stood with the pot of coffee in one hand and her other hand on her hip. We were all halfheartedly glancing over our menus. I had decided before I went inside that if they offered apple pancakes that I'd be ordering them. Luckily they were listed next to blueberry and banana as options. I liked blueberries, but bananas were evil. I hadn't eaten one since I was nine and took a big crunchy mouthful of one. That's right, crunchy. Now we all know bananas shouldn't be crunchy. Thankfully, I had the common sense to spit out my mouthful, only to discover a cluster of black worms. Suffice it to say, bananas and I have not gotten along since.

"Yeah, so we've been looking at places in the county. There's one we're quite taken with that's just lovely. Frey and I were there Friday, and we're taking the boys to see it today. Blake's actually the one who spotted the place to begin with." Mom pointed to Blake as she said this, in case Doris had forgotten which one of us he was.

"Whereabouts is it?"

"It's at the end of Wakefield Road," Blake answered.

Doris's expression changed, and she seemed to pale somewhat. "You don't mean the old farmhouse at the very end, do you?"

Blake gave her a quizzical look. "Yeah. That's the one. Anything we should know about it?"

"Umm … well … no, not really. It's just, well, no one's lived there in a long while." Doris put the pot of coffee down on the table and took out her pad and pen. "So, what'll you folks have this morning?"

An hour or so later, when we were back at the motel, I got the chance to ask Blake something I hadn't wanted to bring up in my parents' presence.

"Okay, so what the hell happened at breakfast? Whattaya make of Doris's reaction?"

"Hard to say. Maybe it was her dream home or something."

"I dunno. Seemed like something more than that."

"Think about it, though. She said she didn't even know the place was up for sale, which I betcha anything means that she was saving up and hoping to buy it herself someday. You heard her say how all the places in town are so boring and the taxes are high. Plus, she's got a boyfriend—they probably live together, and I bet they've driven out on weekends and looked at the place together and made plans for it in their heads and everything."

I nodded. "That makes sense." I thought about it for a minute. "Shit, we probably ruined her day."

"It's not like it was intentional."

"True enough." I took a deep breath and let it out slowly. "Still, would be cool if there was something really interesting about the place."

"Don't worry, I'm sure there will be."

Chapter Two

The drive out to the house on Wakefield Road was a long one, much longer than I had anticipated. Of course, as with most things in life, when you look forward to something, it takes a far greater length of time to arrive (like every Christmas until I was ten). I checked my watch as we made the final turn onto the dirt road. Fourteen minutes from the motel to the turnoff—and these were ideal driving conditions. I could just imagine the time it would take in the winter, and I frowned knowing that my parents were likely to be thinking the same thing. I put down my window a crack, and the fresh spring air wafted into the car. I could hear the robins and sparrows (along with what I would later identify and have become one of my favourites, the Northern Parula warbler) singing in the densely thick pocket of trees on either side of the road. There was a heavy concentration of birch trees on the outermost part of the wooded areas. Since they did not have their leaves yet, I could see far into the woods and spot the scraggly black spruce trees that absorbed all the light from the sky, making the core of the forest look cold and menacing. A chill ran up my spine, so I closed my window.

"Feels like it should be warmer," I said to no one in particular as the power window slid into place.

"It will be at the house. There's no shade around the place at all really. It just sits out and soaks up the sun. I think we'd be smart to put solar panels up—save us a ton on power." My mother said this cheerily as she turned around in her seat to see me as she spoke. She was always cold, and the idea of a warm house and plenty of sunshine appealed to her. I could already picture her out on the porch on hot summer afternoons, sipping iced tea with lemon and listening to the loud cry of the cicadas.

I was still lost in my thoughts when I heard my father announce, "And there it is, boys." I leaned forward and looked between the front seats out the windshield. The house was better than the picture I'd had in my head, and much to my surprise, appeared to need very little renovating at all.

The real estate agent was standing next to her vehicle, a maroon Dodge Journey, with large ReMax magnets stuck to each of the front doors. A big smile flashed across her face when she saw us getting out of our car. She had to be in her mid-forties, but she was wearing so much makeup it was hard to say for sure. She gave the impression of being professional—wearing a well-coordinated pant suit and silk blouse with a matching scarf—and spoke in such a manner as she exchanged pleasantries with my parents, introduced herself to Blake and me, and then led us up the front steps. As Judy unlocked the front door, she glanced over her shoulder and smiled at me.

"This house would just love to have two handsome young men living in it," she stated, still smiling. There was something unsettling about her smile. It took me a few minutes to discern what it was, but then I realized: it wasn't that it was fake, it was permanent—like it had been glued on. She'd been flashing that smile so many times over the years, it got stuck in place. I caught Blake's eye as we stepped inside the foyer. He bit his lower lip and raised his eyebrows. I chuckled.

"And here we are," she said as she stepped into the house, throwing her hand up in a grand gesture.

"Oh sweet, tin ceilings," Blake said. All four of us stopped and looked at him oddly. His face went a tad red. "What? I just think they're cool."

The wide foyer became the main hallway, narrowing after the closets to either side of the front door. Off to the left of the hall was a small room suitable as an office, den, or guest room. Across the hall was the living room, a very large space with heavy oak trim and a working fireplace. At the end of the living room was a connected dining area. The oak continued through there as well. The dining room connected to the kitchen via a short hallway. Actually, upon going through this secret passage of sorts, we found ourselves in what once must have been a pantry. A wall had been removed to make the room open to the rest of the kitchen, but I heard my father saying it wouldn't take much to put the wall back up. The kitchen was far bigger than I was used to. There was a long counter and an island that billowed out at one end to look almost like a thermometer when seen from above. It would make a perfect casual breakfast area.

A doorway went out of the kitchen at the back of the house. Not wanting to go outside yet, we headed to the hallway and ascended the staircase. At the top of the stairs, to the left was the master bedroom, with an ensuite bathroom at the back. Of course, my parents loved the idea of a large bedroom with their own bathroom. Who wouldn't?

The hallway went to the end of the house, but there were no other doors or windows along that way save for the small window at the end of the hall that overlooked the backyard. About three quarters of the way along, the hall branched off with a right turn. Going almost to the end of that hallway was a doorway, which opened into a good-sized bedroom with a large window that faced the backyard and a walk-in closet with a bookcase built on its door. The room was long and narrow, but I really liked it, even though it would need to be painted a different colour (the current mauve was pretty but hardly my taste). Back in the hallway, we went straight down from the door along the remainder of the passage, which, if looked down on from above, would almost form a lower-case 'h.' To our right was a doorway into a third bedroom. There were two windows overlooking the cul-de-sac. Otherwise, the room was completely empty, with no closets or built-in units.

"What's the deal with this room?" Blake asked Judy.

"It's another bedroom, or it was at one point at least. The last people who lived here didn't have kids, so they removed the closets and turned it into a games room. Apparently a pool table fit quite nicely in here. As you can see, the whole room was done with this lovely wainscoting," she pointed to where clear pine went halfway up the walls, with a deep ledge all the way around, "and special track lighting. They had it all set up beautifully, but they didn't end up staying for even a year."

"Why was that?" my mother asked curiously.

"Oh, well, there are a lot of stories. Some people just can't live in a house for whatever reason. It's too remote, it's too big, it's just not them. You know how some people can be," she replied. "A house that's perfect for one family just never seems to take to another. Or rather, the family never takes to it." Judy saw the puzzled look on my mother's face. "Tell you what I think, though." At this point, Judy was whispering as if there were other people around who might hear. "I think there was a little bit of cheating going on, and I don't mean with the billiards," she said with a sly wink that made my skin crawl.

"Oh," my mother nodded.

"Anyway, it's a great room, and I'm sure one of you boys would be right at home in it. Just picture a few posters on the walls, a bed, and a computer desk, and you're already moved in." Judy kept grinning as she ushered my folks back into the hall.

Blake gently grabbed my upper arm as I was starting for the hall. "Hey."

"Yeah?" I turned to face him.

"Dibs on this room, okay?"

"You're older; you get first pick."

"You sure you don't mind?"

"Nah. I want the other room anyway," I said honestly.

"Sweet." Blake smiled that killer smile of his and stood with his hands on his hips, visualizing what he'd do with the space. It was twice the size of his room back home.

Across the hall was the doorway to the other washroom, a spacious facility with a claw-foot tub at one end and a good-sized shower stall at the other. The toilet was along the far wall at the end of a long counter with a faux-granite top. Over the counter stood one of those big square, flat mirrors like a motel would have, complete with large, round lightbulbs along the top. (Blake and I didn't think too much of that, but it was a small thing and could be changed easily.)

"And so, this is the final room of the house, not counting the cellar," Judy announced.

We looked over the white porcelain fixtures and the blackish-grey accented trim. With the exception of the tub, everything was far too new to be in a house of its vintage.

"When was the bathroom redone?" I asked.

"Actually, never. It didn't exist at all until about ten years ago. The previous owner changed a lot of things. This room was actually a storage area, and probably a bedroom long before that. The former owner only summered here, and he often had overnight guests so he had the washroom put in to save them from going downstairs in the middle of the night or from having to go through the master bedroom to take a shower."

"I'm glad for that," Blake mumbled.

"Seems like an awfully large place for a summer getaway," my father said.

"Yes, well, the previous owner did stay here for a few months his first winter, but he decided he just couldn't handle it and rented an apartment in town. He checked on the place regularly throughout the winter to ensure that it was maintained until he was caught out here in a snowstorm." Judy trailed off a bit, and her eyes looked distant as she spoke. "But, anyway," she said, snapping herself back into it, "lots of work has been done here, and really, a person could move in tomorrow without a problem. You'd just have to have the electricity and phone hooked back up. Water comes from the well, so when the power is back up and running, the pump will be on again. Still, a person would probably want to have the well checked and the pump inspected properly just to make sure everything is kosher." Judy made an obnoxious snapping sound with her mouth as she smiled and winked again. Blake and I exchanged a creeped-out look.

"May we see the cellar?" Blake asked.

"Certainly. Right this way."

Half the basement was partially finished. I say partially as all that was done was a cement floor was poured and there were three bare lightbulbs attached to the ceiling. The stairs leading down to the cellar were wide and sturdy, albeit covered in thick dust and cobwebs. There was a heavy smell of dampness that reminded me of a used bookstore without proper air circulation and humidity control. It was an oddly comforting and familiar smell, but one I'd gladly be rid of by putting in a dehumidifier. It was easy to see that with better lighting and a good cleaning, from top to bottom, the room would make a decent area for Dad's little woodworking projects. There was ample space for a deep freezer and a built-in wooden rack for preserves. In the centre of the basement, there was a concrete block wall with a doorway in the centre. Beyond the doorway was the unfinished portion of the downstairs. The furnace stood in the middle of the room with a dirt floor and exposed pipes and wiring, including a large piece of conduit with numerous wires taped off that jutted out from the wall. (Judy explained that there used to be a generator in the barn that was hardwired to the house, but once the owner who had installed it stopped using the house in the winter, it became an insurance issue so he had it removed.) There were a few lights on this side as well, and it was encouraging at least to see the house had been upgraded with a two hundred amp entrance and a breaker panel. All the wires and pipes were clearly labelled with what my father referred to as "turkey tags" (small manila cards with a red ring at the tapered end). There being nothing else to really see or have explained about the space, we all headed back up the stairs. I saw my mom peek inside the small washroom off the kitchen, obviously pleased that she'd have a main-level laundry room, as there was just enough space for the appliances to go in.

The external property itself needed little explanation. As we wandered over toward the barn, Judy pointed out the rough boundaries of the lot, which, naturally, we would have to have officially surveyed. The only area that had clearly distinguishable property lines was where our driveway narrowed to the road. As soon as the first corner of the road began, the lot ended. Up to the corner was a thin line of lawn that we'd be mowing this summer. Behind the barn was a stream that, once crossed, led immediately into thick woods.

The barn was a structurally sound outbuilding, measuring about thirty-six by twenty-four feet, complete with hayloft and doors that opened upstairs over the main swinging doors downstairs. It was in need of a paint job, but it was the traditional red barn with white trim and black wrought iron hinges. It wasn't much to see inside, either. There were two stalls for horses, but from the smell of the place, I doubted there had been horses that lived there in a long, long time. I walked inside one of the stalls and felt the smooth, worn wood beams along the sides. Years of weathering the elements had turned everything inside a grey colour that reminded me of old driftwood. I returned to the large cement floor and pondered all the fun projects I could do out there.

All too soon, I found myself back in the Focus and starting along Wakefield Road. We were heading back to the motel, all of us talking about the house, the potential, the rooms. We talked as if we already owned the place. One thought kept nagging at me, though: *What was so bad about being storm-stayed in your own house for one night?*

My parents put a bid in for the house the next morning. Blake and I had managed to persuade our parents to allow us to miss the next day of school and spend another night at the motel in Stapeton. It didn't take all that much effort. We felt closer as a family than we had in a very long time.

Mom stayed by the phone all day in the motel room, anxious for any word from Judy. Dad was off at work, so Blake and I were left to our own devices. We asked if we could have the car and journey around town to get a feel for the area. Mom gladly handed over her keys and told us to enjoy ourselves, giving us twenty bucks for lunch somewhere. Mom was always freer with her money when she was excited and looking forward to something. "Just please keep your cell phone on," Mom told Blake as we got in the car.

Blake started the two-litre engine of the little Ford and backed out of our spot in front of room number five. As we headed into the heart of the town, the digital readout on the car's stereo informed us it was 9:34 a.m., still too early for some shops to be open, but that hardly mattered as we weren't really planning to do any shopping anyway. We were just out to get a feel for the town on our own terms—drive by the high school to see what it looked like, find the key points of interest and usefulness as we went along. We made note of where the banks, video stores, grocery stores, convenience stores, and gas stations were. Blake hadn't mentioned it to our folks, but he planned on dropping off resumes around town that morning. Not being sixteen, I wasn't likely to have much luck but I figured it couldn't hurt, and every place that Blake went into, I followed, handing in my own thin resume. My father had already gotten a mailbox at the post office in town in lieu of having it delivered at the end of the road. Dad was in town every day of the week, and he preferred the security of having his mail at the post office, so we used that mailing address and Blake's cell phone number on our paperwork.

After handing out some resumes and filling in applications, Blake decided it was time for a break. He parked the car along the shoulder of the central street through the main commercial district of the town. The air was warm for so early in the day, and the sun was breaking through the clouds. Outside the car, the world smelled damp and earthy, with the faintest hint of chlorine, making me picture a kid's plastic wading pool sitting out in a backyard with grass clippings floating in its unmoving water. Some crows made their raucous calls in the distance, and some blue jays made their squeaky-clothesline sounds back at them. Dirty clumps of snow still hung on in certain areas where drifts were once thickest, litter clinging to the icy edges. It felt strange to walk along a town street that I didn't know. Stranger still to be there on a school day. I felt a sense of guilt for not being at school, like I was doing something bad. The fact that I had my parents' permission made no difference. It just felt wrong.

We walked along the sidewalk, not sure where we were going. It didn't really matter. We passed a large church (St. James United, the sign read. Services at 10:30 every Sunday morning. Everyone welcome) and then a collection of small stores. Once we had gone by Danielle's Dos (a hair and beauty salon), we turned left and walked over to the town park. The park was really nothing more than a large area of greenery in the centre of town. Four separate paths led to a stone garden in the middle (the remaining bits of flowers from the previous season all wilted and wizened from the harsh winter), which had bits of life in the form of crocuses pushing through the decay. There were wooden benches and trash and recycling cans at either end of each path; picnic tables were scattered throughout. Beyond the park was the high school—a large red-bricked structure that was filled with students and teachers at that hour on a Monday morning.

"Wanna walk over?" I asked.

"Are you kidding? No chance in hell. We'd look like idiots. We'll drive by later on, but the last thing I wanna do right now is have someone see the two new guys wandering around the school."

"Okay then. Where should we go?"

"I dunno. There's not much here really, is there?"

I shrugged my shoulders. "Nah, but maybe that's good."

Blake cocked an eyebrow at me. "Whattaya mean?"

"Well, just, maybe we'll find something we really like instead of always being just busy. Seems like we're always so busy keeping busy, we don't even have time to think if we like what we're doing."

Blake thought about this for a moment and nodded. "Good point."

We went back to the car and drove around the town some more before venturing out farther. Fifteen minutes from town was a decent shopping mall, so we went there and grabbed some lunch at the food court. I had been craving a Mozza Burger from A&W, so I made a beeline for the fast food joint as Blake settled on some independent little health-food setup, where he picked up a tofu sprout burger with feta cheese and black olives (he claimed it was really good). After lunch, we went into the music store and browsed through the new releases.

The mall was dead after the short boost over the lunch hour. Few people roamed the stores and hallways, mostly seniors and women with strollers. The scent of perfume from a display at the entrance to the Sears store mixed with the yeast from the Subway restaurant to give the mall an unpleasant aroma of leavening orchids. The air was so stale that it was a welcome relief to have the music oppressively loud in the store, as it distracted you from thinking about the odour. Also, the smell in the blackened walled world of CDPlus was more of a plastic one, with the added scent of dust burning on the incandescent lights overhead. I tried not to think of all these things as I flipped through row after row of compact discs, not sure what I was hoping to find.

I was still in a daze when Blake stepped up behind me and said, "Find anything interesting?"

"Nah, well, nothing I have to have anyway. How 'bout you?" I looked over my shoulder at him briefly before flicking through the choices again.

"Yeah. I need some tunes with energy. Gonna get some Kesha, Adam Lambert, Nickelback, and some classic Tea Party," Blake said as he eyed more titles. "You see anything you want, let me know and I'll get it for you."

"Get it for me?" I asked, surprised.

"Yeah, sure."

"Why?"

"Cuz I feel like it. Besides, they're going out of business; everything's dirt cheap." Blake smiled and walked down the aisle.

"Thanks," I said in a whisper as he strolled away.

I continued scanning the titles until I found one I wanted in the new releases. A few minutes later, after double-checking other possibilities, I headed over to Blake with my selection. He saw that I had a disc in my hand and said, "Oh, cool. You found one. Whatcha gonna get?"

I handed him the case and waited for some sort of comment about my choice. "Right on. Just be a sec," he stated and walked up to the cash register. I waited while he bought the music, and then we started out for the car.

"Thanks again for the CD," I said as we got back on the main road heading toward the motel.

"No prob. Didn't realize you liked Justin Bieber." I was glad to not detect any criticism in his voice.

"Yeah, well, I've got that song 'Eenie Meenie' stuck in my head, and I kinda like it. Dumb, huh?"

"Why's it dumb?"

"I dunno, just figured you'd think it was."

Blake shook his head. "I like that song, too. Put it in if you want." Blake motioned toward the stereo with his head.

"No, thanks. I don't feel much like listening to it right now."

Blake eyed me carefully, taking his eyes from the road for only a split second. "Something bugging you, little bro?"

All I could think about was the house. I wanted to be there. I wanted to be home. I wanted to find out why we were able to afford it. I needed to know why the previous owner couldn't stay there in the winters. Why no one had lived there year round in a very, very long time. "Huh? Uh ... well, no. Nothing really. Just some little things keep nagging at me is all."

"Like what?"

"Well, why do you think we're able to afford such a great place? And if we are, why aren't more people in line to buy it?"

"Who knows? I mean, it could be just that the location and the age of the house are turnoffs for a lot of people. Plus, you saw the houses for sale in the papers we went through—it's a buyer's market right now.

Prices are down, and there's lots to choose from. But, if you don't care about all that factual kinda crap, may I suggest one other thing?"

"What's that?"

"For once, luck is on our side."

We drove around the high school before returning to the motel, but it didn't look that much different than any other school we had seen. Lots of bricks, big dark windows, and not enough parking spaces. Cars were lined up on either side of the street and all the way along the chain-link-fenced wall of the soccer field. Parking wouldn't be an issue for us as we'd be taking the bus to school every day. I wasn't looking forward to that, but it wasn't that big a deal. By midafternoon, we arrived back at the motel.

Mom hadn't heard anything yet about the house. She told us how she tried to keep busy working on her puzzle book (she had successfully completed half the puzzles while we had been gone). She had kept the television on for company for part of the morning before turning it off and cracking the window to let some fresh air inside the stuffy little room. She tried listening to the local radio station for a while, but country music was really not her thing (it would take us all awhile to get used to the idea that we couldn't get a wide variety of different types of music stations in Stapeton like we took for granted in the city) so she had shut it off and listened to the passing traffic and the birds instead. She seemed glad to have us back and talked to us about our day.

Dad arrived home from work shortly before five o'clock. He didn't look nearly so worn-out when he came home from the new job as he had from his old one. He still suffered from pain in his leg, but he didn't appear to be hiding it as he always had in the past (when he could hide it, that is). He somehow just seemed more relaxed.

After supper (Chinese takeout we ate in Mom and Dad's room), Blake and I headed to our own room. We knew that no matter what happened, whether we heard about the house or not, we had to leave the next day to go back home. There was still a lot to be done there. I wasn't looking forward to packing everything up (a great deal can accumulate after being in the same house for twelve years) and all the fun of lifting and lugging the furniture and appliances into a cube truck and unloading and placing them all on the other end. I doubt anyone ever looks forward to that part of a move. I wasn't dreading it, as I knew that all my things would be going to a better place, that I'd have a bigger room with more privacy, and that, from day one, I was going to have my room just the way I wanted it—well, pretty much anyway.

I was lying on my bed watching a rerun of *Degrassi: The Next Generation* and thinking of how I was going to set up my new room when someone knocked on the door. I checked my watch and saw that it was five minutes after seven as I got up and headed for the door.

Chapter Three

After supper, I had changed into my old, faded-blue jeans and a long-sleeved, navy blue, button-up plaid shirt. They were comfortable and warm, but not something I would purposely wear out in public. I expected to see my father or mother on the other side of the door, so you can imagine my surprise when I opened the door and found a boy who looked to be about my age. He stood with closely-cropped, dark brown hair above deep brown eyes and the slightest little smile on his face, which exposed a dimple on his right cheek.

"Hey," the guy said, "my mom wanted me to run these fresh towels over to you. Said she forgot to leave bath towels this morning."

"Oh. Thanks." I took the towels from him, relieved that he seemed just as awkward as me.

"You guys moving in to the old Wakefield place, are ya?" he asked me, making polite small talk. He was stocky, not at all fat—just solid, reminding me of the wrestlers on the Olympics. He was a smidgen taller than me, about five feet eight inches I guessed, and he probably weighed about one-sixty. He didn't seem very comfortable as he kept shifting from side to side in his camouflage cargo pants, the chain connected from his back pocket to a front clip *thwapping* against his outer thigh as he moved. The hood on his black sweatshirt was squished against the stiff neck of his puffy yellow vest. He had an easy, *I-don't-give-a-shit* aura about him, and there I stood looking like I just jumped off a hay wagon. All I needed was a long piece of straw sticking out of my mouth to complete the look.

"Yeah, we hope to."

"Cool. That place rocks."

"Yeah?"

We both stood, not knowing what to say next.

"I'm Shane, by the way," he said, offering me his hand to shake. I wasn't used to a guy my own age shaking hands upon introduction. Usually when kids are introduced, they sort of nod and say "Hi" or "Hey" or "'Sup?" and nothing more. I looked at my armload of towels and stammered, "Uhhh," as I put them down on the chair inside the door. When I turned back to face Shane, his face had gone a tad red, and I thought I heard him say something under his breath that sounded like, "Idiot."

"I'm Caleb," I said as I shook his hand. "I didn't wanna drop the clean towels," I added dumbly.

"Yeah, well, there's always more if you need them—or anything else. Just come to the office and let us know."

"Thanks."

Shane stuffed his hands in his pants pockets, his thumbs left out—hooking onto belt loops—and rocked back on his feet. "Right. Okay, well, nice to have met you, Caleb. Have a good night." He walked backward a few steps and turned to leave. I thought I heard him mutter something to himself as he left.

"Hey, hang on a sec," I said, having no idea where I was going with it.

Shane spun around, the gravel beneath his sneakers making a gritty sound as it dragged across the asphalt. He didn't say anything but waited quietly for me to speak.

I didn't know what I was going to say, but I knew I wanted to talk to him more. "Um, I was just wondering, if you aren't doing anything, maybe you wouldn't mind showing me around the town or something." I felt like such a moron. What an incredibly inane thing to say.

I was relieved to hear him respond, "Sure."

"Cool. Just give me a sec, 'kay?"

He nodded.

I dashed into the room and yelled to Blake in the washroom, "Back in a bit." I grabbed my jacket and closed the door behind me. Shane stood in the same spot, all his attention on the pebble he was kicking on the ground. The air was cooling off at this time, and I could see my breath against the darkening night.

We didn't say anything to each other in those first few steps. As we started past the motel office, Shane said, "Just let me run in and tell my mom I'm heading out. Be right back."

"Okay."

I stood in the chilly night air waiting for Shane to return. I kicked at one of the million small stones left over from the winter parking lot sanding. I breathed into my hands and rubbed them together before deciding they were best kept in my pockets to keep warm. When I looked up from the stone bouncing between my sneakers, I saw Shane standing just inside the door of the motel office (which led into his house), watching me with a smile on his face. He opened the door and came toward me. "Having fun?" he teased.

I gave the rock one last kick and replied, "A blast."

"Come on, I'll show you what other exciting things our little town has to offer."

We began to walk toward the business area of town, talking about trivial things like the cold weather and the quiet streets. After what seemed like forever, we began to talk more casually.

"So, ahh ... which room is gonna be yours?"

"The one at the back of the upstairs." Thinking it an odd question, I asked, "You know the layout of the place?"

Shane smirked. "Yeah, well, I spent the night there once last year."

"Your family friends with the owner?"

"Umm ... no." He chuckled nervously. "See, it was early fall, and the people who were renting the place for the summer had left. Well, some guys at school dared each other to spend the night there. I kinda overheard the conversation—it was in the cafeteria at lunch—and they heard me laughing cuz they were all talking about the place like it was really scary and should be on that show *Most Haunted* or something. So this one guy named John, he's kinda the group leader, turns around and goes to me, 'You think you're so tough, I'd like to see you spend the night there.' So, of course, I had to put my money where my mouth is and said something clever to him like, 'Name a night.' Guess he thought he was really smart, cuz he goes, 'Hallowe'en.' After some discussion, it was agreed there would likely be cops checking on the place that night, so we settled on November tenth—the next day being Remembrance Day and not having school, so we could all easily make excuses as to where we'd be and all."

"With my luck, I'd still get caught and have a B and E on my record," I said.

"Yeah, well, I thought about that, and I told them that I wasn't going to vandalize anything to get in. John tells me there's a way to get in through a basement window that usually gets boarded over for the winter. All I had to do was pry off the boards and slip inside, next morning—nail it back in. So, that's what I did."

"Note to self: get that window replaced."

Shane laughed.

"Seriously, though, what's the big deal about spending the night in that house?"

"There isn't one, and that's just what I was out to prove. See, lottsa people around here claim that the house is, well, not exactly haunted, but it makes people feel strange." I raised an eyebrow at Shane. "I know, it sounds like some stupid hick-town nonsense, but there are some people who won't set foot near that place once the leaves start to change colours. Hell, some people won't even go there in the summer."

"But why? What's the story?"

We were walking by the town coffee shop. Shane stopped and grabbed my sleeve as I was continuing onward. "Hey, you drink coffee?"

"Yeah. Sure."

"Let me buy you a cup, and I'll tell you all I know about the Wakefield place."

I nodded. "Cool."

I followed Shane into the Stapeton Coffee Shop (which I would later learn everyone called Stape's) and up to the counter.

"Hi, Shane," the girl from behind the speckled counter said as we approached. She was likely three or four years older than us, with auburn hair and trendy new glasses with thick, dark sides.

"Hey, Heidi. Slow night?"

"You see it. We'll pick up when the game lets out." She was referring to the senior boys' hockey game at the arena. "Who's your friend?"

"Oh, this is Caleb. His family's new in town."

"Welcome to Stapeton, Caleb. What do you think of our fair hamlet?"

"Umm, well, so far everyone seems really nice."

She laughed. "Good answer. We're not much for excitement, but we're usually pretty nice."

I smiled, not knowing what else to say or do.

"You boys have a seat, and I'll bring some coffee over. Give me something to do."

"Want anything to eat?" Shane asked me as we headed to a table.

"No, thanks. I'm good."

I sat down on one of the swivel chairs as Heidi brought over two cups and saucers and filled them both with coffee. She placed two spoons on the table and said, "Need anything, just shout."

We both thanked her, and she headed back over to the counter. She picked up a novel from by the cash register and opened it to her bookmarked page. I could faintly hear her turn the pages of *Angels and Demons* in the background.

"Thanks for the coffee," I said as I rested my spoon on my saucer, having not needed it.

"My pleasure," he said as he poured a packet of sugar into his white (actually it was more greyish from years of dishwasher cleanings) cup. He added a single milk from the small dish of creamers on the table and stirred it in as well. He tapped his spoon two times on the side of the cup before resting it on his saucer. The only other sounds were coming from the humming of the display case where the pies and cakes turned on a spindle and a refrigerator somewhere at the back of the kitchen.

"Okay, let's backtrack. You need to know the whole story. Now, believe what you want, I'm just going to tell you what I've heard and been told myself. I'm not making any of this up—which isn't to say someone else didn't. Regardless, the place, Wakefield House, has character, and that, to me, goes a long way."

Shane pulled me in instantly. I didn't know why he was being so nice to me, but I wasn't complaining. I already felt like we were good friends. I sipped at my coffee, only taking my eyes off him momentarily.

"Taste okay?" he asked.

"Yeah, it's really good."

"You sure I can't get you anything to eat?"

"Thanks, but I'm fine. You go ahead if you want anything."

"Nah. Tell you the truth," he leaned in and whispered, "the food here pretty much sucks; I'm just addicted to coffee." He took a big drink and leaned back, continuing on with his story. "Anyway, back to the house. First off, the facts. This is the stuff that is true, not exaggerated or anything. Okay?"

"Fire away. I'm all ears."

Shane smiled and took another drink, carefully returning the cup to the indentation in the saucer with both hands.

"The house was built in 1927 by a man named Tavis Everett."

"Tavis? Never heard that name before," I said, interrupting.

"Yeah, kinda unusual. It's just Travis without the 'r.' Some people say it wrong, like the woman's name, Avis—but it's Tavis. Anyway, he built the place with his father, Leonard. Tavis had gotten married the year before, and his wife, Blythe, was pregnant with their first child. That's really important, so remember it."

"Gotcha. 1927. House. Pregnant Blythe."

Shane went on, "It was fall when the place was completed, and Leonard, whose wife had died the previous winter, stayed with his son and daughter-in-law that first year. It was a particularly harsh winter, and the location of the house made it even more difficult to get out and into town for the basics. The few cows Tavis kept had died, and his father came down with pneumonia that he never recovered from. During all this time, Blythe got closer and closer to having her baby. She kept away from Leonard for fear of catching something and making the baby ill. Tavis worked all day trying to keep his little farm from falling apart and looking after both his wife and ailing father."

"What an awful way to start out."

"It gets worse. About halfway through January, Blythe goes into labour, so Tavis rigs up the horses and heads up the road to get the midwife. Wakefield Road was a lot longer back then, and the midwife's house was about two miles from them. You probably remember seeing the large red barn a ways before turning onto your road." I nodded that I knew which one he was speaking about. "Well, there used to be a house there, and that's where the midwife lived. By the time Tavis returned home with her, Blythe was screaming upstairs. Leonard had been trying to get into the room, having fallen into constant hallucinations on account of the high fever he had developed. Tavis was able to get his father under control, and the midwife, I wish I could remember her name, I used to know it, anyway, she took over with Blythe."

I sipped my coffee but kept my eyes locked on Shane. I was absorbing all of this information and loving it. Although Shane could've been saying almost anything, and I think I would have paid close attention. He had a really interesting voice, and he spoke so much more intelligently than most kids my age.

"The labour went on for a long time, but finally, shortly before midnight, the baby arrived. Toby Joshua Everett. Tavis was ecstatic that his wife had a boy, and he headed into town, despite the hour and the weather, to celebrate at the local pub with his friends. When he returned shortly before dawn, he was quite drunk. Now, the story goes that when Tavis returned to the homestead, he discovered Leonard had found his rifle that had been hidden in the cellar.

"Nobody knows exactly what happened after that. The midwife had locked herself in the master bedroom with Blythe and the baby sometime after midnight when they heard the first shot. All that anyone knows is that Leonard spent the rest of his days, which weren't many, at the hospital with what would likely now be considered severely advanced Alzheimer's.

"There are many different theories about what took place that early January morning, but I don't think anything happened then. Nothing really important, anyway."

"Whattaya mean?"

"Well, some people have said that Tavis shot his father. Others say that Leonard was trying to kill himself. And then there's the third and most interesting theory. Some people say that Leonard was actually Toby's father and that Tavis somehow found out, so he went and tied his father in the barn during a snowstorm and it was being out in the cold like that that brought on Leonard's pneumonia. I personally don't believe that version at all, but it makes for an interesting twist, don'tcha think?"

"I'll say." I waited for Shane to continue. He took his time, finishing his coffee before going on with the story. I felt tortured. "So, what do you think happened?" I prompted.

"Like I said, nothing. Not then anyway." Shane leaned forward in his seat, resting his elbows on the table. "Flash forward sixteen years. It's 1943. Tavis and Blythe have two more children now. Their first daughter, Violet, was born in 1928. Their second daughter, Ivy, in 1930. Tavis is working at the steel mill that used to be located down by the waterfront. We're at war, and there's lots of work to be done in the industry. Tavis would have gone to fight, but he had poor vision in his left eye as he was nearly blinded when some cinders got in it a few years earlier. Toby was still too young to enlist, so he was taking over most of the chores around the house that Tavis used to do. Milking the cows, haying the fields. I forgot to mention, the sides of the road leading to the house were mostly all open fields, pastureland, before 1950. The new owners, not being farmers, they didn't keep the land cleared except for the meadow behind the house.

"Anyway, back to the story. In the fall of 1943, Tavis decides to take Toby hunting with him in the forest on their land. Tavis went hunting every year to help shore up the supply of meat the family would have for the winter. Toby had often gone on his own, but it was the first time the father and son had gone together because the other kids were finally old enough to look after things. Before that, either Tavis or Toby had to remain around the farm all the time. So, now that the other kids were able to tend to all the chores, Tavis and Toby packed up their rifles and supplies, planning to camp out in the woods until they got their deer. No one knew that when they headed down the path over the stream and into the forest, it would be the last time anyone ever saw Toby."

This revelation gripped me. "Whoa. What happened?"

"Tavis comes home the next day and barges into the house. He's yelling like a madman that he's lost Toby. Tavis explains to his family how Toby spotted a ten-point buck and went after it. Tavis tried to find his son, but there was no trace of him. He called and called for him and spent the entire day searching, to no avail. Toby had vanished.

"Of course, there are theories about this, too. Some believe the story as is and chalk it up to a tragic occurrence. After all, these things do happen. We hear about similar things on the news almost every day. Others think Toby ran away from home and joined the army, lying about his age to get in. And others suggest that foul play may have befallen the boy.

"Anyway, naturally, there was an investigation and a search, but winter weather hampered the efforts and a few days later Toby was slated as officially missing and presumed dead. There was a funeral, and everyone commented about how pale and pathetic Tavis looked. Shortly thereafter, everyone went back to their own lives. And, what with the war still on and all those missing boys overseas, they soon forgot about Toby. The Everetts stayed until spring, but Tavis couldn't handle living in the house any longer and the family moved closer to Blythe's relatives in the Canso area. Tavis never bounced back from the loss of his son and drank himself into an early grave. After that, no one ever heard from the family again."

"What about the new owners?"

"The next people to own the house were the mayor of Stapeton and his family. They thought by living out there, they could help expand the town limits and make a lot of money creating a subdivision for families, now that the war was over. But, as you can tell, that never happened."

"What did happen?"

"The mayor, fellow by the name of Stanley Hardwicke, moved his family out two weeks after Christmas. After living there for a few months, he said the house was too cold to be lived in during the winter. This was after he'd put in an all-new oil furnace and running space heaters in all the rooms nonstop. Said he didn't want his kids to get sick from the cold, so he moved them back in town and put the place back up for sale. A few more people tried to make a home of the place over the next few decades, but not one of them lasted through their first winter. Finally, a guy from Ontario, named Royce Stillman, bought the house and rewired the whole place, replaced the Hardwicke furnace, and installed electric baseboard heaters, as well as servicing the chimney and bringing it up to code for fires. He even hardwired a generator out in the barn and ran the wiring underground so if the power went out, it instantly would come on and keep the place heated. Royce stayed late into January and thought he had the problem solved, not being cold one day in all the time he was there. Then, according to stories, he was in the back bedroom one day—your room—and suddenly his teeth started to chatter. Ice formed on his freshly poured cup of tea, and a thick frost covered the windows. He presumed that the power was out and the generator had failed to kick in, so he bundled up and went out to the barn to check.

"As he stepped out the front door, he noticed that the streetlight he'd had installed over the driveway was on, which meant that the power wasn't out. He gazed at the lamppost for a few minutes to see if it was flickering before returning inside the house. When he opened the door, the house was lovely and warm. Upstairs, in the back bedroom, his tea now sat at warmer-than-room temperature. Everything seemed fine and as it should be, so Royce sat back down at his desk and skimmed over his work on the typewriter page to remind himself where he had left off. He was writing an article for the local paper about Wakefield Road and the house he was living in. He, too, had heard the stories and had studied up on the history of the place. And that's when things get weird."

Shane lowered his voice and leaned in closer to me. I could smell the coffee on his breath and the faintest hint of his deodorant or bodywash—a scent I didn't recognize, but liked—that was still clinging to him from the morning. I didn't say a word, just waited for the next thing to come out of Shane's mouth. "When Royce went to type, he found three keys in a clump by the ribbon. He unhooked them, thinking it strange that they should be stuck as he hadn't typed since he had come back inside. With them back in their place, he tried once more to type, and once more found the same three keys clumped together. This time he examined them closely. The three keys were the 'T,' the 'J,' and the 'E.'" Shane looked at me and, adding dramatic tension, held out the first three fingers of his right hand. He bent one finger down for each of his next three words: "Toby. Joshua. Everett."

I shivered in my seat, wishing Heidi would return and refill my cup with hot coffee.

"Shit," I said in a barely audible whisper.

"Royce tried to shake it off, just an odd coincidence, right? I mean, he hadn't checked the letters before, maybe they were three different ones … maybe he had miscounted. Maybe he just needed a new typewriter. We'll rationalize anything when we refuse to believe the truth. Still, Royce had a major case of the heebie-jeebies, so he went downstairs for a bit and made a fresh pot of Irish Breakfast. As the water boiled on the stove, he told himself he was being silly. Irrational. He laughs at himself for letting his imagination get the better of him."

"Um, okay, not to sound picky, but how do you know all these details?"

Shane sat back and took a drink. "Fair question. Like I said, a lot of this stuff could be fact mixed with fiction; I'm just telling you the story I know. I'm not elaborating on anything I was told. Believe me, the facts are good enough on their own without me making up more of them. But, with regard to all of Royce's actions that day, well, I heard it all secondhand, but my mom swears it's exactly as Royce told her."

"Your mom knows Royce?"

"Not really well, but he stayed at the motel—wait, I'm getting ahead of myself. I'll fill you in on the details later on, okay? I gotta finish the story first."

"Yeah. Sorry." I shook my head at myself, feeling like a tool for interrupting.

"No, it's cool, man. I woulda asked the same thing." Shane smiled to let me know he wasn't frustrated that I had thrown him off course. He leaned back in and continued. "Anyway, so Royce makes tea and takes a cup with him back upstairs. As he gets to about the halfway point on his way up the steps, he feels a sickening chill snake up and down his spine. He keeps going, trying to laugh at himself again, but not really pulling it off. At the top of the steps, his heart sinks a bit as he finds it cold again, not freezing like before, but nowhere near as warm as it should be. He decides the furnace isn't doing its job well enough, so he turns the dial on the baseboard electric heater and listens to it begin to lightly tick and hum into action. Satisfied, he continues down to his study—the back bedroom. He sits down in his desk chair after turning up the heat in that room as well. His work is progressing, and the room is heating up nicely. Having had too much tea, he needs to use the washroom, so he goes down to the end of the hall to the newly constructed bathroom. When he returned to the back bedroom, he stopped just inside the doorway, his heart jumping at what he saw—the room emptied, save for a pile of leaves scuttling along the floorboards. He managed to turn and run, not even thinking about it, all the way outside. He got in his car and was ready to take off, only to remember that his keys were still in the house and, worst of all, in the back bedroom."

"God, this is creepy."

"Hey, man, don't sweat it. Like I said, they're all just stories. Hmm. Maybe I shouldn't be telling you all this. I mean, you're gonna be living there." Shane suddenly looked guilty.

"No, it's cool, Shane. I mean, I'm gonna hear it all at some point anyway. Better from you than someone who's out to just try to scare me. Besides, I want to hear more. I think it's fascinating."

"You sure? I mean, the back bedroom is gonna be your room and all."

"Really, it's okay. Kinda neat actually. Besides, I don't believe in ghosts anyway."

"No?"

I shook my head. "Do you?"

"Well, yeah. I mean, not like white sheets saying 'Boo' or anything, but yeah, I believe there's something. I mean, there's gotta be."

"I dunno. Maybe. Tell me more—did he go back for his keys?"

"I'd hate to disappoint you and tell you he said 'Screw it' and walked to the nearest house and called a cab, which is what most people say they woulda done, but I don't think so. I woulda done just what Royce did. I woulda told myself I was just feeling off, and that, since I was the only one home, there was nothing that could hurt me inside that house. So, like Royce, I woulda gone back in to get my keys.

"So, Royce steps back inside the house and calls out 'Hello?' which is odd really, seeing as how he knew he was the only person there. He tiptoed back up the stairs to retrieve his car keys. He found the hallway empty and warm. As he made that right turn down the hall toward the back bedroom, he detected an odour in the air. He couldn't place it at first, but the more he inhaled, the more distinguishable it became. The hallway smelled like leaves. You know, that smell of dry leaves in the fall?" I nodded. "That's what it smelled like. Royce took a deep breath and turned to face the doorway of the back bedroom. He braced himself on either side of the doorframe, holding it with all his might as he peered around and looked down the narrow room." Shane paused for effect. "Everything was just as Royce had left it. He stepped inside and took his keys from the desk. Then he noticed the one thing that wasn't right. A single oak leaf was pinned under three letters on the typewriter. And I don't need to tell you what three letters they were, do I?"

"T. J. E.," I said.

"Exactly. Royce turned and walked out of the house, coming directly to the motel and checking in. He went back to the house the next morning, accompanied by a police officer. Royce made the excuse that he thought things looked out of place when he came back from being in town the other day and wanted the cops to check things out. Everything appeared to be in order, so Royce thanked the officer and proceeded to pack up his belongings. He closed the house up that night and didn't return to stay overnight until the spring. What should be noted is that he was never again alone overnight in that house. He was quite wealthy and was able to afford to hire a housekeeper. He also had many friends constantly staying for one or two nights, sometimes even a week or more, during the warmer months. He always closed the place the weekend before Hallowe'en and didn't return until the first weekend in May. If there was ever a chance of one of those freak May snowstorms, he came into town and stayed at the motel, getting a room for his housekeeper as well."

"Did he ever see any strange things again?"

"Just once, and that was by accident that he was even there. It was in March, just about eight years ago. The weather was unseasonably mild, so he thought he'd go check on his summer place. He felt brave, as it had been over five years since his fright and nothing had happened out of the ordinary since then. But, he had never been there alone since that time, either.

"He drove up to the house and unlocked the front door. The air inside was musty from being closed up for so long, but otherwise everything was fine. He recalled having left some of his housekeeper, Gerta's, mustard pickles down in the cellar, so he went down to get them. After grabbing the large Mason jar from the top shelf, he started back up the stairs, surprised to find the door closed at the top. Thinking it was the draft, he turned the knob and pulled, but found that the hook was through the eye on the other side. Naturally, you would think someone would have to have locked you in, but Royce remembered leaving the hook up against the doorframe and, as it was old, it stuck in a well-formed groove from years of doing just that. Royce told my mom how he hated the sound it made when it clanged against the wood if someone were to drop the hook in normal fashion. Anyway, Royce figured the draft that closed the door jostled the hook loose and it just so happened to fall through the eye—perfectly timed."

"Yeah. Right," I scoffed.

"Stranger things have been known to happen," Shane said, stretching in his seat, his back arching and his hands finding each other behind his head. He returned to his normal seating position and continued with his story. "Royce, not wanting to panic, knew that he could take the door off its hinges and get out. He went back down the stairs and put down his pickles, taking up the toolbox. As he began to work at the door, a storm started outside. March, as you know, is probably the most unpredictable of months, and it doesn't take long for a March storm to amount to a big mess. The hinges on the old door were rusted and seized, and unfortunately, Royce's can of WD-40 was under the kitchen sink. He worked away at the hinges as best he could, and almost two hours after he first went downstairs, he was able to free himself. This was only after he cut himself when the screwdriver slipped from under the top bolt on the hinge and took a hunk of flesh off the palm of his left hand.

"With no power, there was no water to clean the wound, so Royce took a bottle of Scotch from the cabinet over the fridge. He winced from the pain as the liquor spilled over his bleeding hand, and that's when he first looked out the window and the panic set in. He hurriedly put the bottle away and forgot all about his pickles as he darted for the door.

"He locked the house and ran to his car. The snow was deep and blowing wildly. Royce got his car started, no problem, but he had to wait for the defroster and defogger to do their jobs before he could see to move. As soon as he had any visibility, he edged along the road. Everything was white, and the road was slick. He went slowly, terrified of going off the road. He barely moved at all. He tried using his cell phone, but there was no signal out that far—and with the weather, those old analogue phones weren't much good anyway.

"As he got to the first corner, he just about cried out in frustration. His tires began to spin wildly under him. The car was not able to go farther. The only thing he could do was back up. He tried numerous times to get through the bad section, but the car slid backward on every attempt. He sat in the car, debating his options. He could try to walk to the road, stay in the car, or go back to the house. None of the prospects were good, but only one was viable. He had to return to the house and face his fears. As he went back, he told himself how he had been under emotional distress those years ago and that there was nothing really at the house to be frightened of. He'd prove to himself how everything could be explained with rational thought and sound reasoning. So, with a false sense of self-confidence, he unlocked the front door.

"He got a fire going and found some dry food he had left in sealed containers in the pantry. His hand was still throbbing, so he cleaned it again and wrapped it in a dish towel. He returned to the fireside with the bottle of Scotch and poured a glass. He was feeling rather pleased with himself, despite his circumstances. Everything was fine—until it got dark."

I thought of glancing at my watch, knowing it was getting late and really no one had any idea where I was. I resisted the temptation, as I feared it might seem rude. Besides, I was fascinated by the story Shane was telling me. I couldn't wait to get back to the motel and keep Blake up late retelling the story to him. I had been so intent on listening to Shane that I hadn't even noticed the other customers coming in and out of Stape's. I discovered I had a full cup of coffee again, and it made me realize that I hadn't been aware of Heidi either. How many cups of coffee had I been drinking all this time? Every time I went to take a sip, I got a mouthful. I was going to be wired.

"When darkness settled, Royce was a bit more on edge. He tried to remain awake as long as possible, but it had been a tiring day and his eyes soon gave in and shut. He fell asleep in his chair, but woke suddenly at half past three in the morning. He'd heard a bang from what sounded like the second floor of the house. He convinced himself it was a shutter loose in the wind or shingles ripping from the roof or just the house settling. No matter what, he wasn't going upstairs to check. He looked into the fireplace. Only embers there, still glowing. He got up to stoke the fire and put on some more logs, and that's when he became aware of something—a blanket slid off his body and landed on the floor. He picked it up and examined it closely. He didn't recognize the blanket as one of his own. It had a red and black checkered pattern and a faintly familiar scent to it—"

"Dead leaves," I whispered, finishing Shane's sentence.

The boy nodded. "Now, you'd think he'd be scared, but he wasn't.

First thing he did was call out 'Gerta?' half expecting to glance out the window and see her little silver Saturn in the driveway outlined in the moonlight. When there was no spotting her car, he called her name again. 'Gerta?' He'd not told her he was going to the house, but she knew her employer well after so many years and would likely recall their conversation a few days prior regarding the pickles. Gerta was a bit hard of hearing, so Royce lit a candle on a brass holder and, shielding the flame from any breeze, went up the stairs.

"He called for her again, thinking maybe she'd gone to sleep in her bedroom, the one at the front of the house. The second floor was frigidly cold, and Royce said he felt a heaviness in the air, a deep sadness filling him. He turned down the hall and headed for Gerta's room. As he met the doorway of the back bedroom, his candle flickered wildly. He turned toward the room to see what was causing the draft, and he swears he saw two people's shadows against the wall. He froze and tried to comprehend what he was seeing. He waved a hand in front of his candle, and only one of the shadows was disturbed—his. The other shadow seemed to move closer.

"He was so scared that he didn't turn away and run, but tiptoed back down the stairs and to his chair in the living room. He said the shadow seemed to slowly follow him along the walls. He grabbed his bottle of Scotch and made his way to the front door. He dared to set his eyes up the staircase to see the shadow standing in the centre. Royce locked the door and ran to his car. He swears he heard crying as he left the house."

"Whoa."

"The high winds had drifted the snow, so he could get his car up the road far enough that he could see the streetlight in front of the next house. He was able to slowly make his way into town and banged on our door at five in the morning. He never stayed in the house again."

"That's one helluva story."

"Yeah."

"But there's one thing you forgot to tell me."

Shane looked puzzled. "Oh?"

"What happened the night you stayed there? Is there any truth to the stories, in your mind?"

"Some people believe every word of these stories to be fact. Others, not an ounce of it. I leave it up to you to decide. Personally, I wouldn't give it much thought. When I spent the night there, nothing bad happened at all."

"That's good, as far as I'm concerned."

Shane laughed. "Yeah, I suppose it would be."

"So come on—what happened?"

Shane shifted in his seat. "All right, well, I went in through the basement window after school on the tenth. Other kids were there to watch me go in. They were going to stay in their cars overnight to make sure I stayed put. I had no intention of giving them the satisfaction of me running out of there, even if it was close to being hell on earth. 'Sides, I figured it was just me in an empty old house. No biggie.

"The cellar door, I had been told, was replaced the next spring at Royce's request. Despite the fact that he never planned on staying in the house again, he wanted the door replaced by a modern and unlockable one. This was good for me as I could access the main floor of the house easily.

"Once on the main floor, I went to the living room and waved out to the kids, letting them know I was inside. That wasn't enough, though. John pointed up and yelled, 'Back bedroom.' I nodded and went upstairs. I didn't notice any change in temperature up there, and I didn't feel anything other than a little guilty for trespassing and that I really shouldn't be doing this. But, oh well.

"So I go into the back bedroom—it's larger than I imagined from the descriptions people gave—and wave out from the window. John seemed angry I had made it that far, but it wasn't dark yet so I know he was counting on me still chickening out.

"Even though I wasn't scared, I didn't plan on getting any sleep that night. The other kids had said it was against the rules to take anything inside with me, but I had snuck in a mini Maglite, hiding it inside my sneaker until I got in the house. I knew the juice was turned off for the winter, and I wanted to have some light—just in case."

"I don't blame you. So then what happened?"

"Tell you the truth, I was pretty bored. I was inside, all alone, while I could hear the other kids outside laughing and having fun. I've felt like that a lot, though, so it wasn't anything new. I figured I might as well explore the place, so I wandered around the rooms and checked the whole place out.

"As the evening wore on, I found myself sitting in the corner of the back bedroom, holding my Maglite so that no one could see any light from outside. I felt cold and alone, but still not scared. I guess I fell asleep, because the next thing I knew, I heard a crow outside and saw the first crack of dawn. I went downstairs and opened the front door. The few kids that remained were asleep in their cars—mostly passed out from drinking. I went up to John's car and rapped on his window. He grumbled at me as he rolled down the window and spit out on the driveway. All he said was, 'I knew the stories were all bullshit.' Then he started his car and drove off. I was left standing there by myself. I went back in the house, shut the door to lock it, and slid out the basement window. I nailed it back in place and began my long walk home."

"Assholes didn't even give you a ride."

"Nope. But, whatever. I proved my point, and since then, all the mystique of the place has vanished. Kids never talk about it anymore. The last couple who had the place altered a few of the rooms, but they didn't last one month in the winter. When asked why they left, they said something about the place being too cold and remote and that they were feeling isolated and depressed. So, who knows? All I can say from my experience is that Wakefield House is cool." Shane smiled and took the last sip of his coffee. He noticed his watch and said, "Eek, guess I've been talking your ear off. Sorry. Hope it's not too late for you."

It was nearly eleven, but the time had flown by. "No, that was really fascinating. Thanks for telling me all that stuff. Neat to have a house with history."

"Yeah." Shane fidgeted with his spoon.

"Guess we'd better get going, huh?"

"Yeah. Probably."

I dug into my jeans and pulled out a well-crumpled five.

"Whoa, man. It's on me," Shane stated.

"Thanks, but that's not necessary."

"Really. It's my pleasure. You can buy next time if you want, okay?"

I grinned and stuffed the worn picture of Wilfred Laurier back in my Roadrunners.

Shane dropped a couple of loonies and a toonie on the table, and we left the coffee shop. We walked along the sidewalk to the motel and continued talking about Wakefield Road and my upcoming move. Once we arrived back at the parking lot of the motel, I had no idea how to properly end our evening together.

"Umm, look, I know we barely know each other and everything, but you're a really cool guy and maybe, once we move in, you could come over and hang out. If you want."

"Sure, that'd rock." Shane stepped up to his front door. "So, I'll see you at school?"

"Ahh, yeah. Guess we're gonna start next week."

"Cool. Your first day, if you want, we could meet up before class; I could introduce you to some friends."

"That'd be huge. Thanks." Neither of us knew what to say next. "Well, I'd better go," I said. I turned and headed for my room.

"Caleb?"

"Yeah?" I replied, turning back to face Shane, but still walking.

"Good to know ya."

"Yeah. You too."

Shane smiled and went inside. I couldn't help but feel pretty good about my evening as I unlocked the door to room number five.

Chapter Four

"Where were you all night?" Blake wanted to know as I removed my key from the door and entered the dark room. Blake had been watching TV, but he shut it off and clicked on a lamp as I stepped into the room.

"Sorry, I hadn't expected to be gone so long. I was just talking to this guy named Shane. His mom owns the motel. We went over town and got a coffee." I took off my coat and threw it over the back of one of the chairs. I kicked off my shoes, holding the edge of the dresser for leverage.

"Oh yeah? That's good. He seem like an okay guy?"

"Yup. He's cool."

"Friend material?"

"Yeah," I replied as I flounced on my bed. "I think so."

"Awesome."

"Penguins win?"

"Up by two in the third period. Wanna watch the rest of the game?"

"Gee ... let me think."

Blake snapped the TV back on. The score was still the same. We watched the game intently, and Blake casually mentioned, "So, our bid was accepted."

I looked over at my brother. He was trying not to grin.

"No shit?"

"No shit. We can move in this weekend."

I made a fist and rapped the nightstand twice. "Wow."

"Better make sure you get a good rest tonight cuz we're gonna be packing and lugging the rest of the week."

"That's the only sucky part."

"Ahh, nothing to it. We'll make it fun," Blake said, and I knew he was right.

"This is gonna be good, isn't it?"

Blake knew I meant way more than just the move. Even though I was happy, I felt anxious and nervous too. Blake could sense it. Maybe he even felt the same way.

"Of course it is."

"Know what time we're heading out in the morning?" I asked.

"After breakfast. Probably around nine. Dad's gonna stay on here and come home after work on Friday. Mom and Dad are both kinda stressing right now, so I figure the more we can do without being asked, the bigger help we can be."

"Agreed."

Seconds later, we were both cheering as Crosby scored and our boys all but locked up the victory, with seconds left in the game. I crossed my arms behind my head and stared up at the ceiling. Life was good.

We had a celebratory breakfast the next morning. The sky was dull and threatening to rain, but our spirits couldn't be dampened. I had a stack of apple cinnamon pancakes and a tall glass of orange juice. After a mouthful of syrup-drenched pancake, I said, "Last night I went over to town with this kid named Shane. His mom owns the motel we're staying at. He talked to me about the house we're buying and all the history of it and stuff."

"History? Like what?" Mom wanted to know.

Blake, sitting next to me, kicked my shin lightly. His facial expression did not change as he kept eating his bacon, but I knew from years of dinner-table conversations that that little kick meant, "Change the subject."

"Oh, nothing much. You know, just who used to live there, stuff like that. We mostly talked about how easy it would be to get stuck out there in the winter during a storm."

Blake nodded as he ate. I had filled him in on what Shane had told me after the game had ended. He'd found it all interesting but didn't think Mom and Dad needed to know all those extra tidbits of information regarding Wakefield House. He was pleased I had avoided telling anything to my parents that might cause them undue stress or discomfort. He should have known I had no intention of telling them all the stories; I just wanted to mention that I had met someone to hang out with and that the house had a name.

"Yeah, I best start shopping around for a plow for the truck," Dad said.

I took a swig of OJ and said, "Oh, one thing that's kinda cool; apparently everyone around here calls it Wakefield House."

"But weren't the original owners a family by the name of Everett?" my mother commented.

"Yeah, but it's been Wakefield Road since forever. Even when the Everetts built there, it wasn't known as the Everett place, always Wakefield House. Just one of those things, I guess."

"Sounds better than Everett House," Blake stated.

Mom, in a gushy sort of tone, said, "Never thought I'd have a house that had a name. It's so very English."

Dad rolled his eyes and chuckled.

The rest of that week was spent packing things up in and around the house back in the city. Mom had to go about getting our school papers transferred to the Stapeton school board and registering us for the remainder of the semester at our new school. She also had the unenviable task of finding a suitable realtor for the house.

Blake and I spent the bulk of our days boxing and sorting things. We ended up finally getting rid of a bunch of junk that we had no need to move. Sixteen bags of garbage and recycling went to the roadside by the time we were all done packing up on Saturday night. All that was left were the big furniture items that we needed to load onto the truck. Dad took one look at all that needed to be moved and said, "Screw it. I'll hire someone. We'll all be too tired for work and school on Monday if we attempt to do this all ourselves. We'll load up the essentials and camp for a few days until this can all be delivered."

It was decided that we'd pack up the half-ton with the basics and do just what Dad said—camp—for a few days. Mom would return on Tuesday night to let the movers in on Wednesday (Dad having called and arranged the time). When the movers were done, Mom would give the house one final inspection for anything that might be left behind and then give it a thorough once-over cleaning, after which she'd drive out to meet us and we'd begin our new life at Wakefield House.

Blake and I loaded up the truck early Sunday morning and started out for Stapeton by midmorning. Dad had already run off a set of house keys for each of us, so we were off long before our parents were ready to leave. Despite all the good that was coming from the move—the new house (which was both bigger and nicer than the one we had, and actually had a yard), the new job for Dad, and the chance for all of us to start over—I think my parents were a little sad about leaving the old house. After all, it was their home for twelve years. There were a lot of good times and fond memories there. I was the only one who didn't seem to mind at all leaving the place.

We sat quietly in the cab of the old Ford as we drove along. Blake began to reminisce about the little house in the city. "You know, I'm gonna miss the old house. I know it's just a building and all, but it's got a lotta good memories. I guess that's good, though. Means that when I think back on the place, I'll do so fondly." He kept his highway speed at a consistent 110.

"Learned to play basketball in that little driveway." Blake laughed. "I remember Dad setting up my tent in that tiny backyard and spending the night out there with me the week before I went to my first sleepaway camp."

"I don't remember that."

"Yeah, you woulda been six. I was eight. I remember I was really scared to go and Dad told me how much fun camping out with the guys could be, so he proved it by setting up that old orange vinyl tent in the yard and staying out there with me all night. We played games and roasted hotdogs and marshmallows over the little Coleman stove. I had wanted a real fire, but of course, being in the city, you can't do that, so we pretended the little green stove was our campfire." Blake licked his lips. "God, now I want a hotdog."

I laughed. Blake didn't say anything for a while, so I remained quiet. I tried to think of something special about that house that meant a great deal to me. I was left drawing a blank. I had lots of good times there, but I couldn't pinpoint a moment when I loved that house.

We drove on, the sky clearing off from the morning rain, the blue tarp flapping on the box of the truck where it wasn't tied quite as snugly as it should have been. The radio was set to a classic country music station that Blake only ever listened to when driving the half-ton. Don Williams was on singing about catching catfish.

"Kissed for the first time in that house," Blake said some time later.

"Oh yeah?"

"Yup. Becky Oates. She was over to work on a science project with me one weekend. We were in grade six. I had been thinking about kissing her all day, and finally I just did it. I said her name, and when she turned to look at me, I kissed her."

"What did she say?"

"She just kinda smiled at me, her eyes all big and sparkly. We kept on working, but when her dad came to pick her up, she gave me a kiss on the cheek and ran off."

"Did you two ever go out?"

"Nah, not really. It was grade six, after all. Nobody really went out. We danced a few times after that and hung out some on the playground, but that was it. Junior high came the next year, and we each were in different groups of friends. Now we're just strangers, really. But, every now and then, if we pass in the hall, we sorta smile at each other."

"That's kinda cool."

"Yeah. I'm gonna miss that."

"I wish I had some memories of the house like that." I felt rather down. Blake had done so much more living than I had. I always admired his ability to just be himself. Be natural. "Hell, I just wish I had a memory of a kiss."

Blake looked over at me momentarily. "Hey, don't sweat it, Caleb. You'll get there. You musta had times when you thought about kissing someone."

"Sure. Lots of them."

"So, what stopped you?"

"I just ... it's hard to explain."

"See, you're thinking too much about it. Think too much, and when you do finally kiss, you're gonna be so focused on what you're doing that you won't even enjoy it. Just shut your brain off and go for it. Odds are you'll remember it a lot better cuz it'll be good."

"Yeah, I'm sure you're right."

"Of course I'm right, I'm your big brother," he laughed.

"I'm just such a loser about this stuff."

"You're not a loser. And hey, when you do get your first kiss, I expect to be the first one to hear about it."

"You will be."

"Even if it's at 3:00 a.m., I wanna know."

I chuckled. "Yeah, you'd love to be woken up at three for that. I can just hear you. *You what? That's great ... but couldn't it have waited till breakfast?*"

Blake laughed. "Okay, well, you know what I mean, though. You can talk to me about anything at any time. Okay?"

I smiled at Blake. "Yeah."

My memory flashed back to a bike ride we took together when I was nine years old. I had hit the curb and flown over my handlebars, landing in someone's driveway. My knees and wrists were all cut up and bloodied. I was in a lot of pain. Blake had gotten off his bike and sat down in the driveway with me, holding me close and letting me soak his shirt with my tears. When I was done crying, he took the water bottle from his bike and cleaned my wounds, taking off his T-shirt and wiping away the bits of dirt and sopping up the blood. He tore one sleeve off his shirt and used it to wipe my tearstained face. I remember a kid going by slowed down to stare, and Blake angrily saying, "What the fuck you lookin' at?" It had been the first time I ever heard my brother use a big swear, and despite my pain, I remember thinking how cool he was. And how lucky I was.

There wasn't much more in the way of conversation after that. I didn't feel much like talking anyway. As always, I was analyzing everything. Sometimes I think so much about things that I feel sick to my stomach. I try to keep myself distracted when that happens. Reading a good book is my only refuge when I wake up in the middle of the night and my mind starts to race, but during the day, I can usually find some way of keeping my mind occupied. Working on engines always helped. I concentrated my thoughts on the fun I could have in that barn working on mowers and, hopefully, one day, a car. I don't know how much time passed while I was completely zoned out.

"Caleb?"

"Huh?"

"We're here, bud."

"Oh." I had been so deep in my thoughts, I hadn't registered that we had even gotten off the highway, let alone turned on to the gravel road leading to our new house.

"You okay?"

"Yeah, I'm fine."

Blake took a deep breath and let it out slowly. He stopped the truck and put the transmission into park. He took off his seat belt and turned to me. "Listen, I meant what I said earlier."

"I know."

He waited for a second and, seeing I had nothing to say, said, "All right, let's get this stuff inside before it starts to rain again."

I slid out of the cab and untied the knots on my side of the tarp. We dragged the cover onto the ground and dropped the tailgate with a thud. Blake went up to the front door, unlocked it, and removed an envelope taped to the door.

"What's that?"

"Dunno." Blake ripped open the envelope and pulled the letter out from inside. After scanning it briefly, he said, "Just a letter from Judy welcoming us to our new home." Blake folded the letter and stuffed it into the back pocket of his Old Navy carpenter jeans.

He returned to the truck, and we began taking boxes into the house. Every box was clearly labelled, and we took each one directly to its predetermined room. The boxes at the front of the truck bed, which were the last to be unloaded, had my name printed in black Sharpie on them. I made another trip up the stairs and, for the first time, entered the back bedroom as my bedroom. The room was, of course, empty. There were no signs of leaves and no odours that were out of place. The temperature was a mild eleven degrees outside, and it felt about the same inside, though inside the house was damper. The house had been closed up for some time, and the dampness and mustiness were to be expected and would soon dissipate once we got our things moved in, cleaned, did some painting, and cooked meals.

When I had placed the last box down on the floor of my room, I sat on it and looked over the walls. I heard Blake coming down the hall. He poked his head around my doorframe and grinned. "Break time," he said and handed me a cold Coke from the cooler.

"Thanks." I cracked the can open and took a long glug of the sweet cola. Blake hunkered down and sat on the box next to me. He looked around the room and said, "So, this is the famous back bedroom."

"Yup. This is it."

"Only thing scary is that god-awful colour." Blake scrunched up his nose at the purplish-grey walls. "Least my room is a nice dark green. I don't think I'll change it right away."

"Nah, your room is cool. I've gotta change the colour in here first thing."

"We'll go in to the Home Hardware after school tomorrow. What colour you thinking of?"

"I dunno. Not sure really. Maybe a greyish blue. Like a slate colour, or some nice chocolate brown—that would be warmer."

"That'd look good."

"I'm not sure, though."

"Well, we'll get some samples tomorrow and go from there. I'll help you paint whenever you want."

"I appreciate it."

"No prob. I'm gonna need your help building a closet in my room."

"Yeah. Next weekend's project."

"You got it."

I finished my Coke and said, "Sucks we have to camp until Wednesday. I hate sleeping on the floor."

"It's only a few days." He playfully hit my thigh with the back of his right hand. "C'mon, let's go down to the kitchen and grab something to eat. Mom put some sandwiches in the cooler."

We were still eating our picnic-style lunch (ham and cheese, tuna, and peanut butter with homemade strawberry jam sandwiches—all nice and cold, the white bread getting almost soggy from being near the ice pack) when Mom and Dad arrived shortly after two o'clock. They had packed the Focus up with everything they could think of to make the next three days easier: the microwave, a hot plate, the toaster oven, some kitchen basics, the sleeping bags, and some groceries. Blake and I had already plugged in the little bar fridge that we had kept in the basement of the old house, so we could keep a few things cold, like the soy milk and some meats. (Dad had been out Friday afternoon to make sure the power and phone were back on and to meet with the inspector to make sure the water in the well was safe to use. Everything was good to go.) We were camping, but we were having fun. It was almost like a mini family vacation.

That night I took a long, hot shower. I liked that Blake and I had our own bathroom to share. We no longer had to worry first thing in the morning that Mom or Dad would be in there, forcing us to run downstairs to the little half-bathroom just so our bladders wouldn't explode. The only thing Mom said to us was that we weren't to turn our bathroom into a locker room. We had to keep it clean and neat at all times. In fact, Mom said that with the way the house was set up upstairs, she felt as though she never needed to come down the hall toward our rooms at all—offering us a great deal of privacy.

We didn't turn the bathroom into a locker room, but we did have a pretty relaxed policy on usage. The only time we shut the door was when one of us was actually in there using the washroom; otherwise the door was open. I'd be in the shower, and Blake would shave at the sink. It helped cut down on time used up in the morning waiting for one person to finish before getting to begin your own routine. Plus, it was a good time to talk as we got ready for school. But I'm getting ahead of myself.

The first night in my room, I almost expected something to happen. Nothing did. I was too sleepy to fight my eyes from closing, so I gave in and lay there with my eyes closed and the faint sounds of a light breeze whistling around my window. In the morning, I woke early—just after six. The sunlight was pouring in through the panes of my not-yet-curtained window. I wished I'd thought to have tacked up a towel or something to block the light so I could get that last crucial hour of sleep. Knowing I was not going to get back to sleep, I got up and tried to work the kink out of my back. I heard a couple good cracks and walked over to the window. I squinted out the sunshine and saw my new view. Before my eyes stood a panoramic vista of beauty—the tawny fields that stretched out, bordered by rich green woodlands; the babbling brook cutting through the centre; and the sunrise, glowing coppery and vibrant over the entire thing. I caught something moving in the corner of my eye and found two deer sauntering through the high grass on their way to the stream for a drink of the crisp, clear water. I was glad the sun had woken me from my slumber. I had moved to a place where deer walked freely in my own yard, where I could stand at my window in my underwear and not fear being seen, and where I could really appreciate the simple wonders of nature.

I felt selfish watching the deer all by myself, so I ran down to Blake's room and knelt down by his head. "Blake! Blake!" I called out in a whispered yell.

He grumbled a bit and opened his eyes. "What's up, bud?"

"You gotta come to my room and see something. C'mon." I tugged at Blake's arm. He groaned.

"All right. All right. I'm coming."

Blake followed me down the hall to my room. I waved him over to the window, grateful that the deer were still there. "Look," I said as I pointed out.

"Oh, wow." Blake seemed as thrilled as I was, which made me glad I had woken him up. "What an amazing view."

"It's a good sign, don'tcha think?"

Blake smiled at me and ruffled my hair. "Yeah. I'd say so."

I was in the shower when Blake came into the bathroom.

"I'll be out in a minute," I called out.

"No worries. I'm gonna shave."

When I finished washing the shampoo out of my hair, I snapped open the door of the shower stall and nonchalantly walked over to grab my white, fluffy towel from the bar opposite the sink and counter. It was odd at first, I'll admit, having my brother see me naked. It's not that I really cared or was ashamed or anything; it was just something

I wasn't used to. I tied my towel around my waist and joined Blake at the sink. I took my toothbrush from the cup and squirted a gob of Aquafresh on it.

"They thought of everything except putting in a second sink," I noted.

"Hey, I'm not complaining. It rocks we have our own bathroom."

"True."

Blake held his neck, making the skin tight as he dragged the razor across the stubble. He ran the back of his hand over my cheek. "Grab a razor, Caleb."

Without a word, I took one of Blake's disposable razors from his black bag of toiletries. That morning he showed me how to shave. It'll probably sound silly to most people, but I felt kind of cool shaving with my brother. When we were done, I asked, "Honestly, do I look better?"

Blake put his arm around my shoulder and looked at the two of us in the mirror. "This high school won't know what hit 'em."

I laughed.

"I'm gonna take a shower. Sink's yours."

When I had gotten dressed, I headed downstairs. Dad was in the kitchen drinking a cup of coffee. Something seemed out of place to me, and then I realized what it was. No newspaper. Dad always read the paper in the morning, having it folded on the table in front of him while he drank his coffee and had his toast. I could see the crumbs covering his plate and knew the toast had already been consumed.

"Morning, Dad."

"Hey, Caleb. Sleep well?"

"Not too bad. You?"

"Like a log."

I went to the coffeemaker and poured myself half a cup. I made myself some instant oatmeal in the microwave and sat at the island counter to eat.

"Weird to see you without your paper."

"Better get used to it. I can't get it delivered out this far. Guess I'll have to listen to the CBC morning news."

"Did you bring a radio?"

"No. Guess I'll be living in ignorance for a few days."

I chuckled. "Speaking of living in ignorance … any idea how I'm gonna keep up with the hockey scores?"

This time Dad chuckled. "Already looked into it. Gonna have a dish put up next week, and you'll be happy to know we can actually get high-speed Internet out here, so that's coming too."

"You're the man," I said.

"I have moments." Dad smiled and took a sip of his coffee. In rare form, my father put down his mug and asked me, "How you doin', Caleb?"

"I'm good."

"No, I mean it. Really? You've been so agreeable to everything. Never complaining. I know this is a big adjustment for you, too."

"Everything's good, Dad. I mean it. I love the house, I've already made a friend, and this morning I watched two deer from my bedroom window. Honestly, I'm really glad we're here."

Dad gave me a warm smile and finished his coffee.

Blake and I were taking the truck to school that first day because Mom, despite doing everything else perfectly, had forgotten to get us added to the bus route. She said she would call and make the necessary arrangements to get us on the list, but until then, we'd have to take the truck to school. That suited us just fine. We felt bad about stranding her without a vehicle (as Dad would have to use her car to get to work), but she said she would be busy cleaning and putting things to rights around the house anyway.

School was to start at nine-fifteen, so we left the house at eight thirty, not knowing exactly how long it would take us to get to the school and figuring we'd have to go to the office and find out where we were supposed to go for our classes. I hoped that I'd have some classes with Shane so I wouldn't feel completely vulnerable.

Once we found out where our homerooms were, we headed out of the office and split up. Blake said to me, "Keep cool, bud. See you at lunch."

"Right. Take 'er easy, Blake."

Just about every kid I met in the hall looked at me, knowing I was new, that I wasn't one of them. The fact I was holding a piece of paper with my class numbers on it, making me look like a total tool, didn't help either. Lockers banged, and the public announcement system garbled out something about intramural floor hockey. The school smelled of dozens of different shampoos, deodorants, and hair gels applied that morning. The halls were wide and long, with orange and yellow locker doors in a pattern along either side. The school obviously hadn't seen a renovation since the seventies, and everything had a tired, worn-out appearance.

I headed up a flight of stairs and down the hall to room 285—my new homeroom. The door was open, and about a dozen kids were sitting around talking. Naturally, I didn't recognize a soul. There would be more kids coming as it was just a minute after nine, but the ones already in the room glanced at me and looked away again, probably just thinking I was merely passing through or dropping something off. I went over to the teacher's desk and handed Ms. Hastings my transfer papers. She smiled at me and said, "Nice to meet you, Caleb. Feel free to sit wherever you want during homeroom. I don't assign seats unless I'm forced to. I'll see you last period in the afternoon for science, and the rest of the day you follow around with your classmates and you'll find where you're supposed to be." She signed the papers and handed them back to me. "Good luck."

"Thanks," I said as I readjusted my hands on my shoulder straps. I walked over to a desk, close enough to the other kids that I didn't appear intimidated by them, but far enough away that let them know I didn't need them to notice me either. Ms. Hastings went back to busily making notes in her big red binder.

I looked around the room, thinking about how small it felt and wishing I was anywhere but there. One of the kids from the group, who was sitting on a desktop with his feet on the seat of a chair, turned around and said, "Hey, you gonna be in this class?"

"Yeah, you'd think with under two months of school left, they'd let me slide into an extended summer, but no dice."

He laughed. "That sucks, man. I'm Ryley. This is Adria, that's Hunter, over there's Drew, this is Laura, and that's Moira," Ryley said, turning and pointing everyone out to me. Each one smiled and said "Hi" or "Hey" in return. A couple of the girls put a hand up chest high and made a little wave, too.

"Cool. I'm Caleb."

"Welcome to Stapeton Junior High, Caleb," Ryley said.

"Yeah. Welcome to hell," Drew joked.

"It's not that bad, Drew," Laura laughed nervously.

"No, it's not that bad. It is ugly, way outdated, and the dances bite the big one, but it's our home away from home," Ryley said.

"So, basically, it's just like my last school."

Ryley grinned. "Yeah, you're gonna fit in just fine."

I smirked. Thankfully, the first few people I met seemed nice.

"So where ya from?" Adria asked me.

"Halifax."

"Ahh ... city boy. That explains the backpack."

"Huh?"

"It's no biggie, just the way you were carrying your backpack when you came in, over both shoulders and you were sorta leaning forward, pulling on the straps when you walked. Kinda a city kid thing, right?" Ryley noted.

"Umm, yeah. I guess. Never really thought about it."

"Whereabouts you living in Stapeton?" Hunter wanted to know.

"Actually, I'm a bit outside Stapeton, living at the end of Wakefield Road."

"No shit! You're living in Wakefield House?" Ryley asked loudly.

"Mr. Shaw, watch the language please," Ms. Hastings instructed.

"Sorry, Ms. Hastings, but Caleb here just moved into Wakefield House."

"Oh good. Nice to have someone living out there again. Such a beautiful spot."

"Not to mention creepy," Laura added.

"Had any weird stuff happen?" Drew asked.

"Nah. I heard all the stories, but I don't go for that stuff. It's just a house."

"Wait till you spend a winter there," Moira said.

I wanted to laugh, but couldn't. I didn't want to offend these kids in any way, and obviously they, for the most part, believed the stories.

"Tell you what, I ever do see or hear anything unusual, I'll let you know," I said.

Changing the subject completely, Ryley asked me, "So, what kinda music you listen to?"

From then on, everything was fine. My living at Wakefield House was a novelty, an interesting little bit of information. There were more important things to learn about me: what music I liked, what I liked to do for fun, and those other really probing questions that are important when you're fifteen. Proof, once again, that kids are the same, no matter where you go.

More students began to fill up the room. Soon everyone was taking his or her seat as the two- minute warning bell rang, meaning *get your ass to homeroom*. I was glad that when the bell rang, Ryley sat down next to me.

"This is just routine roll-call bull before first period. Whatever you do, don't say 'Present' when she calls your name. It's incredibly lame."

I laughed. "No worries."

As the final bell rang, the last of the students rushed into the room—Shane being one of them. He saw me and smiled.

"Hey, Shane," I said, glad to see my friend. He went to the back of the room and took one of the few remaining seats.

"You know Shane?" Ryley asked me.

"Yeah. Met him last week. We stayed at the motel."

"Right on. Shane's one of our group. You should hang with us at lunch."

"Thanks. I will."

"Cool."

At lunchtime, in the cafeteria, Ryley, Shane, and the rest of the gang filled me in on all the stuff I needed to know about the school. Blake found me, and I introduced him to my friends. He smiled and said "Hi" and went to hang out with a few people he had met.

"Oh, my God," Moira said once Blake walked away from us and across the room. "Your brother is a total hottie."

"Most definitely," Adria (pronounced add-REE-ah, in case you were wondering) agreed.

Laura was slowly dragging her scoop-side-down spoon out of her mouth as she said, "Damn. Girls, look at that ass."

They all looked over at my brother as he sat down with some other older kids. Moira focused her attention back at the table to see me chuckling. "Don't laugh. You're pretty cute, too."

"Yeah, he is. Let's see his butt," Adria teased.

"Oh, it's good. Checked that action out during third period," Laura stated.

I blushed and laughed it off. It was nice to be around people who were so relaxed. We kept talking all through lunch. And, before I knew it, the bell was ringing again.

When the day was over, I was standing outside by the truck, waiting for Blake. I didn't have keys to get inside the truck, and I didn't want to lean against it and get dirty from all the mud that had splashed up from Wakefield Road, so I paced around.

"Hey, Caleb," a voice I recognized said.

I turned around and saw Shane.

"Hey, Shane. Survived my first day. Your friends sure helped to make it easier."

"Yeah. They're a good group. Everyone sure has taken to you. Especially the girls. I could hear them giggling and stuff when I was at my locker."

"Anything I need to worry about there?"

Shane laughed. "No, they're all pretty harmless. Adria kept mentioning how much she liked your hair." He was referring to the fact that I still had some blond at the tips, which when gelled correctly, looked rather cool, but I had no intention of redoing them once they were clipped off at my next haircut. "I thought about putting some colour in mine. Well, actually I did and I messed it up, so I ended up shaving it all off. Made for a cold winter," he confessed.

I chuckled. "I'd be afraid I'd cut my head open."

"Yeah, well, it was either that or come to school looking like a complete douche, so I took the chance of personal injury."

I laughed. "Must feel kinda bizarre, all stubbly like that, though."

"Nah, not really." Shane took off his white Butler Bulldogs ball cap and said, "Feel for yourself."

I hesitated for a moment and then went ahead and placed two fingers on Shane's scalp. I rubbed them back and forth. "Weird."

He stood up straight and put his cap back on. "You get used to it. Sure takes care of ever having bed head." He smiled.

I saw Blake approaching with his keys at his side. "Hey, Shane. Need a lift home?"

"Nah, thanks. I like to walk."

"You sure?" Blake double-checked as he got into the cab and slid over to unlock my door.

"Yeah. Thanks though."

"See you tomorrow, Shane," I said.

"Call me later on if you want."

"Okay."

I hopped up into the truck and rolled down the window. "See ya."

"Laters."

Shane adjusted his backpack and turned for home.

"Good day?" Blake asked as he backed the truck out of its spot.

I rested my arm on the canyon-red vinyl of the windowsill and replied, "Yeah, it was a really good day. How about you? Any problems?"

"Nope. Not a one."

"There are some really cool people here."

"Yeah. You seemed to have met some nice kids."

"Yeah. Makes it a lot easier. How 'bout you?"

"I met a few guys that seem okay, and there are a bunch of really hot girls. For a small town, there's a lot of eye candy here."

"Yeah, that's the truth." I nodded and grinned. "Speaking of which, all the girls you met at lunch think you're gorgeous. Moira in particular."

Blake smirked. "She the one with the glasses? Kinda artsy?"

"Yeah. Why?"

"She's cute."

After dinner that night, I sat out on the front porch step and reflected about my day. I could picture Ryley, the unofficial leader of the group, sitting there on that desk in his perfectly faded Guess jeans and black T-shirt, with his slightly spiked black hair that was thin at the sides. He had blue eyes and a sense of natural self-confidence I envied. Ryley was good-looking and he knew it, but he wasn't cocky about it.

Hunter and Drew reminded me of the guys at my old school.

Hunter was shorter than the other guys, but he had a decent build and a very square jaw. Funny the things that stick out in your mind. He gave me the impression that he'd do whatever the group wanted, just to be sure he fit in.

Drew gave off the same sort of aura. He was taller than me and heavier-set. He had a surprisingly deep voice and soft brown eyes and hair.

Laura, Moira, and Adria all seemed very relaxed and easy to get along with, too. Moira tended to be a tad hyper at times and was apt to speak rapidly and incoherently now and again. She had auburn hair and dark-rimmed glasses, reminding me of one of my mother's Lisa Loeb album covers. Laura was blonde (dyed—she had dark roots) and tiny, both in weight and height. Adria had brownish hair and was a bit taller than Moira, being about the same height as Hunter.

I didn't get the impression that anyone in the group was dating. Everyone seemed to be just good friends. I could detect some attractions, though, and they all flirted with one another to a certain extent.

My mind kept going back to Shane. I'd never felt so comfortable around someone so fast before. Even though I felt good being around him, I always felt a little more vulnerable too—and that wasn't something I was accustomed to feeling. Not when I was with someone I thought of as a friend, at least.

I noticed, as I was thinking, that I was rubbing together the two fingers that had touched Shane's head. I could still feel those hard bristles of his hair and smell the faint scent of his cologne. I wondered what it was that he wore.

Blake came outside and sat next to me. "What's up, bud?"

"Nothin'. Just thinking."

Blake nodded and took a drink from his can of Coke. He offered me the can, but I politely refused it with my hand.

"Be nice when we get the stove out here and I can cook us a real supper. Microwaved meals just aren't the same."

"No kidding, huh?"

Blake gave me his patented, reading-me glance. "You okay, Caleb? You seem so far away these past few days."

"Hmmm? I'm fine. Just got a lot on my mind."

Blake swallowed some of his soda and played with the pull tab on the can's lid. "Maybe you should give Shane a call. Must be kinda nice to have someone your own age to talk to."

"Yeah. I might in a bit. I just wanna sit here for a while."

"Rather be alone?"

"Nah. This is good."

Blake smiled at me and turned his gaze to the dirt road in front of us and the field beyond. It was a warm evening, with a gentle breeze that brought the scent of hyacinth to your nose just long enough to enjoy its fragrance, without being overpowered by it. The spring peepers were making their calls that sounded like a million shouts of *"Pick me. Pick me."* The sun was just starting to set, and the sky was this amazing colour of orange. Everything about the time and place seemed to be perfect. As we sat together on the step, I thought about it and thought about it, and was just about to speak when my dad opened the door and said, "Suppose we'll get the rain they're forecasting?" as he sat down in one of the Adirondack chairs in the screened-in area of the porch.

And, like that, the moment had disappeared.

We only had one phone hooked up until the movers brought the others on Wednesday. I took the handset of the old black rotary-dial phone (it was in the house when we moved in, and it was hardwired instead of having a jack. My father had suggested ripping it out, but my mother had said she liked it so there it remained) off the cradle and sat on the counter as I flicked through the local phone book and found the number for the motel. Dialling was a ridiculously time-consuming process, and since there was no redial button, I hoped the line wouldn't be busy on the other end. I had no idea what I was going to say or what we would talk about, but I wanted to hear Shane's voice. I took a deep breath.

"Kelly Street Motel."

"Hello, is Shane there, please?"

"Speaking." He sounded so professional on the phone I didn't recognize his voice.

"Oh, hey, Shane. It's Caleb."

"Hey, man. What's up?"

"Nothing much. Just sitting here on the kitchen counter wishing it was Wednesday and all our stuff was here."

"Oh, you guys pretty much camping out till then, huh?"

"Yeah, it kinda sucks but ..."

I talked to Shane for almost an hour that evening. I honestly can't remember what all we said to each other, and I don't think it's really important. I just enjoyed having someone to talk to. When I hung up the phone, Mom came into the kitchen and said, "I don't think I've ever heard you on the phone for so long before. You and Shane have a lot in common?"

"I dunno. Some stuff, I guess."

"Does he like cars and fixing things?"

"I dunno. Cars, yeah. Not sure about fixing 'em."

"Does he like to write?"

"Umm. I think so. I'm not really sure."

Mom laughed. "I've never understood how, or what, men find to talk about for so long and still not manage to know anything about a person."

I shrugged my shoulders.

"I'm pleased you've made a friend already, Caleb. Once we get the place set to rights, feel free to have him out for an evening. I want you and Blake to have friends in whenever you want. This is a warm and happy house, and I want it full of people."

"You could have a killer party out here," Blake said as he entered the kitchen. "No one to complain about the noise, and tons of room for people to crash."

"Well, let's not rush into any parties," Mom suggested, "but having friends over is great."

"How about if I ask Shane over for the weekend?" I inquired.

"Sure. That'd be fine."

"Cool. Thanks, Mom."

I jogged upstairs and flopped down on my temporary bed. Having nothing else to do, I put in my earbuds and listened to my MP3.

Chapter Five

When I arrived home from school on Wednesday, still going back and forth with Blake in the pickup (there having been delays with the paperwork for the bus route), I found the house filled with furniture. The movers had arrived shortly after ten o'clock that morning, and Dad had been there to get almost every item put in its proper location. There was still the basic organization to do, but at least all the things were on the correct floors. Mom had arrived after lunch and had spent the better part of her day getting the kitchen and master bedroom set up, taking a break from one to work on the other and then going back again.

I was overwhelmed at first upon entering my room. There were piles of boxes and all my bedroom furniture splayed out in front of me. I dropped my book bag to the floor and let out a deep sigh. I wasn't going to be able to relax until everything was set up properly, so I immediately began to push and drag my stuff around. Blake came in and helped me move the chest of drawers and my desk, as well as helping me put the bed together. Once I had those things in the correct place, I went down to his room and helped him do the same with his things.

By the time I went to bed that night, I was exhausted. I had just about everything where I wanted it, and the room had come together nicely. I hadn't tacked up any posters yet because I still wanted to get the walls painted, but I was pleased with how things were laid out. My headboard was against the inside wall, so I could lie in bed at night and look out the window, my nightstand to the right of it. My desk was opposite my double bed on the outside wall, and my dresser was at the other end of the room, just inside the doorway. I had all my clothes put away neatly, hanging up most of my shirts in the large closet and using two of the shelves inside for the items I wasn't sure what to do with yet.

My curtains must have been put in a box with the things for the living room, which hadn't been unpacked yet, so I once again went to sleep with the moonlight flooding into my room and knew that the sunrise would wake me in the morning.

When I woke the next day, having had a sound sleep in my big comfy bed, I remained under the covers and glanced around the room. It wouldn't feel finished until I had the walls changed and my posters and things up, but it was starting to feel like my room. I reached a hand over my head and touched the wall behind me. It felt rough. I sat up and turned around, kneeling on the bed and eyeing the wall carefully. I could see the slightest line running down the wall, and there was a minute tear at the top where the wall met the ceiling. I stood up and pulled at it, surprised to find wallpaper peeling back in my hand. Someone had painted over the wallpaper instead of taking it off.

Slowly, not wanting it to rip apart, I peeled the paper back with both hands. I had to stop and move my bed out so I could continue. Finally, the paper tore, leaving a messy sawtooth design over the wall. The wall itself, however, was in good shape and, much to my delight, a pleasant shade of brown—a rich, chocolate milk-shake colour. I picked at the paper with my fingernail, trying to get it to lift so I could continue removing it, and eventually was able to grab hold and peel more back. By eight o'clock, I had nearly half the room uncovered.

After school, Blake helped me finish the project. We were very careful not to disturb the plaster underneath (all the other rooms had been redone with drywall over time) as we soaked and stripped the remainder of the wallpaper from my room. When it was all done, we patched a few small nicks and stood back to admire our work.

"It's a good colour. Still wanna change it?" Blake asked.

"Nah. It's good. I think I'll leave it for a while. I was actually leaning toward a colour very close to this anyway. Thanks for your help."

"No prob."

"Now I gotta figure out where to put my posters."

"I'm gonna go work on my room. Need me, just holler."

"Okay. Thanks."

Blake headed down the hall, and I went to retrieve my tubes of posters from the closet.

I took my time placing things. My Sidney Crosby posters (I have two, an action shot and one with him holding the Stanley Cup after their win against Detroit in 2009) went together on the inside wall. My Mustang went over the bed. The Penguins pennant went over the desk, and my *Bullitt* and *New Moon* (I had just finished reading all the *Twilight* books) adorned the other vacant areas of my room. I put my curtains up, finally, and decided that, for now, everything was done for decorating.

I unpacked my boxes of books and loaded up the shelf on my desk and the one built into the headboard of my bed. Most of my books were paperbacks, but there was the odd hardcover as well. I placed my Harry Potter collection directly above my head, the well-worn novels not exactly in mint condition from my repeated readings. Blake got me hooked on the stories when I was ten. The books were actually his old copies that he gave me. I still remember the first time I heard the story of *The Philosopher's Stone*.

Blake was in charge of looking after me while Mom and Dad had gone to a play with friends—*The Mousetrap*, I believe it was. Blake was babysitting for the first time, and I wasn't feeling well. Also, I was a little scared, as there was a bad storm starting and the power on our block went out. I was lying in bed, rather nervous, and feeling sick to my stomach from the onset of the flu. Blake came in and sat on the bed with me, putting a cold compress on my forehead. He left for a moment and returned with a book in one hand and a kerosene lamp in the other. He set the lamp on the nightstand and lay down next to me on the bed. He began to read to me from what he said was the neatest book ever. It was in those feverish moments that I first heard of Hogwarts and potions and magical powers. I fell asleep against my brother, my head on his shoulder, sometime later. He continued to read to me, night after night, until the novel was over—which you know, if you are familiar with the book, took a fair length of time. I savoured every moment of those evenings being read to by my brother.

When he finished the first story, he gave me the book and told me to start reading it again, from the beginning, by myself. That same night I turned back to page one and heard Blake's voice in my head reading me the story a second time. As the story progressed, however, his voice was replaced by my own, and I understood how the same story can change, ever so subtly, by merely the voice that you hear telling it. I've loved books and writing ever since.

I went down to Blake's room to see how he was coming along. He had almost everything finished, and the room looked awesome. He was busy at his computer when I came in.

"Hey, looks good in here," I said as I walked over to the desk.

"Thanks. It's coming."

"We online?"

"Yup. All systems go. I'll be off in a sec if you want to go on."

"Nah. Thanks. I don't have anything I need to do."

"Your new friends must have MSN or something. You can chat if you want."

"Thanks. Not tonight. I don't like hogging your computer."

"I've told you, you can use it whenever you like. If I need it desperately for some reason, I'll let you know. I doubt I'll be around much this summer to use it anyway."

"Whattaya mean?"

"Well, I'm waiting to hear back from this volleyball camp in PEI. If I get in, I'll be gone most of July."

"How come you never told me this before?"

"I dunno. I thought I wouldn't get in, so there was no point getting my hopes up talking about it. But I found out yesterday that they added five more spots, so I've got a pretty good chance of being selected."

"That's awesome. I hope you are." I meant it, but at the same time, I was going to miss having Blake around for a big part of the summer.

"I shoulda told you before. I don't like keeping things from you. Sorry."

"It's cool, Blake. Forget it."

"Anyway, if I do go, feel free to use the computer all you want this summer. Just make sure you update McAfee and hide any porn on your flash drive."

I laughed. "Not a problem."

For the first time in our new home, we sat around the table for dinner. We ate, from our good dishes, a meal that came out of the oven. After supper, I put the dishes into the dishwasher and went to the family room and clicked on the TV. The satellite wasn't hooked up yet, so we only received two snowy channels. I wasn't interested in either of the programs, so I turned the television off and went up to my room.

I called Shane using the only stored number in my cordless phone thus far. A few seconds later, he was on the other end of the line, and I invited him to come over for the night on Friday. He sounded enthusiastic, and we talked for some time before hanging up. I couldn't wait for classes to end the next day.

Shane and I waited by the truck for Blake to arrive after school had ended. Shane had tossed his sleeping bag and book bag into the truck's eight-foot box, and we made plans about what to do that evening. Blake approached the truck and unlocked his door. "Sorry I got held up, guys, but, for what it's worth, I got her number," he beamed.

"Whose?" I asked as we climbed into the cab.

"Sherri Witt's."

"Uh-oh … you better not let Ryley find out," Shane teased. "He's had a thing for her for years."

Blake laughed. "He's got good taste, but she's looking for a man, not a boy."

"I dunno, Blake. From what I hear, she likes the young ones. She was dating a ninth grader last year," Shane said.

"Maybe you just look immature to her," I suggested.

Blake smirked.

We drove along the road home, Shane sitting between us.

"I like this truck," Shane said as we bounced over a pothole.

"Yeah, it's Dad's baby," Blake stated. "This is our last day with it. Monday, we start taking the bus."

"Too bad you guys can't get your own ride."

"It'd be nice, but it's expensive—even if Caleb can fix a lot of the stuff himself."

"You fix cars?"

"Well, I do a little tinkering."

"You never told me that. How'd you get into it?"

"We had this old lawnmower that didn't work anymore, and Dad had put it out to the curb to get rid of it. I hauled it back into the shed and started to take it apart, trying to figure out how it worked. I dunno how, or why, but I found it interesting and kept at it and at it, trying different things, learning the parts, and piecing it back together over and over again. Eventually, I got it going again. Just trial and error mostly."

"That's cool."

"And we had this neighbour down the street who was always working on this old Corvair he kept in his garage. He let me come down on Sunday afternoons and assist him. I learned a lot from him about cars."

"So, you wanna be a mechanic someday?"

"It's definitely where I'm leaning. The community colleges have some good courses, and they're so much cheaper than university. If I can get my course and do well at the work placement, who knows, maybe I'll luck into a job."

"That'd be great."

"Yeah." I suddenly felt like I was dominating the conversation. "How 'bout you? What do you think you'll do?"

"I love to draw and paint. Recently I've started with charcoals. I think maybe I'd like to try art school, but I dunno, there's no money in it. Mom wants me to paint a picture for each of the rooms at the motel, but I'm not sure I want other people to see my work yet. I'll most likely go into accounting or something. I'm good with numbers."

"Must be nice. I suck at math, and I can't even draw a stickman," I stated.

Shane laughed. "I love to play the guitar, too. You play anything?"

I shook my head. "Nah. I was in band in grade seven, and they wanted me to play the trumpet. It gave me a headache so I quit."

"What about you, Blake?"

"I've always wanted to learn to play the guitar, but that's about as close as I've gotten. You play acoustic or electric?"

"Acoustic."

"Good man. Keep it pure," Blake said.

When we got to the house, I led Shane up the stairs to my room so we could dump our stuff before grabbing something to eat in the kitchen.

"Whoa, does this place ever look a lot better," Shane exclaimed as he went up the stairs. My mother was still busily painting in the dining room, making the room a much lighter, more inviting area by changing the walls to a honeydew green from the maroon.

We threw our things down in the corner of my room, and Shane said "Crosby fan, huh? I don't really follow hockey all that much, but I was glued to the TV for the gold medal game. That was intense."

"Tell me about it. US ties it up with like two minutes left. Goes into overtime, and Sidney snaps it in for the gold. So good."

"You into other sports, too?"

"I like pretty much everything, especially hockey, baseball, and football. You?"

"Baseball's cool. I'm a big NCAA basketball fan. I kinda jumped on the Butler bandwagon last year. I've got a soft spot for underdogs."

"Hate to tell you, but we're all Duke fans here."

"God. Next thing you'll tell me is that you like the Patriots and the Red Sox."

I laughed. "Not a chance. Cowboys and Yankees."

"Phew. Dodged a bullet there," Shane joked.

"Why? What are your teams?"

"In baseball, it's gotta be the Braves."

"Yeah. They're cool."

"And football, well, I don't have a favourite team. I like a lotta players on a lotta teams. If I had to pick one, I'd say the Steelers cuz that Troy Polamalu is crazy good."

I nodded.

"Into the *Twilight* series?" he asked, seeing the *New Moon* poster (it was mostly tones of black and gold with a full moon and a wolf howling at the top of a mountain).

"Yeah. I read the books before it got really big and, well, kinda got sucked into the movies, too."

"That's cool. I like them, too. Haven't read any of the books, though."

"Not into books?"

Shane shrugged. "Not really. I mean, I don't dislike reading or anything; it's just I find it takes me so long to read a book that if I'm not totally into it after the first fifty pages, I just move on to something else."

"What's your favourite?"

Shane stopped and bit at his left index finger. "Hmmm. I guess I'd hafta say *Redwall*. Medieval mice kick ass."

"I've read a bunch of that series. They're awesome."

Shane, changing the subject completely, as if a lightbulb had gone off over his head, asked, "Hey, you don't skateboard, do you?"

"Nah. I tried it once and busted my wrist. I figure I'm a better spectator. It's a great sport, though."

"Yeah, definitely. My cousin, Marty, is really into it. I've gone to some of his competitions. It's incredible. Some of those guys are amazing. Marty snowboards, too. He was the one that got me into it. I try to go a few times every winter."

"I've never done that."

"Oh, my God, man. You'd love it. It's really simple to learn, too. Next winter, I'll take you."

I smiled and nodded. "That'd rock."

"I like the colour in here. Sure beats the mauve."

I laughed. "Yeah, I didn't even have to paint. That awful colour was painted on wallpaper. All I did was soak and peel it off."

"Wait—you mean this is the original colour?"

"Well, I kinda doubt that. But it was the colour under the wallpaper. Why? Is there something significant about the colour?"

"Of course. A house like this, every single aspect has a story to tell."

I sat down on the end of my bed and gestured toward the wooden chair at my desk. He took the cue and sat down to tell me more, sliding the chair out and sitting on it backward, resting his arms on the back of the chair. He put his chin on his hands, and I noticed how long his eyelashes were as they caught the sunlight glinting in the window.

"Well, apparently, when Toby was twelve, he had a horse named Cocoa. She was an old mare that didn't have much energy left, and Tavis had been able to buy her cheap from another farmer. Toby loved that horse. He painted his room as close to a match to her coat as he could. He'd look out from his bedroom window and see her in the yard, and on nice nights in the summer, he stayed out in the barn with her, sleeping in the loft."

"That doesn't sound creepy or anything. Kinda nice, actually."

"It is, no question, but the following autumn, the horse got quite sick. Tavis had the vet out a bunch of times, but there was nothing really he could do other than suggest euthanasia, which, back then, most often meant a shot to the head. Toby was devastated, but being a farm boy, he was realistic about things. He spent one last night in the barn with her and said his good-bye before going to school. When he came home, the horse was dead, Tavis having shot her out in the pasture.

"Being a large animal, it was going to take some time to get her buried. Toby immediately went at it when he came home. Tavis tried to help, but the boy pushed his father away. It was something he needed to do on his own.

"The vet's son arrived a short while after Toby got home and, without a word, joined in the shovelling. The boys didn't speak the entire time and didn't finish the job until well after dark.

"Tired, sore, and with bloodied hands, they finished burying the horse. The vet's kid went back home, and Toby went inside the house. No one ever spoke about Cocoa again, but the boys spent a lot of time together after that, becoming best friends.

"Now, what does this all have to do with the paint? Right?" I nodded as Shane asked the questions before I could. "Supposedly the next owners of the house—that mayor's family, remember?"

I nodded. "Yeah."

"Well, they tried to paint over the brown, but the paint wouldn't take to the walls. Figuring they got a bad batch, they tried again with new paint, but the same thing happened. They figured there had to be something in the existing paint to cause the problem, so they papered the room with plain wallpaper and painted over it. I just assumed, after all these years, someone would have replaced the plaster with drywall. Guess not, though, huh?"

"It seems really strange that no one ever did. I mean, everything else in the house was modernized."

"Funny, isn't it? But there are a few possible explanations. One: people didn't live in the house long enough very often to bother. Two: the paper was thick enough that it covered all the plaster imperfections, so maybe a lot of people didn't even know that it wasn't done. Three: people, even the ones who did stay here, like Royce, tended to avoid the back bedroom or not use it at all. And four: maybe people always just liked it as it was. Or, hell, maybe it's just one big coincidence."

"It's weird: I was leaning toward painting this room a shade of blue, but when Blake and I picked out samples, look at the one I had decided on," I said, opening my nightstand drawer and handing the paint chip to Shane. He put it against the wall and saw the colour was an exact match. Then he flipped the paper over and read the paint colour's name.

"No way," he mumbled.

The paint was called "Cocoa."

We headed downstairs for a snack. I grabbed a bag of pretzels from under the counter and set them on the island. Shane and I crunched down on the salty knots as we drank our cans of Coke. My mom came into the kitchen, and I introduced her to Shane.

"It's a pleasure to meet you, Shane," Mom greeted him warmly. "I'd shake your hand, but I'm afraid I'd get you all painty." She showed us her hands covered in spots of latex paint to confirm what she was saying.

"I really like what you've done with the house. Looks great," Shane complimented.

"Thank you, Shane. It's been a lot of work, but it's a labour of love." Mom went to the sink and began washing her hands, scrubbing them hard with Fast Orange to get all the paint off. "Have you been inside before?"

"Umm, yeah. Once."

"Your folks friends with the owners?"

"My mom knew a guy who had it years ago, but no, we don't know the people who had it before you."

"We were fortunate that the last people did so much work to the place. Hardly anything that required immediate attention." Mom dried her hands on a raggedy blue towel and got a cold drink from the fridge.

"It's a great spot out here. Winters can be tough, but I'm sure you'll enjoy it."

Mom smiled. "What do you boys have in mind for the evening? Anything exciting?"

"Not really. Thought maybe we'd watch a movie or something," I replied.

"Are there any kinds of food you don't like or are allergic to, Shane?"

"Only thing I'm allergic to is cats. As far as food goes, I'm not too picky, but I don't eat red meat or pork." Shane laughed at himself. "Guess that does sound kinda picky, but my mom loves it cuz I eat every vegetable she puts in front of me."

"Is chicken okay?" Mom asked.

"Yeah. I love chicken."

"Good. I think we'll keep it simple and do Shake 'N Bake tonight. I'd appreciate it if you guys would set the table."

"Sure, Mom. No prob."

"I best get back in there and finish up. We'll eat around six thirty, so there's no rush," Mom said as she headed for the door.

"Ms. Mackenzie?"

"Yes, Shane?" she stopped and turned around.

"Thanks for asking about the food thing. I hope it's not a problem."

"Not at all. We're used to that sort of thing around here, aren't we, Caleb?"

"Yeah. Blake can't eat dairy and my dad is allergic to shellfish, so we tend to be careful about food."

"See, you fit right in. So don't give it a second thought. Okay?" Mom smiled warmly at Shane, and I knew she liked him.

"Okay."

My mother went back in to her painting project in the dining room.

"Your mom's really nice."

"Just outta curiosity, what's with the meat thing? Your parents vegans or something?"

"Nah. My mom eats meat. My dad did, too, but he died of cancer when I was ten. The reason I don't is that there's a history of heart disease in the family, so I'm being careful now about fat and cholesterol so I won't, hopefully, have issues later on. Plus, it kinda creeps me out—I mean, they're mammals and we're mammals …"

"I'm sorry about your dad. I had no idea." I had never mentioned his father before, and neither had Shane. I had assumed there had been a divorce or that he took off when Shane was an infant.

"It's okay, man. I shoulda told you before, but I don't like to talk about it much. It's kind of a conversational bomb to drop."

I was at a loss for words. I had never known someone my age whose parent had died. I knew of kids whose parents were divorced, but never one who had a parent die. I had no idea what to say or how to change the subject without seeming crass.

"See what I mean," Shane said after my momentary silence.

"Sorry, I just don't know what to say."

"It's okay, Caleb. Really. I know it must be weird to figure out how to say something after that, but it's really all right. We haven't known each other very long, but I knew when I first talked to you that night at Stape's that you were a good listener and that you're someone I can trust. Of all my friends, if I ever do wanna talk about my dad, I'll talk to you." Shane took a deep breath and let it out, changing the tone of the conversation after. "Right now, what I really wanna do is check out the DVDs you guys have."

"Sure. Follow me."

That evening we watched *The Transporter* with my brother. Mom and Dad spent their evening relaxing in the freshly painted living room, having a glass of wine by the fire and likely getting a little high from the paint fumes still permeating the air. At nearly midnight, Shane and I headed upstairs. Back in my room, Shane began to unroll his sleeping bag. He glanced around and asked, "Where should I put this?"

"I'll get the inflatable mattress from Blake's room. Be right back."

"Okay."

I went down to Blake's room and found him on the computer, downloading some pictures of swimsuit models.

"Hey, Blake. Can I borrow your blow-up mattress?"

"I'd say yes, but it's got a hole in it that I needa patch. Won't be much good to you tonight."

"Isn't that the same chick on your poster over there?" I asked as a woman in a string bikini, nipples just barely covered with little yellow triangles of material, appeared on the screen.

"Yep. That's her. Man, what I wouldn't give to nail her. I'm on MSN with Jordan. He gave me the link to this awesome site. Nothing but bikini babes."

"I'm glad I didn't wait too long to come down here. You might have been preoccupied," I joked.

Blake chuckled. "You might be right."

"You got anything else Shane can sleep on?"

Blake was still busily typing messages to Jordan. "Huh? Uh. No. Why don't you just let him sleep on your bed?"

"I couldn't do that."

"C'mon, he's in his own sleeping bag."

"Yeah. I guess."

"Goddamn. Would you look at the ass on that …" Blake said aloud as he clicked open another thumbnail.

"I'll leave you to your website."

"Okay. Have a good night, bud. Close the door on your way out, 'kay?"

"No prob. Night, Blake."

I went back to my room after shutting Blake's door. As I went up the hall, I could see Shane. He was back to me, taking off his shirt. "Whoa, that's cool," I said out loud as I entered my room, not meaning to.

Shane checked over his shoulder and grinned at me. "Got that last year." He had a tattoo on his left shoulder blade.

"My mom would kill me if I got a tat."

"My mom wasn't too keen on it, but she said, 'It's your body.' I don't want to get any more, I don't think. I just really wanted this one."

"Musta hurt."

"Nah, not too bad."

"Why a dragon?"

"I've always loved dragons. Ever see that movie *Dragonheart*?" I shook my head. "Anyway, it's one of my faves. Dragons are so strong and mysterious, and yet they have this tortured existence—well, in literature at least. Plus, I just think they're cool, and kinda beautiful."

"I used to have a dragon earring, but I lost it."

"I like the little black hoop you wear. I thought about getting my nipple pierced, but my cousin Marty, the skater, he got his done, and he said it was like super painful so I scratched the idea. 'Sides, you've gotta have a fairly decent upper body to pull one of those off anyway."

"There's nothing wrong with your build," I said.

Shane smirked a bit and rubbed the back of his neck bashfully. He was standing there in just his silver chain necklace with an ankh on it and his jeans, which were flattering to his physique. I tried to think of something other than him, so I quickly added, "but the air mattress, that's another story. Got a hole in it."

"Sucky."

"Sorry."

"Okay, well, if it's cool with you, you mind if I put my bag up on the bed?"

"Sure. That's fine. I'll try not to kick you off in my sleep. I've been known to thrash," I admitted.

Shane laughed. "I'll kick back if I have to." He spread out his sleeping bag on the left side of the bed and unbuttoned his jeans. He took them off and tossed them over on his duffle bag. He was wearing black boxer briefs with the Nautica emblem in the centre of the waistband. He unzipped his bag and crawled inside, partially zipping back up afterward.

"This place doesn't feel the least bit creepy to me anymore. Strange to think how people can be scared of a place that seems so ... normal," he said as he stared at the ceiling while I got out of my clothes. I was standing at my closet, my back to Shane and the room. I was well enough hidden by the dim light, the distance, and my stance, to hide the erection I was sporting (that would have been very visible once my jeans came off). I closed my eyes and tried to think of the most unpleasant thoughts I could muster to make it go away, but when you're fifteen, it really has a mind of its own and nothing seemed to help. I made my way over to the bed without ever being able to be seen face on. I sat on the bed and squirmed under the covers, snapping off the lamp as I did so. I stayed on my side, back to Shane, so I wouldn't pup a tent in the blankets that he could see.

"Never thought I'd be sleeping in here again," Shane said.

"I bet. Must be kinda weird."

"It's funny. It's actually kinda nice. I think not being alone makes a big difference." Shane was quiet for a moment. "Thanks for inviting me over, Caleb."

I rolled over on my back and looked at Shane in the dark. "I'm glad you came." My eyes adjusted to the darkness, and I could make out the lines of his face. "I never thought it would be so easy to make friends."

"I don't get it. You didn't have a whole bunch of friends in the city?"

"Nope. I mean, I had kids at school I could hang around with, but no one really that I trusted as a true friend. No one I could talk to about anything important. If it weren't for Blake, I don't know what I woulda done."

"Your brother kicks ass. I don't have any siblings. Always wished I had a brother."

"Blake's pretty great at being a big brother. He's taught me a lot. Like last week, he taught me how to shave."

"Yeah?" Shane reached over and ran the backs of the fingers of his left hand over my right cheek. "Smooth. Musta taught you well." My face tingled and I blushed, thankful for the dark room. "Those are the kinds of things I feel awkward about, ya know? I mean, how is my mom gonna know how to deal with stuff like that? What's she gonna do, demonstrate on her legs?"

I laughed out loud at the mental image. Shane laughed, too. "Seriously, though, it's something I think about. Like there's this kid in one of the classes, Gordon Hale, and his face is covered in fuzz, but I guess he either didn't know it or didn't know what to do about it until a bunch of kids starting making fun of him, leaving Fuzzy Peach wrappers on his desk and calling him names in the hall. He came to school one day, and he had all these cuts over his face from where he had tried to shave off the fuzz—and, of course, the kids made fun of him for that. Poor guy couldn't win."

"People are so mean."

"Yeah, and stupid. I feel bad for Gordon cuz, you know, kids will never let that die. That kinda thing sticks with people."

"Well, at least you don't need to worry about anything like that happening to you. You've got some cool friends who'll stick by you. Right?"

"Yeah. I guess. But, some things, some things are just harder to talk about than simple stuff like shaving and shit. You know? Like things that are really personal—they're weird to talk about with friends."

"Sure ... but I hope over time, we'll be good enough friends that we won't think anything is too weird to talk about."

"That'd be cool."

I yawned loudly. "Man, I'm tired. I've gotta get some sleep, bud."

"I like how you and your brother do that."

"Do what?"

"Say 'bud.'"

"We do?"

"Yeah. You call each other 'bud' all the time."

"I didn't realize that. I'll try to stop."

"No, don't. I like it."

"Oh."

We were both quiet.

"Caleb?"

"Yeah?"

"Have a good sleep."

"You too."

Our conversation ended, but I kept thinking about a ton of things. I was still awake when Shane's breathing became regular and steady—the sounds of deep sleep. It must be hard to lose a parent at so young an age. I could only imagine my grief if my mother or father died. It had to be difficult to go on living, but Shane seemed to do so admirably. I could understand his feelings of loneliness and being scared sometimes. It's not easy growing up for most of us. It's even harder when you don't have anyone to talk to.

I brushed my fingers over my cheek where Shane had touched me earlier. I knew I had never felt about anyone the way I felt about Shane. As much as it scared me, it also made me feel really good.

The next day was bright and sunny. The temperature was a balmy eighteen degrees, and the forecast was calling for sun all weekend. Shane and I slept in until almost ten before taking turns hitting the shower. When I got back to my room after my shower, I found Shane lying across the end of my bed on his stomach, still just in his underwear, listening to my MP3.

"It's all yours," I announced as I held my fluffy white towel firmly at my side, even though it was knotted well. I felt insecure enough without the added dread of having my towel slip down and exposing Caleb junior.

Shane took the headset off and smiled at me. "Good tunes. I love dance shit like that."

"Yeah? I'm not much for dancing, but I went to a mock rave last year and really liked the music."

"Mock rave?"

"Yeah, it's like the real thing, only it's in a place with lots of chaperones and junk. Supposed to cut down on the drugs and crap. They gave it this churchy name too, *The Brave Rave,* cuz I guess you're brave if you don't have to do drugs or something. It sounds lame, but it was fun."

"Why do people do that? Give stupid names to stuff? Just call it a rave and let people know there will be chaperones—leave it at that. God. It's like Safe Grad—great idea, lose the lame name."

"Exactly."

"Drugs are so stupid anyway. I've got this cousin, she's right into smoking pot. All she ever does is talk about it and meet up with other kids who do it. It's incredibly boring."

"You ever try it?"

"Yeah, a coupla times. Not my thing at all. It smells so frickin' bad, it made me wanna puke."

"Any of the gang into drugs?"

"Nah. Unless you call guzzling energy drinks and coffee being into drugs."

I laughed. Shane slid off the bed and said, "I'm gonna hit the shower."

"'Kay. Towels are in the cabinet."

"Thanks."

I waited to hear the shower running before taking off my towel and getting dressed. I surprised myself by gelling my hair—I never normally bothered on the weekend unless I knew I was going out somewhere. Most weekends I just wore my white Penguins or Cowboys hat.

I finished playing with my hair as Shane came back to my room. Water ran down his face in beads, splashing over his chest and continuing to trickle down to his navel. He was almost totally hairless except for a thin dark line below his belly button leading down toward his crotch. I tried to take in all this information in a split second so as not to stare at him and have him make some comment. Quickly and out of the blue, I said, "I'm gonna head down to the kitchen. Make us some coffee."

"That'd be great. I'll be down in a minute."

"What a great day," Shane said as he finished his coffee, placing the green pottery mug down by the sink.

"Yeah. Wanna go for a walk or something?"

"Okay."

I debated whether or not to put on my jean jacket but opted not to bother. It was warm and would likely get warmer.

"Could we check out the barn?"

"Sure. I haven't been in there since we moved down."

We headed outside and over to the side door of the barn. With nothing inside, the door wasn't locked. I stepped into the building and smelled the damp, closed-up air travelling through my nostrils. Although I hadn't noticed it the last time, I could detect an underlying odour of hay and animals.

"It's a lot bigger than it appears from outside," Shane said.

"No idea what we'll use it for."

"Be a killer place to work on a car or something."

"That's what I was thinking. I'd love to get some old beater and fiddle around with it. On those warm summer days, open the big doors at the front and be able to get a breeze as I work in the shade."

"I can picture you doing that."

"I dunno. It probably won't happen. Fun to think about, though."

"If you want it bad enough, you'll make sure it happens."

Shane strolled over to the stalls. "There used to be stalls along both walls in here. Royce ripped all of them out except for these two cuz he thought he might have a horse someday. The rest of the space he used for storage. Originally he planned on converting it into a garage and renting out a loft apartment up top, but as you know, he didn't stay year round and didn't bother pouring more money into the place."

I climbed the ladder to the hayloft and, still holding on to its rungs, called down to Shane, "You gotta come up here."

I got off the ladder, and Shane made his way up. He stood next to me on the platform and looked around. "What's up?"

I walked over to the corner and pulled a piece of paper out from between two boards. I examined it carefully. "Never mind. I thought it might be something interesting. It's just an old receipt."

"A receipt? For what?"

"Uh … it's pretty faded. I can't really make it out."

"Step out of the light," Shane said, referring to the sunlight that beamed in on me through the slatted window at the peak of the barn. "Maybe it'll be easier to read."

I stepped back toward Shane, out of the sunlight. "Looks like H. K. *something* brand. I can't decipher the rest. Mean anything to you?"

"Nah. Sorry. Good eyes to spot it, though."

I tucked the receipt into the pocket of my Levis. We went back down the ladder and outside, making our way toward the stream.

The ground was marshy and made squishing sounds underfoot. I dreaded the idea of getting a soaker but didn't want to go back home to put on boots. Fortunately, I had worn my old sneakers and not the new ones I had gotten for school.

"This'll be wood-tick heaven in a few weeks' time," Shane stated.

"I hate those things. Aren't they out now?"

"Everything's a coupla weeks later out here. When flowers are out in town, give yourself about ten days before you start to see blossoms in the country. Surprised a city boy like you would even know what a wood tick is," Shane teased.

"Very funny. I've had a few encounters over the years. Evil little things."

"Well, you better get used to checking yourself for them regularly out here. Gotta check my dog every time he comes in. Found a few on him last year. Trick is to get the entire thing off."

"You gotta dog? I never heard him."

"Yup. He's pretty laid back—doesn't make much noise."

"What kind is he?"

"German shepherd."

"Cool. Is he friendly?"

"You kidding? He's a big softie. But, don't get me wrong, he wouldn't put up with anyone hurting Mom or me. He's very loyal."

"What's his name?"

"Astro. When I was a little kid, I was a big fan of Astroboy. Usually I just tell people I'm a Houston fan. Not many people think naming your dog after a really bad cartoon character is cool."

"That's okay. I had a goldfish named Scooby-Doo," I admitted, causing Shane to laugh out hard. "I was like six and incredibly stupid."

We crossed the stream to the other side and followed an overgrown, but still clearly detectable, path into the woods. We walked a ways into the forest, but suddenly found ourselves surrounded by trees that made it very dark. Branches crunched and snapped in the distance as some sort of animal made its way along. The woods were richly aromatic, with damp pine needles on the ground and lush moss growing on stones and fallen trees. Birds sang all around us, and squirrels nattered at one another. Chipmunks were scurrying about and stopping to make their deep sucking alert sound every so often—warning others of possible dangers or perhaps relaying a message about a good spot to eat. One never knew with chipmunks.

"If you're really patient, you can get chipmunks to eat outta yer hand," Shane informed me.

"Really?"

"Uh-huh. They like black oil sunflower seeds the best. I've been feeding them for years. I've had chickadees and nuthatches eat from my hand too. They know me so well now that when they see me in the backyard with my orange container of seeds, they come right over." Shane chuckled. "One time I was sitting in the backyard, and a little chipmunk came over and stood on my shoe just waiting for his treat."

"That's neat."

"Yeah. I love animals. I'm actually kinda surprised you guys don't have a dog or something."

"We did, but she died a coupla years ago, and we all took it pretty hard. 'Specially my dad. We just figured we couldn't go through that again."

"Sorry to hear that. It's too bad, though. I think of all those poor dogs out there in shelters or bad homes, and it makes me sad. I know it's hard when they die, but that's only because you loved them so much. Think how much joy you had when they were alive. It far outweighs the pain. And, besides, think how great a life you can give the dog."

"I know what you're saying. Maybe down the road we'll get another one. They sure are great company. I often thought it would be nice to adopt a greyhound or a whippet."

"Yeah? Well, with all this land, they could run for days."

"True."

We scuffed along the path, having gotten a fair distance into the woods. The sunlight was almost completely blocked out by the spruce trees. The birds we could still hear singing were no longer close, but back in the distance. A chilly breeze slithered through the forest, and I found myself wishing I had put on my jean jacket. I stopped in the path.

"Um, Shane?"

"Yeah?"

"Let's go back."

"Okay. It's kinda pointless to go much farther anyway. It's just gonna go deeper into the woods and to the start of the stream."

"Maybe in the summer, we can follow the stream to the end, but right now, maybe it's just me, but I feel uneasy being in here."

Shane looked up at the trees. "It's not just you."

We turned and headed back down the path, reaching the meadow much faster than I had anticipated. Shane checked his watch when we got back to the stream cutting through the field. "Whoa, do you realize we were gone for three hours?"

"No way." I checked my own watch, and sure enough, Shane was right. "Holy crap. That doesn't seem possible."

"Time flies, I guess."

"Where have you two been all this time?" Mom asked as we entered the kitchen. "I made sandwiches for you. They're in the fridge."

"Thanks, Mom. We went for a walk in the woods. Kinda lost track of the time. It didn't feel like we were gone very long," I said.

"Well, it's a beautiful day. And I certainly won't complain that you're spending too much time outside. Just please let somebody know where you're going next time, okay?"

"Sure, Mom. Sorry."

Around four o'clock, Shane's mom came to pick him up. Ms. Radnor came into the house and chatted with my mom for a few minutes, complimenting her on the house and all the work she had done. They had a cup of tea together on the porch; Mom had been in town that afternoon and picked up her wicker set. She seemed pleased to so quickly have a person to sit and enjoy it with. Closer to five, Shane and his mother, who insisted I call her Felicia, left in their light blue Chevy Aveo sedan. They weren't gone for more than a few minutes when I found myself already missing Shane's company.

That night I went on the computer and chatted on MSN with Ryley, Adria, Moira, and Hunter. While we were chatting, I had a message window pop up for a private conversation with Shane. He had appeared to be offline, so I was surprised when the screen popped up.

*weird bout time thing 2day.*he wrote.

yeh. think theres sumthin 2 it?

dunno. prolly not.

And that was all we said in our private window. His appearance changed to online, and he joined in our chat group. It was strange. The time thing had been on my mind all day. I was glad Shane obviously couldn't shake the feeling that something was off about it, too. We didn't discuss it, but neither of us mentioned the time thing to anyone else in the group.

Chapter Six

The weeks rolled on to the end of school. I found it somewhat difficult to shift teachers and classes so late in the school year, but I managed to pull off average marks in the mid-seventies, having my best showing in English with an eighty-three. Blake had hit the books hard and eked out an eighty-five average, allowing him to finish the year with distinction.

There was a dance to end the school year, and I went with my group of friends. Ryley was right: the music was pretty lousy, but we all had a good time knowing that we didn't have any more junior high to deal with ever again.

After the dance, we hung out at Stape's, which was crazy with kids, and talked about what we were all doing that summer. Nobody had any major plans. Laura and Moira were going to a camp for a few weeks as junior counsellors, but otherwise everyone was remaining around the area, so we'd likely see a lot of one another, which was cool by me.

Blake had been accepted to attend volleyball camp on Prince Edward Island, taking place at the university, so we went as a family to take him to the ferry for PEI. We walked along the waterfront as we waited for the boat to arrive. Mom and Dad went to the terminal to get coffee, which gave Blake and me a moment alone before he would be gone for a month.

The sun was bright and hot, causing him to shield his eyes despite having his sunglasses on. "You gonna be okay while I'm gone?"

"Yeah. Gonna miss having you around, though."

"Month goes by fast. I'll be back before you know it."

"I guess."

"Do me a favour while I'm gone, okay?"

"Sure. Name it."

"Try to have some fun." Blake stopped walking and turned toward me. We faced each other, and he said, "I mean it. Have some fun, Caleb. Enjoy the summer. It'll be gone all too quickly. Hang out with your friends, stay up late, be adventuresome. Do something that'll make you remember this summer as the best one you've ever had."

I smiled at my brother and nodded. "I'll see what I can do."

Blake ruffled my hair with his large right hand, placing it on my shoulder after and pulling me toward him. He gave me a strong hug, and I held him tight.

"I want you to tell me all about camp when you get back."

"You got it, bud. We'll take off for a day, just you and me. Deal?"

"Deal."

Blake's ferry was ready for boarding, and we headed toward it. Mom and Dad were approaching us, holding their coffees. Mom held Dad's cup as we took Blake's things from the car. Blake put on his backpack and held a duffle bag in one hand, a suitcase in the other. Mom gave him a hug and a peck on the cheek, Dad patted him on the shoulder and told him to have a good time.

"No worries, Dad. It's gonna be a blast."

The horn sounded for the ferry, encouraging all foot passengers to get on board. "Well, I'll see you in a month." Blake smiled a bright, wide smile and looked directly at me. "Remember what I said, Caleb."

"I promise."

"All right." Blake winked at me and shrugged his shoulders. "I'm gone. Have a safe trip home."

"Bye, honey," Mom called out.

We watched my brother get on the boat and go inside. We waited till the ferry launched and was well on its way out of the harbour before returning to the car and heading for home.

The house felt strange without Blake there. Devoid of energy. Although I liked having time all to myself, I wished more than anything that Blake was back home. It made me realize how much I was going to miss him when he eventually went away to university.

There was little in the way of conversation that night at the dinner table. Without Blake around, I hardly spoke at all. In the evening, Mom worked at her quilt, Dad flaked out on the chesterfield watching a baseball game, and I paced back and forth between them, not knowing what else to do.

I wandered down to Blake's room and sat in his computer chair. I surfed around the web for a while and saved anything I wanted kept on my flash drive. I updated the firewall and virus checkers and turned the monitor off, leaving the hard drive on, as always. I spun around in the swivel chair and looked at Blake's room. His walls were covered in posters of sports and girls and music. I went over to the punching bag that hung from the rafter at the end opposite the window and punched the white canvas bag halfheartedly. I wondered if Blake had arrived safely at camp.

As I lay in bed that first Sunday night of summer vacation, I thought of my promise to Blake. I needed to have more fun and to stop thinking so much. I knew that. I'd always known that. It was just hard for me to do. I needed to work on it. I needed to do something adventuresome. But what? There was hardly any likelihood of something exciting happening, and practically anything fun cost money. Whatever. I needed to not worry about the details. I'd hang out with my friends and let each day bring its own surprises. I needed to just let things take their own course.

I closed my eyes and tried to clear my head. I took a deep breath and let it out slowly. I repeated this action three times. As I drifted off to sleep, I heard a fourth breath being let out slowly. I considered turning on my light for a second but decided against it. I told myself I was being silly and, letting my mind drift, soon fell asleep.

In the morning, I called Shane to see what he was doing. We made plans to hook up with Ryley and Adria that afternoon and hang out at her place. I knew I'd have to go into town earlier than that if I wanted a ride, because Mom was working at the drugstore at noon (having gotten a part-time position the week before). Shane said I could come over to his place and we'd go over together to Adria's. With plans made, I got ready for my day.

When I arrived at Shane's, I followed him downstairs to the TV room. He lived behind the office of the motel in a very small house, apartment-sized really, so we were almost never there. I had only been to his house once before that day, and that was just briefly.

"My room's a war zone right now," Shane explained. "Otherwise, I'd let you see it."

"That's cool. I never figured you for the messy type."

"I'm not usually too bad, but I've been working on my drawing a lot lately and have let things kinda get outta hand."

"I'd love to see some of your work sometime."

Shane rubbed the back of his neck. "Ahh, I dunno. I don't usually like to show it to anyone. Stupid, I guess, but it's kinda like letting people see you naked. Dumb, right?"

"No, I understand. I bet it's awesome, though."

Shane, perhaps embarrassed and wanting to change the subject, asked, "You wanna play *Halo 3*?"

"Sure, but I suck at it."

Shane laughed. "I'll try not to let you die too quickly."

We met up with Ryley and Adria around two. Laura was going to come over as well, not having to leave for camp until the following week. We hung out in Adria's backyard listening to the radio and talking. The air was so clear and warm it would have been a crime to stay indoors. We threw a Frisbee around for a while and talked about thousands of essentially meaningless things. We made plans to go to the movie that night, and I fought the urge to call Mom at work to see if I could get a ride home afterward. I decided to just roll with it, and if Mom couldn't get me, I'd just crash at one of my friends' houses or, worst-case scenario, I could walk the fifteen kilometres home. I wasn't going to worry about it. When the show was over, my father came to get me without any issue. He even asked me if I had had a good time and if the movie was worth seeing.

As I was lying in bed that night, I felt pretty good about myself. The day had been fun and didn't cost me much at all—just six bucks for the movie (thanks to the student discount). I kept thinking about my friends and the fun we'd had that day together. We didn't do anything exciting or wild, but just sitting around, talking, and throwing the Frisbee was fun. I never would have thought that in the space of a few months, I'd have so many friends. They liked coming over to my house because there was so much room to move about and it felt so away from everything. Sure, it was inconvenient if you forgot to pick something up in town (you usually ended up making do without), but that was about the only major drawback. I'd had the guys all over one Sunday in early June, and we played *Risk* all day and into the evening. Drew finally finished conquering Ryley's armies in Australia to win the game. The entire gang was out a few times for movies.

It was in the light shining off the television that I could look around the room at my friends and sense a sort of tension that only exists for teenagers. I could tell who liked who as more than friends, but nothing ever seemed to come of it. I think everyone was too scared of ruining a good thing but wishing they took a chance at the same time. It seemed all the girls liked Ryley, but I think anyone would because he's handsome and confident and fun to be around. Drew definitely seemed to like Laura, and Moira might have liked Hunter, too. They all flirted playfully, but that's all that ever happened.

As for me, I still couldn't stop thinking about Shane. I liked the way he smiled, how he smelled, how he looked with his shirt off (especially when we were swimming at Hunter's and his shorts were all wet and clingy), and how nice he was. And I kept thinking about how he touched me that first night he stayed over—how his fingers glided over my skin so gently.

I knew what all these feelings meant, and it scared me. I told myself I was confused, that I was so happy to have a best friend like Shane that I was mixing it up with other feelings. So I found my best friend attractive. So what? Maybe I was just jealous and wished I could look like that. Even if that wasn't the case, I was a teenager, and I was just having fantasies. I mean, my hormones are raging all the time. Big deal.

But why didn't I think about one of the girls? They were all attractive. Or what about Blake's pinup models? They were insanely hot and seductively posed. But as much as I told myself this, it was Shane that I thought about. It was Shane I saw when I closed my eyes.

I heard Blake's voice in my head telling me not to think so much. The panic attack that had been setting in began to wane. I closed my eyes, and this time when I pictured Shane, I grinned. I pictured him lying on my bed in just his underwear, the grey cotton stretched over his firm, round butt, the black ink of the tattoo standing out against his smooth skin. I let a hand slide under the covers and muffled a small groan before falling asleep.

Sometime around four o'clock, I awoke, needing to use the washroom. (I knew I'd regret having that big glass of water before going to bed.) When I returned to my bedroom, I took a look outside at the beautiful moon splashing its white light over the tall grass of the field. Something caught the corner of my eye—a light flickered in the barn. I was afraid that there might be a fire, so I hurried downstairs and out the kitchen door. I hadn't thought to take a flashlight with me, but there was ample light from the moon to guide me toward the barn. I opened the side door and clicked on the light switch, but none of the sixty-watt bulbs snapped on. I flicked the switch up and down repeatedly, stupidly thinking this would fix the problem (like pushing an elevator button over and over is supposed to make it come up faster, right?). "Perfect," I muttered to myself and stepped over the threshold. There was next to nothing to illuminate the inside of the barn, just the sliver of moonlight creeping in around doorframes and through the small windows. I considered opening the main doors, but I knew it would create a fair bit of noise and I didn't want to wake my parents. If there had actually been a fire, I wouldn't have cared, but there appeared to be nothing out of the ordinary.

I slowly walked around the inside of the barn. The air was heavy (very close, my grandfather would have said) and humid. I was wearing only my boxers, but I was still sweating. I wiped my brow and, against my better judgment, called out, "Hello?"

There was a subtle clank from the hayloft, as if something were dropped from a short height. I went to the centre of the barn and turned my attention upward to the loft. I was half expecting to see some stray cat, like in a horror movie, pounce out of the night or maybe just show me its greenish eyes glinting in the dark. Of course, nothing happened.

I tried to think what could possibly have made that sound. The barn was empty, save for the new Blue Holland ride-on lawn mower my father purchased the previous week (and which had become my new favourite toy) and the gardening tools and supplies my mother stored in one of the old stalls. I might have thought it was one of Mom's hoes or rakes or edgers that had fallen over if I hadn't been so sure the metallic clank sound had come from the loft. I sighed, knowing it would bother me if I didn't investigate. I wasn't keen on doing so, but I was curious enough to grab the first rung of the ladder and make my way slowly up to the top. After all, I had come out to the barn at four in the morning in my underwear, and I'd be damned if I wasn't going to figure out why. In all probability, I'd encounter a mouse or rat or maybe even a raccoon.

As I poked my head over the top, I couldn't see a thing at first, my eyes still adjusting to the dark. I stepped up onto the platform and winced as a splinter went in my big toe. "Motherfucker," I grumbled and held my foot up to remove the long shard of spruce from the floorboard. A droplet of blood immediately spilled out, and the wound oozed for a few minutes. Something in the corner glinted, and I forgot about my foot, heading over to see what it was. Hanging on a nail was a horseshoe. I didn't remember seeing that when Shane and I were up in the loft back in the spring, but it might have been there. I hadn't been up since then, so I surmised that it was possible perhaps we both just missed it—the colour would have blended in with the walls. As I knelt down to be face-on with the horseshoe, it made the sound again, moving in a gentle breeze that snuck in from a torn shingle on the roof of the barn, causing it to hit a protruding nail to its right. Then the air was still. I took the horseshoe from the nail and held it in my hand. I wondered if it was from Cocoa. I took the horseshoe with me back to my room. I put it on a piece of white paper and laid it on my nightstand. Rust flaked off the metal, and my hand sparkled with the orangey dust left behind.

Shane came over the next day, and I showed him what I had found.

He thought the circumstances of my finding the horseshoe were rather odd, and I showed him exactly where I had found it.

"Man, I woulda remembered if I had seen that up here. There's no way that was here when we were up a few months ago. Only thing that was here then was that receipt you found, remember?"

"Yeah."

"Do you still have it?"

"I have no idea. If I do, it's probably in my jeans."

"You haven't washed your jeans in almost two months?"

I chuckled. "Well, not that pair. I hardly ever wear those anymore cuz they're kinda faded and have some rips."

"Those are the best kind of jeans."

I laughed. "C'mon, let's go check it out."

We went inside the house, and I grabbed my old Levis from the bottom of the closet. I kept all my jeans in milk crates stacked sideways in the closet. It was a good system because I kept them sorted by colour and style (okay, so jeans are my favourite clothing, and it's the one thing I can't resist buying when the price is right. I've been lucky to get most of my name-brand denim at used clothing stores—so I'm thrifty and I can afford to have more pairs that way).

I found the snug blue pair of 501s and dug my hand into the back right pocket. I pulled out the brownish piece of paper from a few months before. "Here it is," I said, holding it out for Shane to take.

"H. K. brand. I can barely make out some of the figures at the bottom. Looks like five dollars or something."

"You honestly think there's a connection between the two things?"

"I doubt it, but I'd hang on to them both."

"Good idea." I took the receipt and placed it inside an envelope from my desk. I put the envelope under the horseshoe to keep it from falling onto the floor or blowing away when I had my window open. "Well, guess that's all for today's excitement," I joked.

Shane's deep brown eyes looked at me, and I felt my cheeks flush. "What's wrong?"

"Huh? Nothing."

"You sure? You look really warm. You feeling okay?"

"Yeah. Fine."

Shane stepped over to me and placed his hand on my forehead. "Hmm. You don't feel like you've got a fever. Probably just the humidity."

"Umm. Yeah. Probably." His fingers slid across my skin as he took his hand away. I felt this incredible tension. "So, whattaya wanna do this afternoon?"

"I dunno. It's so nice out, we gotta do something outside."

"Definitely. Any ideas?"

"I'd really like to explore the woods again. Let's throw some food and water in a backpack and go for a hike."

"Sure. Sounds good."

We went down to the kitchen and put some granola bars, bottled water, and a few other supplies in a knapsack. We sprayed ourselves with insect repellent and sunblock and threw the containers in the bag in case we needed to reapply later. For good measure, I brought along my compass.

"It must be pretty cool to have the place to yourself during the day," Shane commented.

"Yeah. It can be kinda lonely when you're not around, though." I hadn't meant to say that; I had meant to say *when no one else is around*. Or had I?

Shane smiled. "I'd come every day, but I wouldn't want you to get sick of me."

"You kidding? I'm always paranoid that I'm boring you."

"Only boring people get bored," he stated bluntly. I had never thought of it like that before. "So come on. Let's hit the woods."

We went out the back door and headed for the stream. No one was going to be home until supper, so I locked the door on our way out. As we made our way along the overgrown path to the woods, I quickly checked my watch, making a mental note of the time.

"Sure is peaceful in here," Shane said as we walked along the old trail. The air was heavy with the scent of pine trees and trapped pollen in the branches of the spruce. A pileated woodpecker, looking almost prehistoric, pounded away at a dead birch tree. The air in the woods was humid, and we were both sweating almost instantly. The trees blocked out most of the light from overhead, but enough filtered through to allow occasional boxes of sunlight to form on the ground in random patterns like pixels on a computer screen. I cursed myself for wearing sandals, as pine needles kept collecting on and between my toes. Shane was having the same issue, but neither of us mentioned it.

As we were walking, I suddenly felt a hand on my shoulder, stopping me in my tracks. Shane pulled me over to him and pointed off to the side of the trail. A deer was walking through the deeper woods. We watched in silence until it was gone from sight. Shane's hand was still on my shoulder.

"Oh, hey. Sorry," he laughed awkwardly.

"Good eyes to spot the deer."

"Lucky."

We continued walking until we reached a steep slope. Carefully navigating our way down, holding on to tree trunks and roots as we went, we reached the bottom and heard a trickling sound. Ahead of us was a small clearing and a waterfall. We sat down on a fallen tree that appeared as though it had been there forever for the exact purpose of being a bench, but had somehow managed to not rot. We ate some granola bars and drank some water.

"It's really nice down here," I said.

"Yeah. I'm glad we kept going."

"Me too."

"I'd like to paint this."

"Yeah, you should, man."

"I dunno. It's just a thought. I have lots of 'em. Most I don't know what to do with."

"I hear ya. I'm trying to take Blake's advice and stop thinking so much—just do stuff. You know, take more risks."

"Easier said than done."

"That's for sure."

Shane picked up a stone from the ground and played with it, keeping his focus solely on it. I wanted him to talk to me, but I didn't know what to say.

"Shane?"

"Yeah?"

"Thanks for hanging out with me and stuff." I looked over at him, trying to get his eyes on me for a moment. I was pleased that it worked.

He turned his head and replied, "You don't have to thank me for that. I like you, Caleb. Like you a lot. You're a really cool guy. I knew that from the first time we talked."

"It's funny. When I first met you, I never figured we'd be friends. I thought you were way too cool to hang out with me."

Shane shook his head. "You're so hard on yourself, man. What gives? I mean, the gang all likes you, your family all obviously love you so, I mean, why don't you think more of yourself?"

I shrugged. "I dunno. Guess I'm still trying to answer that myself."

His expression turned to a genuine smile. "We'll keep working on it then."

I grinned.

Shane headed over to the waterfall and caught some water in his cupped hands. He splashed it over his face and called me over. "It's really warm!"

I stood by him and leaned my head into the waterfall, getting my hair wet and shaking my head as I stood up straight, spraying him with the moisture that came off my hair. He put his hands up defensively and laughed. His white T-shirt and beige cargo shorts were now covered in a splattering of rain. His wet eyelashes caused his eyes to sparkle. His smile showed his white teeth. He was so beautiful. I went with my instincts and leaned in, kissing him on the lips. They were soft and moist and sweet.

Surprising myself by what I had done, I stepped back quickly.

Shane looked at me, stunned. "You kissed me."

"Yeah. Shit. Sorry. That was dumb. I don't know why I did that. Please … forget it, okay?" I pleaded as nonchalantly as possible, even though my heart was pounding so hard I was sure it had to be visible.

"I can't forget it happened, Caleb." Shane's voice was serious, and it frightened me a bit. I knew I had just lost the best friend I had ever had.

I felt sick to my stomach. All sorts of scenarios raced through my mind—none of them good. "Please. I'm so sorry." I felt myself on the verge of crying; my limbs started to shake from panic.

"Caleb," Shane looked me deep in the eyes as he spoke, stepping toward me. For a moment I thought he was going to hit me, but he took my face in his hands instead. "I don't want to forget it. Not ever." Shane slid one hand down to the small of my back, and the other moved to the back of my neck as he leaned in and kissed me. Softly. Passionately. Slowly. When our lips finally parted, he was smiling. "You're never supposed to forget your first kiss," he said gently.

Having been given the courage to do what I had yearned to do for so long, I wrapped my arms around him and held him tightly against me. We stayed in the clearing for some time, watching the water for a while as the stream ran over the shiny stones and snaked its way out of the forest and into the field.

As we walked back along the trail toward the house, we held hands. The sensation of feeling Shane's hand in mine is one I'll never forget. In such a simple gesture, I knew so much about him, and even more about myself. We began to talk openly, on a level where I had never conversed before.

"So, when did you know you're gay?" Shane asked me.

At this point, we were walking side by side, no longer holding hands, but still close—there may have been daylight between us, I can't be sure.

I considered his question before answering. "Well, I guess I've known for a coupla years now, but I kept giving myself excuses like telling myself that when I saw a guy I thought was hot, I was really just jealous and wished I looked like him, right? Like, I wish I had his build, instead of, I wish I had him on top of me." I laughed at myself and shook my head. "God, it seems so dumb when I say it, but in my mind it always made sense."

"I know exactly what you mean. Hell, I voted for Jaydee Bixby over two hundred times to win 'Canadian Idol'—and I don't even like country music." Shane chuckled. "But that boy is so cute."

I smiled and scuffed at some pine needles. "So, I guess, really, I've always known. I mean, I've always liked guys. Girls are cool as friends, but I don't want to, umm, you know, *be* with them. All my crushes have been on guys, but I always made excuses, like I said, and suppressed my thoughts. It's been making me miserable."

"Yeah. I get ya. It's so stupid, too. I mean, there's nothing any different about us—we just dig guys when the majority of guys dig girls."

"Exactly. So, when did you know?"

"Kinda like you, I've always known I was different. I mean, I did the whole making-excuses thing too, but I got to a point when I just said, 'Screw it. I like guys, and that's cool.' But it's one thing to tell yourself that; it's a whole new ball game when you tell other people."

"You think Ryley and the other guys would accept us?"

"I dunno. I think they would, actually. I'm pretty sure of it, but not 100 percent. Plus, I've always been scared that it might change things. You know?"

"Yeah," I sighed. "I'm not ready to come out yet. Are you?"

"Well, to be honest, my mom already knows."

"Really?" I was amazed.

"Yeah, and she's fine with it. She's had gay friends over the years, and it never made a bit of difference to her. She just wants me to be proud of who I am cuz that's how she and Dad raised me."

"That's awesome. You're lucky."

"Too bad it has to be considered lucky to have my mother keep loving me after she found out I'm gay. I've read so many stories about kids who've been kicked out of their homes and stuff. It pisses me off."

"Me too." I wondered how my own parents would react. "So, how long has your mom known?"

"I told her a few months ago, before I met you."

"Was she shocked?"

"Not really. I was sitting in the kitchen at the table, and she sat down with me. I hadn't planned on telling her then, but we got talking about a bunch of stuff, mostly Dad, and it got kinda emotional. I told her how much I miss him and want to make him proud of me, and she was saying all I have to do is be myself to make him proud. Saying things like how I helped her so much at the motel without being asked and stuff was making them both proud every day. I ended up saying something like 'Would you still be proud of me if you knew I was gay?'"

"What did she do?"

"She smiled at me and said, 'Even prouder,' which kinda made me lose it. I asked her if she knew, and she told me that she always thought it was possible because it was possible for anyone. Then she gave me this big hug and told me that she'd be there for me any way that she could."

"Wow. Your mom rocks."

"She's pretty amazing. What kind of reaction you think you'll get?"

"No idea."

"Think they might already know?"

"I don't think so." I hadn't thought of that before.

"Hey ... you wanna know the real reason I haven't let you see my room?"

"Yeah."

Shane laughed. "Cuz I've got this big Zac Efron poster on my wall."

I chuckled. "Good reason. Kinda hard to explain that one."

"No shit."

"He is awfully cute."

"You're right." Shane lightly bumped against my side. "Not as cute as you, though."

I turned about three shades of red. "Shut up," I said.

"So, what's the story with that hot hockey player on your walls?"

"Sidney Crosby?"

Shane nodded.

"What do you think? I'm a Penguins fan." Shane caught the expression on my face and roared with laughter. "But seriously, I've always been a hockey fan—but I kinda adopted the Pens as my team after Crosby started playing."

"Can't say I blame you. And hey, you can put his picture up for the world to see cuz no one would think twice about it, right."

"It does make it easier."

"Have you seen Taylor Hall, the draft pick for the Oilers?"

"Yep."

"Amazing lips."

"And how about Tyler Seguin? Those eyes? Whoa."

"Okay ... so the big question is, Team Jacob or Team Edward?"

"Oh, Jacob all the way," I answered easily. "Taylor Lautner is *so* hot. You?"

"Jacob. He's got that whole dark and brooding thing going on, which is hot, and then ..."

"He takes his shirt off," I finished, laughing.

Shane chuckled. "So, we're definitely going to *Eclipse* when it comes out this summer, right?"

"Yeah. It's a date."

Shane took my hand in his again, and we continued talking about our favourite celebrities and sports stars as we walked toward the meadow.

I checked my watch as we crossed back over the stream. It was getting close to five, and both my parents would be home shortly. Time had gone by all too quickly that afternoon, and I hated to see it end. As we walked by the barn, I got a strange chill despite it being so hot. I stopped in my tracks.

"What's up?" Shane asked, sensing my unease.

"Just got a weird chill."

"As we passed the barn?"

"Yes."

"Same thing happened to me."

"Musta been a breeze catching our sweat, making us cold," I determined.

"Yeah. Good call."

Shane agreed with me, but neither of us believed my explanation.

"Could we go in the barn for a second?"

"Sure." I walked over to the barn door and opened it, stepping inside and holding the door for Shane. "Expect to see something in here, did you?"

"No." Shane pushed me against the wall and kicked the door closed behind him, all in one fluid motion. He kissed me and pressed against me. I had never known what it felt like to be kissed with such passion and, I guess, lust, at the same time. Shane's tongue played with mine, and his right hand cupped my left buttock. I was aware that I had an erection and that he probably felt it against his leg, but I didn't care. I kept kissing him as he ran a hand under my T-shirt, his palm against my bare skin exciting me further. I slid a hand down his back and onto his firm bubble butt, squeezing it. All those horny times alone at night or in the bathroom seemed like such wasted efforts compared to this. We heard a car coming down the road, and our lips parted. We were both panting a bit from the intensity of our actions and from the fact it felt like about forty degrees with the humidity inside the barn.

Licking my lips, I whispered, "Wow. That was awesome."

"Uh-huh." Shane wiped his brow with his forearm. "We'd better go inside … get something cold to drink."

"Good plan."

As much as I think we both wanted to stay in the barn, it was probably good that we were interrupted. Now we had something more to look forward to later. We headed out of the barn, and as I closed the door, I thought I heard a deep sigh from above. I shut the door and followed Shane to the house as Mom's car parked in the driveway.

That evening, we went for another walk into the woods for some more alone time. We made out again in the clearing, practically running to get there. As it began to get dusky, we decided, as much as we wanted to stay, we had better get back. As we started up the hill from the clearing to the upper path, Shane spotted something.

"Hey, you see this?" he asked, pointing at the trunk of a very large oak tree.

"What is it?" I leaned in to see.

"Check it out: it's a heart with the initials T. E. plus C. H. written in it."

"Guess we aren't the first people to discover this spot, huh?"

"Yeah, but think about it for a sec, Caleb. T. E. That's gotta be Toby Everett."

"Whoa. Cool. I wonder who the C. H. is."

"Too bad we don't have any way to find out."

"Strange we didn't notice that before."

"True, but it is at the bottom of this big ass oak tree, so we'd only see it going up the hill."

"But something made you see it this time."

"Umm, yeah, well, last time you went up first, and I got distracted watching your butt." Shane smirked, making me go beet red. Satisfied with himself, he said, "Knew I'd make you blush."

That night as Shane slept, I lay awake, enjoying the warm breeze coming in my open window. The moonlight shone into my room, casting everything in a silvery hue. Something scratching made me look at the window itself. Against the screen, I saw a leaf. I recalled one of Shane's stories and nudged him. He mumbled incoherently and rolled over, his sleeping bag's vinyl making sweeping sounds as he moved. He didn't say anything, just pulled me toward him and held me against him. I could feel his hot breath against my neck. I watched the leaf carefully, listening to it scratch against my screen. I fell asleep and told Shane about the leaf in the morning.

"I bet if we had never heard any of the stories about this place that all of these things we think we hear and the things we see wouldn't even register as being out of the ordinary," Shane suggested over breakfast.

"You're probably right."

"Plus, all the stories take place in the fall and winter. Nothing really is ever said to have happened during the summer."

"Good point. And most of the stuff, I'd agree can be chalked up to coincidence or whatever, but those nights I heard the sighs, I dunno. I didn't imagine them."

"I'm not saying you did. And, believe me, I think it's odd some of the things that have occurred, but nothing that makes me believe the stories are true."

"True or not, I'm glad you're with me," I said.

Shane smiled and chomped down on his toast.

Mom entered the kitchen and poured herself some coffee. "Morning, fellas. Whatcha plannin' on doin' today?"

"We're going into town to see a movie with the gang tonight. Heading to Hunter's after to sleep over."

"Sounds good. I've got to run some errands later this morning. I can give you guys a ride in then if you want."

I looked to Shane to get his opinion. "We could hang out at my place. Maybe see if Ryley's around."

"Okay," I said and turned to Mom. "Yeah, that'd be great."

"Good. Eleven o'clock all right?"

"Sure. We'll be ready."

It was nearly ten when we finished with breakfast, so we went upstairs to get our things for the night. I pulled my sleeping bag down from the shelf in my closet and started to put clothes into my overnight bag. I reached into my drawer for my swim trunks, and Shane said, "Caleb, would you do me a favour?"

"Sure." I turned around to see Shane as he made his request.

"Could you wear your light blue shorts with the flowers up the side instead of those boring black ones this time?"

"Umm. Okay." I rummaged around the drawer and found the pair Shane had referred to. I had only ever worn them once before—the first time we went swimming at Adria's back in late May. I had noticed all the other guys wore really basic, solid-colour trunks. so I hadn't worn the flower ones since. "These, right?" I asked, holding the shorts up for confirmation.

"Yup." Shane's eyes twinkled.

"You like these?"

"You look really hot in them." I never thought of myself as good-looking, so it was weird having someone tell me I looked hot, but it was a weird I could handle.

"I do?"

"Trust me."

"Okay. You got it." I tossed the blue trunks with the white flowers up the side into my bag and finished my packing. I walked over to Shane and gave him a kiss, and then we headed downstairs with our things.

Hanging out with the group was a blast. I barely thought of anything at all, which was a welcome change. Shane and I discussed how to handle things and agreed it was best to just be relaxed and casual, like we always had been before. We were both tempted to come out and be ourselves to our friends, but neither of us was prepared for that yet. We managed pretty well, but we couldn't shake the feeling that we were somehow lying to everyone. We talked about that to great length on one of our many walks through the woods that July.

"By not saying anything, it makes it seem like we're ashamed or something," Shane noted. "And I'm not ashamed of who I am."

"Me neither."

"And if our friends don't accept us, then they were never really our friends to begin with, right?"

"Yeah, that's the way I figure it."

"So why's it so hard?"

"I was reading on a website about how it's best to tell people one at a time; that way you can really talk to them and get an honest reaction," I said.

"Was it the P-Flag site?"

"Yeah. How'd you know?"

"I must have that page memorized. It's a great site." Shane kicked at a pinecone, sending it deep into the woods. We heard it crash into some dried leaves off in the distance.

We didn't talk anymore about coming out as we descended the pathway to the waterfall. We had gotten into the habit of rubbing the oak tree for luck as we passed by. We sat on our fallen tree and listened to the summer day. Cicadas reminded us of how hot it was with their high-pitched wail. We straddled the log and faced each other, having to lean in to kiss as our knees were touching. Shane seemed distant. Distracted.

"You okay?" I asked, placing my hand on his thigh.

"I'm just trying to find the courage inside of me, that's all. Trying not to be scared. I mean, I'm happy with you, and I'm not afraid of that—it's just …"

"It's how other people will treat us. I know."

"Yeah."

"This is our space," I said, gesturing to the clearing. "While we're here, we don't have to think about anything else. Let's just enjoy being here together. Okay?"

Shane grinned at me. He leaned forward and kissed me gently on the cheek, resting his head on my shoulder after. "Deal."

Chapter Seven

The end of July seemed to arrive suddenly. Before I knew it, Mom and I were on our way to pick up Blake at the ferry, his volleyball camp being over.

It was overcast and drizzly that day, and the drive seemed to take much longer than I remembered it taking a month earlier. It was well worth it just to see Blake getting off the boat. He was carrying his things and sporting a wide smile as he walked the gangplank down to the dock. He looked fantastic, all tanned and toned—wearing new khaki shorts and a tight white UPEI T-shirt that was nearly transparent from the rain.

"Wow, you're looking buff!" I told him as he gave me a hug.

"It's sooo good to see you, bud," he replied.

"You could at least hug your mother first," Mom said, feigning hurt.

"Hey, Mom." Blake gave her a big hug, picking her up off the ground. "That do?"

Mom laughed as her face reddened (see, I come by it honestly). "Oh, honey, it's so nice to have you home."

"It's a ferry terminal, Mom," Blake joked.

"You know what I mean," she laughed playfully, slapping his shoulder. "You had a great summer, didn't you?" she asked.

"Oh, my God, it was awesome. I'll tell you all about it on the drive home. I'll say this for now—I know where I'm going to university. UPEI rocks."

I was happy for Blake. The fact that he'd had an incredible time was stamped all over him. He looked refreshed, reenergized. For the first hour of the ride home, he talked a blue streak, answering one question after another and telling us stories of games he played and people he met. He promised to show us pictures when we got home. Finally he put his hands up and said, "Okay, stop. Enough about me. Now I wanna hear how your summer has been so far, bud. Tell me anything and everything—or at least as much as you're willing to admit with Mom in the car," he kidded. "What have you done so far?"

I shrugged my shoulders and merely said, "Nothing much."

After dinner that night, Blake showed us all his photos from camp, sticking his SD card into the side of the television to give us the slide show. He pointed out the different people and explained the different game shots that had been taken. They'd spent some of the nicest days playing beach volleyball, and there were some pretty good-looking guys in those shots, all shirtless and sweaty.

In one of the group photos, Blake was standing next to an attractive blonde girl who had her arm around his waist. Mom noticed and said, "Oh, she's pretty. Who's that, Blake?"

"That," Blake began, "is Chloe. She's such a sweetheart." Blake paused the screen and stared at the picture.

"You two look good together," Mom added.

"Our team played hers in the coed beach volleyball tournament. Wish I had pics from that day—she looked so hot in this little pink bikini."

"Where's she from?" Dad asked.

"Out west. We exchanged e-mail addresses, but I'll probably never see her again." Blake was quiet for a moment. I knew that he really liked her. "At the end of camp, there was a dance, and we went together." Blake hit the play button and showed us a picture of the two of them all dressed up. If I hadn't known him, I would have guessed he was in his early twenties from the photo. He looked so mature and handsome, with an equally attractive date on his arm.

"Sounds like you had a killer time," I said.

Blake nodded. "Yeah. It was amazing. I'm sorry it's over, even though it is nice to be home."

"It's good to have you back," Dad said.

My parents went to bed at their usual time, around eleven. Blake was in his room unpacking and sorting things that needed to go in the laundry. I went outside and sat on the steps, sipping a can of Coke and wishing Shane was there with me. I heard the front screen door stretch open behind me and turned to see Blake. But Blake wasn't there. The door was closed. I shook my head and went back to stargazing. A few minutes later, I heard the door again, and Blake said, "Great night, huh? I missed nights out here while I was gone." He sat down next to me on the step.

"Missed having you around," I let him know.

"You keep your promise to me?"

"Yep. Did my best."

"Good stuff."

When I didn't volunteer any information, Blake asked, "So, what'd you do while I was gone?"

"Like I told you before, nothing much."

"Oh c'mon. I don't believe that for one second."

"Okay, well, nothing really interesting then."

"I don't believe that either. What gives, Caleb? It isn't like you not to talk to me. Are you mad at me for some reason?"

"Mad at you? Course not."

"Just don't feel like talking, huh?"

"I just don't know what to say, that's all." I took a drink from my Coke. "I do have one question for you."

"Anything."

"Are you really going to go to UPEI next year?"

"If I can get in, I sure hope to. Why?"

"It's just so far away."

"Is that what's bugging you?"

"Sorta."

"Hey, listen, bud, I'll never be more than a phone call or an e-mail away. No matter what's going on, you can always talk to me."

"It won't be the same, though. One month was bad enough."

My brother, I think, was surprised by my admission. "Look, a lot can change in a year. Who knows, maybe I'll end up wanting to go to college in the city. I can't be certain."

"But, no matter what, this is gonna be our very last year together in the same house—ever."

"That may be true, but we're brothers. You'll always have me in your life."

"It just seems to be happening so fast."

"What does?"

"Everything. I dunno." I played with the pull tab of my can.

Blake shifted his gaze from the sky to me. "Look, I'm not trying to bug you, but I'd love to hear one thing that happened while I was gone that was cool. What's been the highlight of your summer so far?"

I smiled slyly at my brother.

"Oh, it's something good." He grinned. "C'mon. What is it?"

"Well, you gotta promise me you won't ask me any details and stuff if I tell you, okay?"

"I swear."

"You mean it?"

"I promise I won't ask anything."

"All right." I couldn't wipe the smile off my face, and looking at Blake made me blush more, so I turned my focus to the distance, somewhere beyond the driveway and into the night as I said, "I got my first kiss."

"That's awesome, Caleb." Blake's voice was soft and sensitive. "I'm so happy for you."

"Yeah, well, it isn't much, I guess, but to me it means everything."

"And it should." Blake ruffled my hair with his hand, keeping his promise and not asking me a single question.

"So, tell me about this Chloe girl."

As I was lying in bed that night, I could hear Blake down the hall, still putting things away in his room. It was nice to hear him in the house again, to know he was just down the hall. I found myself wishing I had told him it was Shane I kissed, and said those words out loud that were screaming inside of me. My mind began to race, and I knew I wasn't going to be able to sleep for a while, so I reached over and pulled the chain on my nightstand lamp. The light came on and then went out. I grumbled at the prospect of having to go down to the kitchen to get a lightbulb to replace it, but I knew I had to. I swung my feet over the side of the bed and went downstairs. I got a forty-watt bulb, not being able to find a sixty, from the cupboard over the refrigerator and returned to my room. I replaced the bulb and turned on my lamp. A cold breeze came in the window, so I closed it and got into bed.

I felt like reading to distract me from my thoughts, so I turned to find a book in the headboard. My eyes caught something, and I looked toward my *New Moon* poster. A shadow moved on the wall. I turned swiftly, hoping I'd see Blake, but no one was there. I turned back and looked at the shadow again, deciding it had to be caused by something in the room. The shirt on the back of my desk chair, perhaps. I got up and took the shirt off the chair, tossing it on the floor. Still the shadow remained. I waved my arms to see if I could add to or alter the shadow in any way. Nothing happened.

I went over to my window and glanced out, but with no trees close to the house, there was nothing to create a shadow from outside either. I opened the window a crack and felt cold air rush past my arm and out the window. Out, not in. I shivered and closed the window. I turned back to my wall and saw that the shadow was gone. I crawled back under the covers and grabbed a book from the shelf. I was unable to concentrate on the words, so I put the book back and turned off my light. My life was confusing enough as it was, but I began to feel that some of the stories Shane had told me might actually be true.

When I got up the next morning, I stretched and went down the hall to the washroom. Blake was taking a shower, so I brushed my teeth and shaved, waiting for him to finish. When he stepped out, he grabbed his towel and dried his hair before tying it around his waist.

"Morning, Blake."

"Hey, bud. Sleep well?"

"Once I got to sleep, I did."

"Something keeping you up?"

"Yeah." I put down my razor and wiped my face with a cloth. "Do you ever get cold chills?"

"Nah, not that I can think of. You feeling okay?"

"I feel fine. It's just … forget it."

"What?"

"Well, there've been some odd things happening while you were gone. Some before you left. Nothing major and nothing really scary, just odd stuff. Ya know?"

"Like what?" Blake began brushing his teeth.

So I told Blake about the night I found the horseshoe and about the receipt that Shane and I found back in the spring. I told him about the shadow on my wall and the cold chills, before I said, "And we also found a heart with initials in it carved into a tree in the woods."

"What initials?"

"T. E. and C. H."

"And you think the T. E. stands for Toby, don't you?"

"Well, it makes sense. What do you think?"

"I think that if they are Toby's initials that he found himself a sweetheart, but there's a lot to be said for the power of suggestion, too. I mean, I really don't see much connection between all of this— nothing that couldn't be argued about and picked apart anyway. Sorry to disappoint you."

"I'm not disappointed. I hope you're right. Life is confusing enough without being haunted," I joked.

Blake eyed me in the mirror. "You sure you're okay, Caleb?"

"I'm good. Just overtired."

"You and Shane hang out a lot while I was gone?"

"Yeah. Rest of the gang, too."

"I'm glad. I like Shane."

"He's the best friend I've ever had, 'sides you."

Blake smiled. "You ghost hunters get very far in the woods? I still haven't even gone in them."

"A fair ways. Up to where the stream starts at a waterfall. It's a pretty good walk, but you can make it there in about a half-hour."

"You'll have to show me sometime."

"Love to."

"Good."

"I'm gonna take a shower." I took off my shirt and turned to the stall.

"I missed this when I was gone," Blake said.

"What?"

"Talking to you in the morning."

"Me too."

"I'll have the coffee on when you get downstairs."

"Thanks, bro."

I dropped my shorts and stepped into the shower.

As I ate my breakfast on that first day of August, I tried to shut the idea that school started in one month from my mind. The back-to-school sales had begun, and I knew that soon Mom would want to take Blake and me shopping to get us new clothes for the start of the school year. Mom always made a special thing of it and would take one day to go with me and another with Blake. She had a budget, and we had a list of what were our needs and what were our wants. Mom was pretty flexible and fairly supportive, even if she didn't always understand our taste. We actually ended up having a good time together, and it almost made the notion of going back to another year of classes and tests and assemblies worthwhile.

Since we no longer lived in the city, I assumed Mom would be taking us both on the same day this year to save a bit on gas. I saw that the tenth had been circled on her kitchen calendar (an erasable one that was always stuck to the freezer door of the fridge) and a question mark written next to it.

"Mom, what's happening on the tenth?" I asked her as she took her waffles from the toaster.

"I was thinking that would be a good day to go into Halifax to do our clothes shopping. Does that work for you?"

"Fine by me. Blake coming with us?"

"I was going to ask you about that. I don't mind making two trips in, but if you'd like, we could all three go in together that day."

"That's cool. With the price of gas, it would be stupid to make an extra trip."

"Well, I would if it made it easier for either of you."

"Nah, that's fine, Mom. I'm looking forward to it."

Mom beamed. "So am I."

After breakfast, I went out the back door and started along the path to the stream. I reached my hand out and felt the tall grass tickle my palm as I walked, the dry timothy growing high to either side of the trail. I stepped over the stream at its narrowest point and continued on into the woods. I hadn't been back there by myself ever, but I felt like I needed to be alone. I took my time, taking in all my surroundings, as I headed for the waterfall. Birds chirped and sang in the distance, and the hot smell of pine needles wafted up to my nose in the humid woods.

I hadn't seen any traces of deer since that one I saw with Shane a while back, but there were signs of porcupines and skunks and raccoons along the way. The forest was quiet, save for the birds, and the air grew heavier as I reached the slope to the waterfall. I rubbed the heart for good luck on the way down the incline and stopped at the bottom, hearing the babbling sounds coming from the waterfall. I sat down on my log and listened carefully to my perfect world—my secret place where everything was good and right. I licked my lips, thinking of Shane kissing me. Closing my eyes, I could almost smell his cologne, a scent that I had begun to think of as purely his own, despite seeing bottles of Chrome in department stores.

The air was so humid, even though it was just ten in the morning, that I peeled my grey T-shirt off my sweaty back and set it down on the ground. The sun poured into the area around the falls, the only area not completely blocked out by dense overhead foliage. I lay back on the log, keeping one foot on the ground for leverage, and soaked up the heat. I covered my eyes with my arm, shielding out the sun. I was imagining Shane there with me when I heard something that made my heart skip a beat. I sat bolt upright, certain I had heard someone's voice in what sounded like a whisper, carried in the wind. But there was no wind at all, and I was alone.

I called out, "Blake?" and heard no reply. Thinking I had perhaps drifted off to sleep momentarily and dreamt it, I walked over to the waterfall and splashed the sun-warmed water over my face. I decided it was time to leave the clearing. As I walked back up the hill, I stopped and carefully examined the heart on the oak tree. I wondered if Toby had spent a lot of time in these woods. A sadness filled me as I thought of the boy, knowing he was just a year older than me when he died. I stood there, staring at the heart carved so many years ago, and felt a lump in my throat. I didn't know Toby, but I felt sad for the loss all the same. I thought of how his life was cut short and how scared he must have been, being lost in the woods. I thought how sad it was that his body lay in some unknown location in the very woods I was standing in, having never received a proper burial. The forest was lovely, though, and there are worse places you could find for your final resting spot.

I looked at the other initials, C. H., and wondered how I would have felt if it had been me losing someone so special. I couldn't imagine losing Shane. The mere idea in my head made me feel sick to my stomach. I was only fifteen, but I was pretty sure that what I felt for Shane was love. I didn't know how I could know, but I did. I loved him. How did C. H. go on after losing Toby? Was C. H. still alive? So many questions. So many thoughts.

I kissed my hand and placed it on the heart. "I wish I coulda known you, Toby. I bet we woulda been friends," I said to the tree. I took a deep breath and glanced around the forest. Everything was so lush and aromatic, I breathed it in greedily.

As I made my way along the path to home, carrying my shirt in my right hand, I felt glad to be alive. Yes, I had a lot on my mind, but that didn't need to be a bad thing. Eventually, I knew I would be past the hardest part and just be able to live my life like everyone else lived his or hers. Every life has ups and downs, obstacles and barriers, but as long as you are true to yourself and have people in your life who love you and respect you for who you truly are, then you can make it through even the darkest days. I was telling myself all sorts of positive things like that as I walked along.

It seemed to be taking a long time to reach the field, but I wasn't walking very fast so I didn't think too much of it. A *crack* from behind me made me jump. I turned around and saw a brown rabbit hopping over some twigs. I smiled and watched it hop off into the woods. My expression changed instantly from joy to fear as I heard a thin whisper coming from the deep woods. There was only one word that was said:

Caleb

A chill caused those little hairs on the back of my neck to stand, which I hadn't believed possible, despite all the horror films I had seen that claim otherwise. My nipples became hard, and my body quivered. I put my T-shirt back on and looked over the woods, trying to see deeper into them. "Hello? Somebody there?" I called out. There was no reply. A crow flew off from the top of a tree, cawing as it went. I kept walking toward the meadow, not letting myself speed up and give in to the fear. When I arrived at the opening, the heat felt so overpowering that sweat instantly soaked my T-shirt, causing me to peel it off again. I reached the house in a few moments and went in the kitchen door, feeling drained and in dire need of a cold drink.

"Whoa, Caleb, you're dripping with sweat. It isn't that hot, is it?" Blake asked me. He was standing just inside the pantry door when I came in (Dad having put a wall back up a month before, giving us back the original food storage area. He also cut and framed in a proper doorway from the kitchen to the dining room).

I didn't answer him right away, heading to the fridge and grabbing the partially-filled pitcher of iced tea. I drank directly from the container. After downing about half the pitcher's contents, I wiped my mouth with my arm and said, "It's boiling out." I poured the rest of the iced tea in a glass and set the pitcher in the sink. I sat down at the table with my glass and mopped my brow with my shirt.

"Did you call for me while I was walking?" I asked, hoping for the simplest explanation to what I'd heard earlier.

"No, I've been on the computer most of the afternoon. Why?"

I decided against telling Blake any more at that time. "No reason. Just thought I heard someone call my name. That's all."

"Where've you been all this time?"

"I was in the woods, at the waterfall."

"For four hours?"

"Was I gone that long?"

"Yup. Fall asleep or somethin'?"

"I don't think … I mighta nodded off for a few minutes. Guess I just lost track of the time."

"Huh." Blake rummaged through the pantry. "Would you rather have a chicken stir-fry or chicken casserole for dinner? I gotta use up the leftovers in the fridge."

"Couldn't we have something cold? It's too friggin' hot to turn the stove on."

Blake's eyes lit up. "I'll make us a chicken Caesar instead. Good thinking, bud."

"What were you doing online for so long?"

"Talking to some of the guys from camp and Chloe. Your friend Ryley was on looking for you. I told him you were out and signed you off."

"Thanks. Sorry about that."

"No prob. You guys going to see *Eclipse* tonight, are ya?"

"Yeah."

"That looks cool. When do you want a drive in? Sixish?"

"If you don't mind."

"Not an issue." Blake began to chop up romaine lettuce he'd taken out of the fridge.

I put my glass in the dishwasher and asked Blake if there was anything I could do to help.

"No, thanks. Just stay and keep me company while I get things ready."

"Sure thing." I turned and sat on a stool on the other side of the island so I could be closer to Blake as he worked.

"Hey, turn around again for a sec," Blake instructed, motioning with his finger to spin.

I cocked an eyebrow and turned, wondering why. "What's wrong?"

"I thought so. Hold still, Caleb. You've got a tick on you."

"Seriously? Can you get it off?"

"Yeah, no sweat. Just don't move around, okay?"

"I won't."

I stayed motionless as Blake grabbed a bottle of extra virgin olive oil from a shelf in the pantry. He poured it onto my back, soaking the nasty little bastard trying to burrow under my skin.

"What's that gonna do?"

"It'll make it so it can't breathe and it'll back out. It isn't in too far, but it would be if we waited much longer."

"How come I can't feel it?"

"Cuz they do something to the skin when they bite that causes it to go numb."

"Is it out?"

"Yep. Now I just gotta yank the little sucker off."

Blake slid open a drawer and rustled around until he found the strawberry huller. He proceeded to use the huller to carefully pull the little insect off my back. He dropped it in a jar and filled the jar with water. He screwed on the lid and turned the jar upside down.

"Thanks."

"No big deal. Just glad I spotted it."

"Me, too, believe me."

"You'd better go wash your back. Get the oil off. Don't wanna get a bad burn."

"Yeah. Good idea. Thanks, bro."

I went upstairs and took a long, hot shower. All I could think about the entire time was hearing that distant voice calling my name in that painfully sad whisper.

Blake dropped me off at Shane's place just shortly after six. Astro greeted me as I went downstairs with Shane, tossing my things on the pull-out sofa down there. We always stayed down in the TV room when I came over because Shane's room was rather small—and his mom's room was right next to it. The sofa bed pulled out into a double, and we each slept in a sleeping bag on top of it. Astro slept wherever Shane was and would curl up on the floor next to his side of the bed, snoring loudly. He'd try to sneak up on the bed sometimes, but there just wasn't enough room. Shane would have to pretend to get upset with him and say, "Astro, get down!" in a stern voice. Astro would sulk a bit and come over to my side of the bed. I'd pat him and tell him he's a good dog, and Shane would joke, "Sure, make me out to be the bad guy."

After the movie, we went for coffees at Stape's before splitting up and all going our separate ways. Ryley walked with Shane and me down the main street.

"Thought you were going over to Drew's tonight?" Shane said.

"That was the plan, but his family and Hunter's are going camping tomorrow, and they'll probably leave early so I opted out."

"Wanna come hang with us?" Shane invited.

"If that's cool with you guys." Ryley looked back and forth between us, making sure.

"Definitely, bud," I replied.

"Sweet. Now I don't have to go home."

The three of us headed to the motel and went in the back door. Since it was nearly eleven o'clock, we had to be sure to keep quiet and not disturb any of the guests. There were only two cars parked out front of the twelve-unit motel, and I wondered how the business survived at all. It only ever filled up once or twice a year.

Down in the basement, we played the Xbox 360 for a time before leaving the television on Much Music as we got ready for bed. Ryley put the sofa cushions on the floor and used them as a makeshift mattress.

"If Astro bugs you too much, just tell him to go find his brain," Shane told Ryley.

Ryley laughed. "His brain?"

Shane chuckled. "Yeah, my dad used to say that when Astro was a pup and getting into mischief, he'd say, 'Go find your brain, boy' and poor Astro would go searching the house for his elusive brain. He can't focus on anything else until he finds it."

"Has he ever found it?" I asked, laughing.

"Well, he's brought me different things before, like his bone or his ball—almost always a 'B' word, but so far, no brain."

Astro looked around at the three of us, somehow seeming to know he was the brunt of some joke. He grumbled and rested his chin on his front paws. Then he farted loudly.

"Oh, God! Astro! You didn't!" Shane groaned.

We all roared with laughter.

When we had turned out the lights, we began to talk, as guys often do only once it's dark, about more serious things.

"I've got a problem, guys. Maybe you can help me out," Ryley said.

"We can try," I offered.

"I've got a major crush on Adria, but I don't know what to do about it. I mean, if I ask her out and she says no, then things will be awkward; and if she says yes and it doesn't work out, things will be even more awkward. I dunno. I really like her, but I don't want to screw things up, ya know?"

"I know exactly what you mean," Shane said.

"Stop thinking about it and just go for it," I suggested. "If there's stuff to deal with later, you'll deal with it later."

"If only it were that easy," Ryley said.

"If it's any consolation, man, I think Adria digs you, too," Shane stated.

"You think?"

"Hell, yeah. Every girl in the group likes you, Ryley. Hell, practically every girl in the school does."

"Screw off," Ryley said bashfully. "I know I don't have to ask, but you guys won't say a word to anyone about this, right?"

Shane yawned. "That's a given, man. Anything you say to us stays with us."

"Yeah. Definitely," I agreed.

"Back at ya, guys."

"Shit. It's late. We better get some zees," Shane said after pressing the Indiglo feature of his Timex.

Being more tired than I had realized, I fell asleep within minutes.

On the ride home the next day (Ryley having gone back to his place and Shane coming with me), I filled Shane in on what had happened when I was in the woods the day before.

"I told you, Caleb, I was on the computer all afternoon, and no one else was home. I don't think anyone was calling for you," Blake reminded me as he steered the truck around a pothole.

"I know what I heard, though. I'm positive someone called my name."

"Maybe the sound was carrying from somewhere else."

"But why would it happen to be my name if it were just a carried sound? There can't be that many other Calebs around here, are there?"

"You're the only Caleb I've ever met," Shane said. "It's not really all that common a name anymore. It's a nice name, though," he was quick to add. "And you think you heard it twice?"

"Well, I'm not sure. I was down by the waterfall, and I thought I heard something, but I mighta been partially asleep. On the way back, though, I'm positive I heard someone say, 'Caleb,' and I got really cold."

"But you were sweating like a pig when you came in the house," Blake said.

"I know. The minute I stepped outta the woods, I started to bake. It's so weird."

"Maybe someone was in the woods looking for their dog," Blake suggested.

"I dunno. Pretty odd name for a dog," Shane said.

"True."

"Well, there's gotta be some sorta explanation." I paused for a moment. "You don't think it was Toby's voice I heard, do you?"

"God. You're paranoid. Toby's dead. He died over sixty years ago. So, no, I don't think you heard his voice, Caleb," Blake said, scoffing at my idea. "If anything, I think it's the power of suggestion, mixed with an overactive imagination."

It wasn't like Blake to speak to me that way, and I was too surprised to respond.

"Don't be so quick to shoot down the idea," Shane told him, sounding a bit angry. "Who's to say it isn't possible? There have been too many odd things happening since you guys moved here to just wave it all off as nothing. Maybe there's something to all of this. I don't know what, but I certainly wouldn't discount all the things that have occurred as pure coincidence. The brown walls hidden in the back bedroom, the horseshoe in the loft that Caleb found at four in the morning because he saw a light in the barn, and the receipt we found in the loft the first time I visited—which I still can't make sense of. And let's not forget the shadow that shouldn't have been on the wall, the cold chills, and the screen door opening on its own."

Blake scratched at his stubble. "Moonlight in a torn curtain, a drafty old house, and the wind."

"Okay, but what about the heart we found going to the waterfall? That's connected to all this stuff, too. I know it is. We just need to figure out the sequence and the significance."

"Exactly," I said, feeling better that someone believed in me. I was frustrated with Blake's failure to look at things from my perspective.

"What are you guys? The Hardy Boys or something? C'mon, none of this makes sense. It's all just a bunch of nothing that you're reading *way* too much into."

"What? Hardly. Listen, I'm in Toby's old room. I'm the one who keeps having all these experiences. You think I'm enjoying all this? Hell no. If I wasn't worried, do you think I'd even waste your time talking about it? I just feel like if I don't tell the two of you about it, I'll go crazy. Of all the people I'd … forget it. Never mind." I was so pissed off with Blake I couldn't say any more. I knew that Shane would know I wasn't upset with him in the slightest. Shane's eyes were on me, and I had to look away, out the window.

Blake parked the truck in the driveway and shut off the engine. Shane, sitting between us, sat quietly as Blake held the steering wheel with one hand and removed the keys from the ignition with the other. Blake turned his face toward me and said, "I'm sorry, Caleb. I didn't mean to sound like such an asshole."

"You certainly did a good job succeeding despite yourself then," I shot back.

Blake, almost inaudibly under his breath, mumbled, "Shit."

"I don't know what to say to make you believe me, but I am sorry," he went on to say. "You know that I'd never purposefully hurt you, right? I just don't think you need to get yourself all worked up over ghost stories. I don't know what to say to make you feel better or that will make any difference, other than trying to rationalize all that's happened here."

"So you do admit that things have happened?" I challenged him.

"Nothing's happened to me. Or Dad or Mom—that I'm aware of. But I believe that you've had some strange things happen to you."

"I just don't understand what's going on. Is there something bad here? Something evil?" I asked no one in particular.

"No. There is nothing bad or evil here. There's just a lot of sadness," Shane told me. "You don't need to be scared, okay? You've got me on your side, and whatever is going on, we'll get to the bottom of it together. I promise."

"Hey, look, I'm in your corner, too, Caleb. I mean that. I may not get what's going on, but you can always count on me to be on your side—all right?" Blake told me, hoping to make some amends for his curt tone earlier.

I nodded. "I hope so."

"Know so," Blake confirmed.

He held his eyes on mine, and I replied, "Thanks."

"Okay, now," Blake said as he clapped his hands together, "I'm barbecuing potatoes and chicken burgers tonight, so let's go in and get things ready."

"Sounds good," Shane said.

As we walked up the steps to the house, Blake ruffled my hair. He didn't have to say anything more. I knew we were okay again.

"I'd mess with yours, too, but you'd have to let it grow some first," Blake teased Shane as we went inside.

As we were lying next to each other in my room that night, I held hands with Shane. For the first time, I felt that someone understood me better than my own brother did. I was still a little hurt at how Blake had treated me on the way home, and though he had apologized, I couldn't get over the idea that he hadn't instantly believed me. I knew there was a lot to be digested and that a great deal of it could indeed be picked apart and analyzed so as to totally discredit me, making me appear a complete fool, but I never expected my brother to be the one to make me feel that way. I forgave him; that was instant, but forgetting wasn't so simple.

"Thanks for sticking up for me today," I said, squeezing Shane's hand in mine, lacing our fingers.

"I'm your boyfriend—that's my job."

"Boyfriend. I like how that sounds."

"Me too. I've wanted to say it for a while now."

I rolled over on top of Shane's sleeping bag and kissed him. We ended up making out for a bit, but stopped before we got carried away, afraid of the noise we might make. Even if it was a big house, there were certain sounds it seems a parent always hears.

As we settled back down, I asked, "You really do believe me, don't you?"

"Yes. I really do."

I sighed. "Weird. I say I don't believe in ghosts, and yet, well, it looks as if I must."

Shane shifted uncomfortably in his sleeping bag. "There's something I need to tell you."

"Okay." I always get nervous when someone says that. My stomach instantly churns up its contents and makes me feel the need to use the washroom. Gross perhaps, but true.

"You remember how I told you I spent the night in here last year?"

"Yeah. You said nothing happened."

"No, if you remember correctly, I told you nothing *bad* happened."

I sat up and turned on the light. "Go on."

Shane sat up next to me and continued. "Well, I was sitting over in that corner," he pointed, "and it was really late at night. All the kids were outside, and I felt alone. Really alone. I was sitting there, hugging my knees against my chest, and all I had to do was think and all I could think about was my dad. I was in a really bad place at that time. I hadn't been painting or drawing at all, and the only thing I felt inside was this rage. I was so angry. Angry that my dad was dead, that my mom was depressed, and that I couldn't just be myself, ya know?"

I nodded and listened intently. Shane's voice was thin and barely audible as he spoke.

"I was scared when I was in here, but not because of any ghosts or anything. I was just scared that my life was going to go on as it had been, that each day was going to just keep getting darker and darker until I lost it completely. I couldn't face that, and I didn't have anyone I felt I could trust to talk to about it. I didn't even have Ryley and the gang to hang out with until after Christmas. Before then, I was always a loner, a kid who didn't even register high enough on the scale to warrant insults or teasing. I was just a closeted kid with no hope.

"I was sitting there, kinda crying to myself, thinking of all the crap I had to deal with and looking for any possible signs of hope. I cried more when I couldn't find any, so I took the hunting knife out from the strap I had around my leg and sat, watching the blade glimmer in the moonlight that came in here."

I knew what Shane had thought of doing that night, and I couldn't keep my eyes from watering. I felt so scared for that boy who sat in my very room less than a year ago.

"The blade was razor-sharp, and I cut my finger when I touched it. I watched the droplet of blood roll off and land on the floor, and it became so real what I was thinking of doing. I didn't know how I had gotten to that place, how I had even begun to consider suicide, but there I was. With tears streaming down my face, blurring my vision, I held the knife to my wrist to make the first vertical slash.

"But something caught my eye, and I looked up on the wall. There was a shadow there. A person's shadow. I turned around, expecting to see John or some other kid standing there, preparing to laugh at me for crying or just trying to frighten me. But there was no one. The house was silent. I listened carefully to hear footsteps on the stairs or a creaking door. Anything. But it was so quiet, my ears started ringing.

"That shadow was still on the wall, but I just figured it was the moonlight hitting something. At that point, I really didn't care too much. I started to press down on the blade, breaking the flesh. Quickly the shadow moved as I cut myself. I was crying, thinking it wouldn't be long before all this pain was gone, but then something happened." Shane's voice broke, and he had tears in his eyes as he kept talking. "I felt these arms around me, like someone was sitting on the floor next to me. It felt like someone was hugging me. Like someone cared. And for those few seconds that it lasted, I wasn't scared at all." Shane's wet eyes met mine, and I pulled him to me, holding him tightly.

"I'm so glad you're here," I whispered. "I can't imagine life without you."

Shane sobbed onto my shoulder, finally releasing the pain he had held all to himself for so long. We sat like that, holding each other, for some time.

"Do you think it was Toby that you felt with you that night?" I asked finally.

"I honestly don't know, but I like to think it was. I don't know why he would care about me, but I'm sure glad he did. I feel like I owe it to him to help him. If that makes sense."

"Of course it makes sense. Besides, anyone who looks out for my boy, I'd like to help, too."

"I think we need to try to figure out the connection of the stuff we've seen and heard. Maybe we can do something to help Toby find peace."

"Yeah. We should go for a walk in the woods tomorrow, see if we can get any more leads."

"Sounds like a plan."

"Think we'll find anything?" I asked, lying back down.

"I dunno, but whatever does happen, at least we'll be together." Shane put his head down on the pillow next to me, keeping direct eye contact with me. "I really care about you, ya know."

"I really care about you, too."

Shane kissed me gently on the lips and nestled in beside me. "Night, Caleb."

"Night, Shane."

Exhausted from his reliving of that night, Shane fell asleep almost instantly. I watched him sleep and couldn't recall ever seeing anything I thought more beautiful in my entire life. I kissed his forehead tenderly and closed my eyes. I was no longer scared of the idea that Toby's presence might be in the house and woods around me. If anything, I felt comforted by it. No ghost could be scary that would hug a lonely fourteen-year-old boy. I wanted more than anything to help Toby, if it was possible. There had to be a reason he wasn't at rest.

"Thank you, Toby," I whispered into the quiet of my bedroom. I listened, half expecting to hear a reply. Crickets chirped outside, but otherwise, the night was still.

On our walk through the woods, we carefully examined things as we drew nearer to the slope down to the waterfall clearing. Nothing appeared any different, and the forest was serene and tranquil. We were a bit disappointed that we found nothing of interest and heard nothing unusual on our journey that day. We spent some time at the clearing before turning around and returning home. We were going in to town that night to meet up with Ryley and Adria to hang out.

Blake came to pick me up around midnight and asked if Shane was coming back with us.

"Nah, he can't tonight. The motel is busy, and he hasta stay and help out his mom."

"Oh. Well, that's good. That the motel is busy, I mean."

"Yeah."

"Maybe you and me can hang out tomorrow," Blake suggested.

"Sure. That'd be cool."

"Anything you'd like to do?"

"Hmmm. Not really, I guess. You?"

"Well, I heard there's batting cages by the driving range in New Minas. It's about a forty-five-minute drive from here, but I thought we could check it out. Maybe grab some food somewhere and catch a flick in the evening. Sound good?"

"Yeah. That sounds awesome."

Blake smiled at me. I knew he was still feeling bad about the other day and was trying to make it up to me. "Good. We'll head out after lunch, okay?"

"Perfect."

Baseball was the one sport that both Blake and I loved to play. I enjoyed watching him play volleyball and compete in track events, but I never had any inclination to participate in those things. Baseball was by far the most aesthetically pleasing sport. The crack of a wooden bat (not those awful aluminum ones) as it made contact with the ball, the whack that erupted when the ball soared into the sweet spot of the catcher's mitt, the smell of the freshly cut grass, and the dust from the dirt between the bases. A batting cage was a poor substitute for playing the actual game of baseball, but it was still fun.

We spent over an hour in the cages and then killed some time at the driving range at the same location. We grabbed a slice of pizza before the movie and afterward got some food from a Mr. Sub and took it to a picnic park to eat. We sat on the tailgate of the old Ford and ate our subs, washing them down with Cherry Coke.

"This has been really fun. Thanks, Blake."

"My pleasure, bud. It's nice to spend some time with you again. Feel like I haven't been much good to you this summer."

"Don't be stupid."

"I mean it. I feel like you're pulling away from me, like maybe you're getting yourself ready for when I go away next year."

I shook my head. "No, it's not like that at all."

"We don't talk like we used to, though."

"I guess I don't know what to say. I mean, after last time ... you didn't exactly respond the way I expected."

Blake hung his head. "Look, I know I screwed up, and I still feel bad about it."

"I know. Figured this was kinda your way to try to patch things up." The sky was turning this amazing purplish-orange colour as the sun went down. The first of the streetlights began to hum as their bulbs flickered into action.

"No. I really just wanted to spend some time with you, like I promised."

"Oh. Right. I forgot about that. Sorry." I did feel bad for making Blake's promise to me sound like something he felt obligated to do.

"Don't be." Blake crumpled up his sub wrapper and stuffed it back in the paper bag. "Look, can we just start fresh? Forget the other day?"

I nodded as I wiped my mouth with a napkin and stuffed it into the bag.

"Cuz I really am on your side, Caleb. I want you to know that."

"I know."

"So you know you can talk to me about anything, right?" Blake sounded like he was getting at something.

"Yeah. I know. It's cool." I saw that Blake appeared awkward. He rubbed his hands together over and over again. "Something on your mind?" I asked him.

He studied my face carefully. "I need to talk to you about something, but I'm afraid you'll take it the wrong way or get mad at me, so I don't know if I should say anything or not."

I put down my bottle of pop and took a deep breath. "Just say whatever it is you need to say. I promise I won't get mad."

Blake tried to fix his eyes on mine, but I turned away, gazing at the skyline to free myself from his caring expression. "I just want to tell you, first of all, that I'm really glad you're my little brother and that I love you, Caleb. Nothing can ever change that, okay?"

I hadn't predicted him saying that. I found a lump forming in my throat. I couldn't look at him. I knew what he was going to say next, but after what he'd just finished saying, I knew everything was going to be all right, too. Not being able to speak, I nodded. I tried to fight back the tears that came up before he could say another word.

"If I'm wrong about this, well, I don't mean it to hurt you in any way, but I think that first kiss you told me about was with Shane.

Right?" Blake's voice was soft and caring. It was the same-sounding tone he'd used when I was small and had a bad dream, running into his room and crawling under the covers with him so I wouldn't be scared anymore. I trusted him completely.

"Yes," I whispered.

"Do you want to tell me anything?"

I nodded again as a tear spilled out and ran down my right cheek. I took a moment to gather the strength to say those two little words that I'd never actually had to say before. I turned to face my brother. "I'm gay."

Blake slid down the tailgate next to me and put an arm over my shoulder. It's hard to explain the overwhelming surge of emotions I had when I first spoke the words aloud. I felt like I could laugh and cry all at the same time. I looked at my brother with what I can only imagine looked like absolute desperation. If no one else on earth were going to love me unconditionally and stand by me against all odds, I needed it to be him. I knew, just from his expression and posture, that he had my back. Inside, I wept, but on the outside, I did my best to remain strong, stoic, and able to take whatever came next. I wasn't ever going to allow myself to feel weakened by something so central to my being. If anything, it was going to make me stronger. I knew if I spoke, however, the words that came out would tremble. I waited for Blake to speak.

He smiled at me and simply said, "I am so proud of you." He pulled me toward him and gave me a hug. I bit my lip as hard as I could.

Sitting back in my spot on the tailgate, I casually wiped at my eyes and asked, "Not that it matters, but how'd you know?"

"I didn't. Not for sure. But at camp this summer, one of the guys in my room, Jesse, was gay, and I had no idea until a bunch of us were talking one night about our homes and he mentioned how much he missed his boyfriend. I talked to him a lot and got to know the kinds of things he went through before coming out. A lot of what he said made me think of you, and I thought, if you were gay, I didn't want you to have to go through all that stuff alone. I went online and found a bunch of really good sites that explained what you might be going through and how I could let you know that I was someone you could be open with and not worry I'd tell anyone else."

"You really did all that for me?"

"Of course, I did. Jesse even told me that, if you wanted, you could e-mail him and have someone else to talk to."

"Thank you."

"And, just to let you know, Jesse's pretty hot. If that helps."

I laughed. It was nice of Blake to give me a chance to smile.

"Feel better?"

"You have no idea."

"Good."

"I've still got a long way to go."

"I know. But at least you won't have to do it alone, right?"

I nodded. "That means a lot to me."

"Not to be nosy ... but you and Shane haven't had sex, have you?"

"God." I turned red.

"I mean, it's cool if you ever do, just ... I just wanna make sure you're safe. That's all."

"No, we haven't had sex."

Blake nudged my arm with his elbow. "But you've thought about it, right?"

I went redder still. "Well, of course, I've thought about it. I think about it all the time. Don't you?"

"About sex with Shane? I mean, he is pretty cute and all, but ..."

"Idiot." I chuckled. "You know what I meant."

Blake laughed. "Of course, bud. I think about sex all the time, too. We're guys—it's how we're programmed."

"Have you ever had sex?"

Blake screwed the cap back on his empty bottle. "Yeah."

"Why didn't you tell me?"

"It's not something you brag about when it means anything to you."

"Was it Chloe?"

Blake shook his head. "Nah, man. I mean, don't get me wrong, she has a wicked body and I definitely thought about it a lot, but we just didn't know each other well enough. You know?"

"Yeah," I nodded. "So ... it was Danielle?" I asked, referring to Blake's last girlfriend in the city. They had broken up a few months before we moved away.

"Yeah."

"You two were together for quite a while."

"Almost a year."

"Yeah. So ... I mean, not to be too personal, but ... how was it?"

"It was really nice."

"Glad it happened?"

"My first time?"

"Yeah. Wait ... there've been other times?"

"Well, Danielle and I didn't only do it once," Blake replied.

"Oh. Duh. I meant with other girls?"

"No. Only Danielle."

"Cool. So you're glad it happened, I take it?"

"Absolutely."

"That's good. Umm ... were you safe?"

Blake looked at me closely and replied, "Always. Most definitely. And that's something you gotta promise me you'll be too. Right?"

I nodded. "I think I'm a ways from having to worry about that, but I promise."

"I've got condoms at home. If you ever need any, I've put a bunch in my travelling bathroom bag under the sink."

"Good to know." I scuffed at the dirt on the ground. "So, you really won't be, like, grossed out or anything if you know I'm having sex with another guy?"

Blake shook his head. "Not at all. As long as you're happy and the guy is good to you and you play safe, then power to you."

"Shane's really good to me."

"I can tell. I'm happy for you."

"He's pretty hot, too."

Blake laughed. "I gotta hand it to you, Caleb, he is a good-looking boy."

"It's kinda weird to hear you say that."

"Why?"

"I dunno. I can't imagine most straight guys saying that."

"Only the ones who have something to hide wouldn't. I mean, you can tell if a girl is attractive or not, right?"

"Of course."

"But that doesn't mean you wanna flip her over the end of a couch and bang the living shit outta her, does it?"

I laughed hard. "No. No, it doesn't."

"All right then. It's the same for me with guys."

"You've got a way with words, Blake."

He laughed. "C'mon, squirt. Let's go home."

"Yeah."

We tossed our garbage in the can by the front of the truck and got in the cab. Blake fired up the V8, and we pulled back onto the road.

"You think Mom and Dad will be cool with me? Think maybe they already know?"

"I can almost guarantee you that they don't know. You could say it in front of Dad, and he wouldn't take it in. Maybe if you wore a pink feather boa and a G-string at the time."

"I don't see that happening." I chuckled.

"I'm not sure how he'll react, to be honest. Mom? I think Mom'll be great. You know how much she loves us, and I don't think there's anything that could ever change that. You gotta remember, our parents may have their faults, but they've never been ones to judge other people or say anything negative. Think about it."

I did think about it, and Blake was right.

"I'm not ready to tell them yet."

"That's totally your call, bud. Only thing you need to know is that I'm on your side and that if I can do anything at all for you, I will. Okay?"

"Thanks, Blake." I took a huge, deep breath and exhaled.

"Don't have to thank me. Looking out for you is part of my job." Blake turned onto the highway and sped up to merge with the traffic. "Can I ask you something else?"

"Sure. Anything."

"How did it happen? Your first kiss, I mean. Did you know Shane was gay beforehand?"

"No. I just followed your advice. I stopped thinking about kissing him and actually did it."

"Wow. You're a brave little shit, aren't you?"

I smirked.

"So, what happened?"

"We were at the clearing in the woods, and everything just felt right. We seemed to have this connection like I'd never felt before. And, I dunno, just the way he was looking at me with water running down his face … God, he was beautiful."

Blake gave me a warm smile. "And, how did he react when you kissed him?"

"He kissed me back."

Blake chuckled. "Can't get a much better reaction than that, can you? That rocks, Caleb."

"Yeah. It was pretty nice."

We rode on in silence for a while, the throaty sound of the truck's modified dual exhaust with Rhino mufflers rumbling through the night.

"Blake?"

"Yeah?"

"Thanks."

As I stretched out in bed that night, I felt relieved to finally have talked to Blake about something so important. I was mentally exhausted; having come out to Blake was a big step, a very positive one, but also very draining. As I began to drift off to sleep, I heard the faintest whisper in my ear:

Caleb

I sat up in my bed and inspected the room with my eyes. Seeing nothing, I went down the hall to Blake's room. I tapped on his door and opened it. He was sound asleep in his bed. I walked back down the hall to my room and got back under the covers. I waited patiently to hear or see something, but fell asleep before anything happened.

Chaptor Eight

On the tenth of August, after we had returned home from a successful shopping trip in the city with my mother, I went upstairs to put away my new clothes. It was late by the time we got back, so I stripped down to my boxer briefs and crawled under the covers. I put on my reading glasses and picked up the novel I had been reading the past few nights, *The Talisman* by Stephen King and Peter Straub. It was Blake's favourite book of all time, and I could see why. Halfway through the novel, I found it hard to put it down each night, even when my eyes were so droopy I kept losing my place and had to read the same sentence over and over to make it sink in.

I found myself once more losing the battle with my eyelids and put the book down. I took off my Calvin Klein frames (with Blake's encouragement, I chose the designer frames for my new glasses. They cost a bit more, but I had to admit, they did make me feel better about myself than the previous pair I'd had) and folded them, placing them on my nightstand, where they always went. I glanced over as the glasses made a crunchy sound as they came to rest on an oak leaf that was long off the tree, brown and dry.

I picked up the leaf and examined it closely. I knew it hadn't been there when I went to bed, but it was possible I just didn't see it before. There weren't many oak trees on our land; in fact, the only one I could think of was the one on the way to the clearing in the woods. I didn't think Blake had been there yet, but I wanted to be sure, so I went down to his room and knocked on the door. I opened it when he said, "Come in," to find him sitting at the computer.

"Rafael Nadal, huh?" Blake said, commenting on the newest desktop wallpaper I had put on. The Spanish tennis star was shown in an action shot, pumping his fist and exposing his well-developed bicep on his left arm. It didn't hurt that the angle was slightly from the back, and his shorts were riding up on him at the same time.

"Umm, yeah. He's pretty sexy. You can change it if you want."

Blake shook his head. "It's fine. You put up with my swimsuit screensaver."

"True. Let's just agree to keep the mouse pointer neutral."

Blake laughed. "Deal."

"Have you been down the trail through the woods?" I asked.

"Nope. Not yet. Why?" he spun around in his chair and saw me holding the dead oak leaf in my hand.

"I found this on my nightstand. You didn't put it there, did you?"

"No. I wouldn't do that, Caleb."

"I just found it now as I took off my glasses."

"Lovin' the new frames, right?"

"Yeah. They're nice." I wasn't exactly thinking of my designer eyewear at that moment. "Any ideas?"

"There are a lot of trees around."

"Yeah, but not too many oaks. English oaks in particular. Only one I've seen is on the trail."

"You look it up online?"

"No. Dad's National Audubon Society book."

"You think it's another sign, don't you?"

"Yup."

"You worried?"

"No. Whatever it is that's here, I'm not frightened of it."

"You're sure there is something, aren't you?"

I nodded. "Positive."

"But I thought things only ever happened in the winter. Maybe late fall."

"I don't think ghosts follow a set of rules."

Blake paused for a moment, seeming to absorb what I said and silently agreeing. "Anything I can do for you?"

"No, thanks. I just wanted to check with you about the leaf. I'll let you get back to whatever you're doing."

"You sure you're okay?"

"Yep. I'm really not scared. I just wish I could make sense of all of this."

"Believe me, so do I."

I shrugged my shoulders and turned to go. "Good night, Blake."

"Night, bud. Have a good sleep."

"You too."

I returned to my room and put the leaf on my desk with the horseshoe and the receipt. I thought I understood the leaf and the horseshoe, but the receipt was still a mystery. I got back in bed and tried to connect the dots, but I drew a blank. I turned out my light and listened to the gentle breeze as I drifted off.

———

Shane came over on Sunday, and I showed him the leaf. Like me, he figured it was a sign trying to get us to see the tree on the slope with the engraving. Having discovered it already, we were confused.

"Maybe Toby doesn't know we've seen the marking," Shane suggested.

"I dunno. How could he know my name when I'm in the woods but not know I've seen the tree?"

"Hmm. Good point. What's Blake think?"

"I don't think he's all that interested. I mean, he listens to me and wishes he could help, but he doesn't have any of the experiences like we've had so he can't really get into it as much, you know?"

"At least he's cool about us."

"Yeah."

"Wanna go for a walk?"

"To the waterfall?" I asked slyly, lifting my eyebrows like Groucho Marx (my Dad is a fan, that's the only reason I know to use this analogy) in hopes Shane was thinking the same thing as me.

"Race ya," he said, storming in front of me down the stairs.

He bolted out the front door and I went out the kitchen, saving valuable time and taking over the lead.

"You sneaky little bastard," he called as I ran off ahead of him. I stuck my tongue out at him and heard him say, "Oh, I'm gonna get you for that!"

I jumped over the stream and darted into the woods. I hid behind a tree to pounce out at Shane, but he didn't appear. I stepped out from my hiding place and called for him. "Shane?" I looked toward the entrance to the woods and saw no sign of him. "This isn't funny, Shane! C'mon. Where are you?"

Caleb

A distant voice beckoned me.

"Shane, please don't! That's really mean."

Caleb

The voice repeated, only this time it was much closer sounding.

My mind kept trying to convince me that it was Shane off somewhere calling me, but I knew he wouldn't do that. Nervously, I spun around, hoping to see Shane appear at the opening to the stream and the field beyond, but still he wasn't there.

"*Shane!*" I screamed out. "*Where are you?*"

Caleb

I heard my name once more, the voice sounding as if it were being said right next to me. I turned slowly, not knowing what I could expect to find standing beside me in the woods.

Nothing.

This time, my own voice much softer, I asked the forest, "Toby?"

The woods were silent. A wind picked up, and I heard footfalls behind me. I turned to see Shane coming up the path, still running.

"What took you so long?"

"Ha. Ha. You weren't that far ahead of me," Shane said, panting slightly. "Besides, you cheated."

"Wait, wait, wait. You mean you were running all this time?"

"All this time? I was right behind you."

"Did you call out my name?"

"Nope. Used all my energy running after you. You're pretty speedy."

"Then it was Toby."

"What? You heard him again?"

"Yeah. Sounded like he was right next to me."

Shane took my hand in his. "I'm right next to you." He smiled at me. "You okay to keep going?"

"I'm fine. Just strange how it felt like we were separated for so long. You didn't hear me scream your name?"

Shane wore a mischievous grin. "Now that, I woulda remembered."

I blushed. "Seriously though?"

"No. I didn't hear anything. Sorry. Wind musta carried it away."

"There wasn't any wind when I called for you."

"You're kidding, right? The wind was blowing hard the whole time we were running."

"It wasn't in here. Wind didn't pick up until …"

"Until what?"

"Until I said 'Toby.'"

"You said his name?"

"Yeah."

"And that's exactly when the wind picked up again and you heard me coming?"

"Precisely."

"Seems almost like we're dealing with a time transfer, or whatever they call that in the movies. Like you stepped into a vortex or something."

"Remember that first time we came in the woods and we were gone for a long time, but it didn't feel like that much time had passed?"

"Yup. That was bizarre."

"There's gotta be something in these woods that we aren't getting."

I tilted my head back and looked high into the trees.

We kept trying to decipher what it was we were supposed to do as we made our way to the clearing.

"Think we're supposed to find his body?" I asked.

"I don't know. That'd be pretty tough. These woods are huge, and it's been sixty-seven years. Odds are, if he got lost, we'd get lost, and I don't think Toby wants us to get hurt in any way."

"No. You're right."

We sat down on our log and let the strong breeze cool us off. The sun was warm and pouring into the opening, causing us both to perspire. Shane took his shirt off and tossed it on the ground.

"It's so hot today. Feels a lot better with your shirt off," he hinted to me.

I peeled my T-shirt off and placed it on his. I leaned over and kissed him. He put a hand to the back of my neck, and our bare upper bodies touched as we made out.

That night, Ryley came over to hang out with us. We stayed up late watching movies, not going up to my room until almost two in the morning.

"This'll be my first time to sleep in the famous back bedroom," he noted as he laid his sleeping bag on the air mattress (Blake had finally patched it) at the side of the bed.

"Don't expect too much," I said.

"This place is cool, but I gotta admit it's kinda a letdown knowing all those stories are made up. You gotta have us out this winter during a storm, Caleb. Maybe something freaky will happen then."

"According to the stories I've heard, nothing ever happens when there's a group of people around," Shane stated.

"Hmm. That's true. Oh well. It would still be fun to be here in a storm. Be all stranded and have the power and phone lines go out. We could sit around and tell ghost stories," Ryley insisted.

"What are we—twelve?" Shane asked sarcastically. "Sounds too much like Cub Camp to me."

Ryley chuckled. "You know what I mean."

"You ask Adria out yet?" I asked, changing the subject.

"I almost did the other night, but I chickened out."

"You're running out of summer, man. Not much time left for romance," Shane taunted.

"Yeah, yeah, I know. I was thinking of asking her to the first dance once school starts up, but then I thought that's too far off, and so I was just about to ask her when I felt stupid and kept my mouth shut."

"Bite the bullet and go for it, Rye. I know she likes you," Shane told him.

"I hope so. She's incredible, and she has no idea. I mean, I just start to talk about her, and I get all tongue-tied and feel like a complete douche. It's so frustrating." Ryley mocked pulling out his hair. "How 'bout you guys? Anyone either of you are interested in? You've never told me."

"You've never asked," I kidded.

"Shit, I'm sorry. I shoulda. I mean, we're all being honest with each other, right? You guys know who I like, so come on, spill it, who do you like?"

"You promise you won't tell anyone else?" I wanted to know.

"Of course. I wouldn't trust you if I didn't want you to be able to trust me."

"Fair enough. You wanna try to guess, or should we each just tell you?" Shane asked.

"I'm not so hot with guessing games, but I'll give it three tries and if I don't get it, tell me … okay?"

"Fine."

"All right. Shane … let me think. I bet you like Mandy."

"Who's Mandy?" I asked.

"Mandy Simmons. She's in one of the other classes, but she's right into art and stuff, figured she'd be Shane's type."

"Oh God … Mandy Simmons? Are you serious?"

Ryley shrugged. "It's only my first guess."

"Yeah but … dude … give me a little credit."

"What, is she a heifer or something?" I asked.

"No, not at all," Shane said. "She's just really mousy. I mean, I guess she's kinda pretty in an artsy sorta way, but she is definitely not my type."

"Okay. Let me try again." Ryley rubbed his temples, trying to conjure up the right name. "I'm having trouble here. Is it someone in our group?"

"Yes."

"That's better. Now I think I can see it. It's Moria, right?"

"Nope."

"Dammit. Okay ... Uh-oh, it isn't Adria, is it?"

"No. Don't worry."

"Phew. Had me worried there for a second. So, it's Laura?"

"I admit nothing. You gotta try to guess Caleb's first."

"All right, but then you gotta tell me. I haven't known you as long, Caleb, so I'm just gonna be taking shots in the dark. Umm ... Megan, from homeroom? She's pretty."

"Yes, she is, but no, not her."

"Hmm. This is hard. Oh, what about Moira? You blushed when she said you were cute."

"He blushes all the time," Shane said.

"Nope. Not Moira."

"Crap. I dunno then," Ryley laughed. "How about Hunter?"

"Closer," I replied.

Ryley stopped laughing. "Oh shit. Really?"

"I said 'Closer,' not that it was Hunter."

"Yeah, but you're gay?"

I nodded. "Yup."

"Goddamnit. I wouldn't have wasted two guesses on girls had I known that. It's not fair. I get two more chances," Ryley exclaimed.

I laughed, pleased with Ryley's casual reaction.

"It's only fair; you gotta let him try again," Shane agreed.

I sighed, pretending to be bored by the proceedings. "If you must."

Ryley laughed. "Okay, now, you'll have to permit me the indulgence of an ego boost—is it me?"

I laughed so hard I almost fell off the bed.

"I didn't think it was that implausible," Ryley joked, mocking hurt.

"Sorry, Rye. It's not you."

"Jesus. Well, it's not totally inconceivable that you might like me, is it? Aren't I cute?"

"Yes, actually you're very cute. Hot even. And you're really cool, but you're not the one."

"Heh. Knew I could still get an ego boost if I whimpered." Ryley smirked.

"One more guess," Shane told him.

Ryley looked at me more carefully and then glanced over at Shane. "Oh my God ... Of course, duh!" he slapped his forehead. "You two like each other."

"We have a winner," I deadpanned.

"Hey, that's great. Why didn't you guys tell me before?"

"Guess we were both worried that you might not wanna hang out with us anymore," I admitted.

"God, do I come off that shallow?"

"No, man, we just weren't sure. The more we've hung out with you, the more comfortable we've gotten. Besides, we've only been out to each other for a little over a month. You're the first person other than my mom and Blake to know," Shane informed him.

"Well, I think it rocks. Power to you."

"Thanks, Rye."

"Yeah, thanks, bud," I said.

"Hey, we're friends. Friends stick together. But ..." Ryley hesitated a moment. "I gotta ask you guys something ... you really think I'm hot?" He tried not to smile but couldn't hold it back. We were all laughing a second later.

⁓

During the last two weeks of summer vacation, nothing more happened with Toby. I didn't hear my name being called, and I didn't find or receive any more strange items. I began to doubt the validity of it all. Perhaps my mind had been playing tricks on me the entire time. The thing that still bothered me was that time in the woods when Shane should have been right behind me but wasn't. I didn't think I'd ever understand that. It was the only thing that stayed with me, somewhere at the back of my mind, for the remainder of vacation. It had been the best summer of my life, and I felt as if maybe Toby were offering me a reprieve to let me enjoy it. Or maybe he was pacing himself, planning for something much bigger.

Chapter Nine

Three days prior to the commencement of school for another year, and my first in senior high, I decided I wanted to make a special evening for Shane and me. I planned it so it was a night my parents were going to be out at some get-together with friends of theirs in the city. They would be gone overnight, and that meant Blake and I had the place all to ourselves. I spoke with Blake the day before our parents went away.

"Wanna go for a walk in the woods with me today?" I asked him after breakfast.

"Sure. It'll be the first chance I've had to go all summer."

We put on our sneakers and went out the back door. We crossed over the stream and entered the forest, the concentration of trees immediately blocking out any trace of our whereabouts to the outside world.

"It's really pretty in here," Blake commented. "I can see why you and Shane come here so often."

"I'll show you the waterfall at the clearing, if you want."

"Yeah, I'd love to see it." Blake looked up and took in all the surroundings. "You can barely see the sky at all in here."

I led Blake down the pathway to the waterfall, stopping to show him the oak tree with the carving on it.

"Wow. So this is the infamous tree. It must be ancient. Look at the size of it." Blake felt the rough old bark with his hand. "Still no idea who C. H. is?"

"Nope. No clue."

We kept going down to the falls. I sat on the log as Blake splashed water over his face to cool off.

"God, it sure is hot in these woods," he said as he got his hair wet.

"Yeah. It seems to trap the humidity."

"You guys ever go any farther than here?"

"No. We didn't want to get lost."

"Smart move. Just wondering cuz of the path over there."

"Where?" I asked, jumping to my feet and going to where Blake stood.

"Right there." Blake pointed to a path between two spruce trees that neither Shane nor I had spotted.

"I never noticed that before."

"I imagine you guys had other things on your minds when you came here," Blake hinted. I blushed, giving myself away. "What about those times you were here by yourself?"

"Umm. No. I was always kinda … umm … preoccupied."

Blake laughed. "Try using the shower like every other guy."

"Rather difficult when you share a bathroom."

"Good point. Well, just keep an old towel under your bed or something. Works for me."

"I really wish I didn't know that." I chuckled.

"C'mon, you wanna go down the path a ways? See where it leads?"

"Okay, but if we can't see the waterfall anymore, we turn back."

"Agreed."

I held back the branches growing over the path so I could get past the trees. The section of forest on the other side looked similar to the one we had just descended from—lush and green, humid and still, and blocking out most of the sunlight.

"I wonder how far this goes," I said.

"I'm guessing a fair distance if that kid got lost."

"That musta been scary for him."

"I'd imagine. I read somewhere, though, that once you get really cold, you just sorta curl up and get sleepy. Supposedly, it isn't that bad a way to die," Blake informed me.

"Still, it's hard to think of someone close to our own age dying like that, all alone and out in the cold."

"True," Blake agreed.

Suddenly Blake stopped walking and held on to his stomach. "Ugh," he mumbled.

"What's wrong?"

"I just got this sharp pain in my abdomen."

"You okay? You feel sick?"

"No. It's not like that. It's like … I dunno."

"Wanna turn back?"

"Yeah, I think we better."

Blake and I returned to the clearing and sat on the log.

"You okay?"

"Yeah. I feel better now. That was weird. You ever get a feeling like that?"

"No, but I've never gone that far on the trail before."

Blake eyed me carefully. "Let's go back to the house, all right?"

"Sure."

I followed Blake up the slope and turned back to see the waterfall once more. Something happened on that trail. I wondered if it was where Toby had died. I couldn't understand how I hadn't noticed the path before, despite being otherwise engaged.

Shane came over the next night, and Blake made dinner for the three of us. We were served barbecued chicken in a peach glaze, a rice salad made with raspberries and mandarin orange segments, and steamed broccoli with a white wine vinegar dressing. We savoured every mouthful of the delicious meal and repeatedly told Blake how good everything was as we cleared our places.

For dessert, Blake presented us with large slices of mocha mousse cheesecake with chocolate sauce, cherries, and whipped cream drizzled over the top. They were carefully arranged on chilled glass plates.

We took our desserts into the family room and put on a movie. The warm air blowing in from outside drifted into the front room and, combined with the big meal we'd just had, made me start to yawn. I couldn't even sit up, I got so tried. I curled up next to Shane on the couch and rested my head on his chest. He brushed a loose hair back from my forehead and kissed the top of my head. I drifted off to sleep.

When I woke up, Shane was still holding me, and the movie was still playing. Blake was sitting in the recliner, and I smiled at him sleepily.

"Welcome back, sleepyhead," he teased me.

"How long was I out?"

"'Bout an hour. Missed most of the movie, but I didn't wanna grab the remote from the table and risk waking you," Shane informed me.

"God, you two are so cute together, it's almost nauseating." Blake pretended to retch.

"Someone sounds jealous," I said.

"Yeah, well, I kinda am. This is the first summer in a long time I haven't had a girlfriend. I can't wait for school to start and I get the opportunity to see someone."

"Ugh, school. I don't even wanna talk about it," Shane stated.

"I'm not dreading it this year, but I could use a longer summer," I said.

"Well, you've got forty-eight hours of freedom left. Better make the most of it." Blake leaned down to the side of his chair. "Think fast!" he said as he tossed a can of beer at me.

"Sweet. How'd you score the beer?" I asked.

"It's really not that hard. Shane, want one?" he asked my boyfriend.

"Absolutely."

Blake tossed him a can, and we cracked them open together. The three of us polished off the better part of a two-four of Budweiser in a couple of hours, and I enjoyed the first major buzz of my life. I don't exactly remember what we talked about, but I know we laughed a lot.

When we decided to call it a night, Blake went to his room, and for the first time, Shane and I got in my bed together. I think we both felt almost naughty not having one of us in a sleeping bag, but we soon got over it. We were both still buzzed from our first real beer-drinking experience, and we began to make out. Shane slid over on top of me, and our bodies pressed against each other. I could feel his hardness against my own. We rolled around, each taking time being on top of the other.

Shane licked at my nipple, and I let out a faint whimper of delight. I held his behind with both hands and allowed one hand to slip under the waistband and feel his butt. We rolled over again, and I was on top of him. This time he had his hands on my ass, giving it a squeeze.

As much as I wanted it to go on, I felt myself ready to explode. "Whoa ... stop."

Shane looked at me, lightly panting. "What's wrong?"

I shook my head, my hair damp with perspiration. "Nothing's wrong. I just ... I just wanna slow down for a bit. Okay?"

Shane kissed my lips. "Sure." He slowly slid his hands out of the back of my shorts and placed them on my back. He looked deep into my eyes. "I love you, Caleb."

Without a moment's hesitation, I replied, "I love you, too, Shane."

We began to kiss again, but I heard a heavy sigh and a muffled sound of crying in the distance. Both of us froze.

"Do you hear that?" Shane asked me.

"Yeah. Sounds like crying, right?"

"It's coming from outside," Shane said.

We got up and went to the window. There was a flicker of light in the barn, like I had seen months before when I found the horseshoe.

"You see that?"

"Yeah."

Without another word, we slid on some jeans and ran out into the hot late-summer night. At the door of the barn, we slowed. I put a finger to my lips and gingerly opened the side door. The muffled crying sound became clearer, but still distant. I pointed up to the hayloft and took hold of the first rung. As quietly as I could, I made my way to the top, slinking onto the platform in my best attempt at stealth. Shane was right behind me. I cautiously examined the area around us, peering into dark corners that the moonlight didn't illuminate. I felt Shane's hand on my arm, keeping contact with me as he looked over the other end of the loft. I wasn't really scared, but my heart was pounding in my chest.

"See anything?" Shane whispered.

"No. You?"

"No." Shane's hand tightened its grip on my forearm. "Wait a sec ... there's something over here."

I turned and followed Shane into the darkest recess of the loft.

The thinnest line of light just caught the edge of something, making it sparkle. As we got closer, I became very cold.

"It's freezing back here," I shivered, my breath forming little clouds as I spoke. I wished we'd put on shirts and socks along with our jeans.

"Check it out," Shane urged, kneeling down in the corner. I knelt down next to him and saw a small puddle of water on the floorboard. "This has gotta be really fresh, or these old boards woulda soaked it up by now."

"It's so cold, you'd think it woulda frozen."

"Yeah, but it's only early September. There's no way it's really this cold."

I reached out and touched the tiny puddle with my right index finger. "It's lukewarm."

Shane took my hand and placed my wet finger to his lips. He licked his lips and whispered, "Tears."

I don't know why, but thinking the ghost of a boy roughly my own age was crying made me feel helpless. "We've gotta help Toby."

Shane took my hand in his, lacing our fingers together. "We will."

Any buzz we'd been feeling was gone. We were sober and wide-awake at that point, and I regretted stopping what we had begun earlier.

"Hey, Shane, look … about earlier …"

"Caleb, you don't need to explain. It's probably for the best. I mean, it was hot, and I gotta admit, I really wanna be with you, but I want us to be clearheaded and it should be special."

I nodded. "That's exactly how I feel."

"What should we do now?"

"I'm not sure."

"Should we tell Blake about what happened up here?"

"We'd better. I think we need to go into the woods."

"Now?"

I nodded.

"Dammit," Shane mumbled. "I wish I didn't agree with you."

We talked to Blake about what had happened in the barn, and like us, he couldn't think of any logical explanation and had given up on the idea that he could rationalize all the things that had taken place. The experience he had on the extended path in the forest seemed to have made him accept the idea that Toby was still on the property; otherwise, he would have claimed it was just cramps from something he'd eaten.

"So, how do we go about figuring out how to help him?" Blake asked us.

"I wish I knew. I keep waiting for something to happen that will give us a real lead," I said.

"Too bad Toby can't just sit down and talk with us," Shane said. "Sure would make it a lot easier to help him. Only thing that we've heard him say is Caleb's name, and only Caleb has heard that. I did hear him crying tonight, but that's as far as he's gotten with me."

"Well, you're still one step ahead of me. I haven't heard anything at all. I haven't found anything either. Only thing that happened to me was that weird feeling in the deeper woods," Blake noted.

"Deeper woods?" Shane asked.

"I can't believe I forgot to tell you. Blake and I were down at the falls yesterday, and he spots this path between two big old spruce trees, so we follow it a ways. And as we're walking, he gets this awful feeling in his gut," I explained.

"I felt like someone had stabbed me or something," Blake said.

"So we turned back and came home."

"Whatever it is that we're supposed to do has something to do with that path," Shane stated. "We need to go up there."

"I am *not* going in there at night." Blake was adamant.

"Maybe we need to go at night. Maybe that's the key," I said.

"You have flashlights?" Shane asked.

"Boys, there is no way I am letting you go out there at night. Forget it. If you insist on returning to the woods, I will go with you in the morning, but *not* tonight. Got it?" Blake said sternly. He'd never spoken to me in quite that severe a way before, and I knew he was genuinely worried.

"Blake, I don't believe that there's anything that can hurt us out there. We just need to see if we can get another clue. We've gotta help Toby," I pleaded.

"I really hate all this," Blake grumbled in a nearly inaudible tone.

"Man, it's not exactly fun for any of us, but put yourself in Toby's place. Wouldn't you want someone to try and help you?" Shane asked him.

Blake sighed. "Well, now that I feel guilty, I pretty much have to go. But if anything the least bit off happens, we're outta there; and if I say we turn back, you can't argue. Just turn tail and run with me. Got it?"

"Got it," we agreed.

"But, Blake, aren't we kinda hoping something off does happen?" Shane said.

Blake couldn't help but smile a bit. "Smart-ass. Go get some flashlights and make sure they work really well."

Within five minutes, we were out the back door of the house, clothed more appropriately for foraging in the woods and brandishing our trusty flashlights. We didn't turn our lights on until we reached the stream, as the moon was nearly full and resplendent. Upon crossing the stream, we clicked on our torches and stood, side by side by side, peering into the pitch-black forest.

"This is stupid," Blake muttered. "We do have extra lights, right?"

"Yup. Two of 'em. Plus I grabbed one of Dad's Zippos."

"Did you make sure it's full of fluid?"

"Yep. I topped it up."

"Good thinking."

"Your dad smoke?" Shane asked.

"No. He used to, but he quit. Still has a bunch of old lighters kicking around. He sorta collects them. I didn't bring one of his good ones, just a beat-up old one I found by the fireplace. I think he said it's actually worth something, but the finish is gone and you can't clearly see the markings on it anymore."

"What the hell is this, *Antiques Roadshow*?" Blake said sarcastically. "If we're gonna do this, let's get moving."

We started to walk along the path, but it narrowed quickly and we were unable to walk next to one another, having to go in single file. Two people could walk side by side, but under the circumstances, walking in a line seemed best suited to the situation.

"Should we keep quiet or keep talking?" Blake asked from the back of the line.

"Talking is good," I suggested. Anything was better than thinking how in horror movies the single-file line always had a tragic ending for the person at the front or the back of the line—being consumed by a bloodthirsty, maniacal monster was a popular choice.

We talked about the upcoming school year and baseball and music—anything at all that had nothing to do with our mission—until we reached the waterfall. We carefully negotiated the slope down to the clearing, but I still managed to drop my flashlight. Luckily, it continued working when I picked it up off the ground.

"So far so good," Shane said. "It's really rather nice in here at night."

Shane was right. The clearing was beautiful in the moonlight—the ultrawhite light spilling over the wet rocks behind the waterfall and the log appearing like a bed, with a large clump of moss at one end for a pillow.

"Yeah. It's incredible," Blake agreed without a hint of sarcasm.

We stopped walking, taking a chance to rest on the log momentarily before continuing on. "Wow, it's already after two," Shane announced. "We keep walking, it'll be close to dawn by the time we get back, probably."

"We can sleep in all we want. I'm not the least bit tired yet. Are you?" I asked them both.

"Nope. I'm good to go," Shane responded.

"Me too," Blake said.

"Good. Let's get mov—"

Caleb

I stopped talking in mid-sentence as I heard my name being called in the distance … down the path.

Caleb

"You guys hear that?" I asked, frozen in place. I turned to see both my brother and Shane nodding. We turned our flashlights back on and pushed our way between the outstretched branches of the two spruce trees.

I went in first and stopped on the other side, waiting for the others. My flashlight went dead. I shook it hard, but nothing happened. "Crap. Shane, hand me another flashlight. Mine's toast." I listened and heard nothing. I turned back to the trees and saw no movement. Shane and Blake were gone.

Despite what I had told myself about Toby and not feeling threatened, I was scared. I fumbled in my pocket for the Zippo and spun the wheel under my thumb, the flame shooting up and offering me limited visibility. All I had to work with was the small circle of glowing amber around me. The trail wouldn't light up at all until I entered that area of it, and that would mean it would be black as tar behind me. I swallowed hard, trying to work up the courage to go forward, knowing there was a reason I was separated.

Caleb

I heard the voice calling me again, sounding like it was down the trail ahead of me, not off in the distance, but in the path itself. I wanted my brother and my boyfriend with me. I snapped the Zippo shut, not wanting to start a fire as I pushed my way back through the spruce branches. I expected to see Shane and Blake still standing there, but the clearing was devoid of anyone. I stepped over the stream and wandered around the clearing, trying to take in everything to see if there was something I was meant to notice. I started up the slope and stopped at the oak tree's base, flicking on the Zippo once more to see the carving.

The bark was unmarked.

Shivering, I felt the trunk of the tree, trying to feel for the cut-out bits of fibre where the heart and initials had been placed. I felt nothing at all but the rough texture of an old tree. I heard the sounds of what I thought were two people coming from the clearing. I ran back to find Blake and Shane, but when I got there, everything was as I had left it— quiet and empty. I walked over to the waterfall and slipped on a rock, hitting the ground hard on my right side. "Shit!" I cried out, more angry with myself than in pain. I had gotten fairly wet when I landed, and the water on my skin felt as if it were beginning to freeze. The temperature in the clearing seemed to drop further and further. I wished I was back home, lying in bed with Shane, feeling warm, comforted, and loved. All I felt in the clearing was cold, wet, and alone. And scared. I picked myself up, rubbing my arms in an attempt to warm them.

I ran back through the spruce trees and heard voices when I reached the other side. The next thing I saw was Shane breaking through the path. I practically knocked him over as I ran up to him and hugged him with all my might. "What happened?"

Blake burst through the trees and asked similar questions. "What's wrong? What happened?"

"It was just like that time you were running after me," I said to Shane. "I came through the trees first, and you guys didn't show. I heard my name being called again from right up the path, but I couldn't see anything cuz my flashlight died. I went back through the trees, and you were gone. I thought maybe I was supposed to find something, so I looked around and went back up to the oak tree. Then everything got really cold again. I flicked on my lighter to see the engraving, but it wasn't there."

"It had to be there," Blake insisted.

"No, I swear to you, it wasn't. I checked all over the tree trunk, and there was nothing on it at all. Then I heard footsteps, and it sorta sounded like voices, but I'm not sure, coming from the clearing."

"Did you say voices? As in more than one?" Shane asked.

"Yeah. I figured it had to be the two of you, so I ran back down. I slipped on wet stones and fell. I got pretty wet, and it was so cold I was sure it was gonna start to freeze on me. When I got up, I tore through the branches here, and I heard you guys, and see, look, now my flashlight works again."

"You say you fell and got wet?" Blake asked.

"Yeah."

"But, Caleb, you're completely dry," he told me.

I checked my clothes, touching the areas I knew had to be wet. Blake was right. I was bone-dry.

"That doesn't make sense," I said.

"You're dry in this time. You fell in the past. When you landed, did you scrape yourself or anything?" Shane wanted to know.

"Yeah, I got some scratches. I went down pretty hard."

"Show me."

I flashed my torch on my arm where I knew it had to have bled, around the elbow.

"It looks fine. Does it hurt?"

I moved my arm around. Shaking my head, I replied, "No."

"You did it again—you found the portal."

"Portal? What the hell are you talking about?" Blake asked.

"Like Caleb said, a while back we were running in the woods, and he got ahead of me. I swear I was right behind him the entire time, but Caleb didn't see me and he heard someone calling for him. Three times, right?" I nodded to confirm the detail. "And the third time, it sounded like the voice was coming from right next to him, right on the path. Weirdest part is the wind. It was blowing hard the entire time, but Caleb told me the woods were quiet and that there was no breeze at all. When the breeze did pick up again, I was coming up the path. Somewhere in there, he was in a different time."

Blake tried to absorb all this information. "Hang on a sec. You said that there was nothing carved in the tree, right?"

"Right."

"So that means, going by this time-portal theory, that you had to be back before it was carved. Does that make sense?"

"As much as any of the other stuff," Shane stated.

"But why—what's the point?"

"That's why we have to keep going, to find out," I said.

"God, this is eerie. I think we should turn back." Blake made the suggestion but did not insist.

"No. We need to keep going," I said.

We journeyed on, breaking new ground. At the point where Blake and I had turned back the other day, we felt a sudden chill, but it didn't last and we ventured forth. I held the side of my watch to get it to glow. We had passed three in the morning.

"Guys, I don't think we're going to accomplish much more tonight," Blake said. "We should start back."

"I think you're right. Whatever we were supposed to find tonight, we found. Let's go," I agreed.

"We oughta mark this spot somehow, so we can remember exactly how far we've come for next time," Shane suggested.

"Good call. Too bad we don't have any spray paint," I said.

"Here, tie this around the tree there," Blake instructed, handing me one of his orange shoelaces.

I took the lace and tied it securely to a birch tree. With that done, we began our trek for home. I stopped and checked the oak tree on our way back up the other side of the clearing and found the initials carved in the heart as always.

It was close to four o'clock when we crossed the stream and headed up the path toward the house. We were all tired and barely spoke as we climbed the stairs. Lying next to Shane, I still felt cold and scared, remembering my experience just a few hours before. I took Shane's hand and held it in mine, pressing it to my chest. He snuggled up closer, and I fell asleep as he kissed my ear softly, whispering, "I'll never let anything hurt you. I love you, Caleb."

Chapter Ten

On Tuesday morning, after a long weekend of silence from Toby, I found myself in the washroom with Blake getting ready for my first day of school. It was the first time we had started school on the same day since I began grade seven. Junior high students went for their first day on one day, senior high students on the next. Though we weren't rushing, everything seemed to happen in fast-forward. Shave, shower, dress, breakfast, out the door—all in the space of a half-hour.

The bus was supposed to pick us up at the end of our road, which was about a kilometre walk (that I didn't look forward to in winter). I was pleasantly surprised when my father mentioned something about that very thing as we ate breakfast.

"I've decided not to put a plow on the truck. I don't wanna take the chance of doing any damage to it," he told us. We both knew he loved that truck and planned to keep it forever.

"So, whatcha gonna do?" Blake asked.

"Buddy of mine at work was telling me he's got an old Bronco II … you know, those little jobbies Ford churned out before SUVs were everywhere. It's on the same basic chassis as the old Rangers, I believe. Anyway, says he'll let me have it for five hundred bucks. The body's solid and it's roadworthy, 'cept it doesn't run very well. I thought maybe if I got it here sometime this week, you could have a look at it, Caleb, and see if you couldn't get 'er up to snuff."

I practically dropped my spoon from my mouth back into my bowl of Shreddies.

"Figured I could put it in the barn; let you use it as a garage of sorts. If you get it working, it'll be great cuz it has a little plow attachment on it. Well, it isn't on it now, cuz Hank was using it this summer for off-roading. But if you can get it going, we'll stick the plow on it, and you guys can get the road cleared in the morning up to the bus, park it at the end of the road, and when you get home, plow your way back. Sound like a plan?"

"That sounds awesome," Blake said, "but, um … just one thing, Dad."

"I'm all ears."

"Well, if Caleb gets it running and it's safe enough, could we maybe use it for more than plowing? Like, going to school sometimes and stuff?"

Dad scratched at his chin. "I'll put it like this: if you boys can see to it that it's safe and secure and you never complain about having to plow the road, even if it's at 6:00 a.m. so I can be off to work on time, I think we can arrange something. Insurance will go up cuz you'll have to be listed as the principal driver and someone's gotta put gas in the tank …"

Blake nodded. "I know. I'm trying to get an after-school job. I've actually got an interview tomorrow at four."

"Where?"

"At the Home Hardware."

"Good for you." Dad smiled at us. "I just wanna make sure, Caleb, that you really are interested in working on the Bronco. I was thinking it would be a good experience for you. Never know, you may wanna be a mechanic. And hey, there's no pressure from me, either. I don't want you to think it's either you fix it or you guys don't get the vehicle to use. If there are things you can't do or need help doing, we'll have someone else look at it. Fair enough?"

"Sounds good to me. I'm gonna have to get some tools, though."

"Yeah, we'll pick up some basics on the weekend and get the rest as you need them. And don't worry, I'll make sure we get good quality tools for you, okay?"

"Better than okay."

I could picture those big red metal tool chests on wheels, fully stocked with shiny wrenches and ratchets and screwdrivers. I could see the entire barn converted into my own repair shop, my shingle hanging outside. Maybe someday I'd get into body work, too … Caleb's Custom Cars.

Dad chuckled at my obvious enthusiasm. "That's settled then. I'll call Hank today."

Blake and I walked up the road to the bus. It was too nice outside to be going back to school and be stuck in sticky, overcrowded classrooms. I was looking forward to seeing all my friends, though, and getting Shane's reaction to my new clothes. Also, I was really excited about getting the Bronco to work on, and if that meant going through tedious days of school to get me closer to the time I was in the barn playing with my new toy, then so be it.

"It's strange that Dad would want to get that Bronco, isn't it? I mean, he's never had any interest in what I like to do before," I said.

"Dad's a lot happier now. His job might be more stressful but he isn't in physical pain all the time because of it, and that makes life a lot easier for him. Plus, with Dad, doing something like this, well, it's his way of showing you that he loves you. Besides, I think he'd be kinda proud to brag that his fifteen-year-old son can fix vehicles."

"I hope I don't let him down."

"As long as you try your best, you won't."

"Sure would be fun to have it to use."

"Yeah. Just hope it's not some hideous colour. You'll have to get into body work and painting next."

"I was kinda thinkin' the same thing."

Upon arrival at school, we entered the gymnasium to wait for the assignment of homeroom classes. Blake said hi to my friends before heading over to visit with his own.

"My God, your brother just keeps getting hotter," Moira swooned.

Her eyes were fixated on him as he walked over to his friends and casually bumped fists with the guys.

"I like your new look, Caleb. 'Specially the hair." Laura smiled, referring to the fact that my hair was completely back to its natural colour and was lightly spiked at the front. "You could be in some preppie boy-band."

"Is that a good thing?" Hunter asked.

"It is to us," Laura replied, speaking for the girls. "We appreciate a little effort," she winked at me.

Hunter rolled his eyes.

"No sign of Shane yet. Haven't seen Drew either," Adria said.

"They'll be here soon. Drew's probably taking his morning dump," Hunter suggested.

"Eww, Hunter. Gross," Moira slapped his arm playfully.

"It sucks that we won't all be together during the day, but we've gotta hang out at lunch and share the latest gossip. And discuss the eye-candy situation," Laura said, her attention drifting to focus on this cute guy walking by our group.

"Hey, guys," Shane said as he approached us, shifting his book bag on his shoulder as he spoke. "Whoa, look at you, Caleb, wearing all the new stuff on the first day." He smiled at me, and though he covered it well, I knew he was giving me a complete once-over.

"Doesn't he look good?" Moira said.

"Guys never admit that another guy looks good," Laura explained.

"That's horse shit. Only homophobic morons are stupid like that," Ryley informed her. I was so glad he was my friend. "Caleb looks good."

Naturally, I blushed. "I think we all look pretty goddamn sexy," Drew stated as he joined us. He put his arms over Moira's and my shoulders and leaned in. "Now, what are we talking about anyway?"

Before anyone could respond, the principal stepped up to the podium and started the morning announcements. Shane stood next to me against the wall and whispered in my ear. "You're torturing me right now." I couldn't help but smirk.

When the principal was able to get everyone to settle down enough that she could be heard, she made her opening remarks, welcoming us to another year and cheering for the red and white, the Stapeton Stampeders, and all the other *rah-rah* crap that every school seemed to read from a template at the start of each year—full of false promises and rhetoric. No one wanted to be there—well, not most people anyway. You always have those obnoxious few kids who love school and make me want to puke—running for student body president and student council and being on this committee and that committee, while pulling off marks in the nineties and having parents who make six figures and get them whatever they want.

Don't get me wrong, I'm not bitter, I'm just so tired of that type of person. People who breeze through life without any problems. Kids who never have to move and start at a new school, never have to study their brains out just to eke out a pass mark on an exam, and never have to worry about acne, their weight, being popular, and making the team. Never mind being gay and haunted. (I do realize, however, that some kids give all they've got to school because it's the only place they feel safe or appreciated—that some of them have awful home lives, where alcohol, drugs, abuse, or just plain ignorance dominate. For those kids, I understand the desire to focus their energy on something positive. See, I'm not totally jaded.)

The principal's drudgery ended when she passed the microphone over to the senior high guidance counsellor. He took the mic and began calling out class lists, starting with grade ten. "Ten A, homeroom Mr. Burton …" and proceeded to say the names of the thirty or more kids in the class. Everything was purely alphabetical and partially divided by kids who were in music and those who weren't. When we arrived at our homerooms, our teachers would hand out our personal time schedules, and we'd find out what order the classes we were enrolled in were slated.

I had at least one of my friends in each class, so that was good. Ryley was in all my classes except math, and Shane was in two of my classes, math and history. The only ones from our group I never had a class with were Adria and Hunter, but since they were both band students, it wasn't a major surprise.

The first day back was always the same boring routine. We filled out forms, were handed out textbooks, and were given a rough outline of what we could expect from a particular course by a teacher who was no more enthusiastic to be back at the regular grind of another school year than we were.

One nice thing about being in senior high was that we didn't have to share a locker with anyone like the junior high students did (on account of space). I had brought money with me to make sure to secure a locker that first day—not wanting to lug all those heavy textbooks back and forth any more than necessary. I was assigned a locker just outside my homeroom, which was convenient. Before heading to the bus that first day back, I had four hardcover textbooks already sitting on the shelf of my locker with the orange door.

In the evening, I went into town to spend the night at Ryley's place. The next day was the first day back for junior high, so that meant no school for us. Shane came over, too, and the three of us complained about the various aspects of our first day back at Stapeton Regional High. We ate a barbecue chicken pizza and played some games on Ryley's little brother's PlayStation 3.

Everything felt normal again. I didn't think about Toby and the woods. I never thought of the time warp, or whatever the hell it was. I just laughed and pigged out with my two best friends.

"Did you see the way Adria looked at you today?" I asked Ryley. "She is so into you."

Ryley smiled. "That was pretty cool. I'm gonna call her and ask her out. Maybe tomorrow."

"Call her now, man," Shane urged.

"Nah ... It's kinda late."

"It isn't even nine o'clock yet, Rye. C'mon. Call her."

Ryley looked at me for my opinion. I nodded. "Do it, man."

The funniest little grin pierced Ryley's lips. "Okay, but don't make me laugh or anything, all right?"

"We won't. We promise," Shane said.

Ryley picked up the phone and took a deep breath. "Okay, here goes nothing."

He punched in the numbers to Adria's house. After asking politely to speak to her, he crossed his fingers, waiting to hear her voice on the other end. I don't know what she said, hearing only Ryley's half of the conversation.

"Hey, Adria. How goes it? Yeah. Nah, it was pretty sucky for me, too. Nope. Nah, Shane and Caleb are over. Yeah. No, just hanging out. You? Did ya?" he laughed nervously. "No, we just had pizza—no biggie. Seriously? That's cool. You doing anything fun tomorrow? Oh yeah? That's cool. Nah. We're just laying low." Ryley struggled with his courage, and I was afraid he might chicken out. He looked over at us with a shrug and mouthed, "Shit."

"You can do it, Rye. Just go for it," Shane whispered, trying to pump him up.

"Huh? No, everything's fine. I ... I wanted to ask you something, that's all. Well ... I was just wondering ... maybe, I dunno, if maybe you might wanna go out some time ... just you and me?" Ryley's whole mood changed instantly to be cheerier. "Yeah? Cool. Really? I've wanted to ask you out all summer, but I was ... Yeah"—he laughed—"I was too nervous. Wow, that's cool. Awesome. Yeah, so how's dinner and a movie sound ... other than clichéd?" He slapped his forehead and looked at us, mouthing *God, that's dumb.* "Oh yeah? Awesome. Which night is best for you? Oh, right on. Okay, so how about Saturday? Yeah. Cool. Yeah. No, that's perfect by me. Looking forward to it. Yeah. Me too. Okay. Night, Adria. Hmm? Yeah, you too. Bye."

Ryley hung up the phone and pumped his fist. "Yes!"

"Good stuff, Rye," Shane said.

"Yeah, you guys were right. She said she wanted to ask me out but felt weird about it. She asked me if you guys put me up to this or if you just convinced me I should take a shot. She said she's glad I did." Ryley smiled from ear to ear. "Thanks, guys."

"Happy for ya, Rye," I let him know. "And thanks for what you said this morning. That rocked."

Ryley didn't register at first what I was referring to; he was still so caught up in feeling good about getting a date with Adria. "Huh? Oh, that. That was nothing."

"Still, it was cool," Shane told him.

"Look, you guys are my best friends. Best friends stick up for each other—no matter what."

"Absolutely," I agreed.

"Let's fire another pizza in the oven and watch a movie. You guys game?" Ryley asked.

Shane and I both nodded and agreed. "Absolutely," we said in unison.

When I returned home the following afternoon, I took a book outside with me and sat on the wicker love seat on the porch to read. Mom brought me a glass of iced tea and a plate of apple slices with cubes of cheddar cheese for a snack. She put the small lunch down on the wicker ottoman and sat next to me on the love seat.

"Thanks, Mom," I said, snagging a piece of cheese.

"You're welcome, sweetie. I haven't seen you much all summer, we've all been so busy. Thought maybe we could talk, unless you wanna keep reading ..."

I stuffed my bookmark inside the paperback. "No, that's fine. I can read later. What's up?"

"Nothing. Just wanted to visit a bit."

"Oh. Okay."

"Have a nice time at Ryley's?"

"Yeah, we had fun. Just played some games and ate junk, but it was cool."

"Good. I'm so glad you've made friends here. They all seem really nice, too."

"Yeah, they're awesome. Moving here was the best thing that coulda happened to me." All I could think about was Shane as I spoke.

Mom patted my knee. "Does my heart good to hear you say that." She looked around and sighed contentedly. "I just love it here. I don't think we could have found a better place to live. It's almost like it was meant to be."

"I know what you mean. It's like we're supposed to be here." I crunched on a piece of Cortland and asked, "How you liking it at the drugstore?"

"I like it. It keeps me in touch with the community a bit by meeting so many people, and it brings in a little extra money, which is nice. I'm starting to do some volunteer work at the library next week, too. Who knows, that could lead to something down the road. There's something so rewarding about being around books. You have no idea how much it pleases me that both you and Blake are avid readers." She turned the cover of my book toward her to see what I was reading. "*The Greensky Trilogy.*" She beamed. "Are you enjoying it?"

"Yeah, it's pretty good. We found this old game on the computer called *Below the Root* at Ryley's this summer and I liked it, so I thought I'd give the book a read. Picked it up at that used bookstore in town."

"I love the classics. I have a number if you ever want to read any."

"Thanks."

Mom was quiet for a moment. Her smile had a tinge of sadness in it.

"What's wrong?" I asked her.

She shook her head. "Nothing's wrong. You're just growing up so fast."

I forced a light laugh, "Can't really help that."

"Hard to believe sometimes. My baby is fifteen. Seems like only yesterday I was making you your first little quilt while I was still pregnant."

"How's the one coming that you're working on now?"

"Should be done by the weekend. Your brother will love it on those cold winter nights."

I thought of how no one had wintered in the house for years and years and wondered if we'd even make it ourselves.

Mom placed her hands on her knees and declared, "Well, back to work."

"Thanks for the snack."

"My pleasure. Enjoy the book."

I picked the novel back up and focused my attention on its pages. I read, munching my apple slices and cheese, without taking my eyes from the text until I heard my father driving down the road.

"Hey, Caleb," he greeted me as he got out of the car. "Great day, isn't it?"

"Yeah. How was work?"

"Fine," he said as he came up to the porch. "After supper, I'm heading over to Hank's to pick up the Bronco. Wanna come along?"

"Sure. That'd be great. How we getting it home?"

"We'll tow it behind the truck. Hank's place is only about five clicks or so from here."

"Cool."

"Mom inside?"

"Yeah, she's upstairs working on Blake's quilt."

"It's looking really nice. Have you seen it?"

"Not lately."

"You should. Your mother does amazing work."

"Yeah."

"See you for supper."

"Yup."

Dad headed inside the house, and I finished the page I was reading. I took my plate and glass into the kitchen and ran my book up to my room, setting it on my nightstand. I gazed out my window at the barn, knowing in a few hours' time I'd have a vehicle out there to work on. Wanting to keep myself distracted until that time, I jogged back down the stairs and helped Blake get dinner ready.

Hank's house was fairly new, a home built from one of those kits and assembled in a short period of time. The property was neat, with large gardens of perennials along either side of the paved driveway and the front walk. There was a two-door garage attached to the house and a barn-style shed to the left of the property. Blake and I waited in the truck as Dad went and knocked on the side door. Hank stepped outside and followed Dad back to the truck. Hank hopped up in the box, and Dad returned to the cab.

"Bronco's up at his barn, just around the corner," Dad informed us. He backed out of the driveway, and we continued down the road to the barn.

We pulled into the yard in front of the large brown barn, and Dad turned off the ignition. Hank jumped down from the back of the half-ton and unlocked the side door of the barn. A few moments later, he opened the sliding door at the front. Dad started the truck back up and reversed to the opening so we could tie the Bronco to our truck.

We got out of the cab, and Dad shut off the engine again. The little Bronco didn't look all that bad. It had some rusty spots along the rocker panels and the doorframes, but it was structurally sound. The white paint job was recent, within three or four years, I'd guess, and it covered most of the rust quite well.

"What year is it?" I asked as we looked it over.

"'88."

"So that means it's got the 130-horsepower Cologne two-point-nine litre V6, right?" I asked.

Hank's eyes widened, impressed. "Yes, sir. You know a thing or two about vehicles, I'd say."

"It's kinda my thing."

"Good stuff. I had the tranny rebuilt 'bout four years ago, and it works good. The engine needs some playin' with to make 'er reliable," Hank said. "Once you get 'er going right for ya, you'll be able to have a fun little rig to bop around in."

Blake smiled at me. "Cool, huh?" he said quietly so only I could hear.

I nodded. "Yeah."

We hooked the two vehicles together, and Blake climbed behind the wheel of the Bronco. Dad and I got back in the truck.

"Good luck with her. The plow will be here, ready and waiting, when you want it," Hank promised us.

Dad started the truck, and in no time we were back at our place, unhooking the Bronco and pushing it into the barn. We insisted that Dad steer at that point so he wouldn't chance hurting himself. He grumbled about not being an invalid, but seemed to appreciate the gesture at the same time. Blake and I pushed our new acquisition into the barn as Dad steered it into its new home.

"It's got nice, beefy tires," Blake said once we were all out in front of the Bronco, looking at it, admiring the solid raised white-letter BF Goodrich Mud Terrains.

"Yeah. Hank had them put on last summer to go off-road with, but it conked out before he had a chance to really use them."

I popped the hood and examined my upcoming challenge. I was already eyeing the valve covers as my first attack point (there was an obvious leak around the seal of some screws).

"Whattaya think, Caleb? Gonna be doable?" Dad asked me.

"Hard to tell right away. I'll pick at it and see what I can see."

"I'll leave the keys with you, but you gotta promise me, if you ever do get it running, you won't take it on the road until we get it properly inspected."

"No worries, Dad."

I took the keys from my father and got inside the vehicle, pushing down the clutch and the brake as I attempted to turn it over. I listened to the sounds coming from under the hood and made mental notes of possible problem areas. I'd go online later and find some sites with tips and ideas for repairing a 1988 Bronco II.

As I was lying in bed that night, I thought of all the fun times ahead of me using that Bronco. I envisioned taking friends places in it and going for drives with Shane to get away from everyone else. I knew I'd have a job next summer, doing something, and it would be sweet to have my own vehicle to use. I couldn't wait for my birthday—even if it was seven months away. Shane would be sixteen on March 19, so he'd beat me to the licence line (but then, so would the rest of the gang).

Caleb

I bolted up, my thoughts broken into a million pieces, hearing my name whispered from somewhere outside. I darted over to my window and peered out. Off in the distance, by the stream, I saw a shadow. I kept watching it, expecting something more to happen. The shadow remained the same, standing by the stream. I hurried down the hall and got Blake to come to my room.

"I heard my name again," I said softly to him, not wanting to disturb my parents. "There's a shadow by the stream." I pointed out the window.

"Where? I don't see anything," he told me.

I checked out the window again. "Dammit. It's gone."

"You sure you saw something?"

"Yes."

Blake rubbed his eyes. "Want me to crash in here with you tonight?"

"Umm. No, I guess not. I'm fine. Thanks. Just wish you'd see something sometime."

"I do too. At least Shane has been with you when you found things."

"True."

Blake put a hand on my shoulder. "I'm goin' back to bed, bud. Need me for anything, let me know. And hey, if you ever do get scared, it's cool. You can come down and crash with me anytime you want. Okay?"

"Yeah. Thanks."

I smiled at Blake as he walked back down the hall to his room. I watched the stream for a few more minutes before getting back into bed. I read a couple more pages of my book before I shut off the light. I didn't think I'd ever understand what Toby was trying to tell me or get me to see, but I sure as hell wasn't giving up.

Friday, after school, Ryley and Shane came home with me to spend the night. We tossed our stuff in my room and headed into the kitchen for a snack. Mom had left a big Tupperware container full of Rice Krispie squares on the counter, with a Post-it note attached with the word "Enjoy" written on it, along with a smiley face. We opened the lid and scarfed down the squares, washing them down with chocolate Silk.

"That's a good look for you," I teased Ryley, seeing his moustache. "I bet Adria would like a guy who can grow facial hair."

Ryley laughed as he wiped the soy milk from his upper lip. "Man, I am so nervous about tomorrow night."

"Why? It's just Adria. It's not like you don't know her already," Shane said.

"Yeah, but see, that's the problem, right? I mean, since we know each other already, I'm afraid I won't have anything interesting to say to her, and she'll be bored."

"I don't think you need to worry about that. After you guys get through the first few awkward moments, everything'll be cool. Trust me. Besides, as long as you're polite and respectful, she'll be happy. She knows you'll be nervous. She'll be nervous, too. Just relax and be yourself."

"I know you're right, Caleb, but it's still a lot harder than it sounds."

"Don't sweat it, Rye. You'll be cool," Shane told him. "And we want a full report when the date is over."

"For sure. It'll be too late to call probably, but I'll go online and talk to you. Will you both be here, or are you heading home tomorrow night, Shane?"

"I'll be home. I'd like to stay, but I promised Mom I'd do a bunch of stuff around the motel. Gotta mow and edge the walks. Junk like that."

"Sounds like fun," Ryley said, scrunching his nose.

"Supposed to be hot tomorrow, too. It'll suck. Oh well. No big deal."

"Why don't we all meet online at midnight?" Ryley suggested.

"I'm there," I said.

"Done," Shane agreed. "Say, Caleb, can we see your new truck?"

"Sure. It's not much to look at, but I'm hoping to have it ready for the road this winter."

"That's awesome. I wish I knew how to fix things," Ryley said.

I led the boys out to the barn and opened the door. I snapped on the lights and headed to the main doors, unlatching them and swinging them open, letting the sunlight pour in. Shane turned off the overhead lights once the sunlight filled the barn.

"It's in better shape than I imagined," Shane said, smiling and touching the front right fender with his hand.

"What year you say it is?" Ryley asked.

"'88."

"I'm glad it's white and not some stupid colour," Ryley said. "Can I get in?"

"Sure. It's not locked."

The three of us piled into the Bronco. Ryley flipped the seat back and sat on the short bench behind the front seats. I sat behind the steering wheel, leaving Shane the passenger seat. We rolled down the windows to vent the heat that was trapped inside. The blue cloth interior was worn and stained, smelling of hay from being stored in Hank's barn.

"It's not very pretty inside, but with a little TLC, I bet you could make this a real kick-ass ride," Ryley noted. "Even as it is now, it's a pretty sweet ride. I mean, it will be once you get it going. Just think of the three of us riding around next summer—windows down, sunroof open, tunes playing, girls checking us … I mean, girls and guys checking us out. It's gonna rock. So when you gonna start working on it?"

"Tomorrow, actually. When you guys head out, I'm gonna get to work. There's nothing for homework yet except that English essay, and that's not due till the end of the month. Got lottsa time to pick away at this."

"Blake or your dad gonna help you?" Ryley asked.

"My dad would be the first to admit he's not mechanically inclined. Blake might help some, but he's better with computers than with motors. It's gonna be a learning experience for me. I hope I don't screw up too bad."

"Wish I could help you. It'd be a blast to work on this together," Ryley stated.

"Hey, if you wanna hang out and give me a hand, I wouldn't say no."

"I'm afraid I'd just hold you back. Besides, this is your project. It'll be wicked to tell people you fixed it on your own."

"For sure," Shane agreed.

Blake appeared at the front of the barn. He laughed when he saw the three of us in the Bronco. "You fellas taking off on a road trip?" he joked as he approached the driver's side.

"Just thinking about next summer," I replied.

"Yeah, you guys are gonna have a blast till I take it to university with me." We all went quiet after Blake spoke. "Just joshing, guys. C'mon, supper's ready."

With a collective sigh of relief, we got out of the Bronco and followed Blake to the backyard, where the smell of the barbecue filled the air.

Shane, Ryley, and I threw around a baseball after dinner. The sun was so warm and inviting we hated to go indoors and waste any of it. Shane had a strong throwing arm, and the ball soared over Ryley's outstretched glove and down the path toward the stream. He ran after it and snatched it up in his glove, running back toward us and throwing the ball as he came. I snagged the white orb from the air and heard that lovely smack as the ball landed directly in the mesh of my blue glove.

"Good throw!" I called out to Ryley.

"Hey, you guys have never shown me the path through the woods. Haven't you ever gone back there?" he asked.

Shane and I glanced at each other. "Um. Yeah, a few times. Not much to see really," Shane replied.

"How far does it go?"

"A fair distance. Farthest we ever got was about an hour walk. Path keeps going forever, it seems," I told him.

Ryley looked back toward the forest. "Weird to think that kid got lost in there. Least none of the stories are true. You must be relieved."

I glanced over at Shane again. We were both thinking the same thing. It wasn't fair to lie to Ryley. Shane shrugged his shoulders and nodded. Ryley saw our expressions. "Holy shit. What happened?"

Back inside the barn, we told Ryley everything we had experienced. He wasn't upset that we hadn't told him earlier, saying he would have been cautious too. He couldn't get over the various things we had heard and seen, wanting to see the small collection of items that we had found.

Up in my room, we showed Ryley the leaf, the horseshoe, and the receipt. Like us, the receipt didn't seem to make any sense to him or fit into the rest of the story, but also like us, he knew that it had to be the key to the whole thing.

"So the name H. K. *something* brand means nothing to you?" Shane asked Ryley.

"Sorry. Wish it did. I've never heard that name around here."

"Neither have we." I sighed. "Well, that's all there is."

"You guys have gotta show me the woods now," Ryley pleaded.

"Not tonight. I don't feel up to it," I said.

"No problem. Sometime you will, though. Right?"

"Sure. I just don't wanna go through that again right now. It's kinda draining."

"Don't know how I'd feel if someone called my name out in the night like that." Ryley pretended to shiver. "Creepy."

We didn't talk about Toby anymore that night. We went downstairs and watched a movie, and then went out to the driveway, where we set up the outdoor fireplace. We put lawn chairs out for ourselves and sat and talked while tending to the fire. When it was down to embers, we went up to my room and got ready for bed.

"How you doing, Caleb?" Shane asked me in a gentle whisper while Ryley was down the hall in the washroom. Shane brushed a hand through my hair as he spoke.

"All right, I guess. I just couldn't face the woods tonight."

I closed my eyes and took a deep breath. Shane took the opportunity to gently kiss each of my closed eyelids.

"Whoa, sorry, guys. Didn't mean to interrupt," Ryley apologized as he came back in the room.

"No, man, it's okay," Shane told him.

"Is everything all right?"

"Yeah. I'm just kinda confused about everything right now," I admitted.

"Join the club," Ryley said. "Being a teenager sucks. Everyone talks about how great it's supposed to be, but it's the most confusing, messed up, awkward, and downright stupid time of your life. Your voice changes, your hormones are in overdrive, and you think you're a pervert or something cuz you jack off all the time. You grow this hair on your junk, get pimples, you're paranoid your body isn't perfect, and no one respects your opinion. And, let's not forget the most annoying thing of all—the constant hard-ons in class that you always get the second before you have to go to the front of the room for some reason … Like when Beth Munroe drops her pencil. How am I supposed to look at that perfect ass and not get hard? I mean really! God."

Shane and I were both laughing as Ryley ranted. He chuckled, too, as he concluded, "See, Caleb, we all have crap to deal with."

"What is it about teachers calling on you when you've got a hard-on? Do they somehow know or something?" Shane asked.

"I think they must. Probably gives them a cheap thrill," Ryley mused. "I bet they've got these size charts in the teachers' lounge and all sorts of weird junk. I can just hear that old bitch Mrs. Gordon saying, 'Oh my, that Ryley Shaw, he's got quite the package on him. Makes me wanna take out my dentures and make him a man. Slurp. Slurp.'"

"Gross!" Shane exclaimed, thoroughly repulsed.

"Now there's a mental image," I winced.

Ryley was nearly killing himself laughing.

They slipped into their sleeping bags, and I slid under my covers and turned out the light.

"So, you jack off all the time, huh, Ryley?" Shane kidded.

"That would be the one thing you remembered that I said," Ryley replied.

"So ..." I prodded.

"God. Like you two don't."

"Just try to keep your sleeping bag from getting crunchy," Shane teased.

"Eww. Imagine." Ryley chuckled.

"He's avoiding the question," I stated.

"How many times a day, Rye?" Shane asked.

"I dunno, man. Depends on the day and how horny I am. You two hinting around for a demonstration or something?"

I burst out laughing and threw a pillow down at Ryley. "Go to sleep, perv."

"Night, guys," Ryley said.

Shane and Ryley left early in the afternoon, Ryley giving Shane a lift home when his mom came to pick him up. I watched my friends leave and then went up to my room and changed into my old blue jeans and a T-shirt, getting ready to get greasy as I went to work on the Bronco.

The sky had darkened in the morning, but there was hardly a cloud in sight as I walked out the front door of the house and into the bright summer day. The air was somewhat humid, but not nearly as bad as it had been earlier in the season. Opening the doors to the barn offered me a pleasant breeze as I looked over the little truck, determining my first line of attack.

I chocked the tires with cinder blocks I had brought up from the basement of the house. With that accomplished, I popped the hood and leaned into the grill, peering at the black mess inside the small Ford's engine compartment. I worked steadily, slowly deducing what the key problem areas were. The first point of order was to get the Bronco to turn over. I was still at it when suppertime arrived. I washed my hands in the laundry tub in the cellar, using the pumice soap and scrubbing hard under my nails. My hands were clean, but stained in the grooves with oil.

After dinner, I immediately headed back to the barn, carrying a cold can of Coke Zero with me. The air grew more humid as the day went on, the clouds overhead thickening again, threatening to rain. I wished we would just have a downpour with enough thunder and lightning to clear the air. What we needed was a steady, long rain that could be absorbed into the soil and help everyone's well water rise. We were fortunate that ours was still high, but we had been conserving as much as we could. Many wells in the county had been dry for a week or more. It was a new concept for us to get used to. In the city, whenever we turned on the tap, we had water.

As I slid back underneath the Bronco, for what must have been the hundredth time that day, I heard a rumbling sound off in the distance. I stopped what I was doing and listened, lying on my back on the cold cement floor. A few minutes later, I heard the rumble again. I slithered out from between the front tires and sat, leaning against the bumper. The sky was charcoal grey, completely covered in dense cloud. On the horizon, the clouds were even darker—nearly black, ominously looming over the forest. We hadn't had a real thunder and lightning storm all summer, and I was anxious for it to arrive. Having lived in the city for all my previous storms, I had never really gotten to watch one very well. I got up and grabbed my can of Zero from the workbench. I gulped down the last of it, the soda having gotten warm and dusty from sitting for so long. I tossed the can over into the big bin by the entry door and leaned against the truck, focusing my attention on the sky.

"C'mon. Rain," I urged.

As I watched out the large barn doors, the rain began to fall. The dusty road in front of me became speckled before changing colour completely. Puddles soon formed in every rut and valley in the road. It started out softly, and then suddenly, with a clap of thunder, pounded down. The sound of the rain on the roof was wonderful. The thunder rumbled, and sheets of lightning lit the darkening sky. I closed the hood of the Bronco, deciding I'd done enough for the day, and slid back down until I was sitting again. I pulled my knees to my chest and watched the storm. I wished Shane were there to experience it with me. There's something magical about a thunderstorm.

I could feel the humidity leave the air, my arms becoming chilled. I went over to the workbench and grabbed my old jean jacket to put on.

I stood in the large opening of the barn, leaning on the doorframe, and watched the storm get closer and closer.

The rain on the roof reminded me of the cabin we had stayed in years ago on a rare family trip. We had gone to a lake for a weekend, and it had rained the whole time we were there. My father and mother were disappointed that we couldn't enjoy canoeing or fishing, but I loved the trip all the same. We had a big fire going the whole time, and the cabin smelled of burning birch bark and smoke. We roasted marshmallows and hotdogs and drank hot chocolate. We played board games and, when we got tired of games, found a cozy spot to curl up and read a book. Blake and I shared a room at that cabin, and our beds were under the sloping roof. The cabin wasn't insulated, and we could hear the rain splashing down on the old air-lock shingles just inches from our faces. I hadn't heard anything like it since then, not until that evening in the barn.

I climbed the ladder to the loft and lay down under the slope of the roof. I heard the rain hitting hard against the asphalt shingles, and I closed my eyes, feeling sleepy from the comforting and familiar sound. I drifted off, thinking of all the fun I'd had years ago in that cabin by the lake.

I awoke a few hours later. The rain had stopped, and I was a bit disoriented, forgetting for a moment where I was.

"Caleb?" I heard my brother call for me.

"Up here," I called back. I was still sleepy and didn't want to get up, but I forced myself.

Blake's face appeared at the top of the ladder. "What are you doing up here?"

"I fell asleep. I was listening to the rain on the roof and drifted off."

"Well, you better come inside. It's getting late."

"Yeah, I'm coming." I made my way toward the ladder.

"Don't forget your blanket," Blake said.

"Huh?"

"Your blanket," he repeated and pointed to where I had been lying.

"I didn't have a blank—" I stopped, turning to see what Blake was indicating. There, sitting on the floor next to where I had slept, was a red-and-black checkered blanket. I went back and picked it up, smelling it. I could faintly detect the odour of a horse. "This is Toby's blanket. It's just like what happened to Royce."

"Are you sure?"

"How else did it get here?"

"I dunno. Maybe it was in the Bronco or something."

"Even if it had been, how did it get up here?"

Blake shook his head. "I have no idea."

I went down the ladder and examined the blanket carefully. "Wait … This can't be Toby's blanket."

"Why not?"

"Look, right here." I pointed to a corner of the fabric with a name on it. "Mom made this." She always stitched her initials and the date of completion in the corner.

Blake let out a giant sigh. "Thank God."

We closed up the barn and went in the house, where we found our mother sitting in the living room. She was working on a crossword puzzle and biting the eraser end of her pencil. She saw us come in, me carrying the blanket.

"Hi, sunshine. Have a good snooze?"

"Um, yeah. Thanks. Did you cover me up?"

Mom smiled. "Yeah. I went out to see how you were making out about an hour ago and heard snoring up in the loft. You looked so peaceful I didn't have the heart to wake you, so I came in and got the throw that I made for you. I've been working on it in secret for a while."

"How did you come to pick out this pattern?" I asked, trying to sound pleased.

Mom gave me a look of bewilderment. "It's the one you circled and left on top of my worktable. I wanted to make you a quilt, but since you picked the throw, that's what I made." Mom stopped, suddenly worried. "Oh, no … you thought you were picking out a quilt, didn't you?"

"Huh?"

"I should've asked if you realized it was a throw. It's okay, though; if you like the pattern, I can easily do it for your quilt too. You do like it, don't you?"

"What? Oh, of course. Yeah, it's beautiful, Mom. Thanks very much for making it for me." I had no idea what to say; I was too shocked. I had never even cracked open one of my mother's quilting books.

"You're most welcome. Be honest, though, you thought you were picking out a quilt, didn't you?"

"Umm, probably. I guess I never looked at it closely. Just liked the pattern."

"You still need to pick out the quilt you want. Let me know soon, okay?"

"I will. Thanks again for the blanket."

"You're very welcome."

"I'm gonna head up to bed. Have a good night."

"You too."

I took the stairs two at a time, Blake following behind me. We went down to our washroom and closed the door.

"Okay, what the hell just happened?" Blake asked.

"I never picked this pattern out. I've never even looked through her magazines."

"Man, this is freaky."

"No kidding."

"And your first thought was that it was the same blanket that Toby used to cover up Royce that time he was here in the storm, right?"

"According to what Shane told me, this is exactly what it looked like, like an old hunting blanket. It even smells like a horse," I said.

Blake sniffed at it. "Or wet wool. Probably got damp when Mom brought it out to you. And you've been working on the Bronco. It smells like hay. Mix the two together, and you've got ..."

"Horse."

"Right. The power of suggestion."

"God."

"Still, it is pretty strange. You better go online, see if Shane is around."

"Yeah. I gotta be on at midnight anyway to talk to Ryley and see how his date went."

"Does Ryley know about any of this?"

"Yeah. We filled him in."

"Good. The four of us oughta get together next weekend and see if we can't solve this thing."

I knew that solving whatever this mystery was would require heading back into the deep woods and, most likely, my getting sucked into that other dimension or whatever again. I didn't want to re-experience that, but I knew I'd have to if I ever wanted to be able to help Toby and put all of this behind me.

I sighed. "I'll see what they say."

Blake was downstairs watching the extra innings of a ballgame when, at midnight, as arranged, I went online and talked with my two friends. Not wanting to upstage Ryley, I waited until after he had told us all about his date with Adria before mentioning what had happened to me that night.

*howd it go?*Shane asked Ryley.

it wuz cool. adria & I got along gr8

*found enuff 2 talk about?*I wondered.

yeh. weve got a lot in common. more than I thought.

Shane: *movie any good?*

Ryley: *kinda sucked. didnt matter.*

Me: *wut about dinner?*

Ryley: *that was good. went 2 sams 4 pizza.*

Shane: *u pay?*

Ryley: *i tried but she didnt think it wuz right. I told her id get dinner and she could pay 4 the movie. thats wut we did.*

Me: *cool. after the flick?*

Ryley: *went 2 stapes. coffee & talked*

Shane: *howd she look?*

Ryley: *incredible!!!! she was wearing these nice fitting black pants and a white shirt that showed off her boobs ;-)*

Me: *u dog*

Ryley: *lol*

Shane: *gonna go out again?*

Ryley: *yep. askd her 2 dance nxt friday.*

Me: *good 4 u*

Ryley: *u guys goin?*

Shane: *like 2. dont think so.*

Ryley: *y not?*
Shane: *not fun. cant dance w/ my boi*
Me: *yeh*
Ryley: *that sucks.*
Shane: *u kiss her?*
Ryley: *not really. I gave her a peck on cheek tho & we hugged :-)*
Me: *:-)*
Shane: *nice :-)*
Me: *u guys wanna come over next weekend?*
Shane: *4 sure. Ive done enuff yard work to last a month*
Ryley: *when?*
Me: *how bout after dance?*
Shane: *sounds good 2 me*
Ryley: *im there*
Me: *were gonna hafta go back into woods. Something weird hap 2nite*
Shane: *wtf?*

I went on to tell the guys all about the blanket. During this time, Shane reminded me that Royce's blanket had smelled of leaves, not of horse. Regardless, we were in agreement: we needed to get back at solving the mystery. Ryley signed off after saying good night to us. He was tired and pretty pleased after his date with Adria. Shane and I talked a bit longer.

*u ok babe?*he asked me. At that point, he only ever called me "babe" online, which I thought was really cute.

yeh. im fine. wish u were here to hold me tho
me 2
i luv u
luv u 2
sleep well
u 2

I waited until I saw Shane had signed off before leaving my brother's room. I went into my own room and got ready for bed.

Chapter Eleven

I spent all of my free time leading up to that Friday working on the Bronco. I knew I was getting close to having it running, and I felt myself rushing to get to that point. I forced myself to stop, take a deep breath, and go slowly. I didn't want to do a rush job and end up regretting it later. I knew I could get it going before long. Blake and I would be picking up that plow attachment in no time.

Shane and I did end up going to the dance that Friday night. Our friends convinced us to go—none of them, except Ryley, knowing our reasons for not wanting to be there. We tried to have a good time and danced with the girls for the fast songs. Both of us sat out all the slow pieces.

"This sucks," Shane said as we sat on one of the benches lining the walls of the auditorium. "I wanna dance with you."

"Me too. Thankfully, this'll all be over soon."

"For tonight. But there's a lot of dances throughout the year. I don't wanna go through this every time."

"Me neither."

The music changed, and we went back to the floor to dance to a faster song. There were a few more up-tempo numbers before the last dance of the night arrived, and as usual, it was a slow, romantic song. Moira dragged me onto the floor with her, despite my protesting. Laura grabbed Shane by the arm and said, "I'm not the only girl here who's gonna miss the last dance. C'mon."

I couldn't take my eyes off Shane the entire time he was slow dancing. His eyes were fixed on mine, too. We wanted to be dancing together, but this was as close as we could get.

"Don't look so sad, Caleb," Moira said sweetly. "You're too cute to be sad."

I forced a smile. "I'm not much of a dancer," I told her.

"You're doing fine. At least you aren't stepping on my toes like Hunter always does."

"Yeah, but you'd still rather be dancing with him, wouldn't you?" I said, knowing she had a little bit of a crush on him.

Moira blushed. "Shut up," she giggled, "I bet there's someone here you'd rather be dancing with, isn't there?"

"Umm. Yeah."

She smiled. "Who?"

"I'm not telling."

"Hmm … secret crush? Can I guess?"

The music ended, and the disc jockey said his thank yous and good nights before I could respond to Moira. We all clapped and began to file out of the gym and into the night.

"You're off the hook for tonight, but I'm gonna figure out who you like yet," Moira teased as she walked out beside me.

I tried to smile as we met up with our friends at the bottom of the large cement steps at the front of the school. We talked for a while in the school yard before departing. Ryley and Shane followed me to the car so Blake could drive us home.

"Isn't Adria kinda pissed that you aren't seeing her home or anything?" Shane asked Ryley.

"Nah. She's going over to Moira's place for the night."

"The last dance was torture," Shane mumbled.

"I know. Moira was trying to figure out who I like."

"That's awkward," Ryley said.

"Very," I agreed.

Blake strolled over to the car, grinning.

"Well, someone looks happy," Ryley noted.

"Hi, fellas. All set to go?"

"Yeah. Where were you?" I asked.

"Just talking to Vicki Morgan," he answered proudly.

"Vicki Morgan, as in *the* Vicki Morgan—*the girl I'd give my right nut just to get to say 'hello' to me* Vicki Morgan?" Ryley asked.

Blake nodded.

"Whoa. Man … she is so goddamn hot."

"Indeed she is, and I've got a date with her next weekend."

"Cool, bro. Congrats," I said.

"Thanks, bud."

"I can't believe I know someone who is gonna date Vicki Morgan. She's like … a goddess."

"You guys wanna stop for anything before we head home?" Blake asked.

"Nah. Let's just go," I replied.

I didn't want to get home and have to face the woods again, but it was inevitable, so I wanted to get it started sooner rather than later so it would be over. Even though I was thinking that way, we were back on Wakefield Road all too quickly.

We waited until my parents were asleep before sneaking out of the house, being careful to avoid unnecessary creaking on the steps and gingerly closing the kitchen door. None of us said a word until we crossed the stream and stood at the threshold of the woods.

"Okay, everybody got their flashlight?" Blake asked.

We all took our flashlights out and turned them on. I carried the Zippo in my pocket again and hoped that I wouldn't need it.

"All right. Let's go."

We walked in pairs, Ryley and Blake in the lead, with Shane and me following. I wondered if I walked with Shane the entire time if he would also be pulled into the time differential with me. Selfishly, I hoped so.

The woods were silent and calm. When we did hear a noise, we all shone our flashlights at it and saw a porcupine lumbering over a rock, stepping on twigs as he went. We heard nothing else all the way to the clearing.

"See, there it is," I said, shining my light on the oak tree so Ryley could see the carving.

We continued down the slope to the fallen log by the falls.

"Wow, it's beautiful down here," Ryley commented.

"Anyone need a break?" I asked.

No one wanted to stop. We reached the spruce trees hiding the path.

"Let me go first this time," Blake offered, somewhat nervously. He pushed his way through the branches, and Ryley followed.

"Go ahead, Caleb. I'm right behind you," Shane said and offered me his hand. I clutched it in mine and pushed my way to the others. I reached the other side to find them there, waiting.

"So far, so good," Blake said.

We kept going, the night seeming suddenly darker as the moonlight was blocked out by the trees. I kept holding Shane's hand, not wanting to lose contact with him.

"Whereabouts was it we marked the path last time?" Shane asked.

"Up a ways still," Blake responded.

"Am I missing something?" Ryley wondered. "Or has nothing weird happened yet?"

"Nothing yet. Maybe nothing will tonight," Blake told him. "It's hard to say."

"There's the birch tree," I said some time later when we got to the place we had marked with Blake's orange shoelace.

"Do we keep going?" Ryley asked.

"We've come this far," Shane replied.

We slowly edged our way along the new territory. We turned a slow, arcing corner and stopped. The path ended abruptly in front of us.

"What the hell?" Blake, like the rest of us, was confused.

"Guess that's it. End of the line," Ryley said.

"God, did you have to say it like that?" Blake asked him.

"Sorry. Wasn't thinking."

"So, do we head back?" I asked them.

"I'm not leaving the path, not at night. We'll just end up getting lost," Blake stated.

We turned and started back. I think we were all thrown off by the trail ending and the lack of unusualness we encountered. We were so busy thinking things over that none of us took in the fact that Shane and I now led the group.

"You guys are awful quiet back there," Shane said as we passed the shoelace marker.

There was no response.

"Guys?" I turned around and shone my light down the trail. Nothing.

"Where the hell did they go?" Shane asked, a tremor in his voice.

"I think the real question is, where did we go?" I looked down at my hand, still firmly clasped in Shane's. He saw what I was looking at.

"Whoa. We're together this time. Now what do we do? Do we go back to the end of the path or to the clearing?"

"The clearing. I'm almost positive."

"All right. Let's go." We kept going toward the spruce trees. "Caleb, don't let go of my hand, okay?"

"I won't. I promise."

BANG

"What the hell was that?" Shane asked in a scared whisper.

We both had heard a loud noise that sounded like a gun going off, and we froze in the path.

"Sounded like a gunshot."

"Yeah."

"Has hunting season started yet?"

"No, and besides, who goes hunting at night?"

"Come on, let's keep going."

Caleb

We stopped again, hearing my name being called from up ahead of us. Shane shone his light down the path. It seemed to catch an image momentarily and then the torch went out.

"Did you see something?"

"I'm not sure," I answered. "Looked sorta like a person standing there ... didn't it?"

"Yeah."

The sensation of cold air told me that I didn't even need to bother trying to get my flashlight to come back on when it went out a second later. I knew it wouldn't work. I took out the old Zippo, and we slowly made our way to the clearing by its small yellow light.

Shane made me stop before we broke through the trees. He took a deep breath. "If this is the past, nothing here can hurt us, right?"

"I dunno. I guess that makes sense."

"And if we're here together now, I don't think we can be split up again … right?"

"I honestly don't know."

"Okay. Well, let's just get this over with anyway."

I held his hand firmly in mine as we went through the spruce trees.

The moonlight spilled over the clearing and gave us natural light, allowing me to put away the Zippo. We carefully made our way over the wet rocks below the waterfall and toward the log.

"Listen." I stopped in my tracks, thinking I heard something up the hill.

"What is it?" Shane asked.

"Do you hear that?"

Shane strained to hear. "Sounds kinda like people laughing from up the slope."

We headed toward the oak tree, the pathway dark, moonlight blocked out at that location. I retrieved my Zippo and held it to the oak tree, looking for the engraving.

"See, it's not there," I whispered.

I turned my head to see Shane, grateful that someone else was with me to bear witness to the unscathed tree trunk. A look of fright was on his face. He pointed back at the tree. There, before our eyes, we saw bits of bark being cut into. I don't know if I even breathed as I watched first the T, then the E and the addition sign, then the C, and finally the H being carved. The last thing was the heart around the two sets of initials. When the carving was done, I shone my light in front of me, feeling the ability to move once again. Standing up the path, I saw the shadowy figure of a boy about my age. I held the lighter up and saw a face. He looked right through me.

Caleb

I saw his mouth form the word and heard it run past my ear.

"Toby? What do we do? How can we help you?" Desperation in my voice, I begged the apparition for advice.

Shane held my hand so tight it was numb. I turned to make sure he was okay, and when I looked back up the path, Toby was gone.

I heard crashing sounds in the distance and saw Ryley and Blake in the clearing. Shane's flashlight and then mine came on, and I knew that we were back in our own time. I reached out to the tree and felt the same worn, old markings as always. I checked the ground for bits of bark from the cutting, but there weren't any.

Blake ran up the hill to us. "Are you guys okay? What happened?"

"You guys were in front of us one minute and gone the next. We didn't know what was going on," Ryley explained.

"We just saw Toby," Shane said quietly.

"What did he do?" Blake asked.

"Hang on, did you guys say you saw us one minute and then we disappeared?" I wanted to know.

"Yeah. Your flashlights went out, and when we got up to where you shoulda been, you were gone. Why?" Ryley replied.

"Cuz that's the first time that's happened," Blake answered for me, understanding it himself.

"Things are getting stranger. We heard a gunshot first, and then someone calling for Caleb. We pushed through the branches and heard people laughing. Then we watched the oak tree get the initials carved in it, saw Toby, and heard him say Caleb's name again," Shane said, recounting the events.

"Then what?" Ryley asked.

"Then we heard you guys, and Toby vanished," I finished.

"How do we know it was Toby?" Blake questioned.

"Guess we don't know for sure," I admitted.

"We need to find a picture of him," Shane said.

"Let's talk over the details back at the house, okay?" Ryley suggested.

"Good plan," I agreed.

We jogged back through the woods as quickly and safely as we could, avoiding roots and stumps by flashlight. We gathered inside the barn, not wanting to disturb my parents at such a late (or early, depending on your perspective) hour.

"I can't believe it's nearly four o'clock," Ryley stated.

"I'm still chilled right through." I shivered and stamped my feet.

"Come here." Shane pulled me next to him and held me against him for warmth.

"Is the cold always part of it?" Ryley asked.

"Yeah. Always," I said.

"One thing I don't get," Shane observed, "is if we went back in time and saw the carving in the tree, how come Toby was a ghost and not alive?"

"Did you guys actually see him cutting into the tree?" Blake wanted to know.

"No, we just saw the stuff appear."

"And you said you heard laughter from more than one person, right?" Ryley double-checked.

"Right." I nodded.

"This is seriously confusing," Blake muttered.

"Maybe it's like a puzzle. We need to figure out something more before we are shown something more," Shane suggested.

"I bet that's it," Ryley said.

"But what's next to figure out?" I wondered aloud.

"Let's get some sleep and worry about that later, okay?" Blake yawned. "I'm exhausted."

We all agreed and headed quietly inside the house and up to bed.

We slept till noon. Blake got up and showered, and then went downstairs to make us a pot of really strong coffee. I was the last to shower, so by the time I got downstairs, the other guys were all sitting around the table gulping down the freshly brewed blend of Arabica beans. The kitchen smelled heavenly—the aromas of coffee, toast, and bacon all filling my nose. Without saying a word, Blake poured a cup and handed it to me.

"Thanks. Looks good and strong," I said before taking a sip.

"Yeah, it is," Ryley confirmed.

Blake fried some eggs and turkey bacon for our late breakfast before making another pot of coffee at regular strength.

"Your folks not around?" Ryley asked.

"Nah, Dad works on Saturdays, and Mom has her quilting group meeting this afternoon," I told him.

"Can we talk about what happened?" Ryley voiced timidly.

"Sure," Blake said.

"Okay, so we know we need to figure out the next clue if it's sorta a puzzle, right?"

"I guess so," Shane agreed. "Whatever the next clue is."

"You guys heard a bang last night, like a gunshot—that has to be it. It's the first time anyone's heard that, right?" Ryley wanted to know.

Shane twirled his mug around on the counter slowly, staring at the whirlpool effect it created with the contents. "It's the first time we've heard it," he said quietly. "But Royce Stillman swore he heard what sounded like a gunshot one time, but he figured it was hunters."

"You guys think maybe Toby didn't get lost? I mean, maybe there was an accident. Why else would the gunshot be so important?" Blake asked, looking at us for our opinions.

"Could be that Toby did go off to war. Maybe he was shot and killed over there, and he's trying to communicate that," Ryley offered.

"Or maybe it was hunters, or maybe it was someone setting off firecrackers. We can't be sure of anything," Shane stated.

"They're all possibilities," I suggested. "At this point, I'd say pretty much anything is worth consideration. Let's put the gun thing aside for now. I mean, if that's the first time we've heard it, it can't be the next piece to solve. I think the next thing to do is try to find a picture of Toby to see if it really was him that I saw. Make sense?"

"Does to me," Shane said. "But where are we going to find a picture of him?"

"He went missing in 1943, right?" Ryley asked. "Odds are that a missing boy would get his picture in the paper. Don'tcha think?"

"There was a war on. I doubt they spent much time covering a lost kid when thousands of people were dying each day overseas," Blake remarked. "But it can't hurt to check. You never know."

"Was there a local paper here then? Odds are they'd have been more likely to have had a picture than the provincial paper," I said.

"I dunno. We'll have to do some research," Shane answered.

"What if we can't find a picture?" Ryley asked.

"Then we're no worse off than we are now," I replied.

During school that week, we never mentioned anything about Toby. Any discussions we had on the subject we had on the phone or online. Nothing was turning up in the papers. We searched through the archives in the school library, hoping to find a class photo, but there weren't any before 1953. We went through the database at the town library but still found no leads.

As September waned, we all became frustrated at not having gotten any further in our research. Toby had been silent since that night in the woods with the guys. There was something we weren't doing right … something we needed to understand before we went back there.

On the last weekend of the month, Shane came over, Blake bringing him back after his Saturday morning volleyball practice.

"Oh good, you brought your stuff," I said, noticing the large leather case that Shane held in his left hand. The case contained all his drawing paper and supplies. He tried not to smile when he heard my enthusiasm.

"Well, I got thinking about it and thought maybe it might be a good idea to sketch the different areas along the path and inside the barn, you know, the places where stuff has happened."

"Good idea. Hope you brought some of your work to show Blake. He really wants to see it."

"Umm … I dunno. They're not that good." Shane became bashful.

"And you talk about me being hard on myself," I teased. "Your stuff is amazing, and I know I'm biased, but I know Blake will like them, too."

"Humph," Shane pretended to grumble. "All right."

"These are incredible, Shane. How long have you been doing this?"

Blake asked Shane as he laid the drawings out on the dining room table.

"Ever since I can remember I've been drawing. After my dad died, I started doing it more and more, sorta a distraction and a coping mechanism, I guess. Mom gave me a graphite drawing kit for my thirteenth birthday, and I've just sorta gone from there."

I loved hearing the sound of the parchment as it slid out from the black leather portfolio. Shane removed each sheet carefully, placing the large pieces of paper on the table. I had only seen a few of his drawings before, and I was more than impressed by the ones he now displayed.

"I love that one," I said, pointing to a sketch of the motel front, looking down the cement walkway in front of the rooms, with wispy people going back and forth along it.

"Yeah? I did that when we were super busy one time last summer. Everybody was moving around so fast, I decided not to try to draw them clearly but as they appeared. I wasn't sure how it turned out, but I like the feel of it."

"Mom would like it, too," Blake said.

"Yeah, she would. Could we show her?" I asked Shane for permission.

He scrunched up his face a bit and shrugged his shoulders. I think he was pleased we wanted to show someone else, but it still made him uncomfortable. "I guess," he reluctantly okayed.

I went upstairs to find my mother in her room, sitting at her sewing machine changing a spool of thread.

"Mom, Shane's here, and he brought some of his drawings. Would you like to see?"

"Oh really? I'd love to."

"He's kinda shy, okay, so don't expect him to talk much about them."

"I'm surprised he actually brought them. It can be a pretty nerve-racking experience to expose yourself to other people like that. You musta asked, huh?"

"More like begged. He could use some positive reinforcement. He's got an amazing ability."

Mom smiled. "You're a good friend, Caleb. That Shane is a sweet boy."

I nodded. "Yeah, he's a cool guy."

Mom looked at my face softly, reading me in that way only mothers do.

"What?" I asked her.

She shook her head. "Nothing. I'm just proud of you. That's all."

"What for?"

She stood up and hugged me playfully, squeezing me and rocking me back and forth. "Cuz you're my kid, silly." As she let me go, I gave her the *you're strange* look. "And I know what that look means, too, mister," she said.

I led Mom downstairs to the dining room, where she immediately began to gush over Shane's work. He was bright red and kept trying not to laugh at being so awkward-feeling. Not used to having all the attention focused on him, he'd let out the cutest little chuckle every so often.

"Is this Astro?" Mom asked, pointing to a sketch of a German shepherd.

"Yeah, that's Astro all right. Lazing out back by the Lawn-Boy a few weeks ago."

"He's a gorgeous dog."

Mom examined each picture carefully, finding something positive to say about each one, which wasn't hard as they really were all exceptional. When she was done looking them over, she gave Shane a friendly little hug. "You're an excellent artist. You should be very proud," she told him.

Shane, not used to anyone hugging him except me, appeared emotional. My mother has that effect on people, which is where Blake gets it, I think. There's something just in the way she inflects a word or tilts her head or touches you that makes you feel like you're the centre of the universe for that moment.

"Thanks."

"Tell me something, what inspires you to draw what you draw?"

"Ahh, I dunno." He scratched the back of his neck. "I guess I just draw whatever I find beautiful," Shane replied.

"It shows," she said.

"Well, thanks for all the encouragement," he said. "I think I'd better put everything away now."

"Thanks for showing them to us. Maybe one day you'll let me buy one from you."

"Heh, well, you never know."

Shane started gathering up his drawings and returning them to the portfolio. He'd had enough attention thrown his way, and I knew he wanted it to stop. We politely excused ourselves, and with the art back in its case, we went up to my room.

"Now I know where you get it," Shane told me as he sat on the end of my bed.

"Get what?"

"Those eyes."

"I don't have my mother's eyes."

"Not in colour, no, but in depth, you sure do. If anything, yours are deeper. Sometimes when you look at me, it's like, I dunno, like everything else in the world has stopped, and I just ... I get lost in there." Shane was trembling a little. I sat down next to him, and he put his head on my shoulder. "When I look in your eyes, I can see how much you love me, and I never thought anyone would ever be in love with me ... I think of how close I came to killing myself and how I would never have known you. I love you so much, Caleb. You're better than anything I could ever have imagined, and you're here ... and you're mine. And I'm just so grateful to be alive."

I held him close and whispered gently in his ear, "I'm grateful you're alive, too."

Chapter Twelve

Early Sunday morning, we started out for the woods. Shane had his paper and pencils with him in a backpack he carried over his left shoulder. It was a touch chilly, so we wore our fall jackets with our jeans and T-shirts. Blake was still sleeping when we left the house, and we didn't feel the need to make him come with us. After all, we'd been in the forest lots of times before without him, and he could really cramp our style if we wanted to make out or anything.

The first place we stopped was just inside the forest, where I had experienced that first episode of time transference. I sat down on the wide stump of a long-gone spruce tree on the side of the path. Shane hunkered down right in the middle of the pathway itself and sketched the opening to the forest. I watched his hands move gracefully over the paper, making the quick marks that looked like nothing but which suddenly became a tree so specific in detail that I could tell exactly which one it was.

"That's about the neatest thing I've ever seen," I told him once he had finished.

"I'm not doing a perfect job, just a rough sketch for our own use."

"Looks pretty great to me."

Shane smiled and kissed me.

I took his hand in mine, and we kept going toward the clearing.

The woods were so peaceful and soothing that Sunday morning, it didn't seem possible that they could ever be a scary place. Squirrels and chipmunks scurried about the limbs of the trees, the squirrels stopping to natter at us because we must have seemed a threat to their food supply. Birds could be heard chirping from the highest branches. We could discern the songs of the white-throated sparrow, the purple finch, the chickadee, and the crazy noise of the nuthatch. There were no ogres or monsters roaming the woods. Nothing evil or terrifying dwelled there. The only thing that existed in the forest beyond the plants and animals was an undercurrent of melancholy.

We stopped on the slope to the clearing so Shane could draw the oak tree, with special attention paid to the carving. Once completed, he came down the hill a bit and squatted in the path, just as we had a few nights before.

"We were about here, right?"

"Yeah," I agreed.

"Okay. Now, tell me what Toby looked like. You've never mentioned anything about his appearance other than you saw him ... or at least who we believe was him."

"You saw him, too."

"Not really. I just saw a silhouette. You saw his face."

I let out a large sigh. "Okay. Let me try to think."

"Take your time. We aren't in any rush."

I sat down next to Shane and tried to recall how Toby had looked.

"Try to remember just one thing at first. Focus on a particular feature." Shane was already beginning to sketch an outline of Toby from what his own memory would allow. I watched the shadowy drawing take shape, and the more Shane drew, the more I remembered. I began to describe Toby as Shane drew, getting him to change something if it wasn't how I pictured it in my head. He took out another piece of paper, and we worked solely on drawing Toby's face. When we were done, it was as close to being exactly how I pictured Toby in my mind as possible.

"Damn ... he's pretty cute," Shane said.

I took the paper in my hands. "Wow, this is amazing. I just wish we had a real photo to compare it to."

"At least we have something to work with in case we ever do see a picture of him."

I held the drawing, almost in disbelief. Shane was right: Toby was very attractive—in a down-to-earth, boy-next-door kind of way. His brownish hair was a little floppy at the front, arcing in the centre and coming down to rest about an inch from the far side of each eyebrow. He had a small nose and ears, slightly larger than normal eyes, and a trace scar on his chin.

"Are you sure you didn't just fantasize that he looks like this? I mean, he's awfully good-looking, isn't he?" Shane said, noticing how long I held the picture.

"Hmm? No, I didn't make this up. This is how he looked."

"I was only kidding, Caleb." Shane put a hand on my shoulder to reassure me.

I smiled at him. "I know. I just feel so sad. He died so young. Whoever it is on that tree with him must have been devastated."

"Yeah."

We were quiet as we continued our way down to the clearing.

"Let's just take a break for a bit," Shane suggested.

"Yeah. Sounds good to me."

I joined Shane sitting on the fallen tree.

"Sure is a nice morning."

"Uh-huh." Shane leaned in and kissed me. "Let's not waste it talking."

The sun was high overhead when we got back to the task at hand. Shane sketched the waterfall and the log and the spruce trees hiding the path. With the last drawing done, we pushed through the spruce branches and headed toward the path's end.

At the shoelace marker on the birch tree, we stopped so Shane could sketch the view back to the spruces. You could just make them out in the distance. They had seemed much closer the last night we were there.

The final thing that Shane drew was the tree in the middle of the path, marking its end. "You think we'll actually need these for anything?" Shane wondered.

"Who knows? Can't hurt to have them."

"True."

"And, hey, maybe someday, when all this is behind us, we'll want to frame them."

"You never know."

"Guess we'd better head back now, huh?"

"Yeah. I really don't want to leave the trail."

"Me neither."

After we'd had lunch, we went out to the barn. I opened the large doors at the front, and natural light spilled in, showing the dust floating through the air inside. Shane climbed the ladder to the hayloft and sat down, hanging his legs over the edge of the loft, giving him a view of the entire floor space below.

"What are you doing?" I asked him.

"You've watched me work all morning; now I wanna watch you," he replied.

"You'll be bored. 'Sides, I don't wanna work on the engine when you're here. I wanna spend the time with you."

"We'll still be together. It's not like you can't talk to me or something."

"I thought you were gonna draw the loft, where we found stuff."

"I will. You do your thing; I'll do mine."

"But it won't take you that long."

"C'mon, Caleb. I wanna watch you work for a while, okay?"

I shrugged. "All right, but don't say I didn't warn you you'd be bored."

I took my work clothes from the nails on the inside wall by the door. I unbuckled my belt on my good jeans and removed them.

"Woo, see, it's already fun for me," Shane said.

I turned around to see him and felt his eyes roaming over my body. He was so adorable, resting his chin on his hands on the lower railing of the loft, his feet swinging out over the edge.

I laughed shyly. We'd been in our underwear together in my bed (which was still the highlight of my fifteen-year-old life), but this time I was aware of him watching me and me alone. I grabbed my faded and worn jeans from the nail and put them on, pulling them up until they fit snug against my body. I put on my oil-stained white T-shirt and changed my cap to the old red St. Louis Cardinals one that I'd gotten at the only major league ball game I'd ever gone to, when I was seven (Expos hosting the Cardinals at Olympic Stadium, Cards won five to three). I had worn it religiously for weeks until a friend's beagle had gotten a hold of it and used the bill as a chew toy. The hat was still in decent shape, but the bill was badly frayed and had tiny teeth marks in it.

I didn't expect to have Shane still watching me, but when I turned around and gazed up, he was still in the same position—his eyes locked on me.

"I can definitely see the appeal of dating a mechanic," he flirted.

"Perv. Get to work."

Shane laughed. "Yes, sir."

I kept a small transistor radio in the barn over by the old stalls. I clicked it on and tuned in to an AM station that was broadcasting the Blue Jays game (their play-off hopes were long gone, but it was still nice to listen to the game as I worked). I reached inside the Bronco and pulled the hood release. When the metal sprang up, I headed to the front of the vehicle to unlatch the safety catch and got to work. Shane pulled his feet up into the loft and began to sketch the areas we had found things.

The afternoon wore on. I checked with Shane a couple times to make sure he wasn't bored beyond belief. He just smiled at me and told me he was fine, fixing up drawings and watching me work. I climbed into the Bronco for the sixth time, hoping against hope that this time it would start.

"Here goes nothin'," I said to myself as I got in.

I gritted my teeth and spoke to the truck, "C'mon … please work this time. I'm running outta ideas."

I turned the key, pumping the gas pedal gently. Noises from the engine sounded out, giving me hope. "C'mon, c'mon," I urged, holding the key over to the start position. As if hearing my pleas for help, the engine caught. A thick cloud of bluish smoke spat out from the tailpipe, and I slowly removed my foot from the gas. I listened as, for the first time, I heard the Bronco idle.

"*Yes!*" I screamed out, rapping the steering wheel with my hands.

Shane hurried down the ladder and called, "Way to go, Caleb!"

"Hop in!"

Shane opened the passenger door and got in beside me, offering me a big grin. "I knew you could do it," he said.

I checked to see that no one was looking and gave him a kiss. I hated that I checked first, and it lessened my good mood momentarily. Shane sensed what had happened and said, "No worries. Just listen to that engine."

I pressed down on the clutch and shifted into first. The Bronco lurched out but didn't stall, as I had feared. I drove out into the driveway, honking the horn repeatedly.

At dinner that night, Dad said he'd get the Bronco registered and insured that week so we could go pick up the plow attachment at Hank's next weekend. Before then, all we had to do was get it safety-inspected. I had high hopes it would pass. I knew it would be a while before I could drive it, but I couldn't wait.

The first week of October was unseasonably warm, feeling more like June. Classrooms were sticky and the courses pure drudgery as I eagerly awaited the arrival of Friday. Not only were we going to have the Bronco out on the road (safety-inspection passed, thank you very much, with only a tie-rod end having to be replaced), but it was Thanksgiving weekend—three whole days off and lots of good food to eat.

When Friday finally did arrive and the last bell rang, freeing us from the monotony of Mr. Belmont's history class, I went to my locker and unloaded all the unneeded books from my bag. Once I had just the few that I required over the weekend, I went out to my bus and found my seat next to Blake.

"Did this week take forever, or is it just me?" I asked him.

"It was brutally slow. Top it off, I got another essay assignment."

"Fun."

"Oh yeah, tons."

"At least it's a long weekend, and we'll have the Bronco to use."

"Thank God. I need three days just to catch up on all my work. 'Fraid any pleasure trips in the Bronco are gonna hafta wait."

I was disappointed, I'll admit, but I understood. "You're still gonna go with us to Hank's, though, right?"

"Oh sure. That won't take long. I just meant the rest of the weekend, I really gotta try to get ahead of these assignments. Sorry, bud, I know you wanted to have some fun."

"No prob. There'll be lottsa time for that."

At dinner, Dad told us that he had called Hank and said we'd be over around seven to pick up the plow. Hank would show us how to attach it and take it off, so when we got back to the house, we could remove it until it was needed this winter. Dad also informed us that he wouldn't be going, as his knee was really bothering him and he just wanted to put up his feet and relax. I was actually pleased it would just be Blake and me, though I would never have even hinted at that to my father.

The Bronco started without hesitation, and I found myself going for the first ride in it that evening, with Blake behind the wheel. I listened to the engine as we drove along, hearing it running smoothly and paying attention for any hiccups or misfires. The interior didn't smell as bad as it had when we first brought it home. I had placed linen-scented car fresheners on the air vents, and it had aired out nicely on those summer days when I opened the barn doors. Still, it was stuffy inside, so I rolled my window down and rested my right arm on the sill. I gazed out at my surroundings. The leaves on the trees were all turning, or had turned, into their various shades of red, yellow, and orange, and the drive up Wakefield Road was alive with colour and the sounds of autumn.

"Few more weeks, and it'll be dark at this time," Blake mentioned as we reached the main road. "I always hate it when it gets dark early in the evening."

"Me too." I checked my watch. Six fifty-six. "How does it handle?"

"Good. I'm not real great with a standard, but it drives nice. You did a good job, bud."

"Thanks."

We pulled into Hank's driveway, and I ran up to the door. Hank's wife, Ashley, answered the door and told me he was already over at the barn. I thanked her and got back in the Bronco.

Hank waved to us as we pulled in the yard, getting us to drive right inside the large outbuilding. Blake shut off the engine, and we said our hellos.

"Your old man told me you got it going again all by yourself, Caleb. Good work."

"Thanks. It took a long time, but I learned a lot."

"I'll bet you did." He nodded and rubbed his chin, making a rough sound as his hand went against the grain of his five-o'clock shadow. "Well, this is the plow attachment, and it's real easy to put on," Hank told us and went on to show us how to do it. We had it rigged up in under twenty minutes.

Hank's barn was large and very spacious. He had tools and supplies on racks and shelving in one corner and parts of cars and appliances in the opposite corner at the back. I looked over the space, thinking how I would use it for something a bit more productive than merely storing junk.

"This would make a great place to restore cars," I said.

"Well, that was what I intended to do with it when I gutted it about ten years ago, but, well, I guess I kinda got sidetracked when Melissa was born. Never gave it much thought after that. I might someday, you never know, but I doubt it."

"Musta been a lot of work just to gut it," Blake said.

"It wasn't too bad, really. One fella who had the place back in the sixties redid the inside to accommodate a team of horses and a few sleighs."

"Who had the place, Santa?" I joked.

Hank chuckled. "Nah, fella by the name of Rogers. Apparently he was a helluva guy, too. Used to give sleigh rides to kids during winter carnival and stuff like that. Poor bastard died of a stroke back in the early eighties. The place sat vacant for a long time, and the house had to be torn down. Shame really. Apparently the vet who originally lived here had quite the home. I bought the property through a bank sale. Guess the back taxes weren't paid. Worked out well for me."

"You say a vet owned this place?" I asked, getting a vibe from something.

"Yeah. Large animal doctor. You know, horses and livestock."

"Don't remember the name of the vet by any chance, do you?" I hoped against hope.

"Heh, I'd better know it, only stares me in the face every time I come in here," Hank said and pointed to the sign on the inside of the front wall. "It was sitting out back in a pile of junk when I bought the place. I was gonna burn it with the rest of the scrap wood, but when my wife saw it, she made me take it off the pile. She thought it was a bit of history and asked me to bring it inside and nail it up. I wasn't about to argue with a pregnant woman, so I did as she said. Didn't make any difference to me, and it made her happy, so whatever, right?"

I could only nod and mumble, "Yeah," as I read the sign:

H. K. Hildebrand

Doctor of Veterinary Medicine

"Why you so interested?"

"No reason, just always been fascinated by local history. You know, who lived where and when. That sorta thing."

"You sound like my mother-in-law. She's right into genealogy. As for me, I couldn't care less how many dead people I might be related to, unless they've left me money in their will."

I forced a light laugh. "Well, thanks for the help. We'd better get going."

"No problem. Have any troubles, you know where to find me."

"Thanks," Blake replied.

We got back in the Bronco and backed into the yard. We waved at Hank as we pulled out onto the main road.

"Guess we now know the significance of that receipt, huh?" Blake stated.

"Yeah. It's all starting to come together."

Chapter Thirteen

I called Shane as soon as we got home to tell him about our discovery.

"So, where do we go from here?" he wondered.

"I dunno. I'm trying to figure that out too."

"You think we should go back in the woods?"

"Possibly. I still think there's more we need to know first. I mean, sure, we have the receipt and we know that it was from the vet, but that really doesn't get us any closer to solving this thing, does it?"

"Hmm. No. I guess you're right." Shane sounded dejected. "Wait a sec … I think I know the connection."

"What?" I was encouraged by the change of tone in Shane's voice.

"Remember, in the stories I told you, that the vet's son was Toby's friend, that he helped bury the horse?"

"Yeah."

"Okay, so now I think we need to find out if he's still alive and talk to him, see if he can fill in the blanks for us."

"Great, but how are we going to track him down?"

"That's the tough part. We'll start online, but that's not likely to show us anything. We can try the phone book, too. Maybe 4-1-1 the guy."

"Be helpful if we had a first name to work with."

"True, but beggars can't be choosers."

"You should come over tomorrow. I'll ask Ryley too."

"Sounds good."

"If you need a ride, Blake's got volleyball practice in the morning."

"Thanks. That'd be great." Shane's mom called for him in the background. "Crap, I better go, Caleb."

"Okay. See you tomorrow."

"Love you."

"Love you, too."

I pushed the off button of my cordless phone and told Blake about the Hildebrand connection. We checked the Internet for any clues, but all we could find were athletes with that last name and a bunch of other websites that were not what we were looking for.

"It was worth a shot," I said.

"Yeah. This guy might not even still be alive, you know."

"True, but we gotta find out for sure."

"Why don't you ride into town with me in the morning? While I'm at practice, you could hit the library and see if anything turns up."

"Good idea. I'll call Shane back and let him know we'll pick him and Ryley up tomorrow, okay?"

"Fine by me."

I left my brother to go back to working on his English essay on *Hamlet*. I returned to my room and called Shane and then Ryley. Everything was set, and they were anxious to come over.

Blake's volleyball practice started at nine, which made for an earlier-than-normal start to a Saturday morning, but I didn't complain. We took the Bronco into town, giving it a good run that way and leaving Mom the truck. I was delighted to see Shane waiting at the locked doors of the library when Blake dropped me off. We sat and talked until the doors opened at nine.

"You boys must be working on a project together," the librarian said. Her dark blue Chevy Cobalt was the only car parked in the lot when I had arrived, but she hadn't unlocked the doors until precisely nine. She was a large woman in her mid-fifties named Gloria. She had a kind face and a voice you instantly liked, sort of gravelly but rounded. You knew she wasn't afraid to enforce the rules, but that she was there to help because she liked people and loved literature.

"Yep, thought we'd get here early so we could use the research stations," Shane replied.

"Well, they're all yours. No one has them booked until this afternoon. You fellas need any help, just come up to the desk, okay?"

"Thanks. We will," I said.

She gave us a warm smile, and we headed over to the far corner, where the microfiche and databases were located. I sat at one machine, Shane at the other.

"Good luck," I whispered.

"You too."

My back and neck got sore and my eyes burned, becoming blurry, after spending more than an hour hunched over the desk reading anything and everything that the old newspapers had from the late thirties to the early forties. I noticed Shane stretching and yawning, so I leaned over and said quietly, "I'd love to help you work out some of that tension later," and winked at him. He got this silly little smile on his face and snickered.

"Behave," he kidded, and we went back to work.

Gloria came over to check on us a few times and made sure we weren't having any problems. The only problem we were having was finding what we hoped would be there—whatever that was. I put my glasses down on the table and rubbed a hand over my face before putting them back on and continuing my search.

"Hey, check it out," Shane whispered, tapping me on the shoulder.

I slid my chair over beside him and saw a small advertisement in a paper dated April 1943. It was basically just the vet's name and profession listed on the side panel of a page with the words, *Specializing in large animals*, under his title. The articles in the paper were all about the conflict in Europe and escalating tensions throughout the world.

"Good eyes," I said.

"Thanks."

I sat back down at my own station and scrolled through more and more papers. We had found nothing more by the time Blake came to pick us up. We decided to call it quits for the day and put everything back before leaving the library.

"So, nothing but an ad, huh?" Blake asked as we drove toward Ryley's.

"Nope. Nada," I replied.

"That sucks. I was hoping you'd get a lead."

"So were we. Just hafta keep trying, I guess," Shane said. "Least we have an idea what we're looking for now."

"How was practice?" I asked.

"Same as usual. Drills, basics, techniques, yada, yada, yada. Not anywhere near as fun as beach volleyball."

"Is there anywhere around you can play that?" Shane questioned.

"Not really. Some of the guys and I are trying to get the project off the ground to set one up at the school, but who knows?"

"Gee, it'd be really tough to watch beach volleyball games, wouldn't it, Shane?" I said.

"Torture."

"Hey, no shit. I'd love to see some of the girls get all sweaty and sandy in their little bikinis," Blake added. "But that's honestly not why I want to get a beach court set up."

"Sure, sure," I teased.

Blake laughed. "Whatever. It's an added bonus, true, but I just love the game."

When we got to Ryley's, I hopped out of the Bronco and flipped the seat so I could ride in back with Shane. Ryley passed me his stuff, which I put behind me in the small cargo area, and climbed in.

"How's it going, Rye?" Blake asked as we pulled out of the driveway.

"Pretty good. Have any luck this morning, Caleb?"

"Nah. Shane was there too, and neither of us found anything other than this one ad that Shane spotted in a 1943 newspaper."

"Damn. I was hoping we'd have some killer lead."

"So were we," Shane said.

"And there was nothing at all in the ad?"

"Nope, nothing that we didn't already know," I answered.

"Jeesh, this is frustrating. How the hell are we supposed to know where to look now?"

"That's a good question. But hey, we're that much closer than we were at this time last week, right?" Blake said, trying to keep us optimistic.

"Yeah, but I sure hope it doesn't take us months and months to get to the next step," Shane commented.

"Don't lose faith, guys. Maybe we just need to go back out on the trail," Blake suggested.

"With what, though? We know nothing more than we did last time. Nothing that makes a difference anyway," I stated.

"We can't be sure of that. We're playing Toby's game. Only he knows the rules. It's worth a shot."

"Yeah, but Rye," Shane leaned forward so Ryley could hear him clearly, "don'tcha think Toby would expect us to come back with more knowledge than when we left? Think about it: he left us that receipt way back in the spring, and we just figured out this week what it means … and that was just a fluke."

Ryley nodded. "You're probably right. I just don't know what else to suggest."

"If only we coulda found a picture of Toby in one of the papers or somewhere so we could compare it to the drawing that Shane made," I said. "Maybe then we'd have something to work with."

"I bet if we could track down the vet's son, assuming he's still alive, he'd be able to tell us whether the sketch is Toby or not," Ryley said.

"Which brings us back to our main problem: where to find the vet's son," Blake uttered.

We discussed the various possibilities as we drove home, not coming up with anything that seemed very helpful before parking the Bronco back in the driveway.

"The woods, I guess, are gonna hafta be our next step. Can't hurt anything, I suppose," I rationalized.

Blake sighed. "We don't have a lot of other options right now. Let's grab something to eat and then head out. Okay with everyone?"

We all agreed, though none of us sounded enthusiastic.

By two o'clock, we were making our way up the path entrance to the woods. We stopped inside the forest and discussed what we were doing.

"Last time Caleb and Shane got pulled through together cuz they were holding hands, so I think you guys should do that again. I'm gonna walk at the back of the group, Blake should walk at the front. That way, if something does happen, one of us should be able to see it, maybe get pulled along."

"Good thinking, Rye," Shane said.

"Thanks. One more thing before we get going: I don't think we should stop and rest at all. I think we need to go right to the end of the path and then turn back. That's when it happened last time."

"It may be that nothing happens at all this time," I said. "Shane and I were through last weekend, and we didn't hear or see anything out of the ordinary."

"Yeah, but we didn't know about the vet until last night," Blake mentioned.

"True," I agreed.

"Okay. Let's do this," Shane insisted and took my hand in his.

We formed our procession as Ryley had instructed and began our trek. The woods felt serene that Saturday afternoon, and I didn't expect to see or hear anything, even though we knew a little more.

At the clearing, we didn't stop, pushing forth through the spruce trees and up the extended path to the deeper woods—the shoelace still demarcating our first time there. We were past the point of the birch-tree marker when I heard a thud behind me. We all stopped and turned around to see Ryley holding his stomach, kneeling on the ground.

"Shit, Ryley. You okay?" I asked as we all ran to his aid.

Tears were streaming down Ryley's face. "God, oh God, oh God, it hurts!" he whimpered.

I knelt down beside him. "Ryley, look at me!" I urged. He turned to face me; his vision must have been blurry through the tears. "Tell me what is happening to you."

Ryley kept holding his stomach. He shook his head and wiped at his eyes. "I just had this pain like you wouldn't believe go through my stomach, like I was stabbed with something really hot," he told us, his voice quivering with fear, his big blue eyes wet with fright. He pulled up his shirt and felt around for any sort of wound.

Shane put a hand on his shoulder, saying, "We should get you back to the house."

Ryley shook his head. "No. We need to keep going."

"Are you sure?" I asked.

"Yeah. Thanks." Ryley, with a little assistance from us, stood back up. "Sorry about that." He wiped his eyes with the bottom of his shirt, stretching the fabric to meet his face.

"Nothing to be sorry about," Shane said. "We're just glad you aren't hurt."

Ryley walked around a bit and hopped up and down a few times to get himself back in tune with his surroundings. He rolled his head from side to side and said, "I feel fine now. Let's keep going."

"Hold up a second. This is the same spot where we heard the loud bang," I said to the guys.

"So?" Blake asked.

"So, if that bang was a gunshot, we may have just been shown where Toby was shot," I explained.

"We don't know he was shot," Blake said.

"You think he was murdered?" Shane asked.

"There's no way to know. Not yet, anyway. It could have been that he had an accident or that he shot himself—maybe even on purpose. I think we can be pretty sure of one thing … Toby never got out of these woods alive."

"We all assumed that, though, didn't we?" Ryley asked.

"Yes, but there was always the possibility that he ran away for some reason—like to join the army," Shane answered.

"Is it just me, or do you guys feel like something's wrong?" Blake looked at us and then around the forest. He was right: something felt out of place.

"I know what you mean. I feel it, too," I said.

All of us were scanning the forest as far as we could see, trying to understand why things didn't seem right all of a sudden.

"What are you trying to tell us, Toby?" Shane asked the woods. "What are we not seeing?"

The air grew cold, and the four of us could see our breath in front of our faces. There was a crunching sound of footfalls on twigs, and then silence. My ears rang. Nobody moved.

Caleb

I heard my name called and shouted back, "Toby?" There was no response. The air warmed, and my breath ceased making clouds. Shane gripped my hand firmly in his, letting me know he was still there without me having to look.

As quickly as it had begun, the strange feeling ended. We all knew it without having to say a word. We turned and headed back toward the house. An hour or so later, we were back inside, taking a seat at the kitchen table and sipping at coffee from a freshly brewed pot.

Chapter Fourteen

Blake and I were driving the Bronco back and forth to school on days that it rained and we didn't feel like standing out in the wet waiting for the bus. The wipers smeared across the windshield in intermittent bursts, pushing the heavy mist aside. We drove along in relative silence. It was Tuesday, and we hadn't talked about Toby since Saturday. The radio didn't work yet, so the sound of the tires wicking up water from the asphalt was the only sound we had to listen to between wiper strokes and gear changes.

"Blake?" The wipers swished, the right one sticking a bit where the rubber was loose.

"Yeah?"

"Remember how Hank said that the barn was owned by some guy named Rogers?"

"Yeah. So?"

"Maybe we could track down someone in the Rogers family and find out what they know."

"There's gotta be oodles of people named Rogers. We don't even have a first name."

"Registry of Deeds would. All property titles are on file somewhere."

"True, but we'd have to go into the city."

"Wouldn't that info be online?"

"I doubt it, but we can check. After school, we'll grab Ryley and Shane and discuss our options."

"Cool."

We pulled into the school yard and parked just as the rain started to come down harder. I pulled my jacket over my head and made a run for the doors.

After school, the four of us sat in the Bronco behind the school in the dirt parking lot for students.

"Man, all of this is so time-consuming," Ryley said as we talked about our next move. "I've got a ton of work I'm falling behind on."

"My stuff is piling up, too," Blake admitted.

"Okay, look, here's the deal. We've all got lots of crap to work on for school right now, so let's take a week off and focus on our own problems. I mean, we all want to solve this thing, but it's gonna hafta wait a bit. On Saturday, we'll all get together and look for Rogers, but until then, let's not even talk about Toby. Deal?"

The guys looked at one another and then at me. Everyone seemed to agree with what I had said.

"Sounds good to me, but we all gotta really work at our stuff and not let it slide and then bitch when we're still behind on the weekend, right?" Shane said.

"Definitely. Believe me, I'd much rather be trying to solve a sixty-year-old mystery than work on stupid math assignments," Ryley replied.

"No kidding," Blake agreed.

"Good, so it's settled. You guys come home with us Friday night, and we'll go from there."

It was going to be hard to concentrate on homework with Toby still on our minds, but I knew it was necessary. School really interferes with life.

Having had Thanksgiving on Monday, it was a four-day school week. I managed to get ahead of all of my assignments by working at them all evening every day that week. I was even able to get ones done that weren't due until the end of the following week, providing me with a decent amount of breathing room. I hoped the other guys did the same.

Shane and I were standing outside the Bronco talking, waiting for Ryley and Blake to arrive once the final bell had released us all on Friday. The air was mild, and the leaves scuttled across the pavement.

"I hope we don't have to go back to the library and scroll through more blue screens," Shane said, partially joking.

"Same here, but we may have to. Your mom doesn't know any Rogers, does she?"

"Nah. I asked her the other day, and she said she hasn't heard that name around here in a long time. There used to be lots, but as the generations wore on, they began to move away—going to the cities and out west like everybody else."

"You'd think there'd still be one or two Rogers around, wouldn't you?"

"I know where there's one." I turned around to see Adria and Ryley approaching. They were holding hands and seemed happy.

"God, look how cute you two are," Shane teased. Adria smiled brightly.

"You know someone named Rogers?" I asked her.

"Yeah, my grandmother married a man named William Rogers."

"Small world," Shane breathed.

"Why, what's going on?" Adria wanted to know.

"I'm, umm, doing a research project, and I'm trying to find families that lived in this area during ... during the war. You know, for history," I answered. I chose my words carefully, and technically, I didn't lie.

"Which war?"

"Second."

"Yeah, she lived here then."

"Wow. Sure would be great if I could talk to her," I said, trying not to sound excited.

"Sorry. I wish you could, too, but she passed away two years ago."

"Oh. Sorry."

"That's okay. You didn't know."

"Whereabouts did she live?"

"Well, she lived in town until her first husband died. When Grams got remarried, about six years later, to William, she moved outside of town to his place. It's close to your house actually."

"Really? How close?" Blake jumped in.

"You've probably driven by it a hundred times. The house was torn down a while back, but there's a barn kinda hidden up in behind where the house used to be. It's a big brown one on the corner."

"Jackpot," Shane whispered to me.

"He used to have a team of horses and a sleigh, apparently. He died before I was born, so I really don't know much about it. We moved to town a few years later, and Grams came to live with us until she passed away. She was never the same after William died, Mom said." Adria smiled again as she spotted something. "Speaking of which, there's my mom, now." A silver Mazda Tribute entered the parking lot, and Adria waved politely. "I gotta go, guys. Have a good weekend." She stood on her tiptoes and kissed Ryley on the cheek. "Bye, Ryley. Call me tomorrow."

"I will."

Adria headed for her ride, turning to wave at us, or more accurately, Ryley, before she got in the compact SUV. Ryley let out a big sigh as she was driven away.

"Things seem pretty good between you two." Shane smirked.

"Yep. I am really falling for her … hard."

"That's good, man. You deserve it."

"Yeah, Rye. She's really nice," I said, happy for my friend.

"And she doesn't look bad in those jeans, either," Blake mentioned, giving Ryley a good-natured elbow in the side.

Ryley grinned like the Cheshire cat. "I know, right?"

The four of us gathered in the barn after dinner, sitting in the loft and trying to figure out our next course of action. As we mulled over our options, Ryley's cell phone chimed in his pocket. He flipped open the phone and read a text message. He typed a reply and waited for a response. After a few minutes of back-and-forth texts, he snapped the phone shut and said, "Killer news. That was Adria. She was talking to her mother on the way to the mall after school, and she mentioned we had been talking about her grandmother and stuff. Turns out the real reason her grandmother moved in with them after William died was because he had never changed his will after they were married. All his property was left to a distant cousin, who used to live there years before. A guy named Wendell Hildebrand."

"Holy shit," we all gasped.

"Apparently Wendell had told Adria's grandmother that she could stay in the house as long as she wanted, but after a few years, she found it too isolated and moved into town. The bank took over the place after years of taxes not being paid. It sat uninhabited for so long that it had to be torn down before they could sell the property."

We were all a bit stunned, having learned what we deemed to be a crucial bit of information.

Ryley chuckled. "Adria thought you might be working on your project this weekend and wanted to tell you before she forgot. She didn't think it would be any help, but figured that it was up to you to decide. Little did she know, huh?"

"This is incredible," I replied.

"All right. Now we know to look for a Wendell Hildebrand," Blake said. "If he's still alive, there's gotta be a record of him somewhere."

"Well, if the bank repossessed the property, they obviously have contact information for the previous deadbeat owner. I'm sure they made numerous attempts to contact him and get their money," Shane suggested.

"Yeah, but no bank will ever give us any info like that," Ryley stated.

"No, but if they had to sell the property, they probably would've used a realtor. A realtor would have the previous owner information, and as we talked about before, property ownership is a matter of public record," Blake explained. "We can ask Judy. Even if it wasn't her firm that dealt with the place, odds are that in an area this small, she'd be able to find out who did."

"Good call. Let's check it out," I said.

"Who's Judy?" Ryley asked.

"She's the realtor we bought the house from," I answered.

"Right on. But don'tcha think she'll wonder why on earth we're trying to find out about an old barn's previous owner?"

"Valid point, but we can just use the research project story again," I replied.

"Hell, it's worth a shot," Shane said.

We went into town and stopped outside the real estate office where Judy worked. A note on the door read: "Back in Five Minutes." We sat, waiting patiently, for twenty minutes before the door opened.

"I think I should go in by myself," I said.

"Good idea," Blake nodded.

I waited a bit before going into the small office space where Judy worked, not wanting to make it seem as if I had been waiting for her to return. The air was heavy with the smell of lilac—the kind from an Air Wick spray bottle. I could surmise what Judy had been busy doing.

"Well, hello, Caleb," she greeted me warmly. I was impressed she remembered my name.

"Hi," I smiled back. "How are you?"

"Just fine, thanks. And you?"

"I'm good. Thanks."

"Something I can do for you?"

"Yeah, well, I hope so."

"Well, come into my office and have a seat."

I followed Judy to the back of the room, where her desk was set inside a cubicle. There were stations for two other agents as well, but no one else was around.

"What can I do for you?" she asked as she got comfortable in her chair, folding her hands on her desk in a professional manner.

"Well, I'm doing this research project about the area, and since I'm pretty new here still, I was hoping you could help me out. See, there's this barn up the ways from our place, the big brown one on the corner as you head back into town, and I'm trying to find out where the previous owner is."

"Oh, you mean the Harrison's barn?" she asked.

"Yeah, that's the one. Only I'm trying to find out who had it a while back, after Mr. Rogers passed away. He willed it to a distant cousin, whose family used to live around here. I'm trying to establish the whereabouts of the families who built up this area."

"That sounds like a really interesting project."

"It is, but it's rather difficult to find information sometimes. All I know is the name is Hildebrand."

"Hmmm. I'll have to check the records. I don't know much more about the history of the town than you do, and I've been here for fifteen plus years," she admitted with a chuckle.

"So, I guess you weren't in charge of the barn's sale to Hank?"

"No, not me personally. I'm pretty sure it was our office that oversaw the sale, however. Let me check for you, okay?"

"Thanks. I'd really appreciate it."

"Just a sec."

Judy spun her chair to face the computer monitor to her left. She began to click on various things and type in other information, mumbling to herself as she went. She was scrolling through pages of text when she said, "Ah, here it is. Yup, we sold it all right. My coworker Jerry Becker was the agent. Let's see, hmmm, sold to Hank Harrison, mmmhmmm, ah, yes, there it is. Former owner was one Wendell Hildebrand of Toronto, Ontario. That's all it says. There's an asterisk next to his name … oh … sold on account of foreclosure. Bank received all profits, less commission of sale. Does that help at all?"

"Yes, that's all I needed to know. I can't tell you how much I appreciate it."

"My pleasure. Nice to see someone actually willing to do some footwork for their assignments for a change."

"Sometimes it's the only way to find out what you need," I replied as I stood up. "Thanks again."

"You're very welcome. Have a good day."

"You too."

I went out of the office and got back in the Bronco. "Wendell was living in Toronto when the property was sold to Hank. Guess we know where to search next, huh?"

"Good stuff. Biggest city in the country. Prick couldn't live in some tiny little remote community like Stanley Section or East Chezzetcook. God. This should be easy," Blake bitched.

"Don't be bitter. It is what it is. At least it narrows our search," Shane said.

Blake shifted into gear, and we pulled onto the road. "Well, it's someplace to start."

Our efforts to locate Wendell Hildebrand in Toronto started on the Internet, checking the white pages for any idea as to his whereabouts. We searched for hours, all of us crowding around Blake's seventeen-inch flat-screen monitor. We started as a group but paired off in shifts due to eyestrain. Whoever wasn't at the computer was never far away, usually flaked out on Blake's big bed listening to his stereo or playing cards on the floor. As the evening wore on to midnight, we were all pretty tired. Ryley was alone at the computer, taking off his reading glasses and rubbing his eyes periodically (I was glad I wasn't alone in this habit). After replacing his glasses, we heard him say, "Bingo!" in a loud whisper.

Without further prompting, we all gathered around the computer once more, instantly reawakened and hovering over Ryley like buzzards waiting to descend on a dying animal. Ryley began to read what he had found.

"Hildebrand, Sheldon, age sixty-eight, died suddenly at home of heart complications yesterday. Blah blah blah. It goes on to talk about his work at a children's hospital after getting his medical degree at McGill and so on and so forth. Now, here's the interesting part ..." he was tapping on the monitor as he said this, "he was predeceased by both parents, one of whom was indeed H. K. Hildebrand. And then, look at this," he pointed to the screen again. "He is survived by his brother, Wendell Hildebrand of Halifax, and his sister, Constance (Hildebrand) Durant of Berwick." Ryley turned around and smiled broadly at us. "So, not only is Wendell still alive, but he's living in Nova Scotia again."

"How the hell did you find this?" Blake asked.

"I was on one of the Toronto newspaper websites—*The Toronto Star*, I think it was—and I found a link to this city paper that no longer exists but has a site with all its archived stories. I used their search engine, and bam, there it was. Now that we know this Sheldon guy was a doctor, we could probably find out a lot more about him, but I don't think we need to. Do you?"

I shook my head. "No. The info you got is awesome, though."

"I don't think we need to even look for Wendell anymore," Blake said. Something had clicked for him. I could tell just by the way he spoke.

"Why not?" Shane asked.

"Cuz, guys, look." Blake held the printed copy of the obituary that Ryley had done off and pointed to the words on the paper. "Constance Hildebrand Durant … initials before she was married were C. H. Think about it."

We all gawked at each other, stupefied. We'd all been too tired to absorb the information until Blake mentioned it. We were concentrating so much on Wendell that I doubt I ever would have given Constance a second thought.

"Oh man, this is great. That paper is only a few years old. She could very well be still alive and living in Berwick. We gotta find her," Ryley said.

"And do what? I mean, four strangers can't just show up on an elderly woman's doorstep—especially four teenage guys. She'd call the cops for sure … unless she thought we were Mormons," Shane said, adding the last part for his own amusement.

"He's gotta point," Blake agreed.

"So now what? We dress in black suits and bike down her driveway?" Ryley joked.

I laughed. "No, I don't think so. What we need to find out is exactly where she lives and go from there. But not tonight. We all need to get some sleep. We'll work on this tomorrow."

"Okay, good. I'm beat," Blake said as he peeled off his shirt. "See you guys in the morning."

The three of us left and went to my room. I couldn't help but tease Shane as we got ready for bed.

"Were you checking my brother out?"

"Umm, no, not really. He does have a wicked body, though."

"Hey, a guy can look even if he's attached," Ryley stated. "It's like, you've got your meal, but you can still look at the menu."

"It's true," I said. "Why else do you think we keep you around, Ryley?" I flirted.

He grinned. "I'm like catnip to you guys, aren't I?"

We joked around some more before settling down for the night. With the lights out and Ryley asleep, I felt Shane put his arm over me and pull me close to him. I took his hand in mine, gave it a kiss, and held it to my heart.

We would discover, with little effort at all, that Constance Durant lived in a seniors' complex in Berwick. We weren't sure how we'd approach her, but decided that the next weekend we would go see her and figure it out as we went along. We agreed that only two of us should go in to see her, most likely Shane and me. We thought we could keep on with the story of the history project and that sort of thing. Most elderly people, we had concluded, seemed to thoroughly enjoy talking about the past and would do so without much encouragement. We hoped Constance was like that.

Chapter Fifteen

On Monday night, Shane called me. It felt nice to just be able to talk to my boyfriend again like I imagined most couples talked, but it was hard too, as I realized most couples never had to be afraid to let anyone else know they were together. At school I watched kids kissing and holding hands all the time without so much as a single thought. Straight couples never had to worry that they might be called names or get beaten up, or worse, merely for displaying affection and being themselves. For me, it was always at the back of my mind, and when I was with Shane, it was front and centre. I hated that I couldn't be myself with him, that I had to act like we were just friends. I wanted more than anything to hold his hand and let people see us together—but only if there wouldn't be any kind of negative reaction. I felt like a coward.

"I wish it didn't matter to people," I said.

"Well, it doesn't matter to everyone. Look at Ryley—he's straight and he's cool cuz he's comfortable with himself. He told me that he'd be flattered if a guy hit on him, just like we are when a girl hits on us. People who are hateful only hate themselves."

"I know. What drives me nuts is these assholes who think they're all worldly and say they aren't racist but they still hate us."

"You can be a bigot and not a racist, Caleb."

"Yeah, but it's pretty screwed up, isn't it?"

"Definitely."

"I'm just tired of being afraid all the time. I love you, and I feel like I'm supposed to be ashamed of that or something … and I guess, by not being open, I must be. But I'm not. I mean—God."

"Hey, don't think that way. I know you're not ashamed of us. This isn't easy. We're going to come out, we both know that. We've started already."

"But why can't it just be what it is? Why should anyone have to even come out? I mean, wouldn't it be great if we were just talking casually and said something about liking this boy and no one even batted an eye?"

"That'd be pretty sweet, but it's not the world we live in, unfortunately."

"Why does this have to be so hard?" My voice wavered at the brink of breaking.

Shane could sense my emotions. "I don't know," he said softly. "But we owe it to every closeted kid out there to be ourselves, cuz every time someone comes out it gets that much easier for the next person to do the same thing. No one should have to go through this alone. Maybe, if we can be ourselves, we can help someone. Maybe even just one person."

"That would be nice. I want to help people."

"So do I. And we will."

"Shit." I had to stop talking for a minute and compose myself. I hadn't planned on getting so deep.

"You okay?"

"Yeah. Better now. Thanks."

"Never have to thank me. I'm always here for you."

"We're gonna get through this, right?"

"Count on it." Shane's voice was so steady and confident I felt better, like it really was going to happen.

Friday finally arrived, and school ended for another week. Ryley and Shane came home with Blake and me that night. Blake worked on some homework and then went out with his friends for the evening. He was still casually seeing Vicki, and I was glad that he was still living his own life, as well as being part of our ghost-tracking group. Blake's team had a volleyball game the next night, so we'd be leaving around noon to go to Berwick to see Constance. I was apprehensive about going, but not so much that I considered bailing. We had come so far and had gathered so much information already that there was no turning back.

"Have the woods stayed quiet lately?" Ryley asked me as we lay in our sleeping bags after midnight. We'd spent the evening watching movies and playing games on the computer, never discussing the forest situation until we were in bed with the lights out.

"Yeah, haven't heard a peep since the last time we were in there."

"You think maybe it's over?"

"No, I don't think so. I mean, we really haven't solved anything yet. Sure, we know that the C. H. stands for Constance, but otherwise there isn't much more we know. I'm hoping she'll lead us to wherever we're supposed to go next, or at least give us something so we can return to the woods and see what Toby does next."

"What do you think it was that kept Toby from, well, crossing over—for lack of a better term?" Shane wondered aloud.

"Your guess is as good as mine. Maybe it's his mysterious death he wants us to know about, or maybe we're just supposed to find his remains so we can put him to rest properly," I suggested.

"Maybe he's waiting for Constance to die so they can be together again," Ryley offered. "Or maybe he's just meant to wander, sort of lost and hopeless, because he doesn't know how to cross over."

"Maybe there's no place to cross to," Shane said. "Ever think about that?"

I had to admit, the thought had crossed my mind from time to time. "I've never been what you'd call religious, but I do believe in God," I said. "There's something after this life is done. As for what it is, I don't know what I believe."

"How about you, Rye?" Shane asked.

"I've always felt there's something else, but I don't know if I'd call it God or what. I definitely believe there's more to this world than the mortal plain. I think Toby proves that point."

"I wish I knew that my dad was all right."

Ryley and I didn't know what to say after Shane spoke. We were all silent for a few minutes.

"Tell you what I do know," Shane said. "I know that I'm grateful that Toby came into my life. Without him, I wouldn't be here today and have the best friends a guy could ever hope for."

The words Shane chose could be interpreted on two levels. I knew that he literally meant he wouldn't be here without Toby. The story behind that was for Shane to tell. I merely took his hand in mine and said, "I feel the same way."

"You know, I bet if Toby were alive today, he'd fit right into our group," Ryley said.

"Yeah, I bet you're right," I agreed.

Blake arrived home from practice Saturday morning at ten. He had showered and changed at school, so he was able to join us for an early lunch before we piled into the Bronco and headed for Berwick. Upon Shane's suggestion, we stopped and bought a potted plant for Constance, an orangey-coloured mum appropriate for the autumn season.

When we arrived at the Golden Meadows Retirement Community, we parked on the upper level by the main entryway in the visitors' parking area. Blake turned off the ignition and twisted around to face Shane and me in the backseat, both of us somewhat nervous.

"Okay, fellas, you know what you're gonna do, right?" he asked us.

"Yeah. We go in to the front desk, say we're here to visit Constance Durant, and if we get asked who we are, we just say we're friends of the family who want to talk to Mrs. Durant about growing up in Stapeton for a school project," I recited, having it memorized.

"I don't suspect you'll have any problems at all, but if you do, just keep cool and come back out to the parking lot, and we'll jet, okay?"

"Yup." I nodded and took a deep breath.

"All right, you're gonna be fine. You both look like little gentlemen. Old ladies love that," Blake snickered.

I turned to Shane and said, "Helluva first date, huh?"

The Golden Meadows Retirement Community was the nicest seniors' home I'd ever seen. Everything was new and clean, without smelling antiseptic (or like pee). There weren't wheelchairs lining the halls and people calling out in varying degrees of dementia. There was a large common room to the right, with gargantuan windows that flooded the area with natural light. Groups of seniors sat around tables playing cards, making crafts, and working on jigsaw puzzles. Even the smell of the lunch in the dining hall that wafted through the home was pleasant. I was impressed—and relieved that not every seniors' home was like the nightmarish ones you saw on the news.

We strode over to the front desk and received a warm smile from the receptionist. She probably saw hundreds of people just like us coming in all the time with flowers or some little thing that might bring a smile to their loved one's face for a short period of time. Most often, I suspect the gifts were more penance for the people doing the visiting than they were gifts for the ones being visited.

"How can I help you boys?" the woman behind the desk asked us.

"We're here to visit Mrs. Durant," I explained.

"Okay. Are you relatives of hers?"

"Umm, no, we're high school students doing a project about Mrs. Durant's hometown of Stapeton. We're trying to find out about the history of the families that developed the area, and we'd really like to talk to her about it, if we may."

"Does she know you're coming?"

"No, ma'am."

"All right, I'll tell you what I'll do. I'll go ask Mrs. Durant if she's up to having company, and if so, we'll go from there. Most people are pleased to have visitors, so I don't suspect there'll be any problem, especially if you're here to talk history with her. If there's one thing Mrs. Durant is always up to talking about, it's local history." The receptionist got up from her chair. "You boys wait right here. I won't be a minute."

"Thank you very much," Shane said.

We paced about for what seemed like an hour but was only five minutes. The receptionist returned with a big smile on her face.

"She'd love to talk to you. Follow me, and I'll take you down to the smaller common room at the back of the building. She's having some tea and knitting, and she finds the light better in the smaller room. Between you and me, she's really not that interested in socializing with most of the other guests, refers to them as 'old people.'" She laughed. "Now, I'll tell you, her hearing is good, so you don't have to raise your voices, but she does tire quickly, so please be patient with her, and if she gets too weary, you'll have to excuse yourselves, okay?"

"We will, don't worry. My grandmother was the same way," Shane said.

The receptionist nodded understandingly at Shane and led us into the smaller common room. It was perhaps a third of the size of the main room, with smaller windows and without any large tables set up for gaming or puzzles. The walls were a cheery light green, with yellow accents and white wicker furniture with green floral patterned cushions. Constance sat in one of the three swivel rocking chairs in the corner of the room, the perfect place to sit to see people coming from either direction. A bag of knitting was on the floor to one side; her cup of tea (a proper china cup and saucer, I noted) sat steaming on the small table with the lamp to her right. Her hands held the knitting needles but stopped moving as we drew near, her eyes lighting up.

"Mrs. Durant, these are the boys who would like to talk to you about Stapeton's history," the receptionist said, introducing us.

"Pleasure to meet you, Mrs. Durant. I'm Caleb, and this is my friend, Shane."

"It's so nice to meet such handsome, well-mannered young men. That'll be all, Gidget," she said, waving off the receptionist with one of her hands.

"If you need anything, you can come up to the desk," she said as she turned away.

Mrs. Durant made a face at her as she walked away. "Need anything. Bah. I'll tell you who needs something, it's that Gidget. Needs a good smack on the back of the head to wipe that Goody Two-Shoes smile off her face, is what she needs." Mrs. Durant was grinning mischievously, pleased with herself at having shared her feelings with us. Shane and I both tried not to laugh. "Oh, I'm gonna like you boys just fine, I can tell. Any man who brings me flowers is all right in my book. I take it that is for me?" she said, pointing to the chrysanthemum.

"Oh yes, of course. We had no idea what colour you liked, so we got one that looked the most fallish," Shane said as he placed the plant on the table where the teacup sat.

"It's beautiful. I love orange flowers. Be a dear and place it on the windowsill there."

Shane moved the plant to the large sill in front of the window looking out to the gardens.

"Perfect. Thank you very much. I don't get flowers very often anymore," Mrs. Durant said. "Even if I did, Gidget would probably kill them. She hasn't a clue, poor dear." With a sly smile, she went on to say, "You know, her name isn't really Gidget; I just call her that to make her mad."

"Why Gidget?" Shane asked.

"Oh my, you are young, aren't you? Well, there used to be a series of films about a silly little thing named Gidget, and one of her movies was called *Gidget in Hawaii*, or maybe it was *Gidget Goes Hawaiian*, some such thing anyway. Well, Helen, that's her real name, was wearing this god-awful flowery shirt one day, they call them Hawaiian shirts, don't you know, and since I never liked her and I hate those shirts, I started to call her Gidget because Gidget was small and popular and Helen is large and stupid." Mrs. Durant stated this with such joy I had to laugh. This pleased her even more. "Now have a seat and tell me, what can I do for you boys?"

We sat down on a wicker love seat, pulling it around so we both faced Constance.

"Well, Shane and I are working on a history project of sorts, researching families that helped to establish Stapeton. The name Hildebrand kept appearing over and over, but when we tried to find one of the family members, we got stuck. We finally found something about your brother, Sheldon, who we were sorry to learn has passed away."

"Ah, Sheldon. What a good man he was. He was the baby of the family and always the most interested in taking over our father's work. My father, as you may have learned, was H. K. Hildebrand, a noted large animal doctor." We nodded that we did indeed know this, which made Mrs. Durant smile. "Well, Sheldon used to spend all his spare time with Father learning the basics of medicine. He was a huge help, especially after my father's arthritis got so bad it made walking difficult. Sheldon was certain he was going to carry on the family business until one of his classmates died of polio. That death devastated my brother. From then on, he was determined to help children in the future avoid such tragic fates, so he went into paediatric medicine and became very well renowned in his field. When he passed away, the church was packed with people who had been touched by his life. Hearing all those lovely things at his funeral … I am so proud my little brother helped so many people."

"Wish we could have met him," Shane said softly.

"I wish you could have, too. He was a true humanitarian."

"Could you tell us about what it was like to grow up in Stapeton?" I asked.

"It was much like any other small community, I suppose. The majority of the people were farmers, and the town itself wasn't much more than a street with five or six buildings on it. I was seldom in town, actually, as our schoolhouse was just down the road from where we lived and our church was right next to it. Never really had much reason to go beyond there. Most of those buildings are gone now, all of them I think, except father's veterinary practice. That was a lovely barn he had specially built for his work. We spent hours in there with him, nursing sick animals back to health and shedding tears when they died. Until he went to war, my older brother helped our father with most aspects of the business. They went out on all sorts of calls together. Not me, though. Oh, no. Can't have a girl doing that sort of thing. Pffffft. What nonsense. But that was the times for you. I stayed home and helped Mother with all the cooking and cleaning and all that other unappreciated stuff. And when I left home, I ended up doing it for another forty years with my own family. And what do I have to show for it? Two kids who live out west and never visit and a husband six feet under."

"I can't imagine not visiting my own mother, especially when she's as funny and kind as you are," Shane said. It was obvious buttering up, but Constance didn't seem to mind.

She beamed at him and said, "That's because you're a good son. You won't run off with some trampy thing and call your mother after you get married to tell her about it, will you?"

"No, ma'am. I don't see that being an issue."

"Of course not. Oh well, gotta let 'em live their own lives, I suppose." She sounded a bit disgusted with the idea and flicked a wrist in the air.

"My family recently moved to the house at the end of Wakefield

Road. Did you know the family that lived there while you were growing up?"

"Oh indeed, very well," Constance said, her voice getting softer. She sipped her tea and stared out the window. Her teacup made a clank sound as it rested back in the saucer. It rattled momentarily in her unsteady hand. She rested the saucer on her leg to stop the noise. "There ended up being so much sadness there that the Everetts moved away. I don't think sadness like that ever leaves a home, though. Not really. It gets in the air and lingers … Do you boys know about Toby?" She turned back to see us as we replied.

"Yes. We've heard many stories about him," I said.

Constance turned back to the window. "He was such a handsome boy. My, I can still see his eyes when I think of him. Blue as the sky. He had this voice that made you feel warm inside, so sweet and so gentle, yet manly. Of course, I was madly in love with him. I think every girl in the village was. When there's a handsome boy like that in a small village and you know you're not related to him, well, I guess it's a given that you develop a crush."

"Were you two an item?" I asked her.

Constance turned back to me and sighed. "No, we never were. Toby was a few years older than I was, and I don't think it ever crossed his mind to court me. He was friends with my older brother, and he treated me like a little sister, which was nice but not too satisfying." Constance shook her head. She sighed, seeming to regroup, before continuing.

"When Toby's horse, Cocoa, died, he was devastated. I remember that well. My brother was a rock for him. They were best of friends, practically inseparable. They camped out in the woods, fished, hunted, and went horseback riding. All that fun boy stuff I was never allowed to do."

"Whatever happened to Wendell?" Shane asked.

"I don't think anyone was more devastated when Toby vanished than he was. He looked through those woods, high and low, scouring every inch of them—even after Toby had been pronounced dead. He shut himself off from us almost totally after that, only speaking to me. I was the only one who wasn't surprised to find his bed empty that early spring morning, and I was the only one who got letters from Europe letting me know that he was still alive.

"You see, he ran away and joined the army. He got himself shipped overseas by the summer of 1944. It was in those letters that followed over the next two years that I learned so much about him and what had happened." Constance looked distant. "I can't imagine what he went through." She wiped a tear away from her eye. Shane handed her a tissue from the box of oversized Royale that sat on the table. She dabbed at her eyes. "Thank you. You'll have to forgive an old woman for being sentimental a moment." She cleared her throat and sipped her tea. "The last letter from Europe that I received was an official letter stating that Colonel Hildebrand was being posted to stay on and continue his work with the Canadian regiment in France."

"Colonel?" Shane confirmed.

Constance smiled. "Yes, indeed. Would you like to see a picture of him?"

"Sure, that would be great," I replied.

"Wait here a moment while I go down to my room for the album." Constance got up cautiously from her chair and grabbed her cane. "If it weren't for these darn hips of mine, I wouldn't have to be in a place like this," she grumbled.

We watched her head back to her room just down the hall. When she was out of sight, Shane said, "Whattaya think so far?"

"Hard to say. We're certainly getting information, but I don't know that it's helping any."

"Yeah."

Constance emerged from her room and made her way back to us. It was after two o'clock, and Blake wanted to be gone by three. I hoped we'd learn something more in the time we had left. Constance sat down between us with a large scrapbook in her lap. She opened the cover and pointed to a picture.

"There's the Colonel," she beamed as she tapped the black and white photo of a young man in uniform. "Well, he wasn't a colonel yet, not when this was taken. He sent me this picture after he enlisted. Wasn't he handsome?" she sighed.

He was very attractive, and even though the photo wasn't in colour, you could tell he had piercing eyes. His strong jaw and brush-cut hair were somewhat deceptive in hiding the fact that he was just a sixteen-year-old boy.

"Why didn't he tell anyone else that he was going to join the army?" I asked her.

"He didn't want to be found. He told me he just wanted to disappear. I think he wanted to die and decided that since he couldn't commit suicide that he could die trying to help others—and he told me, to have a son die heroically on the field of battle would be easier for people to accept than if he took his own life. So, off he went. I tried to talk him out of it, not understanding why he felt he wanted to die. He promised he'd explain it to me if he lived long enough," Constance said as she held her brother's picture in her hands. "He comes and visits me every so often, making the drive down from the city. He's lonely and I tell him he should move closer so we could be nearer to each other, but he says he can't. He didn't even move back to Nova Scotia until three years ago. He'll be coming down in a few weeks' time to take me to the Remembrance Day service. We go to that every year. He drives down and takes me to the service, and then we have lunch out somewhere. Usually he stays for the afternoon. Most of the time we just sit in my room and talk. He always ends up in tears. It's a very hard day for many veterans."

"Yes, I'm sure it is. I had a great uncle who served in the war. He was in the air force. Mom said he refused to ever talk about the war or even have it mentioned in his home. He just found it too hard to deal with," Shane said.

"It's a terrible thing. I pray you boys will never see battle." Mrs. Durant flipped the page of her scrapbook, and her mood lightened. "Ah, here we are. You see the boy on the right? That's Sheldon. It's me in the centre, and this is—"

"That's Toby," I stated.

Constance looked at me, surprised. "Why yes. That's Toby. How on earth did you know that?"

"I just had a feeling is all."

"And standing on the end next to Toby is Caleb," Constance said as she finished pointing out the different people in the old photo of kids sitting in the back of a hay wagon.

"Did you say Caleb?" Shane asked, his voice sounding shocked.

"Yes."

"But isn't that your brother, Wendell?" I asked, confused.

"Oh, yes, it is, but you see, no one ever called him Wendell. His middle name was Caleb, and that's what he went by, growing up. On all of his records and things, he is listed as Wendell, but to us he was always Caleb. Never Cal … oh no, he hated that."

Shane and I exchanged a *Holy Shit!* look.

"See, when he left home, he told me in one of his letters that Caleb no longer existed. The boy he was and that we knew was dead. From then on, he was to be called Wendell. It was hard to think of him as anything other than Caleb, but eventually, it just became natural to call him Wendell. He said it was just too painful to hear the name Caleb."

Constance examined our faces carefully. A gentle smile appeared on her face, and she said, "I know the stories of Wakefield House. Every single one of them. At least, I thought I did, until you boys came today. I may be an old woman, but I'm not stupid. I listen carefully to the words people use, and you boys haven't lied to me, I know that, but I also know that you never said what the project was for. It's not for school or a local paper, is it?"

I shook my head. "No, Mrs. Durant."

Her smile broadened. "So, you're here because something has made you curious about where you live. Right?"

"Yes." Shane took a piece of paper from his pocket and unfolded it. It was the drawing of the carving on the oak tree. "What can you tell us about this?" he asked as he handed her the sketch.

She held the parchment in her hands, and her expression changed. The smile left her, and her hand shook slightly. "Where did you see this?"

"In the woods. The forest behind the house. It's carved into a big English oak tree far along the path," I replied.

"And you thought the C. H. was me, didn't you?"

"Yes."

Constance handed the paper back to Shane. She took a deep breath. "Wendell never told me about that. I knew there was a place in the woods that he used to go with Toby. They used to camp out there, at a clearing with a waterfall. They were the best of friends—they sparkled when they were together." Constance was staring at the wall ahead of her. Her eyes were damp and her voice shaky. "I don't know how I didn't see it then."

"Mrs. Durant? Are you all right?" Shane asked.

She gently patted his knee. "Yes. I'm just a bit tired. That's all."

"Maybe we should leave you," I suggested.

Constance cleared her throat. "You know, it's funny. Sometimes it takes a complete stranger to make you understand something that was right in front of you your entire life. In all of Wendell's letters to me, he never came right out and said it, and I suppose I was too naïve to read between the lines."

"Have we upset you?" I asked.

Constance's smile returned. "Oh no, my dear boy. You've made me feel much better. Finally, it all makes sense to me …" and then she looked at each of us again, back and forth, studying us, "and I gather it makes a great deal more sense to you now as well."

"Yes, I think so," Shane responded.

"We can't thank you enough for your time, Mrs. Durant. Is there anything we can do for you?" I asked as Shane and I stood up and turned to face her.

She pondered over my question momentarily. "There is one thing …"

"Name it."

She placed one of Shane's hands and one of mine into hers. "Don't shy away from your fears. You must face them in order to live your life fully. God makes miracles, not mistakes. You remember that."

Shane and I looked at each other. "We will," he promised her.

"And maybe you'd both be so kind as to visit me again one day."

"We'd love to," I told her.

"Thanks again, for everything," Shane said.

"Believe me, it was my total pleasure."

Shane and I turned to go.

"Oh, wait. I want to give you something," she said.

We turned back, and she opened the photo album. Constance removed a picture we hadn't seen before and handed it to me. "Keep this. It's always been one of my favourites, but I think it needs to belong to you boys. There's something about that photo, I've always thought, but I was never able to place my finger on it. Perhaps I just don't have the right eyes to see it. I get the feeling you fellas might."

"Thank you. I'll keep it safe," I assured her.

"I know you will."

"Good-bye, Mrs. Durant."

"So long, boys. Come again, please."

"We will. You can count on it," Shane said.

As we headed for the door, I examined the photograph. Wendell and Toby were sitting, side by side, their legs stretched out in front of them, bare feet making vees, in the back of an old pickup truck. They looked to be about twelve years old. Toby was wearing overalls with a patch on the right knee, and he had a piece of straw in his teeth. He reminded me of one of those prints you see at gift stores, with a typical farm boy with no shirt under his overalls and that sweet, innocent face that breaks your heart. Wendell was dressed in jeans with patches on both knees, but instead of chewing anything, he was wearing a straw hat, tipped back on his head so his cute little face was visible. A bale of hay was situated between them, and the entire bed was covered with pieces of the grass. A bottle of Coke, half full, stood on the bale of hay, perfectly centred. I could almost feel the sunshine pouring down on them. I could hear the cicadas in the distance and smell the sweet hay. I could feel the sweat run down the sides of my face and taste the soda that quickly warmed in the sun. Under me, I could feel the metal of the old truck (though I couldn't tell from the picture, I like to think it was a '34 Ford, the first model year of the V8) and see my best friend sitting there beside me. I knew what those boys must have been thinking as they sat there that day: *Life doesn't get any better than this.*

I pocketed the photo as we stepped outside and made our way to the Bronco. Ryley was flaked out on the backseat, dozing, and Blake was leaning back in the driver's seat with his eyes closed. When I opened the passenger door, they both jumped. Shane and I filled them in on all we had learned as we journeyed back to Stapeton.

Chapter Sixteen

"Holy crap!" Ryley exclaimed. He had woken up fully and was sitting in the front seat again as we headed for home. Shane had just finished saying that Wendell went by his middle name, Caleb, growing up.

"Those are pretty much the same words I was saying to myself when I heard it," Shane said. We were all talking like we had an adrenaline rush.

"So, Toby was never calling for you then, huh, bud?" Blake asked me.

"Guess not." In some ways, I was disappointed to have to acknowledge that fact. Although it had been very unsettling in the beginning, it had begun to feel very personal to me, like I was the only one that this long-dead boy wanted to contact. Like I had been chosen to figure it all out, and no one else was going to be able to do it without me. It deflated me a bit.

"I wouldn't be so sure, though," Shane said. "I mean, yeah, odds are that Toby was just calling out for his love, but you gotta think it strange that there are no other accounts of anyone ever hearing Toby call the name Caleb. And I think it's pretty amazing that sixty years after he dies, a kid named Caleb shows up, and he's a gay kid at that. So, I'm betting Toby was just waiting for someone he could really relate to moving into the house—maybe by warding off unwanted inhabitants all these years." Shane smiled at me and laced his fingers with mine.

"Well, regardless, I think it's pretty kick-ass that Toby and Wendell, or Caleb, or whatever, were gay. I don't know why we didn't think of that before," Ryley said.

"Guess maybe cuz it was so long ago. But really, that just makes it make more sense, cuz they never woulda been out back then, right?" Blake suggested.

"Almost definitely. Constance didn't even know her brother was gay until we were there. She never said the words, nor did we, but she figured it out," I said.

"Was she pissed?" Ryley asked.

"No. Actually, she seemed happy to finally understand," Shane replied.

Ryley, who had been turned around in his seat the entire time and looking at us, grinned. "We're hitting the woods tonight for sure, aren't we?"

"I don't think that's even a question," Blake answered.

We arrived home in a half-hour and had a light supper. Blake left for his game at five thirty, and the rest of us went in with my parents at six thirty to watch him play.

There were a lot of kids at the game, so we sat with a bunch we knew. Almost all of the parents sat in a clump at one end of the risers and the kids at the other. It felt good to just relax and watch my brother play volleyball, like I had done so many times in the city. I'd never had friends to sit with in Halifax, though, so this was far superior. As an added bonus, number seven on the opposing team was a total hottie.

When the game ended (we lost, but it was close), Ryley, Shane, and I stayed behind to catch a ride home with Blake. While he was in showering, we hung around outside the school and talked with some of the other kids. The game-winning team from the South Shore started down the inside steps and burst through the front doors a moment later, all talking excitedly and looking rather pleased with themselves as they trotted down the cement steps and past us toward their bus. There were a number of attractive guys on the team, but number seven was by far the most gorgeous. He was wearing jeans that were snug in all the right places, and Shane elbowed me gently to make sure I had seen. I enjoyed the view but found I'd rather look at Shane. When he turned his gaze back my way, he whispered, "Whatcha lookin' at?"

There was a sweet smile on his face and a twinkle in his eye. I did everything in my power to keep from kissing him at that moment. I hated that I stopped myself.

"You," I whispered back. No one else was aware that we'd even spoken to each other. Shane's hand reached back toward mine, and I felt one of his fingers touch mine before he quickly pulled it away.

Gradually the other kids went off. Our volleyball team members filed past us in staggered clumps, looking defeated and tired. Blake's hair was still dripping from his shower when he opened the door and stepped out into the night. The air was chilly, and you could see the steam rising from Blake's head as we walked to the Bronco.

"Sorry about the game," I said as I got in the backseat.

"No big deal, bud. Just a game. We played hard."

"Yeah, you were awesome out there," Shane said.

"Thanks." Blake chuckled. "Not that either of you two were really watching our side a lot."

"God, were we that obvious?" I asked, slightly worried.

"Nah, not to anyone else, I'm sure. I just happened to look up a coupla times and saw you guys checking out the fellas on the other team. Not to worry, I'm less than loyal when the girls have a game."

Ryley laughed. "No shit, huh? God, there's this one chick from one of the city teams, whoa … she's so hot it hurts."

"Is it that blonde from the Heights?" Blake asked.

"Yeah, that's her. You like her too?"

"You kidding? She's slammin'. And don't forget that brunette on the team from Antigonish. Damn."

"Oh, my God, yes. I was watching her in this game last year and like, she slipped toward the net, and her shorts went up so far you could make out her—"

"Ryley, Lord, man, stop!" Shane laughed. "I'm visualizing that." He pretended to shudder.

"So if number seven's cock had flapped out sometime, you wouldn't wanna talk about it?" Ryley needled.

For that little while on the ride home from the game, we were just teenagers again. I don't recall everything that was said, but I know we had a lot of fun. We drove back to Wakefield House with a sense of anticipation, our excitement filling the cab of the small four-by-four.

We got home around ten and sat in the kitchen to chat with my parents for a bit and get something to eat. I wished they'd hurry up and go to bed so we could hit the woods, but it wasn't like I could tell them that. Finally they called it a night, and we said we'd be going upstairs in a bit but that we might hang out for a while outside, maybe have a fire in the pit or something.

We headed outside to the barn after putting on our jackets. The air was cold, colder than when we had left the school. There was a chance of a frost, the forecast had claimed. I didn't doubt it.

We had stashed our supplies in the hayloft, so Shane and I scurried up the ladder and grabbed the canvas knapsack containing flashlights, matches, my trusty Zippo, two water bottles, a compass, a small first-aid kit, and some snack foods. Shane slipped the sack over his shoulders and held the straps with both hands, reminding me of my first day of school in Stapeton. Shane was wearing a grey hoodie and jeans along with his jacket, and he looked so sweet I couldn't stand it. I pulled him toward me by his belt loops, hooking my index fingers inside them. I placed a soft kiss on his lips, holding him tight against me. "I wanted to give you that earlier."

"I almost held your hand."

"I know."

"Maybe I should have."

"I wanna tell my parents before I tell the world."

"That's cool." Shane nodded and looked down at where my fingers still held him close. "Planning on keeping me here forever?" He smirked and kissed me passionately, placing a hand at the back of my head and bringing me even closer to him as his tongue tasted mine. I knew I was getting hard, but I didn't care because we'd crossed that threshold a while back. I could feel him too, and I wished for some time alone like we'd had before.

"Come on, boys, the windows are fogging up down here," Blake called up to us, pretending to stamp his foot from impatience.

Shane and I started to giggle as we kissed, and we held our

foreheads together, gazing into each other's eyes as I called back, "We're coming."

"No wonder they're taking so long," Ryley teased.

With that comment, any sense of romance was gone—with a healthy, if not a tad crude, laugh. We headed down the ladder with our supplies and made our way toward the stream.

"Man, it's cold tonight," Blake mumbled as we began our trek to the clearing.

Ryley stopped and shone his flashlight on a thermometer attached to a key ring on the outside of his pocket. "It's hovering around zero, maybe plus one."

"God, it's not even Hallowe'en yet, and it feels like winter," Blake griped. I think he realized he was the only one complaining, so he changed the subject. "Where, or when, do you think Toby's gonna talk to us tonight? If at all."

"You can never tell. It's up to him. Would be too easy if it were at the start of the trail every time," I said.

"You think he'll show us something big tonight, don't you?" Ryley asked me.

I'm not sure how I knew, other than gut instinct. "Yeah, I think he will."

We didn't talk much more after that. We made it to the clearing and started down the path between the spruce trees. I had gone through the trees first and was sure I had heard the others behind me, but everything seemed quiet—even for a forest at night.

"Shane?" I whispered. I turned around. "Shane? You there?" I flashed my light around and saw nothing but trees and emptiness. I heard a crunching sound from back toward the spruce trees. I quickly set my light on the path, and it fell on the face of a boy.

It's hard to describe the feeling that went through me at first. Although I believed I was prepared for anything, I felt almost sick to my stomach from fear. My hand started to shake, and the flashlight quivered. The light went off the figure for a second and then back on. But when I found the face again, I stopped shaking.

"Caleb, you okay?" Shane asked with a worry in his voice as he began to jog to me.

"I thought you were gone. Everything was quiet, and when I called for you ..."

"Hey, it's okay. I'm here, I just got stuck on some branches coming through the trees."

"You mean, you weren't just standing in the path at all?"

Shane shook his head. "No, I just got through the trees and saw your light shaking, and I came right to you. I didn't hear you say anything, or I woulda said something back. You were supposed to hold my hand, remember?"

"Shh." I held my finger to Shane's lips. "They aren't with us," I said.

Shane pointed his light down the path I had my back to. "Ahh ... Caleb ... we aren't alone."

I turned and saw what Shane was looking at. There, just ten metres up the path from us, was Toby. He appeared much more clearly than when I had seen him before. He was still rather shadowy, but his features were more easily distinguishable.

"Toby?" I asked the figure, not sure what to say to an apparition.

The boy stood momentarily, and then, slowly, began to drift nearer. Shane held my hand tightly in his.

Caleb

The boy called out.

Caleb

He kept getting closer.

"What's happening?" Shane nervously whispered to me.

I studied Toby's face and smiled at him. I wasn't scared. In fact, I felt very warm inside as he drew closer. "He's not looking at us," I explained. "He's calling for *his* Caleb. See, he's looking past us."

Sure enough, as Toby came closer, he didn't stop but continued on through us. For a split second, I saw this incredible light and felt this intense tingling sensation, like when I was little and grabbed an exposed plug from the wall. We turned to watch Toby go on to the clearing. We followed close behind.

The temperature was much milder back at the clearing, and we could see the moonlight on the waterfall. Shane nudged me and motioned toward the fallen tree. There sat another boy.

"Why didn't you follow me?" Toby asked the other boy.

"Cuz I got a rock in my shoe. Just give me a second."

"We don't hafta go on. There's nothing much up the path anyway."

"I'd kinda like to just stay here. It's so quiet."

Toby sat down on the log by his friend.

"Whatcha thinking?" he asked.

"I dunno. Nothing, I guess. You?"

Toby looked at his friend and grinned. Without saying anything, he kissed him. "I love you, Caleb. Now and forever. That's what I was thinking."

Caleb smiled sweetly. "I love you, too, Toby."

They sat, holding hands, as they tossed pebbles in the stream.

"Wanna head back?" Toby asked.

"No, not really. Only place we can be ourselves is here."

"I know, but when we go off to college, we'll get a room together to save money. Lottsa fellas do that. We'll manage."

"Why are we different?"

"We're not different."

"Yeah, but, you know what I mean. I wish we didn't even hafta think about other people and stuff. Does that make sense?"

"Sure it does. Maybe someday we won't. Hard to say. No matter what, we'll always be together. You can count on that much."

Caleb smiled. "I know I can."

"C'mon. Let's go."

Shane and I followed in the distance as the boys started up the path. At the bottom of the hill, I held Shane's hand in a firm grip to make him stop from going forward.

"Look," I said.

We watched as the boys kissed by the oak tree. Toby swept a hair back from Caleb's eyes. "I wanna do something," he said and pulled a jackknife from his jeans. He knelt down on the path and began to carve into the oak's trunk. Caleb stood over him and watched. When Toby had finished, he rose, and they held each other in a tender embrace.

"It's only one more year until we get out of here. Just one more year," Caleb said, the sound of frustration and exhaustion in his voice mixed with the hope he had for their future together.

"That's not long at all," Toby said, trying to sound cheerful.

They began to leave our line of sight, so we hurried up the hill to the path, but when we reached the top, the boys were gone.

"Damn, we lost 'em," Shane stated.

"Okay, let's think. What did we learn tonight?"

"Just that Wendell is Caleb, and he is, er, was, Toby's boyfriend."

"And that they had plans to live together and go to college."

"Yeah, but since Toby died and Wendell went to war, why is it so important?"

The air grew chillier as we talked.

"Damn. Feel that?" I asked.

"Yeah. It's cold. We're back."

We trudged down the hill to the clearing and through the spruce trees. We could see Ryley and Blake turn around ahead of us as they heard us approaching and saw the flicker of our lights.

"What happened? Something big?" Ryley asked before we even had a chance to catch our breath.

"Well, sorta. We didn't really learn much, but we were right about Wendell and Toby," Shane said.

"You'd think we woulda thought of that earlier, what with you two being gay and everything," Ryley noted.

"No kidding. It's pretty amazing what society has ingrained in us, isn't it?" Blake commented with disgust. "Everyone is straight until proven otherwise."

"There's gotta be something else to report, guys," Ryley said.

"We heard them both talk, which was rather cool, really," I informed them.

"What did they sound like?"

"Just like us. They looked and sounded pretty much the same as us," Shane replied.

We filled in the other blanks as we hiked home.

"What do you think was so important about hearing them talk about their plans for the future?" Ryley wondered aloud.

"That's the part we don't get either. There's gotta be some reason we heard that conversation, but I don't know why," I admitted.

"I think they were trying to tell you that they always felt they were going to have to hide in order to be together, but that still wasn't going to stop them from making it happen." Blake stopped in his tracks as he spoke; it was as if a lightbulb was on over his head. "Yeah, think about it for a second. They were teenagers in the forties. They knew they were gay and that they couldn't be open about it or talk about it. Hell, they didn't even have a word for it, cuz 'gay' only meant 'happy' back then. But, despite it all, they were determined to live their lives. And if they could do it back then, with all the odds stacked against them, why shouldn't you guys be able to now, in a world that's much more accepting?"

"It's an interesting theory, Blake, but I'm already out to my mom, remember?" Shane said.

"And I'm out with you guys. So we're already better off than Toby and Wendell were," I added.

"I gotta say that you could interpret what they said a bunch of different ways. I really don't think that's what it's about," Ryley said.

"I dunno. I was just guessing," Blake mumbled, sounding sad. "I just don't want to see you feeling scared of what other people might say, Caleb. I want you to be proud of who you are. Both of you."

"So do I, and I'm getting there."

"We both are," Shane added.

Back in my room, we didn't waste any time getting into our sleeping bags. We were tired, physically and mentally. I listened as both Ryley and Shane slept. I couldn't get Blake's words out of my head. I wasn't sure what it was Toby had wanted us to derive from what he and Wendell had been talking about, but regardless of that, Blake was genuinely concerned about me. It wasn't that I was surprised by this—he'd always looked out for me—but it made me realize just how completely he accepted me for who I am and how he wanted nothing but the best for me. He knew I needed to come out to our parents before I could really feel good about myself. If I had our parents' support, then it wouldn't matter what anyone else would ever say because the people who mattered most to me would be on my side. The most heartbreaking things can happen to people when they come out, but some of the most heart-tugging things can happen too. I've come across stories where the family is brought closer together with a newer understanding of one another. There are cases when kids are able to form new friendships and help other kids to feel good about themselves. And, perhaps, what is in many ways the easiest thing to read are the instances when it's not an issue at all to the family. The person comes out, everyone's cool, and life goes on.

But I couldn't help think about the possibility that my parents might not accept me. What then? Would I be kicked out? I'd read so many stories where that had been the case. What about those kids whose parents sent them away to be so-called "reprogrammed" as straight? I couldn't even fathom such a thing (and so often it stemmed from "religious" households, which leads to all kinds of questions about what kind of church would encourage and promote hatred on such a scale). Would my parents hate me?

I didn't know what I could expect from them. We used to go to church together every Sunday when I was little. Gradually we went less and less until we didn't go at all anymore, not even at Easter and Christmas. We still said grace before dinner, and I still prayed and had faith, like the rest of the family. We were just not people who needed to go to church every Sunday. So, from a religious standpoint, I wasn't really worried, but there are plenty of nonreligious kids who get kicked out of their homes or abused in some way if they do stay home. I didn't know what I'd do if I got kicked out. The thought worried me so much my stomach began to knot and a panic attack started to set in. I shook Shane lightly, needing to talk myself to a calmer state.

"Shane? Shane? Wake up," I whispered, not wanting to disturb Ryley.

"Hmm? Huh? What's wrong?"

"If I get kicked out, could I stay with you?"

Shane sat up on one elbow and looked at me tenderly. "Babe, you aren't going to get kicked out." He stroked my cheek with the back of his hand. I grabbed his hand and held it against me.

"Please, just tell me I can stay with you if it all goes bad."

"Of course, you can."

I breathed a sigh of relief. "Thank you."

"But, Caleb, it's not going to happen. Your parents are good people. They may need some time to adjust, but they won't throw you out."

"You can't know that, though. I'm their son, and I don't know that for an absolute fact." I was shaky and on the verge of tears.

"Hey … hey … it's okay. Shhh. Don't cry. Shit. I'm sorry, Caleb. I didn't mean to make light of it. Look at me. Hey, look at me." Shane slid his hand under my chin and lifted my face to see his. "You can stay with me as long as it takes if you need to. Even if it goes really well, you might need some time away from them just to let it sink in, and you're most welcome at my house. You always are and always will be. Okay?"

I nodded. Tears streamed down my face and splashed over Shane's hand. He pulled me down next to him and held me tight. He kissed my forehead and rubbed the top of my arm.

"There's gonna come a time when we don't have to hide, Caleb. I swear it. No matter what happens, we're in this together."

"Together forever," I added.

Shane held me close and kissed me. I drifted off to sleep in the safety and warmth of his embrace.

Chapter Seventeen

The first Thursday of November arrived with a cold wind and a light frost. I stood outside the Bronco chatting with Shane as we waited for Blake to arrive after school. The parking lot was about half full with students' vehicles. One section of the lot was always unofficially reserved for a group of rougher kids, who often only bothered to come to school to see if they could get kicked out. There were a lot of kids like these in Halifax, too, but in the city not as many had cars. As Shane and I were talking, we heard a loud bang and then a grinding sound coming from the nicest of the cars in the rough section (affectionately known as "The Grease Pit"). The owner was a guy named Tim Weller. Tim was more than slightly intimidating. It wasn't that he was really tall or really big; he just had this way about him. He might have been decent looking had he cared about his appearance, but he didn't, or at least, it didn't seem that he did. His car, on the other hand, was a thing of beauty. He drove a navy blue 1971 Oldsmobile Cutlass Coupe. The car was in fairly good shape, save for a dent in the left rear fender, but the old eight-cylinder engine had seen better days.

We could hear the endless stream of profanity as Tim slammed his steering wheel with his fists and repeatedly tried the ignition. He got out and lifted the hood, and I knew he didn't have a clue what he was looking for. Here was a guy who wanted everyone to believe he was tough and had a kick-ass car, but he didn't know the first thing about what made it work. It was almost funny to see him reach in and fiddle with wires and knobs, but really it was just sad. I felt bad for him.

"Watch my books, okay?" I said to Shane as I unshouldered my book bag and dropped it to the ground by one of the Bronco's wheels.

"What are you doing?"

"Gonna see if I can help."

"Are you nuts? That's Tim Weller."

"I know, but he doesn't have a clue what he's doing, and the poor old Cutlass is suffering."

"But … well, be careful."

"I will. No worries."

I turned and headed toward the Oldsmobile. When I got there, a couple of Tim's friends were standing with him, trying to help him out.

"Can I give you guys a hand?" I asked as I approached.

"Go stick your hand up your ass," one of the minions told me.

"I plan to, but I like to get it greasy first."

The other minion laughed, somewhat nervously. "Shit, that's good. Got you there, huh, Gary?"

"Seventy-one, right?" I asked.

"Yeah," Tim said flatly, not turning around.

"Original block in it?"

"Yep. Piece of crap that it is," he mumbled. He still didn't turn around.

"Mind if I take a look?"

Tim turned to face me. "And what the fuck are you gonna do?"

"Well, hopefully more than just stand around and stare at it hoping it fixes itself," I replied curtly. To this day, I can't believe that's what I said.

The minion who had laughed before snickered again, only this time it was nervous laughter. He glanced from Tim to me and back to Tim again. I never took my eyes from Tim's until he cocked his head slightly and said, "Be my guest."

I had visions of him slamming the hood down on my head, so I went at the engine from the side and kept an eye on Tim, who still stood at the front of the car.

"Got any tools with you?" I asked them.

"I've got some in my truck. Hang on," laughing minion said. He ran over to his Toyota to retrieve them.

"You know what's wrong?" Tim asked.

"Yeah, I'm pretty sure."

"Can you fix it?"

"Do my best. Won't take long, maybe a half-hour."

"And you're gonna do it?" he asked, sounding somewhat shocked.

"I'm here, aren't I?"

"Ask him for how much," Gary sneered.

"I'm not looking for any money."

"Then what's your game, man? You planning on messing with his engine or something?"

"No … the engine is actually fine. It's the distributor. I'm going to clean it up the best I can and secure the lines. As for my game, I just like to work on cars. Fixed that Bronco over there," I said, pointing to our little Ford.

"Looks like a piece of crap to me," Gary said.

"I'd take that over your Neon any day, Gary," Tim stated and spat on the ground. "Goddamn tuner piece of shit."

Laughing minion returned with the tools and handed me the kit. I began to work away at the problem. Blake came up to the car and said, "Umm, Caleb, I'm heading out now."

"Go on ahead. I'll be finished here soon."

"How you gonna get home?"

"I'll go over to the library. Mom's working today. I'll catch a lift with her."

"Hell, he gets my car fixed, I'll drive him home," Tim said.

"Actually, I need to do some work at the library anyway," I said. "But if you'd give me a lift over there, that'd be great."

"Yeah. No sweat, man."

"Ahh, okay, well, see you later then, I guess," Blake said.

"Yeah. Laters," I said as I ducked back under the hood.

I heard my brother and Shane leave the parking lot. A while later, I stood back and asked Tim to start the engine. He got behind the wheel, and the car came to life with little effort. I closed the hood and handed laughing minion back his tool chest.

"Right on. Thanks, man," Tim said, standing outside his driver door.

"No prob. Just glad you didn't slam the hood on my head."

Tim laughed. "Nah. You're a cool little gearhead."

"Got brass balls, too," Frank (the laughing minion) stated.

"C'mon, Caleb, I'll give you a ride to the library," Tim said.

"Not that you'd know where that is," Gary snipped.

"Check you guys later," Tim said as he got behind the wheel.

"Take 'er easy, Caleb," Frank told me.

"Yeah. You too, man," I replied and got in the car.

The interior wasn't in great shape, but it was restorable. The tan vinyl was splitting on the ends of the bucket seats and the dash was cloudy and cracked in a few spots, but all in all, it was a pretty sweet ride.

"So how'd you get into fixing cars?" Tim asked as we went down the street to the library.

"Had a friend in the city that was restoring a '66 Corvair. I did a lot of watching and listening. Got to help eventually."

"Cool. Sure I can't drive you home?" he asked as we pulled into the parking lot of the library, which was only a kilometre from the school.

"Nah, thanks. This is good."

"All right, man. Keep cool."

"You too. Thanks for the lift."

"Hell, least I could do."

I got out of the car and headed inside the library. I went directly into the washroom to clean the grime and grease off my hands. I stood at the mirror and gripped the counter with both hands, taking what felt like my first breath since I left Shane back at the Bronco. I smiled at myself in the mirror and ran my wet hands through my hair.

Mom was surprised to see me as I approached her at the main desk. She had been busy when I came in, but the line had cleared and no one was demanding her immediate attention.

"Can I get a ride home with you?"

"Sure thing, hon. I'll only be a few more minutes."

"Okay."

I wandered up and down the aisles of books as my mother finished up with whatever it was she was working on. I was leafing through a book on the second world war when she found me.

"All set?" Mom's keys were in her hand, and her purse was tucked under her right arm.

"Umm, yeah. I guess." I was on a section of the book with photographs from concentration camps. I was feeling a bit shaken. You never get used to seeing people being tortured and the inhumanity of war. I have been very aware of the atrocities of the concentration camps as far back as I can remember hearing the word *war*, but in all the time I had seen the pictures and heard the accounts, I had never really let it hit me. Somehow it had always felt distant—remote, like it was something that only happened in another world altogether. As I was looking over the photos that day, I saw one that made me stop and really focus on it. For the first time in my memory, I saw a prisoner wearing a triangle on his chest instead of a star. The photograph was in black and white, but I knew the triangle was pink. The man's eyes were drawn and his skin gaunt, pulling back on the bones. He was on the verge of death, you could tell. At first glance, I would have guessed his age to be in the sixties or seventies, but upon closer examination, I could see he was a man not much older than twenty. His eyes seemed to be locked on mine.

"You wanna take that book home?" Mom asked. Her cheery voice made me come back to reality. I snapped the book shut and stuffed it back on the shelf.

"No." I hurried past her and went out to the car. I was already inside when she opened her door.

"Honey, what's wrong?" Mom put her purse down on the floor behind my seat and stuck the key in the ignition. She didn't turn the engine on. She turned to me, placing a hand on her right knee.

I shook my head and looked out my window. "Nothing."

"Is something bothering you?"

"Nope. I'm fine."

"Was it that book you were reading? Some of those pictures can be awfully hard to look at."

"It's not that."

"So ... it *is* something. Please, talk to me."

I don't know how my mother knew not to say anything more than that, but she did. Had she asked me if there were problems at school or something along those lines, I would have clammed up completely. She just sat, not saying a word until I spoke.

"I'm so scared," I told her, my voice shaky with emotion.

"Of what, sweetie?"

"That I'm going to say something that will change everything—but if I don't say it, it'll be even worse."

My mother took a deep breath. "No matter what it is, hon, you can tell me."

I turned to face my mother, and with the strongest voice I could muster, said, "I'm gay, Mom."

I had never intended when I woke up that morning to come out to my mother that day. Looking back, sometimes it's best when we don't plan things out and just let them happen. I had been terrified to tell her, but I didn't want to come across as if I were apologizing for who I am, either. I held my gaze on her after I spoke, gauging her reaction.

"Oh, Caleb. Thank you so much for telling me," she said in the warmest, most comforting, and loving voice I had ever heard her use.

It was the last reaction in the world I would have predicted, and I couldn't pretend to hide my relief—on a multitude of levels. My eyes glazed over. Mom pulled me to her and held me. "I am so proud of you, my beautiful baby boy," she whispered into my ear. She had a tear in her eye. "I didn't think I could possibly love you any more than I already did, but there it is. I love you so very much, Caleb. More than you can ever possibly know."

We stayed in the parking lot of the library for quite a while and talked. I asked her if she was shocked or if she had maybe already known I was gay. She told me she never suspected it, but that she wished she had, so that maybe she could have done something earlier to help me feel comfortable with who I am and lessen my pain.

I smiled, a genuine smile.

"There it is," Mom said. "There's that sunshine smile. You feel better?"

I nodded. "Yeah."

"So Blake, Shane, and Ryley already know?"

"Yes."

"And they've all been great?"

"Yup. They've been fantastic."

"Mind if I ask, who did you come out to first?"

"Shane."

"Really? That must have been hard for you."

"It was weird, but wonderful."

"What did he say?"

"Umm, well, nothing really."

"Nothing?"

I blushed a deep crimson. "Umm, no. He was kinda too busy kissing me to respond."

Mom blinked at me, and I worried, just for a moment, that I had told her too much too soon.

"Oh, Caleb, I'm so happy for you."

"You are?"

She nodded.

"I was so scared you were going to hate me, throw me out, or something. Or that you'd forbid me to see Shane ever again."

Mom looked very hurt when I said that. Her voice trembled. "I'm so sorry you could ever even think that. I love you. Nothing in this world could ever stop me from loving you. That you could even think ..." her voice broke off, and she held a hand to her mouth to control her emotions.

"I'm sorry, Mom. I didn't mean to hurt you."

"No, this isn't about me. It's about you, honey. I just feel so bad that you ever felt you had to hide and that you've been so scared for so long. You can't know what that does to me inside. But I can just imagine all that you've had to endure and all those thoughts that must have gone through your head. I'm so glad your brother and your friends have been there for you. It makes me very proud of them all, too.

"And as for Shane," Mom took one of my hands in both of hers, "I don't know when I've met a sweeter boy. I love it when he's at the house because you're so much happier. I don't know how I didn't see it before. It's so obvious to me now. You really love him, don't you?"

I nodded.

Mom couldn't keep her tears from coming this time. "Then he's a very lucky young man." Her voice was faint in timbre but strong with conviction.

She hugged me again, and when she let go, she turned on the engine. She wiped her eyes in that way I've only ever seen adult women do, using their index fingers, one for each eye, and wiping away tears like windshield wipers.

"Let's go get something to eat," she suggested happily.

I wasn't at all hungry. In fact, my stomach was sore from stress, but I couldn't do anything other than smile at my mother and say, "Sure. Sounds good."

We sat down at a booth at the Black Cherry Barn and sipped at our waters as we perused the menu. I only felt like something very light, so I had the soup of the day, chicken noodle. Mom ordered the club sandwich and fries. When the waitress left with our orders, Mom leaned forward and asked, "You sure you're okay?"

"Yeah, I feel pretty good, actually. My stomach's just kinda a mess right now."

Mom's thoughtful expression from across the table made my eyes well up, so I turned away and concentrated on the cars in the parking lot, taking mental inventory of the makes and models.

"I'm sure there's a lot on your mind."

I nodded. "What's Dad going to say?"

"I honestly don't know. Your father doesn't say much, as you know, but I also hope you know how much he loves you. He'd never want you to think for a second that he doesn't."

"How am I going to tell him?" I asked, returning my gaze to her.

"Do you want me to?"

I shook my head. "No. No, thanks. It's something I really need to do myself. I'm just not sure how."

"Did you have any plans about how you were going to tell me?"

I chuckled. "No. I never thought I was going to today, that's for sure."

"So, what happened?"

"That book I was looking at. There was a picture of this guy—he couldn't have been that much older than me—in the concentration camps. He didn't look like he had much time left. I noticed on his chest was a triangle, and I thought to myself, here's this guy who's dying because he had the courage to be himself, and if I keep hiding, is his death in vain?" I pinched my eyes shut and peered out the window again, trying not to lose it right there in the restaurant.

The waitress came back with our food, and I could hear my mother's tiny voice saying thank you. Her voice was only tiny when she was trying not to cry. When I turned back to her, she smiled at me again.

"I'm going to make it through dinner without crying, I promise," she said, trying to make light of the situation as she spread her napkin on her lap.

She squirted a glob of ketchup on the side of her plate and dipped a fry in. I took up a spoonful of soup and blew on it before tasting. The hot broth warmed my aching belly, and as dinner progressed, I felt better.

"You know, I've been thinking about how you can tell your father."

"And?" I asked as I crumbled my two-pack of salted Premium Plus crackers into my soup.

"And I think you just need to find some time to talk to him, one-on-one."

"Well, I know that much, Mom."

"Don't be rude, Caleb. I haven't finished."

"Sorry."

"Anyway, as I was about to say, I think you should get him to go for a walk with you through the woods. He's never been in them, and you boys are there all the time." Mom stopped suddenly and looked over at me. "We've never even talked to you about sex."

"Good Lord, Mom, please don't start now."

"Well, I just got to thinking, I mean, you and Shane ..."

"Whoa, Mom. Stop. No, we aren't, so please don't ask. God. Besides, Blake and I talk. He's been answering all sorts of questions for me for years, okay? So, really, please, let's not have this conversation."

"You mean Blake has ... no, don't answer that."

"I wasn't planning on it. All I meant was that I can talk to him, about anything."

"I'm glad." Mom went on timidly, "But you know, your father and I are always here if you have any questions ..."

"Mom, really, thanks, but I'm much more comfortable talking to Blake. No offense. Now, can we change the subject ... please?"

"Ah, yes. Right. What were we talking about? Oh yes, your father. All I was going to suggest was that if you go for a walk together, it will give you a chance to talk. I know his knee is bad, but one walk won't kill him."

"I dunno. Maybe. I've just read so many horror stories … like I was saying before. I'm really nervous about telling him. I don't want to disappoint him."

"Look at me, Caleb, and listen to me carefully. If your father doesn't accept and embrace you for who you really are, I'll leave him."

"What?"

"I'm not kidding. I wouldn't stay married to someone whose love for his own child could change because of the kid's sexual orientation. But I'm truly not worried about that happening. Your father is a good man, and he won't let either of us down. There's a lot about him you don't know."

"Oh?"

Mom nodded. "We talk a lot. More than you'd ever think. He worries about you boys all the time. He just doesn't know how to tell you he cares. He's always found it hard to show emotion—with anyone. It was a long time into our relationship before he really even let me in. I can't tell you how proud of you he is. When you got that old Bronco working, he talked to me long into the night about the possibilities of your future. And when Blake went to volleyball camp, he tried to arrange time off work so we could all go over and surprise Blake at one of his games.

"But it's more than that. He tells me over and over how proud he is to have such responsible, caring, and well-mannered sons. He only wants the best for each of you. He's so glad we moved here because he tells me the sound of you and your brother laughing with friends makes him feel alive inside. When Shane first started coming around, your dad and I were sitting up in bed one night, and he said to me, 'If for no other reason, I'm glad we moved here cuz Caleb finally has a friend.'"

"He said that?"

"He said that."

"Wow." I placed my spoon in my nearly empty bowl of soup and wiped my mouth with a paper napkin from the dispenser on the table.

"So you see, you may not hear it and may not know it, but your dad is always thinking about you. I know he'll be good when you tell him about yourself. I'm sure of it."

"Thanks. I feel better hearing you say that."

Mom smiled at me, and we finished our meals.

When we got home and had parked the car, Mom said to me, "I'm really very proud of you, Caleb."

"Thank you." I hesitated before asking, "I'm not sure when I'm going to talk to Dad, so don't say anything, okay?"

"I would never do that."

"Thanks for everything today, Mom."

"You never need to thank me for being your mother."

I opened my door a crack, just enough for the dome light to come on. I turned back to my mom and said, "You know, I think I should thank you more often."

Mom's eyes frosted over, and I got out of the car. I could see her trying to compose herself, waving her hands at her face, before she followed me inside the house.

I could hear the television on in the den, where my father was watching *Sports Centre,* as I jogged up the stairs and went to Blake's room. I sat down on his bed where he was lying, listening to his stereo. I slipped off his headphones, and not being able to hide my smile, told him what had happened. He gave me a huge hug before I went down to my room and called Shane.

In bed that night, I replayed the events of the day over and over in my head. So much good stuff had happened to me that day, it was incredible. I knew I still had a long way to go, but I wasn't worrying about it that night. I just wanted to enjoy the feeling that I was getting closer and closer to reaching my goal. My mom was better than I ever could have imagined, Blake was supportive and loyal as always, and Shane was, well, Shane was perfect.

In many ways, I looked forward to the time that my father and my other friends all knew that Shane and I were gay. I looked forward to not having to avoid questions of who I found attractive or what I wanted out of life. One day I was going to be completely free to be myself, and

I knew that day was going to come, when at one point it had seemed only like wishful thinking. I couldn't keep from smiling as I lay on my bed, staring at the ceiling with my arms folded behind my head.

A sudden crash made me jump. The noise had come from outside in the direction of the barn. I hurried over to the window and peered out. The lights were on in the barn, and the door was open. The noise I had heard must have been the door hitting the side of the barn as the wind caught it and blew it back. I checked my watch and saw that it was well after two in the morning.

I headed down to Blake's room to check that he was in it. He was, fast asleep, his sheets pulled up tight against him. The moonlight spilled over him from the window near his bed. I stood and looked at him for a bit. I didn't know when I'd last seen my brother sleeping—he looked so innocent and almost fragile. I couldn't bear to wake him.

I went down the hall and toward my parents' room. I could clearly hear my father snoring, and I doubted my mother would be up and around at that hour. A part of me thought it possible that perhaps there were burglars in the barn, but the notion only lasted for a second. I knew it had to be Toby out there and that it was going to be one of those occasions when I was to be all by myself when he communicated with me. I can't say that I was overly fond of these occurrences, but I did my best to convince myself I wasn't scared. I took a deep breath and went down the steps.

Halfway down, I felt a bitter breeze rush up the steps to greet me. I rubbed my bare arms to keep warm and wished I had thought to put a shirt on before heading downstairs.

As I turned into the kitchen, I stopped, almost expecting to see something. All I saw was that Dad had forgotten to put the jug of water back in the fridge. I picked it up from the island and returned it to its shelf in the refrigerator. As I closed the door, I heard the barn door bang again. I looked out the kitchen window. The lights were off inside the barn, and the door was closed. I shook my head, wondering if I had been asleep and dreamt it all. I had had a rather stressful day, despite it being a good one, and I was overtired. Perhaps my mind was just hazy from all the things running through it.

I watched the barn for another minute or so and then turned to head back up the stairs. As I turned, I froze in my steps. The kitchen didn't look the same. There was no island, and the table was gone, replaced by some wooden hutch filled with china and glasses. Everything was different, and I knew I had gone back to seeing Toby's world again. I waited, fearing what I was going to see or hear next. Glancing over the walls, I spotted a calendar, hung in almost precisely the same spot Mom had her calendar hanging. The date was 1943, just two months prior to the time Toby would disappear.

I heard the familiar squeak on the stairs and then silence again before the soft footfalls of someone coming closer started up. I gripped the counter with my hands that were behind my back. The next thing I saw was Toby walking into the kitchen. He stealthily made his way across the floor in his bare feet. He stopped at the door and checked over his shoulder to be sure he had not disturbed the household.

"Toby?" I whispered.

The boy seemed to look at me, but I can't be sure. He held the doorknob, carefully turning it and holding the other side once it opened the door so it wouldn't catch in the wind and make any sound. I watched as the door closed silently. Immediately I went over and repeated what Toby had just done.

Outside, I saw him go to the barn and, once again, carefully open the door and close it behind him. I followed his lead and repeated his actions. Toby was going up the ladder to the loft. The moonlight shone through the window at the front of the barn and allowed me to see him step over the top and hear him walk across the hayloft. Thin lines of dusty sand trickled between the floorboards above and landed on the cement floor below as Toby moved. I made my way to the ladder and climbed up slowly.

Toby's face appeared over the top, looking down at me on the ladder. I froze again, not sure what to do.

"C'mon, Caleb," he said quietly.

There was a rustling sound somewhere below me in the barn. I kept going, and when I got to the top, I stepped over and stood, face-to-face with Toby.

"I was beginning to worry you weren't going to show," I heard a voice behind me say. I stepped away and saw that Toby's Caleb was emerging from the ladder.

"You been waiting long?"

"About an hour, I guess."

"Sorry. My dad was up late, and I couldn't risk leaving earlier."

Wendell stepped closer to Toby and stroked a hand through the boy's hair. "It's okay. I woulda waited all night."

I stepped back to watch the two boys. Hay was stacked all around me, so I sat on one of the bales, half thinking I would fall right through it, as I knew it wasn't really there. But then, if it wasn't there, was I really just standing in the hayloft of my barn at nearly three o'clock in the morning in the dark in November in my boxers?

"Why was your dad up so late?" Wendell asked.

"Cuz I made the mistake of mentioning that I wanted to go away to college next year. He was expecting me to stay home and help with the farm."

"Was he angry?"

"At first, but then he said that it was okay, as long as I paid my own way."

"So we're really going to be able to do it then?" Wendell smiled and sounded happy.

"Yeah, we really are. I told you we would."

Wendell embraced Toby, and they kissed passionately. Wendell's hands slid under Toby's shirt, and he caressed the smooth flesh hidden beneath the cotton. I felt odd watching them, both voyeuristically aroused and embarrassed. This was an intimate moment, and I was an intruder. I decided the decent thing to do would be to go back down the ladder and let them be together. I waited a minute before my legs reacted to my brain's idea. Toby and Wendell eased their way down onto some hay and kissed tenderly, deeply, and erotically. Their clothes ended up in a pile on the old floorboards, and I made my exit. I must admit, it was a hard decision to leave because they were both really cute and it was intensely hot seeing two guys together, but I thought how I'd feel if someone were watching me with Shane and I had to do the honourable thing.

At the bottom of the ladder, I felt a bitter cold go over me again, and my nipples became hard, my skin breaking out in goose bumps. I could see my breath as I held myself tightly, rubbing my arms. My feet were going numb, and my teeth began to chatter. I went over to the nail on the wall and took down my old jean jacket, wrapping myself up in it and holding it closed over me. I realized that if it was there, then I was back in my own time again. I shivered, and though I knew I should go back in the house to get warm, I stayed in the barn.

I kept glancing up at the loft and thinking about the boys who had been up there. Now I was starting to understand the significance of the things we found up there and the sighs and crying we heard. The loft was a very special place for them. It's where they first made love. My mind was drifting when I heard,

"Caleb?"

Somewhat startled, I turned my attention to the door and saw my father standing there.

"What in the world are you doing out here?" he asked as he came toward me.

"I thought I heard someone out here, so I ran out to check."

"I heard the barn door bang—was that you, or was that the reason you came out here?"

"It wasn't me. I've been standing here really quiet to see if I could hear anything."

"It mighta just been the wind. Let's go inside. It's freezing out here."

"Dad ... I need to tell you something," I said, my teeth chattering still.

My father, who had wisely worn a coat, put each hand in the opposite armpit and replied, "What is it, Caleb? Are you all right?" He sounded worried.

The air inside the barn was still, and the lack of movement made the cold even more intense.

"Dad ... I'm gay."

My father studied my face a moment and shook his head. He put his hands on his hips and stepped toward me. I braced myself to be struck, but I kept my eyes open. No matter what happened, I wanted to see it coming.

My father put his right hand on my left shoulder and pulled me to him. He gave me the first hug I could remember from him since I was about eight years old. His strong hand patted my head, and I felt the hot sting of tears in my eyes.

Never good with his emotions, my father quipped, "It's hardly a reason to stand out here and freeze ourselves to death. Let's go inside."

"Are you mad?" I asked as he let me go.

He stood facing me as he answered, "Of course not."

"Disappointed?"

"Disappointed?" Dad sounded surprised I would ask him that.

"Yeah, you know. Having a gay son probably doesn't make you feel very manly. People might make fun of you if they know. I won't give you grandkids. All that stuff."

"All that stuff. Jesus." Dad shook his head again. "First off, there are lottsa ways you could give me grandkids, so throw that out. Second, if anyone ever said anything bad about you, regardless of what it was about, they'd wish they'd never been born. And as for feeling manly … I don't know what could make a man feel prouder than having a son like you. You're a great kid, Caleb. There is nothing on this earth I wouldn't do to try to help you live the happiest, fullest life you can. So as for being disappointed, the only way I would be is if you weren't true to yourself, cuz I hope I've done a better job raising you than to ever allow that."

I was at a loss for words. I swallowed hard, determined not to cry. I nodded. "Thanks, Dad."

"I love you, Caleb. Nothing can ever change that. Okay?"

I nodded my head. "Okay."

"C'mon, let's go inside."

Dad patted me on the back, and we headed for the door.

As I got back in bed, the clock was displaying a time just shy of four in the morning. I knew I was going to be a zombie at school, but I didn't care. I could sleep all weekend if I needed to. The important thing was that I had told both my parents that I'm gay and they still loved me and were going to stand by me. I didn't have to worry about being alone, ever. At that point, even if I had lost all of my friends (except Ryley and Shane, of course), I knew I had the people who mattered most in my corner. I didn't feel so scared anymore.

As I was lying there in the predawn hours, my adrenaline slowly subsided and gave way to sleepiness. As I began to succumb to the sandman, I felt this enormous sense of gratitude, and all I could think to say was something that sounded like a prayer. "Thank you, Toby. Thank you."

Chapter Eighteen

Never have three hours' sleep made me feel so good. When my clock radio came on at seven-fifteen to wake me (I was able to tune in to some New Brunswick stations, thankfully, and could listen to music other than country or the CBC), I opened my eyes to the sounds of The Tragically Hip singing "Music at Work." I love that song. I hopped out of bed and found myself singing along—or whistling. (It's a fast song, and it's hard to keep up with Gord sometimes.) I got down to the bathroom ahead of Blake and jumped in the shower. I clicked on the radio we always left on the vanity and continued to sing along as the hot water splashed over me. When I stepped out and began to dry my hair, I found Blake standing at the sink, shaving.

"Well, you sure look happy today. Have a hot dream?" Blake smirked. "You and the senior boys' hockey team in the locker room or something along those lines?"

I laughed. "No, but that doesn't sound bad. As long as Craig Meisner isn't there ... ugh," I shuddered.

"Ha. Yeah. He is fugly, huh? So what gives, baby brother?"

I tied the towel around my waist and stood next to him. "Nothing much. Heard something in the barn last night, went back in time, saw Toby and Wendell lose their virginity, came out to Dad ... the usual."

Blake dropped his razor in the sink. It hit the porcelain, making a loud *clank* before hitting the water with a *sploop*. "Okay. Back up and start from the beginning."

I told Blake everything. I had to admit I didn't actually see the boys lose their virginity, but I knew that was what was going to happen.

"I kinda wished I did stay after I saw Toby's butt. It was really cute, and he had those little thumbprint dimples at the top of each cheek …" I grinned.

Blake laughed and ruffled my hair. He pulled the plug from the sink and let the water drain. I began to refill the basin as he got in the shower.

I arrived at the top of the stairs to smell the delightful aroma of freshly brewed coffee and pancakes wafting up from downstairs. When I entered the kitchen, I was pleased to find a big mug of coffee and apple cinnamon pancakes waiting for me.

"Oh man, these are sooooo good," I let my mother know.

"I wanted to make something special today," she said, "and I wanted to ask you something, Caleb."

"Sure. What's up?"

"I was wondering if you'd mind if I brought some books home from the library today that you might find helpful. That any of us might find helpful, actually."

"That'd be great. Thanks," I said, offering her a warm smile.

"Good. I wanted to check with you first because I don't want to make you uncomfortable or anything. You'd let me know if I ever make you feel uncomfortable, right?"

"Yeah. No worries, Mom."

"There's nothing to be uncomfortable about," my father said. "Caleb is gay, and we're all going to support him 100 percent." He glanced at his watch and exclaimed, "Oh crap, I have a meeting this morning. I hafta go." Dad hurriedly got up from the table and kissed my mother on the forehead.

"I'm so sorry, dear. I completely forgot," Mom apologized.

"That makes two of us," he replied as he grabbed his black zippered binder from the island. "Besides, there are more important things in life than work." He looked at the three of us at the table, darting his eyes between Blake and me. Mom held his hand on her shoulder as he began to walk away. "See you tonight," he said, giving her a kiss before heading out.

"Wow. That was weird. Nice, but weird," Blake noted.

"Your father and I were up talking for a long time. Been up since four, actually."

"So everything's really okay?" I asked.

Mom smiled at me, "Yeah, hon. Everything's just great." She patted my hand, and we all went back to finishing our breakfast.

Shane came home with us that day after school on the bus. Ryley had a date with Adria and was going with his family to visit his grandmother on Sunday, so he wasn't going to be able to come over at all that weekend. I had talked to Ryley for a few minutes at lunch before the rest of the gang arrived in the cafeteria. He was happy for me that I had come out to my parents and that things were going so well. I didn't get a chance to tell him about how and where I had come out to my father (or my mother, for that matter), merely that I did. Hunter plunked himself down at the table before I could go on, so I changed the subject to how I helped Tim get his car running the day before. Ryley knew I'd fill him in later.

Upon arriving home, we dumped our book bags at the bottom of the steps and went into the kitchen for a snack. Blake immediately went about getting things ready for dinner as we sat around and munched on pretzels and drank cans of Sprite.

"He makes it look so easy," Shane commented, watching Blake stuff the chicken breasts with garlic and other seasonings before mixing up a tomato-based sauce that he poured over all the pieces in the large amethyst-coloured Pyrex pan.

"It's pretty simple, actually," Blake told him.

"And when Blake makes supper, you know it's edible," I said. "When Mom makes it … well, let's just say she's not the gourmet type."

"No, but she does make a great breakfast," Blake mentioned.

"Very true."

Blake covered the dish with aluminum foil and slid it in the oven. "Okay, that's that. I'm just gonna keep it simple and do jasmine rice and peas with it. Okay with you guys?"

"Sounds good to me," Shane said.

"Anything we can do to help?"

"Sure. You guys could set the table, but there's no rush. Supper won't be ready for a coupla hours cuz I'm cooking the chicken at a low temp."

"Consider it done."

Blake sat down at the table with us. I slid the bowl of pretzels over to him, and he grabbed one of the salty knots and took a bite. He washed it down with some of his clear soda and looked at us thoughtfully. "Is it gonna be weird for you guys now that you don't have to hide in front of Mom and Dad anymore?"

"I guess a little. But it'll be nice," Shane said. "It's gonna be odd at first. I mean, it's not like we're gonna be making out in front of them or anything, but it'll be nice if we're watching a movie or something that we won't hafta jump to opposite ends of the sofa when your parents come in the room, and if we wanna hold hands, we won't hafta think twice about it. It's sorta like sanctuary from how we hafta be at school and almost everywhere else."

"Oh shit," I blurted out. "You think Shane will still be allowed to sleep in my room?"

"Crap. I never thought of that either," Shane said. "Whattaya think, Blake?"

"Way I look at it, as long as you don't give Mom and Dad a reason not to trust you, they'll trust you. Worst-case scenario, Shane probably has to sleep down in my room when Ryley isn't around too."

"Yeah. You're probably right," I agreed.

"And on that note, are we hitting the woods this weekend sans Ryley?" Blake asked.

"I don't think so. It wouldn't seem fair," I answered.

"But after what happened in the barn last night, I thought maybe there'd be more for us to see," Blake suggested.

"What happened in the barn?" Shane asked.

"You haven't told him yet?"

"I haven't had a chance to. There wasn't an opportunity at school."

"So, what happened?" Shane asked again.

I told him all about the kitchen changing and the barn and the calendar and everything I saw and felt and heard.

"Whoa. That's awesome. Hot, and awesome," Shane said. "Wish I coulda seen it. I know what Toby was doing, though."

"Whattaya mean?" Blake was asking the question that time.

"Don'tcha see? He set it up so Caleb would have the perfect chance to talk to your dad. I mean, think about it, did you hear the barn door banging?"

"No."

"And your room is closer to it than your parents', right?"

"Yeah."

"So why was it that your dad woke up and went outside and not you?" Blake appeared bewildered at Shane's query. "You see? Toby set it up. He needed you to come out to your father, Caleb."

"But he didn't see me come out to my mother."

"No, that's true."

"And by the time that my dad got to the barn, I was back in real time again."

"That doesn't matter. You know that Toby's been around in our time too." Blake leaned forward in his chair, folding his hands on the table in front of him. "Think back, Caleb. Did anything happen after you told Dad you're gay? Did you hear anything or see anything else?"

I shook my head. "Nope. Nothing."

"Are you sure?" Shane asked, double-checking.

I thought about it and tried to concentrate on the barn as I followed my father out. "It was so cold. I was shaking like crazy, and my teeth were chattering. I was only wearing my boxers and that old jean jacket I keep in the barn." I tried to relive the morning and listened carefully to the barn as I walked behind my dad. I could visualize myself going by the ladder to the hayloft and toward the door. Then I remembered how I glanced up for a split second as I hung my coat up. "Oh."

"What? What do you remember?" Blake needed to know.

"As I walked by the hayloft ladder, I looked up for a fraction of a second. I didn't take it in at the time, but I remember seeing this little white cloud disappearing in the air above the ladder. Like when someone exhales in a cold place."

"See, Caleb. Toby was there. He was watching," Shane said with a sweet smile. "For some reason, he needed to see you tell your father."

"I really think we should go back to the woods this weekend," Blake urged.

I shook my head. "No. Sorry. I'd like to take the weekend off. It's been a pretty stressful twenty-four hours for me, and I'd like to just hang out with you guys and veg for a while."

"Fair enough. I'd say you've earned it. And, if we're definitely not going into the woods, then I guess I'll call Clark and see what's going on with the team. Heard a bunch of the guys were going to some party in Wolfville tomorrow night, and as you know, Wolfville is a university town, which means university girls." Blake raised his eyebrows three times to show his enthusiasm.

"Wait, you mean to say you were going to take a chance on missing a party with college chicks just to go in the forest with us again?" I asked my brother, finding it difficult to believe.

He shrugged. "Well, yeah. I mean, there'll be lottsa parties in my life, but how often do you ever get to help out a ghost?"

Shane chuckled. "He's got a point."

"You two should do something fun this weekend," Blake suggested.

"Like what?" I asked.

"Hell, I dunno. Why not go bowling? They've got glow-bowling in New Minas. It's kinda cool."

I scrunched up my nose at the idea until Shane said, "Hey, that sounds like fun."

"Really?"

"Yeah. I used to love to go bowling with my dad. There was a bowling alley here until about four years ago, and we'd go all the time. Never gone glow-bowling, though. Sounds cool."

"Right on then. Now you've got plans," Blake told us.

"How we gonna get there?" I wondered aloud.

"I'd normally offer, fellas, but I'm not gonna be around." Blake saw the expressions on our faces. "I know, it sucks being fifteen. You don't want your parents to drive you anywhere, and none of your friends have their licences yet."

"Adria's sister has her licence. Maybe we could get Ryley and Adria to go with us and her sister could drive us up," Shane said.

"I'll leave the details to you guys, but if worse comes to worst, you can always swallow your pride and get Mom to drive you up. It's not like she'd be coming in and bowling with you or anything anyway."

"True," I said. "But let's see what Ryley and Adria are doing before we make any plans."

After dinner that evening, Shane and I were in the den watching a movie together. We'd had a hard time choosing but had settled on *Escape from New York*. I'm a big John Carpenter fan, and Shane had never seen it. We were just at the part when the underground dwellers started emerging from the manholes and chasing Snake to the Chock full o' Nuts when my mother called me over to the living room. I went across the hall and sat down with her on the chesterfield.

"What's up?"

Mom was sitting against the corner of the couch sipping a cup of coffee with what smelled like Bailey's Irish Cream in it.

"I just want to know how sleeping arrangements work when Shane is over."

"Oh," I blushed even though I was totally innocent, or at least close to being innocent. "Well, ahh, I sleep in my bed, and Shane sleeps next to me in his sleeping bag."

"Every time?"

"Yes, Mom. I told you, we aren't doing anything. I mean, okay, sure, sometimes we hold each other, but that's it. He puts his arms around me, and we sleep like that. Honest. You're not going to make him sleep in Blake's room or something, are you?"

"No, hon. I believe you, and as long as that is all there is to it, then I think it's fine that Shane keeps sleeping in your room. I just know that sometimes it can be hard to resist doing more."

"God, it's really weird to be talking to you about this."

"I'm not completely naïve, Caleb, and I don't expect you to be a monk or something. I just want you to make sure that you take things slow."

"Don't worry. I plan on it. Besides, Shane is my best friend as well as my boyfriend. Neither of us want to rush into anything. We're just glad to have each other."

"You make a nice couple."

I smiled at my mother. "Thanks."

"He's a cutie, Caleb. You go on back to him."

"So everything's cool?"

"Yes. Just wanted to talk it over with you. Figured it might be something that you were wondering about."

"Thanks. It was." I got up and started for the door. I turned and asked, "Mom, if I were straight and I had a girlfriend, would you let her stay in my room?"

Mom had to think for a minute. "I hope I wouldn't treat the situation any differently. It's hard to say. I doubt many girls would have parents that would allow their daughter to stay over, though. Kinda a double standard, I suppose."

"One of the few that favours me." I chuckled.

"Don't knock it, but don't abuse it."

"No worries, Mom."

"Go and enjoy your movie."

"Thanks."

I went back to the den and cuddled up with Shane. I put my arm behind him, and he rested his head on my shoulder.

When I called Adria and Ryley, they actually sounded like they really wanted to go glow-bowling with us. We met at Stape's around noon, but unfortunately, Adria's sister, Teri, wasn't able to take us so I had to ask my mother. She said she had some shopping she wanted to do anyway and that it would give her the opportunity to drop in to visit her friend, Mary, giving us the afternoon to ourselves. She'd meet us back at the bowling alley at four o'clock.

When she dropped us off, we headed inside and went about getting our shoes, score sheet, and a lane. It was candlepin bowling, which I had only ever done twice before (most of the times in the city, we went to a five-pin alley). The place was actually pretty funky in that it was outdated enough to look almost retro. Everything white, of course, seemed to glow with the black lights overhead. Top-forty music pumped out from the speakers, sounding like the latest compilation albums of *Much Music Dance Hits*. It combined with the crashing pins and rolling balls to make for a loud, but fun, environment. There was a decent crowd there, mostly kids our age and some elementary-aged children with their parents. Everyone seemed to be having a good time.

Adria was sitting next to me on the old bench that rounded the back of our lane. The bench had a pale blue panel and then a white one, over and over. The white panels really stood out against the lights. Ryley was up taking his shot, and Shane was keeping score at the small desk. Ryley's jeans fit him nicely, and I couldn't help but notice.

"Mmm, God, he has such a cute little ass," Adria said and then giggled. She held my arm playfully. "I sound like such a perv, I know, but I bet you guys are checking me out when I'm up there too."

"Well, I can guarantee Ryley is."

"Not you, though, huh? Mister innocent," she teased.

"Nope. Sorry," I laughed.

She thought that was funny. "Sure, sure. You boys are all alike."

Ryley sat back down on the bench as Shane went up to take his turn.

"What you guys talking about?" Ryley asked us as he reached for Adria's hand to hold.

"Oh, I was just saying how cute your butt looks when you take a shot," she said and reached a hand under Ryley's seat to pinch him. He laughed. "But Caleb won't admit that he checks me out when I'm up there."

Ryley said, "His loss," and chuckled.

I wasn't really paying attention to them. Shane was bowling, and I was very interested in watching his ... er ... form.

"Caleb?" Adria pulled my arm again.

"Hmm?" I turned back to see her.

"You zone out on me there?"

"Huh? Sorry. Was just checking out Shane's ass as he took his turn." I smirked and turned back to Shane.

Adria laughed. "Okay, very funny. I was being serious, though, Caleb."

"So was he," Ryley said.

Shane sat back down at the desk and marked in his score.

"Nice job, Shane. What's that, your fourth spare?"

"Nah, only my third."

"Oh, my God, Caleb. Are you gay?" Adria asked me, her voice sounding both shocked and excited.

"Yeah."

"That is so cool. I've got a cousin who's gay. His name's Mark. He's like twenty-five or something, and he's gorgeous. Lives in Quebec. Only get to see him at holidays and stuff." Adria was getting verbal diarrhea. "So, do your parents know?"

"Yes."

"Wow. That's awesome. And they're cool?"

"Yup."

"God. That's great. I'm just so pissed I didn't know before. I mean, maybe I shoulda figured it out cuz you, like, know all the words to most of the Jonas Brothers songs."

Shane roared with laughter. Ryley shook his head, chuckling. I just grinned and went toward the lane to take my turn.

"What are you laughing so hard for?" I teased Shane as I walked by him.

"I didn't realize that liking the Jonas Brothers was a prerequisite for being gay. Guess I better borrow some CDs from you, Caleb."

"Yeah, man. Better start studying up in case there's a quiz," Ryley suggested. He was now laughing so hard he had tears in his eyes. He and Shane reached out and gave each other a high five.

"Oh my God, oh my God, oh my God … you mean?" Adria waved a finger back and forth between Shane and me.

"Yup," Shane answered.

"And you guys are …?"

"Boyfriends," Shane finished for her.

Adria made this high-pitched shrieking sound I can't even pretend to know how to describe. The best I can do is "Eeeeeeeeee," and she ran up and hugged Shane and then me. "This is so cool," she pronounced, practically drooling with excitement.

"Promise us you won't tell anyone else, okay?" I asked.

"Of course. I would never do that to anyone. I'm just so happy you told me." She clapped her hands together and stated, "This is a double date … oh my God. I love it."

At four o'clock, we were outside the bowling alley waiting for my mother. We made tentative plans to go skiing sometime in the winter, and Shane promised to show me how to snowboard. We all agreed for certain that we'd hit the rink on public-skating days. We were still talking about our various skating abilities as Mom pulled up. We immediately hopped in the car to get out of the cold.

"Sorry, guys. I got talking with my friend, Mary, and lost track of time." She looked at us, all apple-cheeked and shivering. "Oh, you're all so cold. Let's say I treat us all to a nice hot cider at Tim Hortons."

My mother had instant and unanimous approval for her suggestion. We went into the drive-through at the local Timmy's and got back on the highway, sipping our delicious hot beverages. Adria slouched against Ryley in the backseat. I wished I could have been back there with Shane. It was one of the rare times when I actually wished we had a minivan.

We dropped Ryley and Adria off at her place and then pulled into the motel to let Shane out.

"Thanks for the ride, Karen. And for everything else, too," Shane said as he unbuckled his seat belt. (My mother had, in unusual fashion, asked Blake's and my friends to call her by her first name.)

"You're most welcome, Shane."

I whispered to my mother, "Be right back."

I got out of the car and walked with Shane to the back door of his house. We kissed and held each other for a minute before saying good-bye. I watched him go inside and then headed back to the car. When I had clipped in my belt, Mom pulled to the end of the driveway.

"Did you have fun today?" she asked.

"Yeah. We had a blast. How about you?"

"Yes, actually, I had a very nice afternoon. I even bought myself a top."

"Good stuff. How's everything with Mary?"

"Oh, you know how she is …"

Mom went on to talk about Mary, her friend from college who always seemed to be having one crisis or another. Apparently this time there had been an ordeal with the oil company over her home-heating bill. How riveting.

When I went up to my room that night, I tried to work on some homework for a while, but I couldn't concentrate. The algebra problems that I was to complete for Monday seemed so utterly unimportant in comparison to everything else going on in my life. Besides, I hated math and knew that I was never going to need to find the square root of *y* after I was done with school anyway. I halfheartedly finished the assignment, knowing I had many mistakes, but honestly not caring.

I tossed my math scribbler onto the floor by my desk and took off my glasses before flopping onto my bed. I stretched my arms up over my head and stared at the ceiling. There was a strong wind outside, and it whistled around my window. I thought of Blake and hoped he was having a good time. I was worried about him, though. I knew I wouldn't be able to sleep until he was home safely. I put on my headset and listened to the radio for some time before taking it off again and grabbing a novel from the headboard. I put on my glasses again, only to remove them and put the book back down a few minutes later. I couldn't seem to keep my attention on anything for very long. I was half tempted to go for a walk, but it was cold and I knew I'd feel drawn toward the forest, which I just didn't need to deal with that night. I got undressed and slid under the covers of my bed. It was already warm from where I had been lying on top for so long. I turned out my light and lay there, listening to the wind. I could hear the fallen leaves scuttle about outside and scratch against the side of the house.

I thought of Toby and Wendell in the hayloft, the sound of the leaves reminding me of the oak tree in the woods. They were so soft and gentle with each other. They made me think of being with Shane. I found myself visualizing Shane up there in the loft with me. I pictured Shane's hands over my bare skin, imagining what he would look like completely naked and how his skin would feel against mine. I let my thoughts go further and got very turned on, needing to address the situation. I was in my fantasy world when I heard a knock at the door. I quickly snapped back to reality and sat up, my erotic visions dashed from my mind.

"Yeah?"

"Hey, bud. Did I wake you?" Blake asked as he opened the door and stepped into my room.

I shook my head. "No. I was waiting for you to get home. Have fun?"

"Meh. It was okay. Danced with a lot of hot girls. What about you? Have fun bowling?"

"Yeah. We had a good time. Thanks for the idea."

"No prob. I'm gonna hit the hay. We'll talk in the morning, okay? Just wanted to check."

"Okay. Gonna watch the Cowboys game with me tomorrow?

"You bet."

"Awesome. Have a good sleep."

"You too."

My fantasy world gone and my eyelids heavy, I took a deep breath and drifted off.

Chapter Nineteen

On Monday, starting the week off in grand order, I stabbed myself with my poppy as I attached it to my jacket. I was holding it firmly, trying to get it on without assistance (and while wearing the jacket—brilliant), and ended up having the pin bend and dig down deep into my chest. I bit my lip to keep the obscenities from spilling out and pulled the poppy out of my skin. I went into the washroom and put disinfectant on the area and then had to change my shirt, as it had quickly gotten a bloodstain. Blake helped me put a bandage on my chest before I put on a clean shirt.

"Great way to start the week," I grumbled as Blake finished taping on the pad.

"I just can't believe it went in so deep."

"With my luck, it's a wonder I didn't puncture a lung," I deadpanned.

Blake made the square piece of gauze lie flat and snug against my skin. He patted my side twice when he was done and said, "There, all set."

I smiled at him. "Thanks." I looked down at the job he did fixing me up. "You're gonna make a terrific dad someday, you know."

Blake had been sitting on the toilet seat lid as he tended to my wound. He stood up and cocked his head at me, "Ya think?"

I nodded.

He grinned and checked his watch. "Crap. Come on. We're running late."

We hurriedly finished getting ready for school and, having missed the bus, ran for the Bronco.

～

Despite the fact that Remembrance Day fell on a Sunday, we didn't have any school on the following Monday, as government employees had the day off. During the week prior to our long weekend, our history classes focused predominantly on the two world wars, especially the second. I found myself fascinated by the subject. I had never given much thought to history when it dealt with the English and French and the colonization of North America, but the world wars were so recent in history, with a few survivors still around to recount the details.

I've always had respect for the men and women who served during the wars, and like all my family, always wore a poppy from the end of October until the eleventh of November. When I was a little kid, we all went to the Remembrance Day service together, and oftentimes, we'd watch a war film when we got home (*The Longest Day* and *A Bridge Too Far* were two of my father's favourites). The last several years, we gathered around the television and watched the ceremony from Ottawa instead of going out to a local service. It was always very moving.

A bunch of my friends were planning on making the most of the long weekend and hanging out at Hunter's Saturday night to watch movies and get some pizzas. I was reluctant at first, but eventually gave in, as the entire gang would be there and it promised to be fun. Having always been so serious, I thought I was entitled to lighten up and enjoy myself for a change. I'd need to after the Friday night I was about to have.

Having chatted with me on the computer, Ryley and Shane came over Friday after school. We had decided it was time to go back into the woods. As per usual, we waited until my parents had gone to bed before slipping out to the barn and collecting our things from the loft. With our supplies at the ready, we began our trek into the forest, walking in pairs and keeping silent. Our torches lit the way, cutting through the darkness in a triangular spectrum of illumination, blackness enveloping the space behind us.

When my flashlight began to flicker, I thought perhaps something was going to happen, but Shane's light was still strong. My batteries had gotten weak. We stopped in the path, and I unbuckled the backpack on Shane's back and removed a fresh flashlight, placing the dead one inside and rebuckling the canvas bag. I pressed the black button, and the light snapped on. We continued toward the waterfall.

The air was damp and a bitter wind blew, but thankfully, the trees sheltered us from most of the breeze. We could hear the highest branches sway in the wind and make a creaking sound as they were forced to the brink of breaking.

At the spruce tree hidden path, we paused for a moment. I reached out and took Shane's hand in mine as we pushed our way through together. Blake and Ryley were right behind us.

"Don't know if I'm happy to see you guys or not," Shane said to them. "Guess we've gotta keep on a ways before anything's gonna happen tonight."

"If anything is gonna happen at all," Ryley added.

"It's a lot colder down here than it was up on the other path," Blake stated as he zipped up his volleyball team jacket (a red one with white leather sleeves and the letters SRHS for Stapeton Regional High School, along with the school crest on the left breast. The right sleeve had his name on it, and the left had his number, 8. Across the back in an arch was the word *Stampeders* in raised white letters against the red field, with a group of wild stallions charging forward).

"Yeah, almost feels like it could snow," I said.

"It's supposed to," Shane told us. "Weather forecast said we could expect two or three centimetres overnight."

"It should only snow on school nights," Ryley joked.

We made our way along the path, hearing and seeing nothing unusual all the way to the end. Without saying a word, we turned around at the tree ending the path and started back. My flashlight began to flicker again, and I grumbled, "Ah, man. Batteries are going on this one, too."

Shane grabbed my arm and stopped me. Ryley bumped into my back, not having foreseen my sudden stop. "Oomph. Sorry, Caleb."

"No prob. I just need another flashlight." As I began to unbuckle the backpack again, I heard Shane shaking his torch.

"Damn. Mine's going, too," he said.

"Ahh, guys. I don't think the batteries are the problem," Blake mentioned and grabbed the lighter from his pocket.

"You see something?" I asked him, giving up my search for batteries.

"No, I didn't see anything, but I'm getting an awful feeling in my stomach."

"Oh man, I really hope I don't go through that again," Ryley said, his voice sounding nervous.

"Shh," Shane whispered. "You guys hear anything?"

We all fell silent and listened.

"No, nothing," I replied.

"Exactly. The wind's stopped."

Blake held the lighter near the ground. He rubbed his fingers in the pathway. "Snow."

As he stood back up, we all heard a tremendously loud bang. Everyone jumped, and my heart rate skyrocketed. I half expected Ryley to fall to the ground in agony again, but nothing like that happened.

What did happen, however, was something far, far more devastating to hear. There was the sound of crying ahead of us in the path.

"What is that?" Blake asked, his voice timid.

The crying continued, and we heard a slow, crunching sound—like someone was crawling in the snow. Then we heard another set of crunches—footsteps. Then there was another loud bang, and everything fell deathly silent.

"Shit, shit, shit," Ryley cursed quietly.

Each of us felt sick to his stomach. Before anyone had a chance to speak, the wind picked up, and our flashlights came back on. The snow had disappeared, and everything felt as close to normal as it could under the circumstances. Leaves rustled around at our feet. I shone my light down in front of me and said to the group, "Check it out. Every single one of them … oak leaves."

We sombrely made our way back to the clearing, not saying a word.

In fact, we didn't speak again until we reached the end of the path and looked out over the field at the back of the house. A gentle snow had begun to fall, and the air was crisp and white.

"It sure is a beautiful night, huh?" Shane commented.

"Yeah," Blake agreed.

"Guess that forecast was right," I said.

We stood on the forest side of the stream at the threshold to the woods and watched the snow cascade on the amber grasses of the field. As snowflakes landed on the stream, they melted quickly, but everywhere else they held fast and blanketed the greying earth with their purity.

"What did we hear in there?" Ryley asked, his voice shaky.

"Pain," Shane said, staring out at the field in front of him.

It was as good an explanation as any, and all that any of us really wanted to say about it at the time. We had heard pain. That was the only certainty we had.

We made our way across the stream and to the house. The kitchen door was locked, so Blake used his key to open it. We quietly entered the house and made our way up the stairs to my room. Shane and I sat at the end of the bed, Blake at the desk, and Ryley on the floor against the wall. No one said anything for a bit.

"We should really talk about what we think we just experienced," I said.

"Yeah," Blake agreed.

"Do you think we heard Toby being murdered?" Ryley asked. "Cuz that's the only thing I can think of, and I really wish that weren't the case. So, please, if you've got any other ideas, I'd love to hear them." When no one spoke, Ryley sighed. He was rocking himself, cradling his knees. "I don't know how much more I can take." His voice was desperate and frightened.

"I know, man. This is hard for all of us," Shane said.

"No. It's not just that. Some days, it's all so black. I just feel so empty, like I'm walking around inside this shell and I'm wondering why can't anyone hear how loud I'm screaming. You know?" He looked up at us to see if we understood. "And so many days, I just think, *well, what's the point?* And I find myself thinking a lot about ..." he sniffed and a tear fell from his right eye. "My parents don't even notice when

I'm not in the room. I've tested them before. I've walked away from the dinner table and gone out of the house—I stayed out till 4:00 a.m. one time. There wasn't even a call on my cell from them to see where I was. Nothing. I don't exist in that house for any reason other than to give them something to argue about. I am so tired of it all. I get to that dark place inside. I think, maybe if I killed myself, they'd have to have some sort of reaction. Maybe that would matter." Ryley wiped at his eyes. "But I doubt it. They'd probably just argue about whose fault it was that I did it."

"Ryley, please promise us right now that you'll never hurt yourself," Shane urged. "Please."

Ryley held his knees again. "I don't want to hurt myself. I really don't. I just get so lost ..."

"I know, man, I've been there. I almost killed myself in this very room just last year." As Shane spoke, Ryley turned his head to see him, surprised by his admission. "I was in a really bad place, too. My dad was dead, and my mom was depressed. I had no friends at all, and I was in the closet—terrified of the idea that I might always be alone. I'd taken a dare to stay overnight here, so I broke in and huddled up in that corner over there," Shane pointed to the other end of the room. "I sat for the longest time, feeling worse and worse about everything, and then I took out my knife and I realized I was really going to do it."

"What stopped you?"

"Toby. He came into the room, or maybe he'd been here the entire time, and he hugged me. I don't know how else to describe it. I didn't hear him or see anything except for this shadow on the wall. I felt these arms around me and this amazing warmth in my heart. I dropped the knife and cried." Shane tried to keep from getting emotional as he retold his story, but his voice did break a bit toward the end, as I'm sure mine would have too. "That's why I really want to help him. He saved my life, and it wasn't much later I met you and the gang and finally had some friends.

"Life's never easy. It never will be. But it can, and it does, get better. Here I am today with best friends and a boyfriend. I never thought I'd have either. You can't give up, Rye. We need you, and your little brother needs you, too."

Ryley took a deep breath. "I know. I try to look out for him as best

I can." He ran a hand through his hair and let his breath out slowly. "If it weren't for you guys, I don't know where I'd be. I guess I can kinda thank Toby for that, too. I mean, I've gotten to know you guys so much better since all this started. Everyone always seemed to think I must be doing fine cuz I've always been able to make friends and stuff, but so much of it is all an act. When I'm around you guys, I can be myself, but when I'm with the group, it's different. When I get home after being with all of them, I'm exhausted."

"Yeah, I think we can all relate to that to a certain extent," Blake said. "I went to a party last weekend, and it sucked. I pretended to have fun, but I wished I was home and hanging out with you guys the whole time. You guys keep it real, and when I'm with you, I dunno, I feel like you actually want me to be around."

"Cuz you rock, Blake," Shane said.

"Thanks."

"Yeah, man. I wish I had an older brother like you," Ryley told him.

Blake went over and put a hand on his upper arm. "Day or night, no matter when, we're here for ya, bud. Never hesitate to call if you need to talk. I don't care if it's the middle of the night."

"Thanks, Blake," Ryley sighed as he ran a hand through his hair.

"Feel better?" I asked.

Ryley put his hands behind his head and smiled. "You have no idea."

It was weird to be at Hunter's the next night and act like nothing at all was going on. Every time I closed my eyes or there was a moment's silence in the room, I could hear that loud bang and the mournful crying. On one of my trips to the kitchen for a refill of pop, I found myself staring into the refrigerator. I don't know how long I stood there before I felt a hand on my shoulder and I jumped.

"Whoa, Caleb. It's just me," Ryley said. "You okay?"

"Ahh, yeah. Just sorta zoned out there for a sec, I guess." I fumbled with the two-litre bottle of Big 8 cream soda and poured myself a glass before returning it to the door of the fridge and shutting it.

"Can't get it out of your head either, can you?" he asked.

I placed my hands on the counter and stretched, shaking my head as I did so. "No. I just keep hearing that crying."

"Me too."

"God." I grabbed my pop and took a drink, feeling the sugary rush flow through me. I looked over at Ryley in the dimly lit kitchen, only the light over the stove being on. I could hear the gang laughing and carrying on down in the lower half of the split-entry home. I was almost angry at the other kids, who couldn't possibly grasp what we had experienced the night before and the months leading up to it. At the same time, I envied them. Ryley seemed to read my mind.

"That's one of those things that's always bugged me too," he said, glancing momentarily in the direction of the stairwell. "It seems so easy for everyone else, doesn't it? I mean, for a lot of them, it seems like their biggest worry is about some trivial little thing—if they even have worries at all. People who are happy kinda piss me off … but you know, I'd love to be one of them sometimes."

"I'm glad you're not, man. Don't get me wrong, I like our friends— they're fun and stuff—but they don't take anything very seriously."

"Who knows? Maybe they will one day. My father always says *'everyone goes through their own brand of shit.'* I betcha anything every one of our friends have crap they're trying to deal with."

Shane came bounding up the stairs and joined us in the kitchen. "What's up, guys?"

"We're just talking about last night," Ryley informed him.

"Yeah. That's been bugging me all day. I still think we need to go see Constance tomorrow. She said Wendell would be there to take her to the Remembrance Day service. We've gotta talk to him, see if he can help us out."

"I dunno, Shane. Remember, she said he always gets really depressed on that day," Ryley said.

"Yeah, and besides, what are we gonna say to him? 'Hi, we've been seeing your dead teenage boyfriend lately, and we'd like to ask you a few questions about him.'"

"I somehow don't think that would be a good opener," Shane noted sarcastically.

We could still hear the other kids downstairs laughing at the movie.

"I so don't want to go back down there," Ryley stated.

"Me neither," I agreed.

"Wish we were back at your place," Shane said. "I think we've got to see exactly what happened before we can resolve everything."

"But we don't know anything more yet," I said.

"Which is why I say we need to go to Berwick tomorrow," Shane reiterated.

"I think he's right, Caleb."

"Okay. Let me use your phone, Rye. I'll call Blake."

After a short conversation with my brother, he agreed to pick us up at nine the next morning. None of us knew what we'd accomplish, but we were all in it together.

Back downstairs at Hunter's, we rejoined our friends. Ryley sat on the floor with Adria, their backs leaned against the base of a chair. He put his arm around her, and she leaned back and kissed him to welcome his return. I sat down on one end of the couch, and Shane resumed his seat at the other end. Adria turned back and smiled at me thoughtfully. She mouthed the words, "You okay?"

I forced a grin and nodded. "Thanks," I mouthed back.

Between the movies, most of the kids went upstairs to get something to nosh on and use the washroom before coming back for the second film—some generic slasher flick. Adria sat down next to me on the sofa and put a hand on my knee. "How ya doing, you?" she asked, genuine care in her voice.

"I'm fine, thanks," I lied, hoping that the lie everyone else believed so easily could work with her.

"Yeah. Right." She whispered the next part. "Why don't you just sit next to him? You both look miserable when you can't be together."

"It's not that easy."

She nodded. "I know. I'm not trying to make light of it, but I really don't think anyone here is gonna have a problem with you two, and if they do, screw 'em—it's their problem, not yours."

"Yeah, until they tell everyone at school, and we get the shit kicked outta us." Some of our friends were coming back down the stairs, so we were forced to end our conversation. "Thanks for caring, though."

"I just want my friends to be happy," she said.

I smiled at her appreciatively. She squeezed my knee as she got up and returned to her spot on the floor with Ryley.

When Hunter put on the next movie and Drew killed the lights, I could see the forest again. In the silent moments as they crunched popcorn and didn't speak, I was away from my friends, back in the woods. I could hear the wind and the snap of branches. I could smell the newly fallen snow on the pine needles. I saw myself, walking along the path, but the path seemed to narrow and darken. A distant sound of crying drew closer. A sudden pain tore through my abdomen. I looked around, and I was back in Hunter's den, watching a horror movie with my friends—everyone waiting expectantly for the gory scenes. Shane slid down the couch and sat next to me, placing a hand on my back and leaning forward so he could make eye contact with me.

"You okay?" he asked.

"Yeah ... I just got this awful pain in my stomach. I was thinking about the woods, and it just hit me."

"We need to go back out there."

"Tomorrow night ... can you come over?"

"It doesn't matter if I can or I can't. I'll be there."

I sat back up, the tension in my stomach easing slowly. I took a deep breath, and everything returned to normal.

Shane whispered to me, "I really wanna hold you right now."

Adria, who must have been casually observing us, motioned for Shane to move down on the small sofa. She and Ryley joined us, forcing us to all squish together. Shane's leg was pressed hard against mine, as was the rest of his right side.

"There, this is much more comfy," Adria announced. "Got three hotties on the couch with me. Life is good." She raised her arms and stretched so she could pull us all closer still. I made a mental note to thank her later.

I was exhausted when I woke up the next morning. I had forgotten where I was for a moment and was surprised that when I opened my eyes, I saw v-grooved pine on the ceiling. Hunter's room was really big, and there was a set of bunk beds in the corner as well as his double bed. I'd claimed top bunk as soon as I stepped in the door the previous evening. Shane was in the bottom bunk, and Drew and Ryley were on the carpeted floor. All the other guys were still sleeping.

Sunlight came in the skylight, and the off-white walls displayed posters of hockey players, swimsuit models (all female, the pity of it), and the odd monster truck or rock group thrown in for good measure. A large clock with the "Miller Time" logo informed me it was just after seven.

I decided that since I was awake, I might as well get up. I leaned over the side of my bed and looked down at Shane. His hair had grown back in (he called it his winter coat), and it looked really good, dark brown and thick. I couldn't get over how beautiful he was. I let my eyes roam over his form under the covers and watched as he slowly opened his eyes, squinting as light hit them.

"Hey," he said sleepily, seeing me above.

"Morning."

He stretched and yawned. "What time is it?"

"Nearly seven thirty."

Shane rubbed his eyes. "Shit. I'm tired."

"Me too. Wanna go get a coffee?"

Shane nodded. "Yeah. Sounds good."

Hunter's house was just a half-kilometre walk from Stape's, so we got up and grabbed our backpacks of clothes, going down the hall to the washroom to change.

Shane walked over to me, placed a hand on my bare stomach, and kissed me passionately on the mouth. I kissed him back and let my hands slide over his back.

"Mmm … God …" Shane softly moaned as we parted lips, and he kissed me again. The hand that had been on my stomach slid around to the small of my back and, to my surprise, went under the waistband of my red Hanes. I was incredibly turned on.

Following his lead, I slipped a hand under his shorts and slowly allowed it to make its way around to the front. Still kissing me, Shane took my arm in his hand, stopping my motion.

"No, babe. Not yet," he whispered. "Not here."

Knowing he was right, I blushed. "Sorry … got carried away."

Shane flicked a hair back from my eyes. "We should get dressed."

"Umm … about that …" I said, looking down.

"Oh … right. Okay, well, I'll change in the shower stall," he volunteered.

Shane stepped into the stall and snapped the door tight. The glass was heavily frosted, and even if I had wanted to see him (which I did, quite honestly), I wouldn't have been able to. I went about changing and waited for him to finish. When we were both ready, we went down the half flight of stairs to the foyer and put on our jackets and shoes before heading outside.

The air was crisp that morning, and it made me wake up fully as we marched along the road toward town. Shane was wearing his San Francisco Giants ball cap and a hooded sweatshirt and vest, along with his jeans. He looked tough and cute at the same time, and I found that incredibly sexy.

No one was around as we walked. There were cars at the Legion and at the church we passed, but the sidewalks were empty. Stape's was quiet as well. I bought our coffees, and we turned tail and started back for Hunter's. I pulled back the plastic tab on my cup's lid and took a sip of the steaming hot black liquid.

"Mmmmm … that tastes sooo good," I sighed after my first swallow.

Shane nodded in agreement as he drank his.

I shivered. "Man, it's cold today."

"Yeah—least there's no wind."

We sipped at our coffees, enjoying the contrasting cold air with the hot beverage. An older-model Chevy Caprice, I'd guess at an '87 or an '88, drove by. It wasn't in great shape, and the smell of its emissions let me know it was burning oil as well as gasoline. Oddly, on a cold day, that can be a pleasant odour.

"Sorry about earlier, making you stop like that …" Shane said, sounding annoyed at himself. "Maybe I need to just let stuff happen, ya know? I mean, be one of those people who goes with the flow and says afterward, '*Oh, hey, so that's what it was like the first time I got off with my boyfriend. Cool.*' But I don't work that way."

"I don't usually either, but when I'm with you, it's different. It's all right, though. I mean, I really like what we've got. I don't wanna rush into anything."

"Me neither. But, I mean, I hope you know, I do wanna do more with you." He looked at me and smirked, shaking his head. "God, I wanna do so much more with you, it isn't even funny."

I blushed.

When we got back to Hunter's, our coffees were gone, and the sun was starting to shine overhead, threatening to melt the snow if it stayed out. We woke Ryley so he could get ready to leave with us when Blake arrived. I left a note on the kitchen counter thanking Hunter before leaving.

"Morning, guys," Blake welcomed us as we climbed into the Bronco. Thankfully, he had the heater cranked, and the little truck was nice and warm. "Tit bit nipply this morning, isn't it?"

"It's brisk," I replied.

We didn't talk much on the way back home, each of us having his own thoughts to attend to. The Bronco moved swiftly over the roads leading to the house. The ride wasn't exactly comfortable in the backseat, and I knew the shock absorbers, which I had debated whether to replace or not, were in need of changing.

As we turned left onto Wakefield Road, I saw a crow standing on the newel post of an old, rotten fence that was collapsing with time. His visage was in stark contrast to the snowy blanket around him. He didn't fly off or make a sound as we rumbled by, just turned his head to watch us go and remained standing guard.

We took turns showering and getting ready to go see Constance. Shane didn't have any dressier clothes with him, so he borrowed some of Blake's.

"Don't you boys look handsome?!" Mom said as we entered the kitchen. "What's the occasion?"

"Well, umm, to tell you the truth, we're going to a Remembrance Day ceremony in Berwick," I replied.

"You are?"

"Yeah. Shane knows this elderly woman at the seniors' home, and we're going to go to the service with her." It wasn't a lie—it wasn't the whole story, but it wasn't a lie.

"How nice. You two aren't going?" Mom asked Ryley and Blake.

"No, we're gonna grab some breakfast while they're with Mrs. Durant. Probably check out a movie after," Blake told her.

"Oh, okay. Well, I think it's great that you're doing this, guys. This Mrs. Durant must be very fond of you, Shane."

"Umm, yeah, well, she's sorta like an aunt or something, ya know? She doesn't get many visitors, and she had a brother who fought in the war, so I thought it'd be nice to go and I asked Caleb to come with me for company."

"That's great."

"Not sure when we'll be back—depends on what movie we see," Blake said.

"All right. Have a nice day and be sure to take your poppies off after the service."

"We will, Mom. Don't worry," I said. (Proper poppy etiquette had been instilled in me from early childhood.)

Mom walked over to Blake and talked quietly with him for a minute while the rest of us put on our boots and coats.

Out in the Bronco, I had to ask, "What was that about?"

"Mom gave me money for gas."

"That was nice of her," Ryley said.

"Yeah ... not surprising, though," Blake replied. "Mom's been slipping me gas money for a while now. I told her she won't need to much longer cuz I picked up an after-school job at the hardware store."

"You did?" I asked.

"Yeah, remember I had that interview a while back? Well, a position finally opened up, so they called me the other day. Good thing, too, cuz it's not cheap having a vehicle, even if your little brother is your mechanic. Besides, I need to start saving money up for next year."

"Small world," Ryley mused. "I just got on at the IGA."

"How? Don't you have to be sixteen?" I asked.

"No, not if you have a parental letter of consent. I'll be sixteen in a few months anyway."

"Wish I could get a job," I said.

"I'll ask the manager for an application form for you, if you want," Ryley offered. "Put in a good word for ya."

"That'd be great. Thanks."

"If I didn't already work for my mom at the motel, I'd be out looking too," Shane said. "So here, take this," he told Blake, handing him a ten-dollar bill.

"I'm not taking your money, Shane," Blake told him.

"C'mon, man. You've been taxiing me around for months. Least I can do is chip in a few bucks now and then. Please, take it."

Blake sighed and took the purple bill. "Thanks."

"Soon as I get my first paycheque, I'll chip in too," Ryley said. "It's only fair."

"Wish I could help out," I stated.

"Just keep 'er running, Caleb. That saves us a ton right there," Blake told me.

"No kidding," Ryley agreed.

Upon arriving at the seniors' home, Blake shut off the engine, and Shane and I scrambled out of the Bronco. We headed inside and up to the front desk. Gidget wasn't there; instead, we found a young woman with shoulder-length black hair. We could hear the sound of a church service taking place down the hall in the small chapel.

"May I help you boys?" the woman asked us.

"Hi. Yes. We're here to see Mrs. Durant. We were here a few weeks ago and promised to come back to see her again."

"She's probably at the service. It's already started, but if you fellas wanna quietly slip in at the back of the chapel and see if you can find her, you can. I'd show you the way, but I can't leave the desk."

"That's okay, thanks. We'll be fine," I said.

The woman smiled, and we headed down toward the room where the hymn music was playing. Just inside the doorway, we stopped and looked over the elderly faces for Constance.

"I don't see her," Shane whispered.

"Me neither."

As we continued to give the room a once-over, I noticed Gidget walking toward us. She put her arms out and placed a hand on each of our shoulders, walking in between us, turning us around and leading us toward the common room.

"Boys, I'm afraid I have some sad news to tell you. Mrs. Durant passed away Friday evening."

We stopped walking and turned to face Gidget, crestfallen. It reminded me of when my father told me that my grandmother Mackenzie had passed away, and I can only imagine how it made Shane feel.

"I'm so sorry. She was very taken with you both, you know. Talked about your visit for days, bragging about the two handsome young men who came to see her."

"H-h-how did she die?" I asked, surprised to find myself choked up.

"She went very peacefully, I assure you. She'd been living with so many different ailments for so long, they just took their toll on her the other night as she was watching *Jeopardy*. One minute, she was criticizing Alex Trebek's penchant for correcting contestants' pronunciation, and the next minute, she was gone."

"I really wish we had gotten to talk to her again," Shane said softly.

"You know, before you fellas came to visit, the only pleasure she ever seemed to get was from calling me Gidget. I only pretended it annoyed me so she'd keep it up. Her spirits were pretty low most of the time, and it was good to keep her fired up—even if it was at my expense. That day you visited, though, that was the highlight of her time here. The plant you gave her was never out of her sight; she even took it with her to the common room and back, for company and a reminder of you both, showing it off to everybody."

The thought that something so small had meant so much to her made my eyes well up. If nothing else, I felt good that we'd given her an afternoon she enjoyed.

"When is her funeral going to be?" I asked.

Gidget shook her head. "She didn't want a funeral. No, she's being cremated and asked that her ashes be buried with her late husband's. I don't even know if her children will bother coming down for the burial. They never once showed all the time she was living here. Only visitor she ever had besides you boys was her brother, Wendell." Gidget stopped talking for a second before going on to say, "You know, it's funny how people can surprise you at times. After your visit that day, Mrs. Durant began to go through all her old letters and things from back during the war. Her eyesight had failed, and she asked me to read many of the letters to her. She'd shake her head as I went over the old lines from her brother and say things like, 'I wish I had understood back then. I was so naïve,' and things like that. Other times she'd just smile and look distant. Once or twice, she even had tears in her eyes."

"Do you know why she was so moved by the letters?" Shane asked.

"Well, I suppose I just assumed it was a very difficult time in her past—knowing how many people died and all."

"Were the letters interesting?" I wondered aloud.

"Oh yes, they were very interesting, but they were sad too, which I suppose I should have expected, them being written during the war. The ones in 1945 were different, though. There weren't many from that time, but the mood of them had changed. That's the time when Wendell was in France and mentioned, more than once, a good friend he had made, named Jean-Luc. Constance nodded and smiled when I read the letters about Jean-Luc. There was even a small photo of the two of them in one of the envelopes. When she looked at it, she said, 'My, wasn't he dashing?' I had to agree, but I've always been a sucker for a man in uniform," Gidget said and laughed.

"We were hoping to meet Wendell today," I said. "Mrs. Durant mentioned he usually came down to the Remembrance Day service with her every year."

"I don't know if he's up for it, but he's here. He's down in her room, sorting things. Let me go and see how he's doing."

Gidget wandered down the hall to the rooms. I gave Shane a doubtful look.

"I can't believe she's dead," he said.

"Yeah. I don't imagine Wendell's gonna wanna see us."

"Probably not, but it's hard to say. If he won't see us, we're pretty much screwed."

Gidget appeared back in the hallway after ducking into Constance's room. She waved at us to come toward her.

"Thank God," Shane muttered.

I took a deep breath, and we walked down the hall together.

Chapter Twenty

At the entry to Constance's room, Gidget put her arms over our shoulders once more and introduced us to Wendell. He rose from his place at the end of the bed and walked over to us.

"Mr. Hildebrand, this is Caleb, and this is Shane," she said.

"Nice to meet you, sir," Shane said to Wendell, offering him his hand to shake. "We're very sorry to learn about your sister's passing."

"Thank you," Wendell replied and shook Shane's hand.

"Yes, she was a very nice lady," I added and offered my hand as well.

"That she was. You boys come in and sit for a spell. I'd like to speak with you," Wendell instructed.

Gidget let her arms fall back to her sides to enable us to enter the room. I thanked her as she turned to leave.

Wendell sat down in the only chair in the tiny bedroom, a wooden rocker, and pointed to the bed. Shane and I sat down at the end of the twin bed on the pinkish-coloured bedspread.

"You know, I was surprised a few weeks back to get a call from Constance to let me know she'd had visitors," Wendell said. He rubbed his smooth hands together as he spoke before buttoning up his wine-coloured cardigan. He took a letter from the table beside him and held it as he went on to say, "She sounded the most chipper I had heard her in a very long time. I owe you boys my thanks for that.

"I couldn't help at first but to wonder who on earth it would have been that was visiting her. I thought perhaps someone was trying to con her, or something of the sort, but she laughed at me and said that it was two young men who lived in Wakefield House. Wanted to talk about history, she said." Wendell leaned forward in his chair, watching our faces carefully. "Was that really the case?"

"Umm, well, not exactly, sir. I don't live in Wakefield House—Caleb does. I live in town. I'm just helping him."

"We're working on a project together," I said.

Wendell pulled a pack of cigarettes from his shirt pocket and withdrew a duMaurier. He struck a match and inhaled the first plume as he waved the match out and dropped it in the small, silvery-coloured tin ashtray on the table to his side. (I had a vague memory of seeing an ashtray like it in a McDonald's in Quebec when I was very young.) He sighed as he exhaled. He must have seen the surprised expression that we tried to hide at his action, because he smiled slightly and said, "At my age, breaking the rules about smoking is the least of my concerns." Wendell tapped off the small bit of ash into the ashtray.

"You've come farther than anyone ever has before with your project," he said behind a greyish cloud of smoke. Shane and I exchanged a look. Wendell sat forward in his seat and rubbed his knees with the palm of each hand, his lit cigarette sticking out in front of his right knee, held between his index and middle finger. "Arthritis is a bastard, boys. Don't ever get old."

"My father has arthritis in his knee, too," I mentioned.

"What's he, around forty? Forty-five?"

"Yes, sir. Forty-three, actually."

"That's about the time mine really began to act up. I put my knees through hell in the war. Some days I can still feel the freezing mud around my legs.

"I was in this small village in France when we were bombed. I was thrown when one of the bombs landed, and I ended up in this pond. It was the middle of winter and bitterly cold. I was unconscious for I don't know how long, but when I woke up, my legs were under the water, encased in mud and badly broken in many places. I couldn't move. I was scared to death—afraid I was paralyzed. I called out for help, but no one was around. It began to snow, and I was sure I was going to either be found and shot by some Jerry or I'd end up dying from exposure. So, despite the agony I was in, I dug in with my elbows and pulled as hard as I could to get loose from the freezing mud. I managed to get my legs free and continued to pull myself along with my elbows. I could see the building I had been standing next to when the bomb hit. There was debris everywhere, and dead soldiers, many of whom were my friends, were all over the streets. The lucky ones died instantly." Wendell sighed, and his gaze became distant. "The only thing I could think of, though, was how much I wanted to get back over to that building and curl up by the enormous fire that was blazing inside it. Everything was burning from the bombing, and the air was thick with smoke. I coughed and cried out for help as I struggled along, finally making it to the building and pulling myself up to the fire. Exhausted from my efforts, I blacked out again." Wendell sat back in his chair and dragged on his cigarette.

"Then what happened?" Shane asked.

We were both fascinated by the story and wanted to find out how he was saved. Wendell was going to make us wait, however. He picked the envelope off his lap and said, "Do you fellas know what this is?"

"No," I said.

Shane shook his head.

"I never told anyone the real reason I left home and went to war. Constance believed what I told her, and that was much more than I told anyone else, but it wasn't the complete truth. She knew I missed my friend, Toby, who disappeared in the forest behind Wakefield House, as I'm sure you boys have heard the stories."

"Yes."

"Yeah."

"But what she didn't know, what no one knows, is what happened between the day they called off the search and the day I ran off to war. And that, my dear boys, is what I wrote down and hold in this letter right here," he said, tapping the envelope. I could feel my mouth watering for information, like Pavlov's dogs for their biscuits. We were so close to knowing. "I wrote it all down and gave it to Constance to keep safe for me. If I died, she could open it, but as long as I was alive, she was to keep it sealed and safe. I could always trust my sister to keep her promises."

Wendell stubbed out his cigarette and sighed. "If I had died, like I had hoped for in those first days in Europe before seeing the reality of death, I wanted to be sure someone else knew the entire story. I'm the only one who knows what happened to this day. All of it is right here," he tapped the letter again, "in this envelope in the handwriting of a heartbroken sixteen-year-old boy I scarcely remember being but have never been able to forget." He looked at us kindly and smiled. "I never thought anyone would try to learn the truth. I've heard all the stories about the back bedroom and the strange goings-on at Wakefield House over the years. I can honestly say I've never known what to make of it all. I could never face going back there again. I haven't been to Stapeton since I left for the war. I vowed I'd never return. I've lost too much in my life to live that close to the greatest source of pain I've ever known." Wendell reached toward us, the envelope in his hand. "Here. This is yours now."

Shane took the letter. "Thank you."

Wendell shook his head. "Don't thank me for anything. To anyone else, that letter is just another story, like the stories that already exist out there. But as long as you know it's the truth, then that's all that matters. I just need someone else to know about Toby." Wendell's voice got smaller. "He must never be forgotten."

"He won't be," I assured him.

There was a silent moment in the room before Wendell began to speak again. "When I came to, I was looking up at the face of a doctor. I had been found and taken to a hospital by another soldier. My legs were bandaged up, and I was basically bedridden for two months as I healed. During that period, I came to know quite a bit of French, as no one in the hospital spoke English and I had to communicate. I got to talking at length with the soldier who had brought me in, a Belgian lad named Jean-Luc, who was fighting with the French army. I thanked him for rescuing me, and he said that when he saw the word 'Canada' on my sleeve, he was sure to take extra care to get me to the hospital safely, as it was a Canadian regiment that aided the battalion his brother was fighting with months before.

"Jean-Luc had gotten shrapnel in his back, and as we regained our health in the hospital together, we became fast friends. The war was drawing to a close at the time of our release, and since I had lost all of my regiment, I finished out my days with a small group of Canadian soldiers who had taken up residence in a little fishing village on the coast. Jean-Luc and I stayed in touch, as we felt a bond between us. It was so good to have a best friend again." Wendell smiled at us and asked, "You fellas are best friends, aren't you?"

I smiled. "Yes, sir. We are."

"Caleb here's the best friend I've ever had," Shane said as he took my hand in his. "And he's my boyfriend, too."

Wendell smiled thoughtfully. "Constance told me when she called that she understood my letters so much better after your visit. Said everything finally made sense to her, and she felt sorry that I hadn't been able to just come right out and tell her. You know, a big part of me wanted Constance to open that letter despite her promise. I wanted her to read the truth and know how much I loved Toby. I never told a soul." Wendell's eyes started to water. "And that has eaten away at me every day of my life." He dabbed at his eyes with a tissue, crumpled it, and stuffed it in the pocket of his right pant leg, clearing his throat as he continued his story.

"I went to visit Jean-Luc in Belgium when the war ended. I stayed in his town at this little motel and worked at a bakery. One day, when I was visiting, Jean-Luc asked me to help him with something in the woodhouse. I went out with him, and he kissed me. As I looked at that handsome boy, I knew I could let myself love again. We moved to Paris a year or so later and were together for six years before we went our separate ways. It was a very hard time for me, but not all relationships are meant to last.

"So, I returned to Canada, moving to Montreal and working for the *Gazette* for some time under a pseudonym. I've been single since Jean-Luc, spending my energies on my work and my volunteering. When I decided to retire, I moved to Toronto to be closer to my brother, Sheldon, and his family. The rest, I guess, you know."

"What kinds of volunteer work did you do?" Shane asked.

"Adult literacy. I used to help people learn to read."

"Wow. That's great."

"It was very satisfying, though at times very trying. I always figured if I could help just one person, I wouldn't have wasted my life."

"I'm sure you've helped many people," I offered.

"Maybe. Who knows? I just hope that I've made some difference." Wendell was quiet. "I'm tired now, boys. I think I'd like to be left alone, if you'd be so kind."

Shane and I stood up. Shane went over to Wendell and shook his hand again. "Thanks for sharing with us."

"Take care of each other," he said as we left the room.

I noticed the amber blooms of the mum were still vibrant as we walked by the potted plant on our way out the door.

We walked down to meet up with Blake and Ryley at Tim Hortons. We bought coffees and joined them at their rounded table with four chairs on swivel posts, allowing us to swing from side to side.

"Okay," I sighed after taking a sip of my coffee. "First things first. Constance died Friday night."

"Shit," Blake mumbled.

"That's what we thought at first too," Shane agreed. "I mean, don't get me wrong, it's sad that she died, what I meant was …"

Ryley cut him off. "Shane man, it's cool. We know what you meant."

Shane looked relieved that no one thought he had been disrespectful, and I went on with the details of what happened.

"So anyway, we're figuring, that's it, right? We're not going to be able to learn anything more. Not with any ease, anyway." I stopped and took another drink.

"We couldn't have been more wrong," Shane continued. "Turns out Wendell was there going through some of Constance's things."

"Already?" Ryley asked.

"Yeah, a lot of these places have such a long waiting list of people wanting to get in, they can't afford to let the rooms stay empty," Blake explained without averting his eyes from Shane's direction.

"So this woman who works there, she remembers us from the last time we visited, and she goes and asks Wendell if he'd be willing to meet us. So we go down to Constance's room and we meet him and he sits and talks to us about the war and how grateful he was that we want to learn what really happened to Toby."

"Holy crap. This is incredible," Ryley said. "What'd ya find out?"

"Well, nothing yet. Not really," I replied. "But he gave us an envelope containing a letter he wrote when he was sixteen, just before he ran off and joined the army."

"Open it, bud," Blake urged.

I shook my head. "No. Not here. We'll wait till we get home to read it."

"Fair enough. So what else did Wendell have to say?"

"Nothing I can't tell you on the way home," I said urgently.

"Right. Let's go," Blake instructed.

It was midafternoon when we gathered in Blake's room to open the letter. I cautiously slid Blake's letter opener (with an acrylic handle holding three shiny coins: a penny, a nickel, and a dime) along the top of the envelope and pulled the folded sheets of unlined paper from their longtime home. I gently set the envelope on Blake's nightstand and sat back against the headboard, a pillow behind me, to read the letter aloud to everyone. Ryley and Shane sat on the bed at the opposite end, and Blake rolled his desk chair over to the side of the bed near me.

As I looked at the page, the first thing that struck me was how similar Wendell's handwriting was to my own.

"It's weird, you know," I said before starting to read. I looked around at the guys. "Wendell was our age when he wrote this back in 1943, and no one has seen it since." It felt to me as if I was going to read someone else's diary. There was this guilty feeling about reading Wendell's words as a boy, but an exciting feeling at the same time.

I guess my voice was a tad shaky as I spoke because Blake asked me, "You okay to read it?"

I smiled at my brother. "Yeah, I just, I dunno. It's weird."

Shane nodded. "It's cool, Caleb. Take your time."

I took a deep breath and began to read:

December 19, 1943

Dear Reader,

    I do not know who it is that will be reading these words or in what year they will be read. All I know is what has happened, and if you read this letter to the end, you will know what happened, too.

    First off, you need to know who I am. My name is Wendell Caleb Hildebrand. As I write this letter, I am sitting at my desk in the only home I have ever known, just outside of Stapeton, Nova Scotia. I am sixteen years old, and I am a fairly typical kid—at least that is what I had always thought. Nothing I ever did seemed anything but ordinary and natural to me. Not one thing. You need to know that.

    I grew up in close proximity to a dozen or so other farms. My very best friend on earth, Toby Everett, lived on the farm located at the end of Wakefield Road. We did everything together, and my childhood was a happy one. As we got older, our friendship grew, and we had a bond like no other. My feelings for Toby grew too, and much to my delight, his grew for me as well.

    We oftentimes went for long walks in the woods behind Toby's house, and on one such day, when we were thirteen, Toby kissed me. I had not known that a boy could kiss another boy, no matter how much he may have wanted to. It was absolutely wonderful. As time went on, we found ourselves sneaking away more often to our place in the woods by a waterfall. Neither of us felt that what we were doing was wrong, but since we had never seen or heard of anyone else like us, we decided we had to hide our feelings for each other from the world.

    Despite this fact, we made plans for our future, and we knew that we would always be together. All of our hopes and dreams came to an end when Toby disappeared.

    According to everyone else, his disappearance in those same woods behind the house at the end of Wakefield Road was just a tragic accident. He had been hunting with his father, Tavis, the weekend he went missing. Toby was going after a buck on Saturday evening. Tavis said that he could not keep up with his son's pursuit, so he returned to the campfire and waited for Toby to return. When Toby failed to come back, Tavis began to search for his son and returned home on Sunday afternoon, during an early snowstorm, to tell his family Toby had vanished. A search party went about looking for him, but with the war on, there are not many men around to assist in the efforts, and after a few days passed, the search was called off. Toby was pronounced dead from exposure, and everyone went on with life. Toby's body was never found.

    I kept searching those woods long after everyone else had stopped. Toby knew the forest too well for me to ever believe he could have gotten lost in it. There were areas of the forest that the searchers had not gone in that I went to. One day, as I was searching for a sign, anything that would lead me to Toby, I started up the far side of the waterfall clearing. There was snow on the ground and no traces of footprints, as the wind had been fierce and the snow fluffy. I was halfway up the path when I heard someone's feet crunching over the snow and twigs underneath. My heart jumped and I turned, expecting to see Toby, but I saw Tavis instead. He stood, his face full of fury, glaring at me.

"You won't find him, you know." Tavis told me this and snapped a twig from a birch tree. His voice was distant, as if he was not there at all. I'm sure he was drunk, as he swayed, holding a branch for leverage. I asked him how he could give up hope so easily, and he told me that some people were just meant to never be found, that Toby was dead, and that if I stayed in the woods, I would likely end up the same way. I knew then that Tavis had killed his son, and although I was filled with anger, I was terrified as well. I realized I was in the woods, on a path that no one else knew about, with a murderer—and that I had to get by him to get out. I forced back the tears that were trying to come out and did not make a sound other than to tell Tavis I supposed he was right and that I had best be going home.

When I walked by him and began to push my way through the spruce trees, I honestly believed I was going to feel something come down on the back of my head and that I would die. I walked as fast as I could out of the forest and jumped on my horse, Midnight, that I had tied inside the Everett barn. Tavis was close behind me the entire time. As I untied my horse, Tavis said to me, "You best leave well enough alone. Finding out the truth about a man could get him killed."

There was no outright confession on Tavis's part, but if you had seen his eyes and heard his voice, you too would know that he killed Toby. You are probably wondering why I never told anyone about what happened or about my suspicions. The fact was, I could prove nothing. My word would never be taken over an adult's.

Now I am filled with rage. I want to hurt someone. Anyone. Maybe even myself. I have decided that I'm going to enlist in the army. I believe I will pass for eighteen, as I am tall and strong. I will go where the fighting is, and I am prepared to never come home. If I should perish, I shall be reunited with my love.

As I sit here, I hope against hope that you who are reading this can do so with an understanding of what I am feeling. I am just a boy who loves another boy. Toby will be my angel on the field of battle, as he was my angel on the fields of Wakefield Road. He will never be forgotten as long as I hold breath or someone reads this letter. That is my pledge to him. Toby Joshua Everett will live on in the hearts and minds of all who knew him and in the places and times that we shared together. I ask you, whoever you are, to do just one thing and to do it with every ounce of your being—love.

While I still grieve, it gives me comfort to know that Toby is safe in Heaven. Perhaps I will be joining him soon.

I must finish this letter and pack my bags. I am leaving as soon as everyone has gone to sleep. I will miss my family and I will miss my home, but I shall never return to Stapeton. I miss Toby too much to ever come back.

Sincerely,

W. Caleb Hildebrand

I put the letter down in my lap and examined the faces around me. No one said anything right away. We were all too moved and shaken by the words on those old pages.

There was nothing that seemed appropriate to say at that moment, so we sat, united in silence, each of us afraid to break it and desperately hoping someone else would. My mother, it turned out, was the one to save us.

"Knock knock," she said as she came into the room. "Whoa, what's with all the long faces?" Mom stopped at the foot of the bed and put her hands on her hips.

"Mrs. Durant passed away," Shane explained.

"Oh my gosh. I'm so sorry to hear that." Mom sat down between Ryley and Shane. "Are you okay, sweetheart?" she asked Shane.

He nodded. "I'm okay. Just feeling kinda, I dunno, blah."

"Is there anything I can do?"

"No. Thanks anyway, Karen."

"Well, if there is, don't hesitate to ask, okay?"

Shane nodded.

"What's the letter?" she asked me.

"It's a note from her brother."

"Oh, well, that was nice of him to give to you."

We all kept quiet, not sure what to say next.

"Is there anything I can do to help cheer you boys up?"

"Umm, no. But thanks, Mom," I replied.

"Okay. I'll leave you alone, but if you guys want to talk or anything, I'll just be downstairs."

Mom placed a hand on Shane's cheek and smiled at him as she got up. She touched Ryley's shoulder as she walked by him. Mom always touched people, just a gentle reminder that she was there.

"I'll just throw something together for supper, and whoever wants any is welcome to it. Okay?"

We nodded and thanked her, and she went downstairs.

"You know, all these years I've listened to the stories about Toby, and I never once gave the idea that he'd been murdered any real merit. I mean, it just didn't make sense to me. Who could kill a kid? Especially one as nice as Toby was said to be," Shane said sombrely. "I never thought it coulda been a hate crime—but that's what it was. Tavis killed Toby because he found out he was gay."

"We still don't know for certain that that's what happened," Blake stated. "Wendell said himself he could prove nothing."

"But it seems so clear from what Wendell wrote in the letter," Ryley said.

Blake responded, "I know, but you have to think of the circumstances. He wrote it when he was in a very fragile state, and perhaps he misinterpreted some things or maybe the tone was different than he remembered. I'm not trying to defend Tavis, but I want to know the facts, if possible, before accusing anyone."

I considered what my brother had said. "You're right. We need to see what really happened."

"I don't think I could handle seeing that," Ryley told us. "Just hearing and feeling it was awful enough."

"Rye, I think we all need to know exactly what took place. It's gonna be difficult, to be sure, but there's a reason the four of us were chosen," Shane explained.

"You and Caleb, you guys were chosen. Blake and I are just along for the ride."

"No, I don't think so. It was you who fell to your knees screaming, holding your stomach—not any of us. And if it weren't for what you heard last time out, do you think you would ever have opened up to us and talked about what you're going through?" Blake asked. Ryley shook his head. "See, Toby's helped us all out. We have to help him, no matter how hard it is to do."

"You're right," Ryley agreed. "I'll go. But," Ryley tilted his head to one side and looked at Blake quizzically, "how has Toby helped you?"

"Huh?"

"How has Toby helped you? I mean, I know he helped the rest of us, but what about you?"

All eyes were on Blake as we awaited our answer. In truth, I couldn't think of anything. I doubt the other guys could either. It was apparent that Blake was racking his brain for a response.

"Maybe there's more that needs to happen before Blake is helped," Shane suggested. "I mean, it was before I met any of you that Toby helped me, and it was just recently that he helped Rye. Maybe what he really does is gives us the opportunity to help ourselves."

We all thought about this and quietly agreed.

Knowing what we had to do that night, we stopped talking about it and focused our attentions on our growling bellies. When we entered the kitchen, Mom was taking the chicken almandine out of the oven. If ever there was a time I wanted comfort food, that was it, and Mom had made my favourite kind.

Our appetites had been larger than we had imagined. We ate the entire casserole, as well as all the multigrain rolls, before we cut into one of the two apple pies Mom had taken from the freezer the night before. We cut large slices and ate them with thick chunks of old cheddar cheese. When dinner was over, we took cups of coffee into the family room and watched episodes of *American Dad* on DVD. My favourite episode, a brilliant parody of *Who's Afraid of Virginia Woolf?* can always make me laugh.

In what seemed like the blink of an eye, it was eleven o'clock, and we were out in the barn putting together our things. We all bundled up in extra layers of clothing, knowing how cold the woods could get. The night was chilly, hovering around zero. The ground was free of snow, but we all wore boots just the same. We took out our flashlights and proceeded toward the stream.

The ground was hard underfoot, a level of frost already setting in. Our footsteps from a previous trek were formed in frozen patterns in the muddy areas around the water. The temperature felt as though it would plummet quickly. Despite the layers we wore, we were all cold.

We stopped on the other side of the brook and merely stood, staring momentarily into the abyss of treelined blackness that we had visited so many times before. Without ever saying so, we knew this visit would not be like any of the others. We would see something that would alter our lives forever. I suppose we felt that way every time we entered the woods with new information, but this time it was different. We weren't excited to get to the next step. The onetime sensation that we were on a grand adventure, that this was all some mysterious game to be played out, was long gone. I can't speak for the others as to how they were feeling inside, but I know for certain what I felt—small, incredibly small.

"You all right?" Blake asked me.

I shrugged. "Doesn't really matter."

As I took my first step into the woods, I was reminded of the film *To Kill A Mockingbird* when Scout says: *"And thus began our longest journey together."*

We made our way to the spruce trees and pushed through to the hidden path, pausing on the other side to be sure all four of us were still present and accounted for. At the end of the trail, we stopped, knowing without saying, that this was now the point of no return. Soon we'd be in another time—all of us or some of us, we couldn't be sure. We stretched and rolled our heads from side to side. I jumped on the spot to force blood to my cold legs. We all stalled for time. Then, we started back.

We were a quarter of the way along when our flashlights went out and the breeze picked up. The air became much colder, and we could see snow on the ground. I didn't let myself stop walking. The guys followed me in single file—I was so glad I wasn't alone. The faint moonlight was our only source of guidance to the halfway point, where I stopped. I heard a voice, a boy's voice, sounding cheerful and full of energy, off in the distance, carried in the wind to me. And that's when things changed.

The darkness evaporated, and the woods were light as if it were only late afternoon or early evening. The wind was still strong and the air cold, but it wasn't snowing. It felt like a typical November day, grey and gusty. There was a crash and a thump, and we all stared down at the spruce trees. A large buck had gotten through and was running in our direction. The voice of the boy was louder and called out, "Dad, he went this way!" and then, bursting through those same spruce branches, was Toby.

If ever there was a naturally handsome boy, it was Toby. Standing there in his plaid shirt and denim jeans, with the polished-wood stock of his Remington .30-06 held in a ready-carry position against his chest, he was absolutely gorgeous.

He ran after his deer, spotting it behind a clump of birches. Toby stealthily approached and raised his rifle, resting his barrel on the stub of a broken branch. He stood, silent. His breathing was perfect. His aim was set. His shot would be pure. I kept expecting it to happen at any moment, to hear the bang and then watch as the deer fell—but all remained quiet. Toby stood still, looking like an Abercrombie and Fitch mannequin that wound up in the forest. What seemed like an hour passed, and nothing happened. Then, without fear, the buck stepped out from his hiding spot and came right out into the open—a truly majestic beast. Toby kept his eye on it, and his finger caressed the trigger. Then I heard the faintest whisper. "Bang."

Toby looked up from his long-held position and removed his finger from the trigger. The buck turned its head toward him and snorted, a small cloud of breath coming out its nose. Toby watched as the deer sauntered off into the deeper part of the forest and out of sight.

A smile formed on Toby's lips, and he turned to go and find his father, who was still back at the clearing. There was a sound of crunching branches, and I looked, expecting to see the buck return from beyond the tree that marked the end of the path. What I saw instead was a man coming over the small hill.

Toby turned and saw the man drawing nearer. His expression did not change.

"Hi, Mr. Hildebrand. Surprised to see you out here today."

The man said nothing until he came closer. "All sorts of surprises in this world," he said with a sneer. He made an unpleasant ticking sound with his tongue.

Toby seemed a bit apprehensive. "Fine day for hunting."

"Is it? Seems to me if I were hunting, I woulda shot that big buck that ran by."

The man stood tall, about six-foot-two, and had dark hair. His pale white skin almost glowed out from under the sleeves of his black coat. I felt uneasy watching him.

"He was a beauty all right. Wouldn't have been right to kill something so beautiful."

The man spat and squinted his eyes at Toby. "Just the kinda talk I'd expect from the likes of a frilly little fairy like you."

"Excuse me?" Toby was instantly on his guard and angry.

"You heard me. I know all about you, you pervert. I found your little love letter," the man tauntingly waved an envelope in the air. Toby glared at him. "Just lucky I found it before my boy read it. The idea that you might pollute his mind too … you diseased maggot. Don't you ever go near my son again."

"I'd sooner die than never see Caleb again. I love him more than anything."

"Shut your mouth," the man stuck a finger in Toby's face. "You can't love another boy—it's sick and unnatural."

"There is nothing sick or unnatural about me or the love I have for your son."

The man was stunned by Toby's conviction and composure.

"Now, I'll take my letter back." Toby held out his hand for the envelope, but when it wasn't returned, he reached for it. In the same instant, the man grabbed Toby's rifle and pointed it at the boy.

"You will never get this letter back, and you'll never see my son again." His voice was harsh but barely audible.

Toby didn't move. "You can try to keep me away for a while, but not forever. I …"

And then Toby's words were cut off by the sound of his rifle being fired. A split second later, he was stumbling backward and bracing himself against the trunk of a birch tree.

"Forever," the man said after firing. He sauntered over to Toby.

Toby slid down the tree trunk and came to a stop in a seated position, his legs out in front of him, at the base of the tree. Tears streamed out of the boy's eyes, and he cried in agony. His hands gripped at his stomach where the bullet had entered, a large patch of red soaking through his shirt.

The man put the gun down on the ground next to Toby. "I'm no thief; you can keep your rifle. Oh … and here's your little fairy letter too. You can enjoy reading it in hell." The man spit at Toby and turned away.

Exerting what strength he could, Toby took up his firearm and pulled back the bolt, causing the empty shell to eject from the receiver and the next bullet to drop into place. He pushed the bolt forward, making the round enter the chamber. He pushed the bolt handle back over to the right-hand side of the stock, just over the trigger, and took the best aim he could. He fired. The bullet zoomed through the cold forest and into the back of H. K. Hildebrand's right thigh, along the side. The man fell to the ground and cried out in anguish. He picked himself up as Toby tried to work the bolt on his rifle to load the next bullet into the chamber, but his bloodied hands slipped and fumbled and he was unable to work the mechanism.

Having heard the shots, Tavis had begun to walk down the path to the deeper woods to see if his son had been able to drop the stag. Tavis was visibly shocked when he came around a turn in the path and saw Toby's legs sticking out in front of a tree, a trickle of blood in the path in front of him.

"Oh my lord," Tavis gasped as he saw his son, now very pale from blood loss, sitting propped against the tree. "What happened?"

"I … I …" but Toby couldn't speak strongly.

Tavis got down on the ground next to his son, taking off his jacket and putting it over the boy to keep him warm. "We've gotta get you to a doctor."

"H. K." Toby pointed to the hill.

"What? The vet? No, son, you need a real doctor. We'll take you up to Doc Lawson's. Get you all fixed up." Tavis tried to keep his voice calm and reassuring so as not to scare his son, but when he looked at the wound, he knew there would be only a short time before the boy bled to death.

Toby continued to point, and Tavis looked up. He saw H. K. Hildebrand on the hill, struggling to get up. A sudden realization dawned on the man. "He did this?" Tavis asked.

Toby whispered, "Yes."

Tavis ran up the hill to H. K. and yelled at the man, "What the hell have you done, you sonofabitch?"

"I saved my son from Satan's clutches," came the surly response as H. K. held onto the side of his wounded leg.

"What the hell are you talking about?"

"Your son is one of those perverted faggots I'm sure you've heard horror stories about. He tried to lure my Caleb into his sick world, so I had to stop him. You'd have done the same if you'd known."

"You don't know what you're talking about. After I get Toby to a doctor, I'm gonna come and get you. Mark my words."

"And you mark mine, Tavis. You so much as suggest that anything happened, I'll not only destroy you, but your whole family. A plague might take your livestock. Your house could burn down. And what if someone were to suggest that you took little Ivy out to the barn for more than just feeding the horsies."

Tavis staggered back. "You sick bastard."

"Your son is the sick one, and he had to be put down like a rabid dog, before his disease could spread. I warned him to stay away, but he refused … so he asked for this. I strongly advise you to consider your options carefully. He might have just enough time to repent, but I don't think that will save his wicked soul. As for you, Tavis, kill me, and you've got two dead bodies to account for … good luck explaining that one. You'll go to prison or hang, and you'll leave your family destitute. I can almost see your daughters whoring themselves now."

Tavis used the barrel of his shotgun to jab H. K. in the chest. When he crumpled to his knees, Tavis brought the butt of his shotgun down on his head. The man fell to the ground, unconscious.

Tavis ran back down the hill to his son.

Toby held in his hand a blood-soaked piece of paper. He pushed it toward his father.

"What's this?"

"Re … read."

"Want me to read it for you?"

Toby nodded.

"Okay. Do the best I can."

Tavis opened the letter and, trying not to smear it with the blood that was on his own hands, read:

My Dearest Caleb,

I am writing you this note so that you'll have something to remind you of how much I love you when we are apart. Of all the beautiful things I have seen in my life, the roses that grow wild in the meadows, the red-winged blackbirds that sing along the marsh, the sunsets that paint the horizon to look as though it is on fire, and the moon that shines its silver light on our waterfall, none of these things can come close to how beautiful you are to me. I loved you before I was born, and I will love you after I die. In between, we shall spend a lifetime together. You are the other half of my heart.

Love, Toby.

Tavis squinted his eyes as he refolded the letter. He put it in his shirt pocket and said, "That was beautiful, Toby. I never knew you were a poet."

Toby looked pleadingly into his father's eyes. "I love him, Dad. And he loves me. I'm not sick."

Tavis put his arm around his son and pulled him close. "I know you aren't, Toby. You're a good boy." Tavis was crying as he spoke. "You've got to fight now. We're going to get you some help."

Toby tried to smile. "Rather just stay here. It's so beautiful." Toby took his father's hand in his own. "I love you, Dad."

Tavis cried and held his son. "Please … you've got so much to live for. You simply must fight." Tavis placed his head on his son's chest and wept. "I love you, son."

Toby's breathing hitched and ceased. His eyes glassed over as they locked on their final vision. The large buck had returned and was standing up on the hill. Toby's hand still held his father's. Tavis pulled his son's limp body against him and moaned in grief. They were like that for some time.

During this time of mourning, Tavis must have been debating what to do. I can't imagine the inner turmoil he was going through. The sky was getting darker and the air colder. Tavis tucked his jacket around Toby carefully and said, "I have to go for a bit, but I'll be back. I won't leave you like this. I …" Tavis couldn't continue. He hurried away toward the clearing.

I walked over to the slain boy and knelt down beside him. I could feel his lifeless body next to me, and when I reached out, I could actually touch him. I sat in as close as I could to Toby and watched as the other guys gathered around him on the ground, too. None of us spoke. We just sat there with Toby, surrounding him with our heartfelt tears and our love until we could hear Tavis returning almost an hour and a half later.

The sky was nearly dark when Tavis came through the spruce trees with a shovel in one hand and a blanket in the other. He squatted down next to his son and spoke softly and tenderly to him. I couldn't make out the words he said, and I don't think I needed to hear them. That was meant to be a private moment.

Tavis gingerly wrapped his son in a red and black checkered blanket and carried him past us and down to the end of the path. We followed at a distance, even though we knew Tavis couldn't see us and our footsteps left no imprint.

Tavis took Toby down the hill behind the tree and went around a corner. On the other end of that short turn in the woods was a dense collection of wild rosebushes, growing in almost a perfect ring. Tavis took his boy to the far side of that area and then rested the body on the ground. He went back to the path and returned a few minutes later with the shovel. He crawled under the rosebushes with the shovel and began to dig in the centre. It was a perfect spot. No one would ever look in the middle of a clump of thorny rosebushes for Toby's body—but I don't think it's why Tavis chose the location. I believe he opted for the place within the roses because Toby would be buried in the forest he loved under the flower whose beauty he wrote of. In the summer, he would be covered with the crimson blooms and the fragrant odour they emitted, and all the year long, the thorns would protect his resting place from animals that might otherwise disturb him.

Tavis spent a long time in the centre of the roses before he emerged and took his son inside the thicket. We could hear Tavis sobbing as he prepared to lay his son to rest. We all got down on our stomachs and looked under the branches to see Tavis cradling his son's lifeless form. He put Toby's head on his shoulder and rocked back and forth, brushing the boy's hair and singing, ever so softly, the first verse of a hymn I would later learn was called "God Sees the Little Sparrow Fall."

Tavis stayed there all night long, holding his son. When the dawn broke, he kissed Toby on the forehead and gently laid the boy in his grave. Although I witnessed it, I can't fully appreciate the excruciating agony that Tavis felt. As he piled earth over his precious son's body, I could tell that his sanity was within inches of leaving him forever. When he crawled out from under the thorns—dirty, bloody, and looking as though he had died too—he stumbled to his feet and began to make his way back to the hidden path. We followed and kept going all the way to the clearing, where he stopped and removed his soiled clothing, burning it in a small fire. He cleaned himself in the frigid waters of the stream and changed into items he had carried in a small sack. He made sure to remove his son's letter to Caleb before tossing his shirt on the flames. He sat and read the letter over and over as his clothing burned.

When there was nothing more than ash left in the fire, Tavis kicked the black sooty mound into the stream and started up the path toward home. When he got to the threshold, he stopped, took a deep breath, and stepped into the meadow. When we saw him enter the house, the sky darkened, and the wind picked up. Snow began to fall, and it quickly accumulated enough to cover the ground.

"Ryley, hand me a flashlight," Blake said.

Ryley took off his backpack and grabbed a torch, handing it to Blake. My brother turned the light on, and we knew that we were back in our own time.

Caleb

Hearing my name being called out was the last thing I had expected. I turned around, and there, standing directly in the path before us, stood Toby Everett.

"Toby, we know what happened, and we're going to make sure other people do too," I told him.

The boy smiled at me.

"That's what you wanted, right?"

The boy's smile faded, and he cocked his head to one side ever so slightly.

Caleb

He repeated the name softly and turned to go.

"Wait, Toby. Wait!" I called out and ran after him. But he had vanished, and I found myself alone in the dark woods. I went back to where the others stood, and we made our way over the brook and back to the house.

Up in my room, Shane was the first to say anything. He sat next to me at the head of my bed and said, "Strange, isn't it? You think you have everything all figured out, and that's when you realize you don't know a damn thing."

We nodded and mumbled in agreement. "What's even stranger," Ryley added, "is that, according to the clock, we were only gone for four hours. It was way longer than that … wasn't it?"

"I'm too tired to even think right now," Blake said. "Let's talk about everything tomorrow."

When we had all gone to bed, I heard Shane whisper, "Seeing Tavis hold Toby like that …" His voice cut off, and I turned to see Shane crying. "I miss my dad so much."

I pulled Shane's head onto my chest and held him, letting his tears slide down my skin. I kissed the top of his head and ran a hand through his hair. After some time, we both fell asleep.

Chapter Twenty-One

The following week at school, I found it hard to concentrate on my work and my classes. I would sit at my desk and stare blankly at my textbooks and binders, replaying the events I witnessed in the woods again and again on those pages.

At home, I sat at my desk and attempted to work on an English essay that I hadn't been able to put much thought into. I became frustrated with it and threw my blue Uni-ball pen at the wall. I folded my arms at my chest and leaned back in my chair. "Screw this," I muttered as I got up from my seat.

I headed down to the kitchen for a change of scenery. Dad was coming up from the basement at the same time as I sat down on a stool at the island.

"Hey, sport. Whatcha doin'?" he asked.

"Getting frustrated with my essay. You?"

Dad set a jar of pickles he'd retrieved from the cellar on the counter before leaning against the fridge and asking, "What's it on?"

"Poetry. We're supposed to pick our favourite poem and discuss its meaning, and then do a short biography of the author."

"That doesn't sound too bad. I've always liked poetry; maybe I can give you a hand."

I was shocked. My father had never mentioned liking poetry or offered to help me with an assignment before.

"Don't look so surprised."

"Sorry, it's just ... well ... do you have a favourite?" I asked, intrigued.

Dad shook his head. "Not just one. Dozens. I'll see if I can find my favourite collection. I know it's probably still packed away in one of the boxes somewhere. When's the essay due?"

"End of next week."

"Okay. Plenty of time."

Blake thundered down the stairs and into the kitchen. "Hey, guys. I'm making fettuccini with mushroom sauce and garlic bread tonight, so give us a hand or ...," Blake pointed to the door and snapped his fingers. He was in a very good mood, and his energy, as always, was infectious.

"I'll help," I offered.

"Cool. Thanks, little bro." Blake ruffled my hair as he passed behind me.

"I've gotta do some digging around downstairs," Dad said. "Call me when it's ready."

I hopped off my stool and took out a knife so I could start dicing up an onion. Blake was whistling as he went about getting supplies.

"All right, so what gives? Why are you so happy?"

"Am I that transparent?" Blake chuckled.

"Not at all."

"Heh. Well, I just got off the phone with Clark, and his sister is best friends with Alicia Hawthorne, who just happens to be one of the hottest girls in grade eleven."

"Cradle robber."

"Pfft. Whatever, man. She's a total fox, and she's got a thing for yours truly."

"Oh, is she the blind girl?"

"Very funny."

"So ...?"

"So, anyway, I called her up and asked her to the dance next Friday."

"I take it she said yes."

"In fact, she did." Blake smirked.

"Whatever happened with Vicki?"

"Meh. She was nice to look at but not so nice to be with. Very high maintenance, with a nasty mean streak. Funny thing is, now I don't even find her attractive cuz I know her."

"So what's this Alicia girl like?"

"I've only talked to her a few times when the gang's at Clark's and his sister has her friends over too, which is, more than coincidentally, almost every time."

"Interesting."

"Yeah. So, anyway, we've hung out a little, and she seems like a total sweetheart."

"That's awesome."

Blake grinned. "So you and your boy goin' to the dance?"

"I dunno. We'll probably go but end up being miserable the whole time we're there, as usual."

"That sucks. Wish I could make it easier for you."

"Thanks."

"I mean it, bud." Blake walked over to me as I chopped up some mushrooms and squeezed my shoulder with his hand for a second. He didn't say anything more. He didn't have to.

We kept working at getting dinner ready and talked about sports, cars, and school. Blake offered me some good advice about my English essay.

"Look, you can always do the basic essay the teachers are used to getting all the time, you know, the typical poem with a bland analysis that'll net you a seventy. Or you can do what the friggin' brainy kids do and pick a more obscure poem and make up a bunch of bullshit about it and back it up with credible sources and get a mark in the high eighties or low nineties—as long as the teacher doesn't find it pretentious. God, like when you hear someone reading their essay and it feels so forcefully smart, like they wrote it with a thesaurus, that you actually almost puke right there in class … you wanna make sure you avoid doing that."

I laughed. "Yeah, I hate that. So, what do you suggest I try?"

"What are the guidelines?"

"To take any poem written before we were born and analyze it, along with an author's bio."

"All right, so what you do is this: find a poem you wanna use and make the author's biography the reasoning behind why the poem was written."

"I'm not sure I follow."

"Okay, say you pick something by, I dunno, Walt Whitman, and then you take info about Whitman's life and tie that info into the poem—make them connect. It's still bullshitting, but it's smart bullshitting."

"Good plan," I said, impressed. "How'd you think of that?"

"You gotta read more into what the teacher tells you than what's on the assignment page. Why else would he tell you to have a biography of the author if he didn't want you to use it in your poem analysis? What your teacher wants to see is whether you're smart enough to figure that part out. If you are, even if the essay isn't great, the extra effort will pay off in a better mark."

"Wow. I'm impressed, Blake. That's a great idea. Thanks."

Blake smiled. "No prob, bud. Now all you gotta do is find a poem to use."

"Yeah. I'll see what I can dig up after dinner."

Dad hadn't had any luck in finding the book he was looking for in the boxes downstairs. I read through a number of books that he did find, but still nothing leaped out at me. I gave up my search for the evening and called Shane before going to bed.

In the morning, after I had eaten breakfast, I went to the last bookcase in the house, hoping to find the perfect poem. I walked over to the living room and pulled the last remaining book of poetry in the house from the built-in shelf at the side of the fireplace. The fireplace was set out from the wall, having been put in after the house was built. The chimney ran up inside the house as opposed to outside and formed the wall at the end of the hallway by my room. At the sides of the fireplace were vents to allow heat to enter the room at the sides, as well as from the front. Above the vents were bookcases on either side, but we only used one side for books. Mom displayed her pink Coalport china on the other side.

I opened the softcover blue book entitled *The Albatross Book of Living Verse* and skimmed over the list of authors in the table of contents. I found a few poems I liked inside the worn tome but nothing that really grabbed me. I was beginning to think it wasn't so much the poems, as the person reading them, that was the problem. I was probably putting too much thought into the whole process. Most kids I know wouldn't bother to expend the energy, picking the first poem they could find that wasn't long and going from there. I just couldn't do that. I like English too much to not care. I tossed the book on the end table next to where I sat on the sofa and sighed loudly.

"Still no luck, huh?" Mom asked as she came into the room.

"No. I'm at a total loss."

"Would you like me to pick some books up at the library for you?"

"No, thanks. I'll find something that'll do here."

Mom sat down on the recliner to the left of the couch.

"Caleb, would you be a dear and lay a fire?"

"Oh, sure." I got up from my seat and went over to the large wicker basket by the hearth that the logs and papers were sitting in. I crumpled up some newspaper and put it all around the inside of the fireplace before adding some kindling and then one large piece of wood. I took the matches from the mantle and struck one of the Seadogs against the box. I took the flame and held it to the newspaper in various spots, beginning at the back and moving forward. When I was done, I flicked the wooden matchstick in the fire and listened as it all began to crackle and snap. I returned the matches to the mantle and sat back down, my hands blackened from the newspaper ink.

"Thanks, hon. It's so nice to have a cozy fire on dreary days like this."

"No problem."

The room began to warm up nicely. The orange glow from the fire reminded me of the sunsets back in the summer.

"This is only the second fire we've had here, isn't it?" my mother said.

I thought about it. "Yeah, I guess it is." It felt strange that this was the case. It seemed so recently that I had last heard the snap of a fire.

"It works well. I had been a bit afraid that the chimney might smoke, but your father said it was clean."

"Huh?" My mind was drifting.

"I said it's drawing well. The fire."

"Oh, yeah. It is."

"You okay?"

"Umm, yeah. Just trying to figure this poem thing out."

"Maybe Shane can help you."

"He's not in English this semester."

"Well, he still might have some books he could lend you."

"No, I don't think so."

We listened to the fire, watching the flames dance over the wood, hearing the sizzle of burning bark.

"Haven't seen him around this weekend. You two are okay, aren't you?"

"Yeah. We're awesome. We just both have a lot of schoolwork to catch up on. Not that I'm getting anything accomplished."

"Maybe you need some fresh air to clear your head. Go for a walk. Who knows? Maybe inspiration will come to you."

"Yeah. Good idea. Anything's worth a shot."

I added another log to the fire and went to the porch. I put on my coat and gloves and headed out the door. Without giving it a second thought, I found myself walking along the trail to the stream, crossing it, and starting my way into the woods.

I hadn't been alone in the woods for a very long time. I checked my watch, finding it just past noon. I made my way to the clearing and sat down on the fallen tree, like I had so many times before. Thoughts of the last few months of my life raced through my head. So much had happened, and there was still so much more to do.

I heard the sound of someone coming down the hill to the clearing, and I looked over my shoulder expecting to see Blake, but it wasn't my brother. Toby walked along the path and right up to me, looking alive and healthy. He sat down on the log beside me and took a pencil and a pad of paper from his back pocket. The air around me grew warmer, and there was a soft golden hue all around Toby that spread over to me and eventually enveloped the entire clearing. I had to take my coat off as I began to perspire in the summer weather.

I kept hoping Toby would say something to me, that this time he could really talk to me. He put the pencil down on the paper, resting them on the log next to him, and cracked his knuckles. He sat down on the ground in front of where he had been sitting before and took the paper and pencil into his lap. He leaned back against the log and brought his knees up so he could use his thighs as a table to write on. He bit the end of his stubby pencil for a moment and said, *"My dearest Caleb,"* as he wrote down the words. *"I am writing you this note because ...* no," and he scratched out the word *"because." "I am writing you this note so that you will have something to remind you of how much I love you when we are apart."* Toby tapped his pen against the paper. "Hmmm ... Ummm ..." He began to write again: *"Of all the beautiful things I have seen in my life, the roses that grow wild in the meadows ...* What else do I like?... Umm ... *the red-winged blackbirds that sing along the marsh ...* something else, something else ... umm ... oh ... *the sunsets that paint the horizon to look as though it is on fire, and ... and the moon that shines its silver light on our waterfall ... none of these things can come close to how beautiful you are to me.* Now what do I say? I want him to feel really special." Toby tapped his pencil against his lips. "Umm ... *If we* ... no, that's not right." He scratched *"If we"* out. *"I loved you before I was born, and I will love you long after I die ...* no ... wait ..." He scratched out *"long."* "I'll love him forever. *Long* makes it sound like it will stop at some point. Okay ... *love you after I die. In between, we shall spend a lifetime together.* Is 'life time' one word or two? I better make it one word. *You are the other half of my heart. Love, Toby."* He hit the pencil hard against the paper to make a period to his letter. "There. Now I'll just redo it neatly."

I watched as Toby rewrote the letter on a fresh piece of paper. When he finished, he kissed the note and folded it carefully. "I love you, Caleb," he said and stood up, smiling. He returned his pencil and paper to his pocket and headed back to the hill. A moment later, he was out of sight. The warmth and the glow began to leave too. I put my coat and gloves back on as the summer colours retracted up the path and left me back in the cold, dreary November afternoon.

I looked around the woods from my seat, rubbing my hands together trying to keep them from going numb. I decided it was too cold to stay any longer, so I stood up and stuffed my hands in my coat pockets. A breeze snuck across the clearing, and I heard a rustling sound. I glanced down at the ground where Toby had been and saw a piece of paper. I stepped on it to keep the wind from taking it and bent down to retrieve it. I couldn't believe what I held in my hand—the rough copy of Toby's letter to Caleb. I read it over and over before tucking it into my inner coat pocket. Smiling, I said to the forest, "Thank you, Toby." I had found my poem.

I stayed up late, writing my essay well into the night. I needed all of the two thousand words (plus or minus 10 percent—I used the plus) to complete my assignment for Mr. Drexell. When I was finished, as with any English assignment, I realized I hadn't done it for Mr. Drexell—I'd done it for me. And in the case of that particular essay, I'd written it for my friends and, most importantly, for Toby.

I crawled into bed sometime after one and placed Toby's letter in my nightstand with the horseshoe. I decided I'd write Shane a note sometime as I snapped out my light. I went to sleep thinking about my boyfriend.

⌒

"Whoa, whoa, whoa, hold up a second here. You mean to tell me you actually found Toby's rough copy of his note to Caleb?" Ryley asked, flabbergasted. We were at Stape's after school having a coffee with Shane while we waited for Blake to finish his volleyball practice.

"Yep," I replied and took a sip of my java.

"Wow. This is a new dimension," Shane said.

Ryley pointed at him. "Exactly."

"But it doesn't really surprise me," Shane stated. "I mean, think about it; even after we learned the truth, Toby still appeared in the path and called for Caleb. Didn't it strike either of you as odd how close he was to us that night? How real he looked? Nothing else was different that time. Nothing in our time changed other than Toby being there. It was almost like …"

"He was in our time," I finished.

"Right."

"Hope you put that letter someplace safe," Ryley said.

"Yeah. I'll show you when you guys come over this weekend."

"Speaking of that, mind if we change locations to my place?" Shane asked.

"No prob. Everything cool?" Ryley asked.

"Not really. I mean, everything's okay, just Mom is having one of her really bad downtimes, and I'm kinda looking after the motel. We won't get any guests probably, but I wanna be there to keep it open, just in case."

"Your mom gonna be okay?" I wanted to know.

Shane fiddled with his cup, spinning it in its saucer. "Yeah, eventually. She just gets times when everything is too overwhelming. It used to happen once in a great while, but since Dad died, it's been a coupla times a year. She's on meds, but they don't always do enough."

"You sure you still want us to come over?" Ryley asked.

"Absolutely. I've been staying out in Room Twelve so I can keep from disturbing Mom while she's resting. It'll give us a good chance to talk things over."

Blake pulled up front with the Bronco, and we saw him get out and head to the door. He joined us at the table moments later.

"Hey, fellas. Sorry I was a bit later than I intended. Had to talk to Alicia for a bit."

"Oh, you poor guy," Ryley teased.

"Got plans for after the dance, Blake?" Shane asked.

"Nothing official ... but I'm hoping."

"All right, well, if you want, we're all hanging out at my place after. You can come and crash with us if you want. We're staying down in Room Twelve."

"Right on. Thanks. I'll be there. Okay if I show kinda late?"

"Yeah. Whenever. We just need to all sit down and talk ... about a bunch of stuff."

Blake nodded. "Good idea." He stood and took the keys from his jeans pocket. "We should get going, bud. Game comes on in an hour."

"All right. You guys wanna lift?"

"Nah. Thanks. Think I'll stick here for a bit," Ryley said.

"Yeah. Me too. Talk to you tonight, Caleb," Shane replied.

"Okay. Later, guys."

"See ya, boys," Blake said.

My brother and I headed out to the Bronco and started for home.

Blake dropped me off at Shane's before the dance Friday night. I went down to Room Twelve, but not finding Shane there, I knocked on the back door of the house.

"Come in, Caleb. Come in," Mrs. Radnor called from inside, waving me in.

I opened the metal door and heard its loud creak as the hinges moved. I stepped inside the back porch and closed the door.

"Don't worry about your shoes," she said as I began to untie one of my brown Doc Martens.

"You sure?"

"Yes. Come in, come in. Let's have a look at you."

I stepped up the three stairs into the kitchen after hanging my jacket on a hook inside the back door.

"Oh my, don't you look handsome," she said.

"Thanks." I smiled at her. "How are you?" I asked the question in a typical, everyday fashion.

"I'm super, thanks. How 'bout you?"

"Couldn't be better."

She tried to make her forced smile seem natural, but I could tell it was taking all of her strength to act normal.

"Shane still getting ready?"

"Yes, he must have tried on at least six different shirts by now."

"Not that it makes any difference," Shane mumbled as he came into the room, playing with a button on his navy shirt. He stopped in his tracks when he looked up at me. "Whoa." I blushed instantly, though I must admit I felt pretty damn good at the reaction I'd gotten. "You look amazing," Shane stated and came right over to me to give me a hug.

"You too," I said as I feasted over him with my eyes. "Sexy," I whispered in his ear.

"You both look wonderful," his mother told us. "I need to get a picture."

"Ahh, Mom," Shane groaned, but his mother had already scurried down the hall. "Sorry, it's just easier to let her get it out of her system," he told me.

"No problem. How's she doing anyway?"

"She's putting on a good show right now, but she'll be in bed the moment we leave."

Felicia came rushing back up the hall with her camera. "Okay, guys, scooch together." We did as instructed and stood side by side. "Oh, come on now, you look like soldiers. Relax already."

We laughed, and Shane put his arm around my waist, pulling me closer to him. We looked at each other, smiling warmly, and then I felt the sting in my eyes from the flash having gone off.

"Ooo, that's a nice one," Felicia exclaimed, checking the view screen on the digital camera.

"Well, we better get going," Shane said. "We're meeting the gang out front, right?"

"Yeah, far as I know."

"Cool. Okay, we're off, Mom. Be back before midnight."

"All right. Have fun. Need any money?"

"No, thanks. We'll be fine."

Shane led me down the steps, where we put on our jackets. I headed out first, saying good-bye to Mrs. Radnor. Shane said something to her at the door and then stood by my side. Astro gave a playful bark from his large fenced-in yard. We proceeded to the school, where some of our friends had already gathered on the front steps.

I hated when we got to school because we had to pretend again. We had to talk as if we weren't anything more than friends. We'd be able to dance with any girl who wanted to dance with us, but not with each other. My mood dropped into a dark place as we entered the gym. I was angry at myself for letting other people's prejudices influence my right to be happy. I sat out most of the dances, just sitting on the benches along the auditorium wall and listening to the music while the happy couples danced under the glitter ball.

"What's up, Caleb?" Moira said, sitting down beside me.

"I'm just in a crappy mood."

"Aww." She held my upper arm with both hands. "Isn't there someone you wanna dance with?"

"Yeah, there is. That's the problem."

"Oh, you poor thing, who is it? No, no, no. I still haven't guessed from last time. Just tell me this much … is it the same person?"

"Yeah."

Moira squealed with delight. "Okay, okay, okay. I betcha I know. It's Dawn, isn't it?"

"Nope."

"Hmmm ... all right ... let me think ... oh, I know, it's Tracy, right? It's Tracy, isn't it? Tell me, tell me."

I shook my head. "No, it's not Tracy."

"Wow. You've got me stumped here, Caleb. Is it someone in our grade at least?"

"Yeah."

"Okay ... someone in your homeroom?"

"Yes."

"Oh my God ... is it Laura?" We looked out on the dance floor, where Laura was dancing with Shane.

"Close," I said.

Moira wriggled in her seat and asked excitedly, "How close?"

I watched them dancing and said, "Umm, well, I'd say about ten ... no, make that eight inches."

Moira looked at them and noticed a couple dancing close to Shane and Laura. "You mean Fran? I never woulda thought her your type."

"She's not," I almost laughed.

"Well, there's no one else that close to Laura except Shane."

I let Moira's words sit there for her to think about for a second. Then I felt her gripping down on my arm harder than before. "Oh my God. You mean ...?

"What?" I didn't know how Moira was going to react, and at that point, I didn't really care.

"Are you gay, Caleb?" she asked in a whisper.

"Yeah."

She leaned in to my side and reached her left hand around my back and squeezed me. "That's so cool."

I chuckled, inwardly relieved. "Well, it works for me."

"Does Shane know you fancy him?"

"Fancy?"

"Oh, sorry. I've been talking a lot online with my cousin in England. Guess I'm picking up her lingo."

"I'd love to go to England someday."

"Yeah? Me too. Actually I think I am going next summer if everything works out."

"You're lucky."

"Well, it's just gonna be the airfare, cuz I can stay with my relatives while I'm there. They live in this little town called Barrows-in-Furness. Isn't that cute? Anyway, my cousin—she's in university and really cool—is going to take me around, show me the sites as well as all the English hotties."

"You dig English guys?"

"Oh, yeah. I am such a sucker for accents." Moira poked me in the side. "Hey, you never answered my question. Does Shane know you like him?"

"Yeah."

"And?" she prodded.

"Umm, well, he's my best friend ... I guess he's kinda flattered."

Moira nodded. "He should be."

The music changed, and Moira's eyes lit up. "Oh my God, I love this song. C'mon, you've gotta dance with me," she said as she grabbed my hand and pulled me to the floor as Katy Perry sang "Firework."

After the dance, we all went outside to the front walk to hang out for a bit. Moira said quietly to me, "You ever wanna talk, let me know."

"Thanks. I appreciate that. I'm pretty lucky cuz I can talk to my family and a few friends."

"Oh, you're out to your family? That must be a relief."

"You have no idea. But it's really nice to know I have friends I can talk to, too."

Moira smiled at me. "You're a sweet guy, Caleb. You're gonna make some boy very happy."

"He already has," Shane said as he walked over to me. The only people left milling around were our group, minus Hunter, who had gone away for the weekend. Shane took the opportunity to give me a gentle kiss on the cheek.

Moira put a hand on her heart. "Oh my God, that is so sweet."

"I know. Aren't they adorable?" Adria said as she leaned back against Ryley.

"Are you kidding me right now?!" Laura spewed.

"Whoa, Laura. Easy," Ryley said.

"No, no, no. This can't be happening. Why are all the cute guys either already dating or gay? I have the worst luck. And to think I danced with you half the night … no wonder you didn't grab my ass at all," Laura said in a mock rage directed at Shane.

All of us laughed.

"Umm … you know, Laura," Drew stammered, "I woulda grabbed your ass."

Laura turned, put her hands on her hips, and replied, "Drew Harrison, is that your way of trying to tell me something?"

Drew smirked shyly. "Umm, I dunno."

"Well, you never even asked me to dance … what gives?"

"Every time I tried to, I got too nervous and bailed. 'Sides, I figured I had pretty stiff competition with Shane, and I didn't want to chance messing up any of our friendships."

"Oh my God, Drew. That's so thoughtful," Moira gushed.

"Yeah," Shane confirmed.

"So … look … we never wanted to lie to you guys …" I started to explain.

"Whoa, Caleb. You don't need to explain anything," Laura said. "We're all friends here."

"Yeah. We're happy when our friends are happy," Adria added.

"You guys all seriously rock," I told them.

"Whattaya think Hunter will say?" Shane asked Drew.

Drew shrugged. "I dunno, but if it's anything bad, I'll drop him."

Laura's eyes grew large, and she smiled at Drew as she said, "I gotta ask you guys, are you both ready to be out at school?"

I shrugged my shoulders and looked to Shane. He reacted the same way.

"I guess we'll just be ourselves. We're not gonna have a pride parade down the main hallway, but I'm tired of hiding," Shane said.

"Yeah. If it comes up, we'll deal with it. Otherwise, it's life as usual," I replied.

"But I think I can safely say for both of us, we'd appreciate it if it was on our terms and no one said anything to anyone outside the group. Okay?"

"Hey, not an issue," Laura said. "Was just kinda hoping to get to see you guys maybe make out a little. That'd be so hot."

We laughed. "Maybe later," Shane joked.

"Guys, I know we've never been as tight as I've been with Hunter, but you gotta know, I'd never do anything to hurt my friends … right?" Drew asked.

"Yeah, man," Shane answered.

I had a totally newfound respect for Drew that night. I was disappointed in myself that I hadn't seen what a good guy he was before.

"Just, well, one question I have, though," Drew said. "Do you want me to kinda gauge Hunter's reaction before he knows? Like sorta bring it up in a nonspecific kinda way?"

"Do whatever you feel is best," I told him. "I trust you."

Drew smiled. "Cool."

"I don't know about any of the rest of you, but I need a caffeine fix," Adria said.

We all agreed and began to walk toward Stape's. Laura walked by Drew, and I noticed she took his hand in hers. Apparently Moira, who was walking next to Shane and me, noticed it too.

"Goddamn it, would you look at that. Now there are four good-looking guys, and not one is interested in me. I sure hope that hot blond guy is working at Stape's tonight. I need some eye candy."

We left Laura and Drew still talking over lattes at Stape's (where the blond guy was working … and was definitely cute. Moira chatted him up a bit and found out his name was Wyatt) as the rest of us headed out. We walked the girls home and then went back to the motel.

The air was chilly, but clear, and I breathed it in greedily. The stars were bright and the constellations easily detectable (providing you knew how to find them—all I could ever find was the Big Dipper).

"I know we talked about it before but what do you guys think really happens after we die?" Ryley asked us as he looked up at the stars.

"Sure. I guess we all do that," I said.

"I never really thought about death until my dad died," Shane said. "I mean, when you're a kid, it's not usually something that you think about that much. But after my dad died, I started thinking about where he was. I know some people think when you're dead, that's it, and for a while I believed that. Actually, I believed that right up till that night in your room, Caleb. Death was the end of all the pain and the hurt. Everything just went away. But that can't be true if Toby is still here. I don't know if he's totally here or not, but enough of him is that makes me believe there is definitely something more to us than merely a body."

"I've always believed in heaven," I said. "Maybe it's just that it's such a comforting concept that I believe it exists. It's hard to know."

"I went to church growing up, so I kinda got brainwashed into the whole heaven/hell thing, but I'm not so sure about that anymore," Ryley told us. "I mean, if it's so cut-and-dried, then how do you explain Toby?"

None of us had an answer to that. The question floated away into the frosty night. We turned into the parking area of the Kelly Street Motel and approached Room Twelve.

We flicked through the channels on the television before turning it off again. The remote control was bolted to the nightstand between the double beds, and the TV itself had an off-switch on the wall like a light. The two beds had brown and green patterned bedspreads that went nicely with the taupe walls and dark green framed prints and carpeting.

"Can we get some room service?" I teased Shane.

"With our low rates, you serve yourself," Shane replied with a grin.

"You guys wanna wait for Blake before we discuss anything about Toby?" Ryley asked.

"Yeah, probably a good idea. No point in saying everything twice," I said.

"Wanna play cards or something?" Shane asked us.

"Sure, anything to kill some time," Ryley said as he paced around the room.

"You all right, man?"

Ryley was biting his nails. "Yeah, yeah. I'm fine. I just, I dunno, I just wanna keep my mind off Toby until we're ready to talk about the situation, and that's hard to do ... as you both know."

"No kidding, huh?" Shane grabbed a deck of cards from the nightstand drawer. "Here, sit down, and we'll play gin or something."

Ryley sat down on the end of the bed, and Shane dealt the cards out. I kept score on the pad of paper provided by the motel, and we played until there was a knock on the door, shortly before one o'clock.

"Hey, fellas," Blake said as he came in and took off his jacket. "Whatcha been doin'?"

"Just playing cards," I answered.

"Cool." Blake sat down in one of the two chairs at the small round table by the window. They were firm, hard-backed chairs with brown cloth, almost tweed, upholstery on the seats. "Anything to drink in here?"

"No. Sorry. Gotta hit the Coke machine in the breezeway between Six and Seven if you want anything."

"I've got something," Ryley said and went for his bag that he'd dropped off earlier in the afternoon. He rummaged around in his blue Nike duffle and retrieved a bottle of bourbon.

"Hello … where'd you get that?" Blake asked, sounding both impressed and a tad worried at the same time.

"My dad has a case of this stuff in the basement, and he has no idea how many bottles are in it, so I took one." Ryley twisted the top off the bottle of Jack Daniels and took a swig. He grimaced and offered it to me.

I took a sniff. "God, man, this smells awful."

"Yeah, tastes like crap too, but you get used to it," Ryley said.

"Rye, man, you drink very often?" Blake casually asked him.

Ryley shook his head. "No. Don't start thinking I'm an alcoholic or anything."

I held the neck of the bottle in my left hand. I wasn't sure I wanted to drink it because if it tasted half as bad as its odour indicated, I'd be tossing it up seconds after I swallowed it.

As if reading my thoughts, Ryley went on to say, "Look, it's not as if I'm trying to be cool or anything. No one has to drink who doesn't want to. I just thought we've all been pretty stressed and maybe we could use a drink. Dumb, right?"

"No, it's not dumb," I said and took a drink. I shivered and felt my stomach roll and my throat burn as I handed the bottle over to Shane without saying a word. He took a swig but didn't react as I had—he just sat there with a tired look on his face I hadn't seen before.

"You all right?" I asked him.

"Yeah." He handed the bottle to Blake. "I'm just worn-out."

Blake took a glug and set the bottle down on the table. "I think we all are," he said. "I mean, here we are, three of us fifteen and the other seventeen, and I don't think one of us feels his age. We've all been through so much shit, and here we are drinking whiskey, about to have a conversation about a kid who was murdered. Is it me, or is everything fucked up?"

"Things are as they are for a reason," Shane said flatly. "I don't pretend to know why, and I don't bother to question it anymore. All I know is that we're here to help a kid who can't help himself."

Blake nodded. "You're right. Let's figure out what we gotta do next."

We began by going over everything we knew for certain, and then we started to discuss the various possibilities for our next course of action. By 3:00 a.m., we still weren't sure of our next move.

"Maybe I need to go back to the woods alone," I said.

"I dunno, Caleb. Seems to me that there's gotta be something you do before he's gonna tell you anything more. He gave you the letter and ..." Shane froze, his face showing that he had thought of something no one else had considered before. "I know what you have to do. You've gotta get that letter to Wendell."

"You think?"

"Sure, think about it. Wendell's dad found it and took it, and Wendell never got it, right?"

"Yeah."

"Okay then, I think it's time he did."

"But how are we gonna find Wendell? All we know is that he lives in Halifax," Ryley said.

"We'll try online. If that doesn't work, we'll go to the nursing home. They've gotta have his address on file," Shane said.

"Sun'll be up soon," Blake noted. "We better get some sleep. Who knows, we might end up in Halifax tomorrow."

We were on the road by eight, tired from a lack of sleep but too anxious to wait. We stopped at Stape's for coffee before going home so I could pick up the letter. To my dismay, it wasn't to be found.

"Are you sure it was in your desk drawer?" Blake asked, checking the spot again after I had looked in it for the tenth time.

"Yes. Positive. I only had it out to work on my essay that one night, and then I put it in the drawer the next morning." I went over to the desk for another check. Then it hit me. "Oh wait, I had it on my nightstand for a while too. I musta put it in my drawer."

I went over and opened the drawer in the stand next to my bed. I pushed pens and papers and magazines around trying to find the paper. I took each magazine out and shook it in case the note was caught between the pages.

"What was that?" Shane asked as I shook one of his copies of *XY* that I had borrowed.

"What was what?"

"Something fell out and went under the bed."

I felt around under the bed, and my hand landed on something crinkly. I slid it out, expecting the paper to be under my fingers, but it wasn't. I picked up the item and showed it to the guys. They all took a look at an oak leaf.

"Is that another sign?" Ryley asked.

"I guess," I replied.

"What's it supposed to mean?"

"Maybe the rough copy of the note isn't what we're after," Shane suggested. We all looked to him for further explanation. "I mean, why would Toby want Wendell to have the scratched-up rough copy?"

"So what are you saying? We're supposed to get the original somehow?" Ryley wanted to know. "It probably doesn't even exist anymore."

"Oh, I'm pretty sure it does," Blake said. "You two check this room over thoroughly, and we'll check the loft in the barn. Odds are if it's anywhere, it's in one of those two places."

"Good thinking," I told him, and we split up.

Shane and I scoured my room, running our hands over the walls to feel for any soft spots. We pressed floorboards for looseness and examined every nook and cranny in my closet, only to find dust bunnies and a few pennies.

"It's not here. Save for tearing down the walls and ripping off the mouldings, we're not going to find it," I said.

"Yeah. Let's go see if they've had any luck in the barn."

I followed Shane down the stairs and stopped suddenly when I heard that familiar squeak in the middle step. I don't know how I knew, but I knew that the note was there if it was anywhere.

"You coming?" Shane asked, turning to see me standing on the centre step.

"Of course. It all makes sense," I muttered to myself.

"What?" Shane started back up the stairs, stopping two down from me.

"When I felt a cold breeze on the steps, it always started here, and when I heard Toby that night, it was the step I heard first. He was trying to tell me then, and I didn't even register it. The note is under the step."

"But, Caleb, Toby was dead when Tavis put the note away. And why would he hide it? I mean, why not burn it if you're worried someone's gonna find it, and if you're not, then why put it where no one can find it?"

"Because someone would eventually find it. That squeaky step was bound to be fixed at some point, and when it was, the note would be discovered."

"Okay, but that step has never been mentioned in any of the stories, and Royce never told Mom anything about a step squeaking either. Maybe it didn't start to squeak until you guys moved in."

I smirked, thinking back to the night I was witness to Toby sneaking out to the barn to meet Wendell—the step had squeaked.

"Trust me, it's always squeaked. I'm gonna get a crowbar and a hammer."

I jogged over to the basement door to get the tool chest. My father had moved it from its usual place inside the door on the shelf leading down the stairs, so I went down the steps to find it. As I spotted my tool kit against the far wall, I heard the door shut at the top of the stairs. I counted to ten, waiting for the lights to go out, but they didn't. I walked up the steps and turned the knob. The door opened easily, and I returned to the stairwell.

The step was nailed down tight, and I knew that to get it off, I would risk splintering the wood. I knew I had as much time as I needed, but there was this frenzied rush inside me telling me to *get inside, get inside, get inside.* I put down my tools for a moment to catch my breath and force myself to slow down. The last thing I wanted was to rush and take the chance of damaging what might be inside the step.

Blake and Ryley ran through the kitchen door behind Shane. The back door crashed to a close, as no one held it. I was glad my parents were both at work that morning, because there would be no rationale as to why I was "fixing" the step when my friends were over and absolutely no way to explain why they all watched with great anticipation while I worked.

I took the crowbar back in my hand and worked it under the lip of the step. I pounded the corner of the bar with my hammer and listened carefully until I began to hear that stringy, fibrey sound of wood splitting and pulling. The elastic sound of the riser lifting off the frame was exciting, and I had to slow myself once more.

The board lifted higher and higher until I was able to get my hammer under it and hit it from the centre, then one end, then the other, until I heard a pleasing *thunk,* and the riser fell toward me, the nails pointing at my torso as it tumbled back. I took the step board and handed it to Shane. He placed it beside the banister, and then I turned to see what I had uncovered.

"Do you see anything?" Ryley asked.

I was blocking my own light and couldn't see a thing. "I need a flashlight. There should be one in the tool kit," I said, pointing at the green chest on the floor in the hall. Blake opened it and grabbed the yellow snake light. He passed it to me through the railings, and I clicked it on, focusing the light into the darkened crevice.

I put my hand down and felt around. "That's odd," I mumbled.

"What?" Shane asked.

"The frame for the step is narrower than I expected. It should be ..." and then my hand felt the side I thought was too narrow, and it moved slightly.

"What is it? You find something?" Blake eagerly wanted to know.

"Maybe. Hang on." I set the light down in the step and pushed against the narrow side. There was a clunk as a piece of wood fell inward. "False side," I let them know, showing them the piece of wood after I removed it. I handed it to Shane and reached my hand back inside the step.

My hand brushed something soft, and for a second, I thought maybe I had found a dead mouse. "I've got something," I exclaimed as I hauled the object out. I removed from the step a chocolate-coloured box with a picture of a horse on the top, a young boy on its back. The softness I had felt was the suede covering on the box. The picture, I was sure, was of Cocoa and Toby.

"Oh wow," I said with awe. I ran my fingers over the small container and sat down on the step below where I had been working. I gingerly lifted the lid of the box. "There's a note," I said, pulling a piece of paper from the box, expecting it to be Toby's note to Wendell, but it wasn't. I read aloud:

This box belonged to my son, Toby Joshua Everett. In it are some of the things he treasured most. They may not be worth any money, but to my boy, they were all priceless, and that makes them priceless to me as well. I consider this box, like my son, buried treasure. Please honour his memory by keeping it safe. - Tavis Everett. April 24, 1944.

"God," Blake gasped.

"What else is inside?" Ryley inquired.

I put down the note from Tavis and looked over the contents of the box. I took out the items, one at a time, letting my fingers and hands really feel each of them as I held them, knowing that Toby had once held them too. There was a jackknife with a marble handle, a lock of Cocoa's hair in an envelope, a lighter with barely any finish on it (just like my dad's), Toby's driver's licence, a brass compass, a fat, black, stubby pencil without an eraser, a blue ribbon for winning first place in the county target-shooting competition of 1941, a set of jacks with the ball, and a photo that lined the bottom of the box.

"Huh," I mumbled as I took it out. "This is the same picture as the one Constance gave me."

I handed it to Shane, who studied it carefully. "Yeah. Guess we can each have a copy now." He handed it back to me.

"Is that it?" Blake asked. "No note?"

I double-checked the box. "Nope. That's it."

"May I see the box?" Ryley wondered.

"Sure." I passed it to him; the contents were all sitting next to me on the step.

"How'd he get this picture in here?" Ryley asked no one in particular as he tried to see where the photo slid into place. Not finding any trace of an entry point, he examined the inside of the lid. He went over to my tool kit and grabbed a jeweller's screwdriver. He slid the flat end into the place where the suede-lined top met the front of the inside. With great care, he pulled the screwdriver back, and we heard a snap as the inside cover fell back and the photo, as well as an envelope accompanying it, dropped to the floor.

Blake picked up the envelope, which had large, dark-brown stains on it and one word written on the front: *Caleb*. He opened it and unfolded the letter inside. He read it silently and nodded. He refolded the page and returned it to the envelope.

Blake patted Ryley on the shoulder, and we returned all the items to the box. I reattached the step, and we went up to my room. I placed the box on the shelf in my closet, putting the note in a Ziploc bag. I put the bag in my pocket, and we all headed out to the Bronco. We left a note for my parents telling them we'd be home late. We had no idea when we'd be back. We didn't care. We knew what we had to do next.

Chapter Twenty-Two

"Hi there, Caleb," Gidget welcomed me as I strode up to her desk. "How are you?"

"I'm fine, thanks. You?"

"Just great. Can I do something for you?"

"Yeah. I hope so anyway. I wanted to talk to Mr. Hildebrand again. He gave me a letter the last time I was here and I wanted to thank him, but I don't know what his address is and his phone is unlisted. Can you help me out?"

Gidget smiled. "I can't give out information like that, but I'll tell you what I'll do. I'll give him a call and see if he'd mind. If he gives me the go-ahead, I'll let you know. That's all I can do."

"I'd appreciate that."

"Okay. Just give me a minute to find his number."

Gidget clicked the mouse at her computer a dozen times or more before picking up the phone and making the call. I listened carefully as I walked in circles around the reception area.

"Hello, Mr. Hildebrand? It's Helen calling from Golden Meadows. That nice young man, Caleb, is here again. He tells me you gave him a letter, and he would like to send you a thank-you but he doesn't have your address. It's against policy to disclose any personal information without consent, so I'm calling to ask you if I may give him your address. Hmmm. Yes. Are you sure? All right. No, no. That's fine. Thanks for your time. Yes. You have a nice day, too. Okay. Bye."

Gidget put down the phone, and I walked over to the desk.

"Okay, here's the thing: Mr. Hildebrand isn't living at his apartment right now, so it wouldn't do any good to send him mail there. The phone number I used was the one for a summer residence in Angler's Cove. He's been staying out there while he clears up things with the lawyer about Mrs. Durant's estate. He said he doesn't get mail there, but if you'd like to drop out sometime, he'd be more than willing to see you. I wrote down the address for you."

Gidget handed me a piece of paper with a street name and number on it.

"I can't thank you enough," I said.

Gidget smiled. "You're very welcome. I do hope we'll see you again around here."

"I'll drop in sometime and say hi."

"Good. And bring that friend of yours too, if you do."

"I will. Thanks again."

"Take care, Caleb."

I smiled and headed for the door. We both knew the odds of me going back were slim to none. As the glass door closed behind me, I sighed and breathed in the crisp November air.

"Any luck?"

Ryley's question hit me as soon as I opened the Bronco's door.

"Yep. I got an address."

"All right. Halifax, here we come."

I climbed over Shane and took my seat behind Blake again.

"Well, actually, we're not going to Halifax," I informed them.

"No?" Blake questioned, looking at me in the rearview mirror.

"Nope. Turns out Wendell is staying at his summer place in Angler's Cove."

"That's only twenty clicks or so from here," Blake stated.

"Yep."

"And he's willing to see us?" Ryley asked.

"Yeah. Anytime."

"No time like the present," Blake said. He backed out of the parking spot, and soon we were on the road leading over the mountain and down the other side to the Bay of Fundy and the small village of Angler's Cove.

⌒

Angler's Cove has an odd shape to it. The road makes a large letter "U" as it bends to make room for the wharf. Both the longer parts of the "U" are on hills. We were barely moving at all (there was no traffic, so it didn't hold anyone up) as I read out the name of the street.

"Angler's Lane."

"How original," Blake muttered.

We wound down around the wharf and up the other side, not seeing the lane anywhere. We found ourselves leaving the village on the opposite side, so Blake turned around.

"Wait, there it is," Ryley said as he pointed to a road sign that was partially hidden by the branches of alders growing in the ditch. Angler's Lane was just about one hundred metres from the start of the descent down to the wharf. Blake made the left turn onto the gravel road, and we heard the splash as mud puddles kicked up under the tires.

"It's really washed out," Blake grumbled as he tried to manoeuvre the little Bronco on the messy road. "We'd better lock the hubs." Blake stopped the truck. "You get your side, Ryley," he instructed.

They hopped out onto the muddy road and locked the front-wheel hubs. Getting back in the cab, Blake shifted into four-by-four and proceeded onward with greater ease. His boots, and Ryley's, were covered in slimy brown muck. You could see how the rain all ran down the hill onto the road from a lack of proper ditching. The shallow culvert that was there was already overflowing from the snow that had melted.

As we passed the fronts of houses, we could see that most of them were closed for the winter. Even the ones that didn't have boards over the windows had that feel of an unlived-in house about them. There were only three places on the road that appeared to be year-round homes: the one at the very end where the road came to a stop, the reddish-coloured cottage on the water side of the road (it had a large ditch in the front and pipes that sent the excess water over the bluff onto the beach), and the white house across the street from it. None of them was the correct place, however.

"You sure it says Angler's Lane?" Blake asked.

I double-checked. "Yup. 17 Angler's Lane."

"So it should be on your side," Shane said.

We were going back toward the paved road, the odd-numbered houses being on the land side, even on the water side. When we reached the end of the road, the last house was number fifteen.

"Dammit. We missed it again," Blake sighed. He backed the little Ford up the road a ways until we came to number nineteen. "Where the hell?" He rolled down his window to get a better view.

"There," Ryley said. He pointed to a dark sign with the number seventeen on it that lay on the ground.

"No wonder we didn't see it. Number on the ground, and the house isn't visible from the road," Blake spat.

He turned the steering wheel hard left and drove slowly up a swampy driveway that was shared with house nineteen. On the right stood a small, olive-coloured house with red shutters (almost appearing as if it were painted with pimentos in mind).

Blake applied the brakes, and the Bronco slid momentarily before coming to a stop. A fairly new gold Honda Civic was sitting in the driveway, the sides muddy and the tires caked with muck. We hopped out of our vehicle and went up to the front door. I knocked and waited for Wendell to answer as it began to drizzle.

"Wish it would just rain," Ryley said. "I've always hated this kinda weather. Feels like we're being soaked with the spray from someone's sneeze."

"There's an image I coulda done without." Shane chuckled.

The door opened, and Wendell smiled. "Ahh, Caleb. I hoped I might see you today. Shane too. How nice. Brought some other friends as well, I see."

"Yes, sir. I hope you don't mind," I replied.

"Not at all. Come in out of the damp."

We followed Wendell into the house. It was toasty and warm inside, and I could smell woodsmoke coming from the living room as we took off our footwear in the porch.

"This is my brother, Blake," I said, making introductions to Wendell.

"Yes, of course. I can see the resemblance. Hello, young man," he said, shaking hands with Blake.

"Nice to meet you, sir," Blake replied.

"And this is my friend, Ryley."

"Hello, Ryley." Wendell shook his hand.

"Hello."

"Please, come in to the living room. I'll put on the kettle, and we'll have a nice cup of tea together, shall we?"

"That sounds great," Shane answered.

We followed our host into the cozy living room, where a woodstove showed a glowing fire at one end over a large red brick hearth. The room was fairly dark, with wood panelling on the walls, old furniture that didn't even attempt to match (overstuffed blue chairs, a gold-coloured sofa, and a brown recliner) scattered around the room, and an old console television that sat on the floor in its large wooden case. The only works of art on the wall were landscapes in cheap gilded frames and a rack for a spoon collection with only four slots filled. The room smelled heavily of the years of woodstove usage and cigarette smoke, with a faint undertone of mustiness. The only windows were behind the sofa, and they were small. All the lamps in the room were lit, but it was still dingy. The tall brass ashtray-stand next to the brown recliner was filled with cigarette butts, so we all avoided sitting there, knowing it was Wendell's chair.

As we sat down, Wendell spoke. "First of all, there is to be no more of this 'Sir' or 'Mr. Hildebrand' business. You are to call me Wendell. Okay?"

"Fair enough," Blake replied as he took his spot in one of the blue chairs. Ryley took the other, and Shane and I sat on the couch.

"May I ask, why did you stop going by Caleb?" I wanted to know.

Wendell smiled. "First, the tea. Then, I'll tell you everything you want to know."

"We don't want to take up all your time," Shane said.

"Boys, time is all I've got left." He tried to smile again. "Sorry, I don't mean to sound depressing. Constance would slap me for that. She'd tell me I should have said, 'Boys, I am happy to spend as much time with you as you shall permit me.' And she would have been right … it would have sounded better. Ah well. Do you lads take anything in your tea?"

———

"I must apologize for the state of this place," Wendell said as he returned with a tray of mugs filled with steaming hot tea. He set the tray on the small table in front of the sofa, causing the mugs to rattle a bit upon settling. They were all clear glass, like the ones people used to get free when they bought twenty-five litres of gasoline at the Ultramar. We added our necessary milk or sugar and sat back in our seats. Wendell slid a duMaurier from his pack and tapped it twice on the side of the cardboard container. "It belongs to a friend of mine, who basically just uses it as a camp on weekends in the summer. She's kind enough to let me use it from time to time. It's especially helpful now as I have to deal with finalizing Constance's estate."

"It's an interesting little place," Blake commented.

"Hah. Interesting. Yes. That's a very good word for it."

He put his cigarette in his mouth and lit it with a green Bic disposable lighter. He exhaled a cloud of smoke in a perfect ring and channelled his next breath through the ring, as if throwing a dart into a bull's-eye.

"Now, about my name …"

We sat and sipped at our tea. The fire blazed away inside the stove, and a clock I couldn't locate ticked loudly every second. In the moments of silence, I could hear the waves crashing against the shore below us. The wind was strong and whistling outside, the rain coming down harder against the roof. The rear coil element of the stove clicked and rattled occasionally as it kept the tea on simmer. The old fridge, with no exterior freezer door, hummed and whirred and made dripping sounds in the background. Every so often, a branch from the chestnut tree would scrape against the window. I was cognizant of all of these noises, and yet I was acutely aware of what Wendell was saying. I didn't miss a single word.

"When I was growing up, I was always called Caleb. My grandfather was Wendell, you see, and when I was born, he was living with us, so it was easier for me to be referred to by my middle name. My grandfather passed away when I was six, but by then everyone was so accustomed to calling me Caleb that no one thought to change it. I've always preferred it to Wendell, myself.

"But after Toby disappeared, I couldn't bear to hear anyone call me Caleb again. The way he said my name ..." Wendell closed his eyes and took a breath. "Anyway, I ran off and enlisted in the army, as you know, and made sure to sign my papers as Wendell. I just couldn't imagine having my drill sergeant yell the name Caleb at me when it used to be said with such affection. I've been using my Christian name ever since. In fact, you'd be hard-pressed to find anything anywhere that even indicates that I have a middle name at all." He drew on his cigarette once more and stubbed it out as he exhaled.

"So you can imagine why I thought for so long that Toby was calling for me," I said.

Wendell stopped squishing his cigarette butt into the black glass ashtray at the top of the brass stand and looked at me curiously. "Calling for you?"

I nodded.

"Please explain."

"I've heard him—we all have—calling out the name *Caleb* in the woods. It's always in this low, sad whisper—even when it's close."

Wendell leaned forward and folded his hands on his right knee. He studied my face, making me self-conscious. "Tell me more," he insisted.

I rubbed the back of my neck with my palm. "I don't know where to begin."

"I think we need to start with what really happened," Shane suggested.

"What do you mean?" Wendell asked.

My hands were getting cold and shaky, so I gripped my glass mug with both of them, trying to stay calm. "What you wrote in your letter ... that isn't what happened. I'm sure it seemed like a good explanation at the time, and I'm sure you really believed it ... but sometimes ... I dunno how to say this," I admitted.

Shane took over for me. "Sometimes when our emotions are too heavily involved, we can't see things as clearly as they need to be seen. We can't stand outside and observe objectively. I think this might be the case with your letter."

"But I know Tavis killed Toby. I know it," Wendell said adamantly. "He might as well have flat-out said it to me."

"While I'm sure it seemed that way at the time, I think you really need to think about what Tavis said to you. I think what he was trying to do was protect you," Blake offered.

"Protect me? Protect me from what? You didn't see the look in his eyes when he spoke. Oh no. No. Tavis killed Toby as sure as I'm sitting here today," Wendell spoke crossly and resentfully.

"No, sir. Tavis did not kill Toby. If he gave you that impression, it was to save you from the truth," Shane stated.

"What are you talking about?"

"Wendell, it was your father who killed Toby," Shane explained.

There was an uncomfortable silence for a moment. The fire hissed and snapped. Wendell glared at Shane and carried the look over to all of us. He spoke in an almost inaudible tone. "My father was a hardworking, loyal, respected member of the community. He was a brilliant doctor for all the animals in the area and a long-standing deacon in the church. How dare you slander his good name with your false accusations? How dare you!"

"They aren't false accusations," I told him. "We all witnessed it."

Wendell sat back in his chair. "You're all mad. Toby died more than sixty years ago. There's no way you could have witnessed anything of the sort."

I took the envelope from my pocket and said, "Then there's no way we'd have this letter, either."

I handed the envelope to Wendell. He opened the note inside and read to himself the words of his long-departed love. A tear rolled down his cheek.

"Have you ever seen that before?" I asked.

Wendell wiped his eyes with a tissue and shook his head. "Where did you find it?"

"Inside a step in Wakefield House," Ryley answered.

"Inside a step? How did you know where to look?"

"Toby showed us," I replied.

Wendell shook his head again. "That can't be."

"Did your father ever tell you that you couldn't pal around with

Toby anymore? That you weren't to go near the Everett place?" Ryley asked.

"No. Never. Father knew that Toby and I were best of friends."

"Look at that envelope. See those dark stains?" Shane demanded. "That's Toby's blood."

Wendell gasped. "Jesus."

I scratched my head, trying to think of some way to get through to Wendell. "Do you remember your father having a black eye, a broken nose, or something like that on his face just after learning Toby was gone?"

Wendell's hands were visibly shaking as he answered, "No. Nothing unusual. He oftentimes found himself at the wrong end of a sick animal that lashed out. It wasn't uncommon for that sort of thing to happen in his profession."

"How about his right leg? Did he limp at all?" Shane asked, picking up on my train of thought.

Wendell squinted. "Come to think of it … it was about that time that Father began to use a cane on his walks. He said he was getting arthritic. Why?"

"Your father was shot in the leg by Toby. That's why he used a cane."

Wendell absorbed the idea. "If what you are saying is true, then why didn't Tavis tell someone what happened? Answer that."

"Simple," Shane said. "You said it yourself. Your father was a well-respected community member, church deacon, university-educated doctor of veterinary medicine. Tavis Everett was, to many people, just a former drunk, hick, farmer with a sketchy past. You know the stories about his father, Leonard. And besides, H. K. threatened him, said he'd poison the livestock and destroy him both financially and socially—suggesting he had molested his daughters."

Wendell shook his head in disbelief. "This is ludicrous." His voice wasn't as sharp that time, almost as if he were considering it all a possibility.

"Can you explain how a note left for you from Toby would come into your father's hands?" Ryley asked.

Wendell rubbed his hands on his knees. "Sometimes Father would go into our rooms and make sure we were keeping everything neat and tidy. He must have found the note the day Toby left it. Knowing Toby, he probably hid it somewhere so I wouldn't find it right away. He'd do things like that so that when I'd discover them, I'd be reminded of how much he loved me."

"Sorta like you just were," I said.

Wendell looked over at me, his eyes moist. "Yes. I suppose so." Wendell sat back in his chair and sighed heavily.

"Our intentions have never been to hurt you," Shane let our host know. "We only want to help Toby."

"And you truly believe what you say? That you saw these events unfold?"

"Yes."

He removed another cigarette from the pack. "All right. You better tell me everything."

"So, you believe us? About your father?" Ryley asked.

"Son, if I didn't, do you really think I'd ask to hear more of something so painful?" He rubbed his temples and put the cigarette between his lips. He flicked the lighter to create a flame and said, "Start from the beginning."

Afternoon turned to night. The wind was fierce, and the rain pounded down relentlessly. We told Wendell everything. All we had felt, seen, or heard regarding Toby. He took all the information in, not saying a word or questioning until we had finished speaking.

"I can comprehend, I suppose, the idea that you saw Tavis, Toby, and my father—all of whom are dead. But how could you have seen me?"

"I don't honestly know. The best I can figure out is that it's like they're images from the past. Like old movies. Some of the actors are dead, some alive. The film plays regardless," I said. "That's the only way I can explain it."

The power flickered and went out. The glow of the woodstove was all we had to see by.

"Wow. That's one nasty storm," Blake said. "We'd better get going."

"No. Please don't," Wendell pleaded. "Stay until it calms down." None of us moved from our seats.

"When I was thirteen," Wendell started to reminisce, "I began helping my father at the animal hospital, and on stormy nights, the animals got spooked so we'd have to stay with them and try to keep them calm so they wouldn't injure themselves. On one occasion, my father was out at a farm some ten miles from home, and I was left at the clinic to tend to the animals.

"There were four horses there at that time, and they all began to get excited as the lightning struck trees nearby and the thunder clapped all around. I was scared of the horses because they were kicking and rearing up on their hind legs—making a racket and looking half mad. I was in a panic trying to keep them calm and seeing to the other animals, as well as trying to keep myself from being too frightened. I was doing a poor job of it all, and then, there in the dark doorway, soaked to the bone from the pouring rain, stood Toby. He had walked all the way over in the storm to help me. He was so good with horses. He got them all to calm down, going from stall to stall for the duration of the storm and stroking their faces, speaking softly to them. And I remember him walking over to me and brushing my cheek with the back of his hand and saying comforting things to me as well."

A clap of thunder sounded overhead. "That's a nice thing to remember," Blake said.

"It's funny, you know. I hadn't thought of that in years."

I got up from my seat. "May I use your phone?"

"By all means. Help yourself."

I walked into the small yellow kitchen with green tiles on the floor. I tried to ignore the fact that the tiles were all stamped with the word Asbestos under the company name. They looked like sample tiles from the fifties or sixties.

I called home and let my mother know that we were safe and waiting out the worst of the storm before coming home. I returned to the living room to see Wendell lighting a kerosene lamp and setting it atop the television.

"May I ask you boys a few questions?" Wendell wanted to know.

"Certainly," I replied.

"Do your parents know you're gay?"

"Yes."

"And that Shane is your boyfriend?"

"Yes."

"And what do they think of it all?"

"My parents think Shane is fantastic, and they're very happy for us. They know we've got some obstacles ahead of us at school and stuff, but they're very supportive with everything."

"And you, Shane? What do your parents think?"

"Well, my dad's dead, but my mother is cool about it all. She thinks Caleb is a really nice guy and wants the best for us."

"I'm sorry about your father."

"Thanks."

"Did he know?"

"Umm. No. I was only ten when he passed away."

"Oh. I'm so sorry."

"It's okay."

"So Blake and Ryley, are you fellas gay as well?"

Blake chuckled. "Nope, and I gotta say, it's rather humbling being a minority member in a room for once."

"Yeah, really, huh?" Ryley agreed.

"But you're both very tolerant of the others."

"Tolerant?" Blake repeated, confused. "I don't tolerate my brother and my friends. I love and accept them for who they are."

"Exactly," Ryley nodded.

Wendell sighed again. "This world has changed so much. Where was the love and friendship like that when I was growing up?"

"In Toby," Shane said softly.

The wind changed direction, and we listened as the storm worked its way out to sea.

"I think you need to go back into the woods," I said to Wendell.

"No. I can't do that. I vowed to never return to Stapeton and especially not to Wakefield Road."

"But Toby needs you. He needs closure that only you can provide."

"I just can't … I'm sorry."

All of us were dejected. We hung our heads and rubbed our hands, each of us trying to find the words to convince Wendell. We knew we were so close.

"We understand," Shane said and stood up. "There's really nothing else we can say. We had better get going. It's after ten."

As we began putting on our coats and boots, Wendell handed me the letter.

"That's yours," I told him.

"No. It *was* mine. I've taken from it what I need. You keep it and keep it safe."

"Are you sure?"

"Positive."

"I am sorry if we've hurt you."

He shook his head. "You haven't."

We thanked Wendell for his time and said good night. After telling a man that his father had committed murder, there was nothing else that really felt appropriate to say.

Blake carefully drove us home over the wet and muddy roads. As I gazed out my window to the blackness, I could visualize the image of Toby calming the horses in the storm. I took great comfort in it.

We pulled into the driveway back at the house, and Blake shut off the engine. As we got out of the truck, Mom opened the front door of the house to us. We ran up to the porch and dashed inside.

"We were getting more than a little worried," Mom said as we removed our wet coats and footwear. "Were the roads bad?"

"Terrible. All the dirt ones are really washed out," Blake replied.

"Well, I'm glad you're all here safe and sound. The temperature is supposed to drop overnight, and all this rain is going to turn to snow. The Weather Network said we might get as much as twenty-five centimetres in the next forty-eight hours."

"Maybe school will be cancelled on Monday," Ryley said. "That'd rock."

"Have you boys had anything to eat?" Mom asked.

"Umm. No. Not really. We had some snack stuff in the afternoon, but nothing major," I replied.

"I'll throw a coupla pizzas in the oven. Can you guys wait a half-hour or so?"

"Yeah. That sounds good."

"Oh my God, pizza. I love pizza," Ryley said dreamily.

Mom laughed. "Okay, you guys get into some dry clothes, and I'll get the food ready."

"Thanks, Karen," Shane said.

"My pleasure."

We jogged up the stairs (the middle one being unusually silent) and up to my room and Blake's to change.

"So, we've pretty much gotta hit the woods tomorrow, right?" I asked as we all met in my room in our dry clothes, all of us in our sleeping attire. Shane had on these camouflage sleep pants and a white undershirt—the kind so affectionately known as a wifebeater—and looked so hot I couldn't stand it. I was in my trusty grey plaid pants and a black T-shirt, as per usual. Ryley was wearing a pair of tearaway pants (he called them snap pants) over his boxers and a white T-shirt. Blake had on these red checkered sleep pants and was putting on his ribbed, heather-grey muscle shirt as he entered my room. I must admit, I was feeling a bit envious of Blake's looks.

"Damn, Blake. You gonna wear that on grad pyjama day?" Shane asked.

"Pyjama day? Like we all hafta wear our pj's to school or something?"

"Yup. All the grads," Ryley confirmed.

"I guess I will be then. Why?"

"Cuz you look superhot like that," Shane told him.

Blake went beet-red. "Shut up," he laughed.

"Oh, and if you actually call them pj's, that will definitely score extra points," Ryley said and laughed.

"You guys are crazy." Blake chuckled, trying to keep from blushing more. "So, what about the woods?"

"We should head out tomorrow after lunch," I said.

"Good thinking. As long as the snow doesn't amount to too much," Shane added.

"We'll cross that bridge when we come to it. Let's get something to eat. I'm starving," Blake suggested.

With our plans roughly made, we went down to the kitchen and feasted. We watched a movie afterward and were awake to see the rain change to snow. By the time we went to bed around two, there was already a good five centimetres on the ground.

As I lay in bed that night next to Shane, I watched the snow falling outside my window. Ryley was sawing logs on the floor at the end of the bed. Shane had his arm draped over me, and his hand was over my heart.

"I love you," he whispered to me in the dark.

"I love you, too."

He kissed my ear and pulled me closer.

"I wish I had a body like my brother," I admitted.

"You've got a great body."

"No, I don't."

"Yes. You do."

"I saw the way you checked him out."

"You think I don't look at you like that? C'mon, Caleb. You're my boy. I mean, sure, I can appreciate another guy's body, and your brother does have a very nice one, but it's you I love."

"I just wish I was hot like Blake."

"You are. You just don't realize it."

"That's sweet of you to say."

"I'm not just saying it. God. I hate it when you put yourself down like that. You should give yourself a lot more credit than you do. You're smart, funny, cute as all get-out, and most of all, you're the most kindhearted, most loyal person I've ever known. Every day I wake up, thankful you're in my life. If you really do love me like you say, then you won't put yourself down anymore, cuz when you do, you're hurting the person I love more than life itself, and I won't allow that. Got it?"

Shane spoke with such passion and conviction, I couldn't reply. I turned to face him and hugged him tightly. When our embrace ended, he put his hands on either side of my face and made me look into his eyes, not that I wanted to look anywhere else.

"Promise me you won't think badly of yourself anymore."

"But I can't do ..."

"Promise me."

"I ... I promise."

"Good." He let his hands slide down my neck and off my body. He leaned forward and kissed me. We continued to kiss as he slid out of his sleeping bag and under the covers with me, quietly so as not to wake Ryley.

"I want to feel you," he whispered between deep kisses, and I felt his hand slide under my waistband. I moaned quietly as, for the first time in my life, someone else's hand felt the skin of my erect penis.

As much as I wanted the sensation to continue, I knew I couldn't keep it from ending soon. I grabbed Shane's arm and worked it back, so his hand could no longer make the stroking motions it had, resting it instead on my stomach.

"What's wrong?" he breathed.

"Not like this. It's too much like the bathroom at Hunter's."

"You feel amazing. Didn't you like it?"

"Are you kidding? It's probably the best thing I've ever felt in my life, but I just can't, with Rye in the room and my parents down the hall. It's too weird."

"I'll cover your mouth with one hand to muffle any noise you make, I promise."

I couldn't help it. I laughed.

Shane was giggling too as he said, "Guess that's not very romantic, huh?"

"Not really. It's oddly kinda hot, but, no, not very romantic."

"Fair enough." Shane flopped over on his back, still snickering.

We looked at each other in the quiet night. The moon was hidden behind a cloud that dropped fat, fluffy flakes of snow on the earth. There was just enough light that I could see clearly into Shane's eyes.

"Whatcha thinkin'?" he asked me.

"Everything. And nothing."

"I know the feeling."

"How 'bout you?"

"Tell ya the truth, I'm kinda hungry. Always happens when I'm horny."

"Me too. Wanna see if there's any pizza left?"

"Yeah."

We flipped back our covers and went downstairs to the kitchen, where we were pleased to discover four slices of pizza sitting in the fridge. We took them over to the table, along with a bag of chips and cans of pop. We went at the food, talking and laughing as we ate. Shane told me about the photographers he admired and the painters he liked best. I talked about cars and my interest in writing from time to time. Throughout it all, we found things to joke about and laughed till our sides hurt.

Fifteen is a strange age to be. One moment you're on the verge of your first sexual experience, and the next, you're playing the latest Xbox 360 game or raiding the fridge at 4:00 a.m. One minute you're checking out some hot guy (or girl, if that's your thing) at the mall, and the next, you're calling your mom for a ride home and asking her, *"What's for dinner?"* You'll be talking with a friend about the *Family Guy* episode where Peter brings home the case of ipecac and trying to remember who went the longest without puking (it was Chris), and later, the same day, you'll be discussing your theories on the afterlife. And what's so incredible about it all is that it all makes so much sense. Sitting there with Shane, I didn't think about anything at all other than how good it felt to be with him, eating cold pizza and laughing at four in the morning in the middle of a snowstorm. Sometimes, all you need to think about is what's directly in front of you.

We went back to bed before sunrise and slept until noon. When we got up, there were nearly thirty centimetres of snow on the ground, and it was still coming down. Venturing into the woods was out of the question.

Chapter Twenty-Three

In typical fashion, the snow turned to rain and melted back enough that school wasn't cancelled on Monday. I awoke that morning to find the temperature hovering between five and eight degrees on the happy side of zero. The sun was shining brightly, and the snow that remained on the ground was slushy. Forecasts called for clear skies and warmer weather for the rest of the week. I went to an uneventful day at Stapeton Regional High and heard all of my friends bitching about school not being cancelled—we'd always all have that in common.

At my locker, just before the homeroom bell rang, Drew approached me. He held my locker door open by resting his arm at the top of the door.

"Hey, Caleb. Can I talk to you for a sec?"

"Sure, Drew. What's up?"

"I kinda talked to Hunter—you know …"

I nodded. "And?"

"Well … he was a real douche at first, but he came around."

"Whattaya mean?"

"Heh. I talked to him in a general sorta way, you know, just to gauge his reaction. He was being stupid, probably thinking it was cool or something. Anyway, I asked him what he'd say if he found out one of his friends was gay, and he was like, 'I wouldn't be friends with them anymore,' and stuff like that. So then I asked him, 'What if it was me? Wouldn't we still be friends?'"

"Holy crap. You said that?"

"Yeah."

"What did he say?"

"He didn't say anything at first; he just got real quiet. Then he asked me if I was gay—and I told him I wouldn't answer him until he answered me first. It took him a while. I could see his brain was working overtime. Then he goes something like, 'Well ... if it was you, I'd guess it would be different.' And I was like, 'Why would it be different?' And he goes, 'Cuz you're my best friend.' So anyways, we talked about it for a while, and I let him know it wasn't me, but that we both had friends who were gay and that if he didn't accept them, then he and I couldn't be friends anymore."

"Wow. Drew ... I don't know what to say." I was completely taken aback. My positive opinion of Drew quadrupled.

He punched me lightly on the shoulder. "Don't have to say anything, man."

Drew smiled, and his teeth showed slightly under his upper lip. Laura stepped over to him and put an arm around his waist.

"Hey, fellas. What's goin' on?"

"Hey, hot stuff," Drew said to her and leaned in for a kiss.

Six months ago, I would never have pictured the two of them together; now they seemed a perfect match.

The first bell of the morning rang for homeroom. I closed my locker door and threw my book bag over my shoulder.

"Have a good one," Drew said as he put his fist to mine.

"You too."

"Later, Caleb," Laura said as she leaned into Drew. Her tiny little frame, accented by her long blonde hair, looked as sultry as she could make it in her low-rise jeans.

"See ya at lunch."

We headed in opposite directions, and I came face-to-face with Hunter at the door to homeroom.

"Hey, Hunter," I said casually.

"Oh, hey, Caleb. How are ya?"

"Good, man. You?"

"All right, I guess."

"Have a good weekend?"

He shrugged his shoulders. "It was a weekend."

We went inside and took our normal seats. Hunter was quiet as Shane and I talked with Moira. I think he was debating what he wanted to say. Finally there was a lull in our conversation, and he spoke.

"Guys ... I just want you to know, we're cool. Okay?" He looked nervous as he spoke.

"Of course we are. We're friends," Shane replied.

"I mean ... you know what I mean, right?"

I nodded. "Yeah, Hunter. We know."

"Good. I didn't want you guys to think I was some asshole or something."

Moira piped up, "Well, you just proved you aren't," and smiled at him.

Hunter grinned shyly.

The second bell rang, and we all turned to face the front of the room as our attendance was taken and we listened to morning announcements.

During lunch, we sat at our usual table and chatted like we always did. I caught Hunter's eye once, and he gave me an awkward smile.

"You okay?" I asked him.

"Yeah. Just ... well, guess I kinda feel bad about stuff."

"Whattaya mean?"

"I was the last person in our group to know about you guys, and I figure it's because you were worried about my reaction. It makes me feel shitty that you'd expect me to be a jerk about everything."

"I'm sorry. We really didn't mean to hurt your feelings."

He shrugged. "I know ... sad thing is, though, you'da probably been right."

"So ... what changed?"

"I realized how lucky I am," Hunter replied, which surprised me.

"Huh?"

"To have such a great bunch of friends, I mean. Did I really want to lose them all over something so stupid? I got thinking about a lot of stuff—especially about what Drew said to me. Would I have been willing to drop my best friend just because he told me he liked dudes instead of chicks? It seemed so stupid when he put it that way. I mean, he woulda been the same guy … just like you and Shane are. And I like you guys."

"We like you too, Hunter."

"Yeah, I know, and I can never figure out why. I'm pretty much a spoiled brat who tries too hard to fit in."

My eyes opened wide, stunned.

"Don't look so shocked. I know who I am. And you guys don't treat me any different. What the hell kinda friend would I be if I treated you different just because you're gay?" Hunter looked me in the eye and nodded. "So, that's my piece. We're cool, aren't we?"

"Totally."

"Good. So, I'm hoping you'll do me a solid."

"Sure. What is it?"

"You think you could kinda get the word to Heather Markus that I'm not an asshole?"

"Heather Markus? I didn't know you liked her." She wasn't the type I pictured Hunter being interested in at all. She was tall and pretty, but seemed rather bookish for Hunter. Of course, the reality is that we don't live in a world of supermodels, and some people we just find attractive, for reasons we can't really explain.

"Umm, yeah. She's always nice to me when we're in chemistry and stuff. She's kinda pretty, too."

"Yeah, she is."

"So, you think you could help a guy out?"

I smiled at Hunter. "I'll do the best I can."

"Thanks, Caleb. And one other thing?"

"Yeah?"

"Can we hang out sometime … just you and me?"

"That'd be cool."

"You guys organizing a playdate?" Moira giggled as she slid over by me.

"God, I hate that expression," I groaned.

"We're just strategizing over 'Operation Heather Markus,'" Hunter explained.

"Oh really? Hmm. Maybe I can help. We're in band together. Want me to ask her if she'll blow your horn?"

"God, Moira," Hunter laughed. "I think we'd better start out a bit more subtle."

‿⁀

On Thursday, I got my English poetry essay back from Mr. Drexell. He'd marked it with an eighty-eight (a very high score from him) and written in red ink on the back of the last page: *Interesting, refreshing take on an old legend. Proving or disputing its accuracy is not possible, but it is a modern way of approaching an old subject, one that obviously has special meaning to you. This is your most impassioned work yet. You have a true writer's grasp of the language. I read this paper four times before grading. Keep up the good work. A. R. Drexell.*

I was pleasantly surprised by my mark and slid the paper in my book bag. As I made my way to the door leaving class that day, Mr. Drexell called my name and asked me to come over to his desk. I made my way through the students pressing to get out of the room and stood at the short end of his desk.

"Yes, Mr. Drexell?" I asked, shifting the weight of my book bag.

"Caleb, I want you to know how pleased I am with your writing."

"Thank you, sir."

"I do have a question … more of a concern, I guess you'd call it."

"Yes?"

"Well, you see, I have no way of substantiating what you wrote— and that is always a concern for me as a teacher. Normally, I wouldn't grade a paper like yours at all, because, well, it could just be all made up. Really good BS for a teacher to eat up. But I've made an exception in your case, and your mark reflects that."

"Umm, yeah. But I didn't …"

"No. Please. Don't say anything more. I struggled with this for a while. Either you're the best liar I've ever had in my class or the best writer. Heh. Sometimes I wonder if there's a difference between the two. I'm going against my better judgment and giving you the benefit of the doubt, Caleb, because your writing has been strong all year. This time, it was impassioned. I'd be remiss as a teacher to not acknowledge that and to not reward you for it. I consider it an interesting theory regarding local history—one that took a great deal of research to delve into. I marked your work based on its strength of argument, its stellar prose, and, as I've already said, its passion. If it is truth or fiction—well, that remains a mystery."

"Sir, while I appreciate your comments, I want you to know I would never ..."

"Stop." He waved his hands in the air in front of his face. "All I want from you is for you to keep writing this way."

Unsure of what to say, I replied, "I'll do my best."

"I look forward to it."

"Thank you, Mr. Drexell."

"You have a good day, Caleb."

"You too, sir."

Mr. Drexell turned his attention back to his white-coiled, red-covered day planner as I made my way to the hall. I put my books in my locker and headed for the bus.

I arrived to an empty house after my walk down Wakefield Road. Mom and Dad were both working, and Blake had volleyball practice that afternoon. I unlocked the front door and stepped inside, tossing my book bag on the floor of the foyer as I removed my coat. I snapped the dead bolt back into place and went to the downstairs washroom.

I stood urinating with the door open, relishing the fact I was alone in the house. A slight chill snaked across my exposed skin, and I shivered as I tucked myself back into my jeans. I washed my hands and went to the kitchen to grab a drink.

I stared in the fridge, willing a desired beverage to magically appear, before settling on apple juice. I chugged a glassful quickly and put the glass in the dishwasher. I glanced out the kitchen window and saw the sun glinting off the fields of snow, the tall tops of the brown grasses poking out from the white sheet.

I took my book bag from the entry and went upstairs. As I turned down the hallway to my room, I felt a sudden heaviness in the air and heard a noise ... noises coming from the direction of my room. There was a scraping, scuttling sound, and my mind recalled the story Shane had told me about Royce believing he saw nothing but a pile of leaves in the back bedroom. As I approached the entrance to my room, I found the door shut and heard the wind under it, the draft licking at my feet in a cold whisper. I placed my hand on the tarnished knob and slowly pushed the door in as I turned the handle. I steeled my stomach to be able to withstand whatever I was about to see. I turned my gaze into the room and saw …

… my bedroom, just as I had left it. I sighed with relief and laughed at myself. I checked to make sure my window was securely shut, and finding it was, I unbuttoned my shirt and took it off as I went over to the closet. I slid the door back on its gliders and took a hanger down. I put my shirt on the hanger and set it back on the rod. I glanced up and saw Toby's box on the shelf. I picked it up and took it over to the bed with me. I stretched out on my side and lifted the lid to once more see the things Toby had cherished.

"Damn. I forgot to give Shane the extra photo," I said to myself as I retrieved the snapshot from the treasure chest. I took the other copy from my nightstand drawer and set it on the bed next to its twin. I continued going through the box, holding each item and wondering what small things in my life would tell someone something about me in the future. I returned all the items to the box and took another look at the photos. I wanted to make sure I gave the one in better condition to Shane. I checked them over carefully—seeing the two boys in the back of an old pickup truck with hay between them and a Coke to share. It looked like something Robert Duncan might paint.

I was examining the photos, side by side, when something peculiar caught my eye. I ran over to my desk and dug out my magnifying glass. I held the magnifier to the photos, slowly going over them until I spotted it. In the photo Constance had given us, each of the boys had one hand completely blocked from view by the bale of hay (Toby's left hand, Wendell's right), but in the photo from the box, I thought I could see a reflection in the rear window of the truck. The light must have glinted off the Coke bottle at just the right angle to make a reflection appear. Regardless of the explanation, there it was. In the window, I could see that the boys were holding hands. I examined the other photo, desperately trying to see the same image, but it just wasn't there. Otherwise, the pictures were identical.

"Incredible," I mumbled to myself. I put both the photos in the box and returned it to the shelf in my closet. As I slid the door shut, I felt another cold breeze run across my body.

Caleb

Hearing my name called out like that again made me freeze for a moment. I knew that if I turned around, Toby would be standing there in my doorway. He sounded like he was right behind me. I slowly spun myself around and found myself looking out into the hallway.

Caleb

This time the voice was farther away. I ran over to my window and peered out. In the distance, on the far side of the stream, stood Toby. He stared at me, as if he were waiting for me to join him. I hurriedly put on a hoodie and rushed down the stairs to the kitchen. I put on my boots, coat, and gloves and raced out the kitchen door. Toby was nowhere to be seen when I reached the backyard, but I kept right on going to the woods and all the way to the clearing, trudging through some deep snow at times.

I pushed my way through the spruce trees and to the end of the hidden path. Still, no signs. "I'm here, Toby. Show me what you want," I called out.

A cold wind blew up from over the ridge. I looked over the embankment, and I knew where I had to go. Toby's roses were down there.

The snow was so deep going over the ridge that it took some time getting down below the hidden path. My legs were numb by the time I got to the roses, my pants having become very wet from my descent. There was almost no snow in the area around the rosebushes. I stared into the brownish mass of thorny growth.

"Toby? Are you here? Please ... talk to me."

I waited for a response, but I heard no more than a crow cawing. I was very cold, having not dressed sufficiently in my haste to enter the woods. I knew I had to get home and into some warm, dry clothes. I pictured the claw-foot tub filled with steaming hot water and me submerging my body in it.

I tried to wade through the snow back up to the hidden path, but it was slick with an icy glaze and I couldn't get any footing.

"Shit," I mumbled, frustrated. I could scarcely feel my legs, and the sun was going down. I feared I would be stuck in the forest for the night. I turned back to the roses and looked at the woods surrounding me. I knew the direction of the field, but no matter which way I went toward home meant a steep climb up the hill, and the snow was deep everywhere. The only direction where the land was flat, or relatively so, was if I were to continue deeper into the woods, and I had no clue where that would take me.

I fumbled around in my pockets for anything that might come in handy. My fingers felt the metal edge of something in my left pocket, and I pulled out my dad's old Zippo. I flicked the lid and rolled the wheel with my thumb. A flame shot up but disappeared. I tried again and again, but every time there was just a momentary flame—the lighter fluid must have dried out. I let the Zippo fall back into my pocket and tried to think of other ideas. Having none, I sat on a rock and put my head in my hands.

I felt a hand on my shoulder and whipped my head around to see Toby. "You all right?" he asked me.

"I'm ... umm ... yeah. I'm fine. Thanks."

"You sure?"

"Yeah, just a little cold."

"Sorry about that."

"Not your fault."

Toby sat down on the large rock next to me. "Well, it sorta is. I shoulda waited till the weather was better or something before dragging you out here."

Still unable to fully comprehend what I was seeing and hearing, I replied, "It's not a problem. Really."

"I'd lay a fire, but I don't have my lighter, and yours is out of fuel."

"I'll be fine." I wondered how long he'd been watching me before he appeared.

"Yeah. I know you will."

Toby was wearing the same clothes he had died in, and when I thought of that, I felt very sad. He was so real, sitting next to me and talking to me ... but I knew he was dead, buried just a few metres from where we sat.

"I don't know what I'm supposed to do next."

"Sure you do."

"No, I really don't. Can't you tell me?"

"Let me put it this way: if you were to die right this second, what would be your last thought?"

"I like to think it would be Shane."

Toby smiled, and the area around us lit up with a warm amber glow. My pant legs felt drier, and I no longer shivered. Everything became brighter.

"So, now you can guess what my last thought was."

I nodded. "Sure, but I've talked to Wendell, I mean Caleb, and he won't come back here."

"He will, now that you've told him the truth."

"How can you be so sure?"

"I can't be sure, but I have hope." Toby's eyes sparkled like droplets of fresh rainwater collected on the leaf of a wildflower. He was so stunning I had to look away.

"What's wrong?" he asked me.

"Nothing, I just ... never mind."

"No. Tell me."

"It's just that you're so beautiful, it hurts to look at you sometimes."

Toby picked up one of my hands and held it between both of his. "You know, I waited for just the right person to move in to the house before I felt I could trust anyone enough to help me. When I first saw you, I knew there was something special about you. I used to sit next to your bed when you slept and look at you. I knew you were the one to help me, and I hoped, in the process, maybe I'd be able to help you as well."

I gazed deeply into Toby's eyes and found myself looking into eternity. Tears welled up in my eyes. "I've been so scared, Toby."

"I know, Caleb. I've been scared for you, too, but I'm also very happy for you. You've got the opportunity to live your life and be yourself. It won't always be easy—it isn't for anyone—but you've got friends and your family who love you and support you, not to mention a really nice fella."

"I know. I'm very fortunate and grateful for all of that, but there's more … I'm scared of losing you."

"Aww, you can't ever lose me."

"But you won't always be here, will you?"

Toby frowned. "I really don't know."

"Why didn't you just, I dunno, pass over into the afterlife? Or whatever it is that's out there."

Toby shrugged his shoulders. "I don't know the answer to that any more than you do. I know that my body is buried over there," he said, pointing to the roses, "but here I am, able to talk to you and touch you."

The glow around Toby grew wider as he spoke, and I felt warm and dry.

"I really wish you were alive, Toby. I think we woulda been great friends."

He smiled at me and held my hand tighter. "We are great friends, Caleb."

I tried to grin as I nodded.

Toby reached up and wiped a tear from my cheek. "It makes me feel good when I see you with Shane. You two remind me of my Caleb and me, except I can't imagine ever doing that to my ear," he said, touching my earlobe.

I chuckled. "I dunno, I kinda like it."

"So do I."

Toby let go of my ear, and our eyes met again. He leaned over and kissed me gently on the lips.

"You taste like that wild mint that used to grow behind the barn. Very sweet," he told me.

I blushed. "Mint Chap Stick," I said, showing him the tube of lip balm in my pocket.

"I hope Shane won't be angry with me for what I did. I just wanted to thank you."

I shook my head. "No. I think he'll understand. I wish we could all hang out. All my friends would love you."

"Someday we will," Toby told me. He stood up from the rock and sighed. "Now, we have to get you back home."

"I'd like to stay with you longer."

"I'd like that too, but it can't be. I need to help you outta here before I hafta leave."

"Where do you go?"

"I don't really know. Sometimes I have control of it, sometimes I don't. The times when I don't, I just sort of vanish."

"Does it hurt ever?"

"No. I haven't felt any physical pain since I died." Toby motioned for me to get up. "We'd better get a move on. I'm not sure how long I can stay."

"But the snow's too deep. I can't get up the hill."

"I know. You'll have to trust me. I know another way."

"Okay."

Toby led me down a narrow path beyond the roses that went deeper still into the woods. We weaved in and around trees and through drifts of snow. I was completely at his mercy, having lost all sense of direction. It was with some shock that I found myself standing next to Toby at the top of the waterfall, looking down into the clearing.

"Wow. Thank you so much," I said.

"I'd love to go the rest of the way with you, but I can't."

"Will I ever get to talk to you like this again? There's so much more I want to say."

"I hope so, but I don't know."

Not knowing if there'd ever be another opportunity, I hugged Toby with all my might. He squeezed me back, and I felt his grip loosen. We parted, and I made my way over to the path and turned to say good-bye.

"Good-b ..." I began, raising my hand to wave. But he was already gone. The melting ice dripped over the rocks at the base of the waterfall. Otherwise, there was silence. I made my way home along the darkened path and reached the house sometime after six. As I stepped inside the back door, I heard the front door close. Blake was just getting home from practice. I followed him upstairs to his room, where he sat down on his bed next to me and I told him what had happened.

Chapter Twenty-Four

"You gonna be all right, bud?" Blake asked me after I finished recounting everything that had happened to me that afternoon.

"Yeah. I'll be fine. It was just really hard saying good-bye today. I mean, maybe I'll never get to touch him again or talk to him again. Maybe not even see him."

"Maybe. But how amazing is it that you were able to do those things at all? Think about it."

Blake's perspective of things never ceases to amaze me.

"You're right. It was pretty incredible."

"Hey … I gotta ask you, what was it like to kiss him? You know, to kiss a ghost."

"I dunno. Real. Like he was alive. His lips were warm and soft and he was very gentle, but it was a friendly kiss, not romantic. His heart belongs to *his* Caleb."

"You gonna tell the others 'bout today?"

"Think I should?"

"I would. But I'd probably tell Shane privately first."

"About the kiss?"

"Yeah. Gotta be honest."

"What if he gets mad?"

"How would you react if Shane kissed another guy?"

"It would depend on the circumstances, I guess."

"If they were the same as yours?"

"I hope I'd understand."

"You expect anything less from Shane?"

"No."

"So, there's your answer."

My brother made me feel better, as always. He ruffled my hair and said, "Oh hey, guess what?"

"What?" I asked, my mood lighter.

"A coupla my friends, girls I'm sorry to say, think you're really cute and asked me if you have a girlfriend."

"What'd ya say?"

"I told them no, you don't have a girlfriend, but you'd prefer to see someone in your own grade." He was chuckling as he spoke.

"What's so funny?"

"My friend Shawna said that she's got a thing for younger guys and would love to break you in."

"Yikes."

"Man, what I wouldn't give to trade places with you. Shawna's hot."

"As hot as Alicia?"

"Different hot. Shawna's sassy hot. Like she'd be real wild in bed. Alicia ... Alicia's just," Blake sighed, "she's incredible. She gets better looking every time I see her."

"You sound serious."

"We just click."

I smiled at Blake and thought how Shane and I clicked too.

"You know, you don't have to cover for me anymore. Like with your friends ... you can tell them the truth."

Blake eyed me carefully. "Are you sure you're ready for that?"

"Yeah. I owe it to Toby."

"Okay, bud." Blake continued looking at me.

"What?" I asked.

"Nothing."

Blake's *nothing* always meant something. I didn't have to ask what it was that time. He smiled at me, and I knew he was proud.

"Boys, dinner's ready!" we heard my mother call out from the base of the stairs.

"Hey, remind me to show you something after supper," I said as we passed by my door.

"Sure. What is it?"

"Remember the two photos of the boys on the truck?"

"Yeah."

"They aren't the same."

"Really?"

We jogged down the stairs and walked into the kitchen. Mom was taking the clay pot out of the oven as we entered. I could smell the roast beef, potatoes, and carrots as soon as I entered the room.

After dinner I showed Blake the photos. He examined them with the magnifying glass and agreed with me—there was a reflection in the truck window glass. The two boys were holding hands in one snapshot, and they weren't in the other.

"The one with the reflection—that's the one from Toby's things, right?"

I nodded.

"Otherwise, they're exactly the same. They musta been taken within a second of each other. Good job to spot it, bud."

"Thanks."

I returned the magnifying glass to its home in my desk drawer amongst note cards, paper clips, a stapler, my glue stick, and the rest of my writing and school supplies.

"You gonna call Shane?" Blake asked.

"I should. I want to … but I'm still worried."

"I know, but the sooner you talk to him, the sooner you can feel better. I'm sure he'll be fine."

"I hope so."

Blake headed to the door. "I'm right down the hall if you need me. Let me know how it goes."

"Thanks. I will."

Blake left my room, and I shut the door. I sighed and picked up my phone. I punched the memory dial button and then the number one. Shane's phone rang a moment later.

"Kelly Street Motel."

"Hey, Shane."

"Oh, hey, you. How are ya?"

I stretched out on my bed, lying on my back with my head on my pillow. "I'm all right. How 'bout you?"

"Whoa. Whattaya mean, all right? You don't sound all right."

"I need to tell you something, and I'm afraid of how you'll react."

Shane's voice dropped instantly. "Just tell me. Whatever it is."

"I was in the woods today, down to Toby's grave."

"Alone?"

"Yeah. Well, see, I was in my room and I looked out the window and I saw him standing in the field, so I didn't waste any time and I just went."

"Okay, slow down. Tell me exactly what happened."

I tried to calm myself down. "All right, so I'm at the grave, and I'm sitting on that big rock near it—the one by the hill. Anyway, I'm freezing cold and I can't get back up the hill, so I'm getting really scared about what's going to happen to me. I've got my head in my hands, and when I look up, there's Toby standing there and asking me if I'm okay."

"Holy crap."

"Yeah, and he puts his hand on my shoulder and sits down next to me and we have an honest-to-God conversation."

"This is incredible."

"I know. And as we're talking, I feel this warm glow all around us, and I'm not cold anymore."

"Then what?"

"We talked. I asked him a bunch of questions, and he asked me some, ya know? It was really weird. Cool, but weird. And he talked about you and how cool you are, 'cept he didn't say cool, he said wonderful or something like that, which you are, and I asked him what we're supposed to do next, and it's like we thought: we gotta get Wendell into the woods. Toby thinks he'll come, but we need to give him time."

"You'd think if anybody wanted him to rush, it'd be Toby."

"No kidding."

"So then what happened?"

"He had to go. He isn't in complete control of it all; he has to obey some sorta, I dunno what it is—cosmic force or something."

"But how did you get out of the forest?"

"He led me through a path that wrapped around to the top of the waterfall."

"Oh wow. That's so cool. Why were you so worried about telling me that?"

I sighed loudly. "Cuz … down by the roses … Toby kissed me." I waited anxiously for some response.

"He … he kissed you?"

"Yeah."

"How?"

"Softly. On the lips. But not like we do—it was more like just a friendly, caring-kinda thing."

"Oh."

"I'm sorry, Shane. I didn't expect it to happen. I really didn't. But that's all it was. Honest."

"Well, I'm glad you told me."

"Yeah?"

"Yeah. You know, it's kinda weird, but it's pretty hot to think Toby is into my boy."

I laughed. "I hardly think that's the case. It was just his friendly way of thanking me for all the work I've done. Plus, he misses his Caleb."

"I miss mine," Shane said sweetly.

We talked for a while longer before saying good night.

When I pushed the off button, I clutched the phone to my chest, relieved and happy. I wished I could roll over and kiss Shane on his pouty lips—maybe more. Being fifteen and horny is a dangerous combination. I went down the hall and took a long, hot shower.

With the weekend came the first day of December. Everyone began to talk about Christmas. Stores all had their Christmas hours posted, and the malls had up their banners indicating how many shopping days were left before the twenty-fifth. Seasonal music played in every shop, and special programs were on the TV. I also discovered eggnog on the shelf in the fridge (my father had a weakness for the stuff, causing it to spontaneously appear as soon as stores began to carry it). Mom was in the kitchen baking her squares, cookies, and cranberry-orange loaves. The whole house smelled of cinnamon, cloves, and citrus. I first detected the pleasing aroma when I awoke on Saturday morning.

Blake had practice that morning, so I got up early to catch a ride into town with him and visit with Shane. When I set foot in the kitchen, Blake was already sitting at the table eating his breakfast.

"Morning, bud. Sleep well?" he asked me.

"Yeah, thanks. You?" I went over to the counter and poured myself a cup of coffee.

"Like a log."

"Sure smells good in here."

"Yeah. Mom's got her first coupla loaves in the oven."

I sat down across from my brother with my coffee. "Must be gettin' close to Christmas if Mom is baking," I said. "Only time of year she enjoys being in the kitchen."

"Well, thank God, really," Blake said.

I laughed. "No kidding. You'll hafta teach me how to cook before you go to university. I don't wanna hafta eat Mom's cooking for the next two years."

Blake chuckled. "I will. No worries." He put his spoon down in his bowl and began to laugh hard. "Remember the time Mom got those pizza pockets?"

I started to laugh, too. "She cooked them in the oven. They were hard as rocks."

"You couldn't cut them, remember?" Blake clapped his hands.

"And you whipped one at the wall to show her how hard they were, and it made a dent in the drywall."

Blake roared.

"I wonder if the new owners have discovered an odd dent to the right of the stove." I added, chuckling. "At least she can bake."

"Everything but doughnuts." Blake smirked as he took his bowl over to the sink. That was all he had to say, and we were both nearly pissing our pants. Visions of black doughnuts with gooey white centres came to mind. Burned on the outside, raw on the inside. My poor mother. We never let her forget it either.

"I'll teach you to cook, bud. It's pretty simple. Can be fun, too."

"What about baking?"

"Sure."

"I'd kinda like to make something for Shane."

"Aww."

"What?"

"That's so cute," Blake mocked me, batting his eyes and resting his head on his hands.

I blushed. "Forget it. It's corny."

"Nah, man. Well, yeah, it is corny, but it's cute too."

"Stop saying that."

"What?"

"Cute."

"Why? What's wrong with being cute?"

"It's embarrassing."

"You'll get over it." He checked his watch. "We better get goin'."

"Yeah. Let's jet."

I'd told Shane I'd be over sometime after ten, not wanting to arrive too early. I sat on the stage of the gym and watched the guys' volleyball practice. I was pleasantly surprised when Shane sat down next to me.

"Hey, you," he said as he plopped down, letting his legs hang over the edge like mine.

"Hi. This is a nice surprise."

"I couldn't wait for you to come over, so I thought I'd come here and see if I could buy you a coffee or something."

"Sure. That'd be great."

"Cool."

"Wanna go now?"

"Sure, unless you wanna watch some of the practice first."

"Nah. I'm done checking things out here."

Shane smiled. "God. Randy Miller is so hot."

"Yeah. Aaron Ashby isn't hard to look at either."

"He's so arrogant though."

"Yeah, but if you taped his mouth shut ..."

"He'd only be half as fun," Shane finished with a smirk.

"Perv."

He laughed.

"Wanna go?"

"Yeah."

We left the gym and walked over to Stape's. Shane bought us each an apple muffin and a coffee. We sat by the front window so we could watch the world go by as we talked.

"Got any plans for Christmas?" I asked.

"We do pretty much the same thing every year."

"What's that?"

"We go to Wolfville to have dinner with my uncle and his family. They've got a coupla kids, a girl a year older than us and a boy who's ten or eleven, I forget which."

"They nice?"

"They're okay. But it sucks going there, cuz they always have all these people in who I have to be introduced to year after year and they all ask the same boring questions. 'What grade are you in?' 'Do you play any sports?' 'Do you have a girlfriend?' It's so lame."

"So I take it you're not out to your uncle's family."

"No. They probably wouldn't be very good people to come out to."

"Oh."

"Yeah. Really churchy."

"That sucks."

"Yup. Oh well, it's just one day of the year."

"Yeah, but it's Christmas day."

Shane took a drink of his coffee. "Christmas doesn't mean that much to me anymore. When my dad was here, it was great, but since he died, well … anyway."

"I'd love it if you and your mom came to our place for Christmas dinner."

"That's really sweet of you, Caleb, but I don't think it's possible. My uncle and cousins are the only part of the family around, and Mom likes to be with them."

"What about your dad's side of the family?"

"Nah. They're all out west, and since he died, they haven't bothered to keep in touch."

"Sorry."

"Hey, their loss." Shane tore at his muffin.

"Couldn't you come, even if your mother doesn't want to?"

"I'd love that, but I should stick with her. You're supposed to be with family on Christmas, so they say."

"You would be at my house. My family's crazy about you."

"Thanks. I dunno, though. I'll hafta think about it, see what Mom says."

"Okay." I nibbled at my muffin. "You wanna come over tonight?"

"Like you need to ask."

I beamed.

"Wanna see if Rye can come over too?"

"Yeah, let's go see what he's doing."

I finished my cup of coffee, and we left Stape's to walk over to Ryley's house.

We hung out at Ryley's playing *Fable 3* until nearly noon. I invited Ryley to join us for the night, so he threw a few things together and walked with us to the motel. Before we had even stepped up to the office door, Blake turned in to the parking lot and stopped the Bronco in front of us.

"We'll just be a minute," I said to my brother.

"All right," he replied from his rolled-down window.

Ryley told us, "I'm gonna wait with Blake."

"Okay."

I heard the door of the Bronco open so Ryley could climb up in, as Shane and I went inside and headed back to his room.

Astro barked happily when he saw Shane, who squatted down and patted the dog's head, talking playfully with him. Astro followed us to the bedroom and hopped up on Shane's bed, flopping down with a thud beside me. I patted the space between his ears as Shane grabbed his clothes and things for coming over. Within five minutes, we were sitting in the truck and leaving the motel parking lot for home.

"What's this crap?" Blake mumbled as we turned at the last intersection before going down our road. Big wet flakes of snow began to hit against the windshield.

"It's not supposed to snow until next week sometime," Ryley said.

"It probably won't amount to anything," I suggested.

"You don't think so, huh?" Blake stopped the truck in the road.

"Holy shit," Shane gasped. We both leaned forward so we could look between the bucket seats out the windshield. We had just driven into a snowstorm. I turned around and saw that it was behind us too.

"It's getting worse by the second. The ground hasn't frozen yet, so the road is gonna be a mess. Dammit. Lock your hub, will ya, Rye?" Blake said.

"You got it."

They jumped out and locked the wheel hubs. The air that swept inside the cab was bitter.

"This feels weird," Shane whispered to me.

"Yeah. Very weird."

The guys got back inside and closed the doors. Blake shifted into four-by-four and made the turn onto our road. He had the four-way flashers on as well as the headlights, but I still don't think a car within two feet of us could possibly have seen us. Visibility was next to nil.

Blake stopped the truck in the road. "Goddamnit. I can't see a thing." He rolled his window down and leaned out, slowly letting the Bronco creep as he steered. Ryley followed suit and leaned out his own window. They'd poke their heads back in for a moment and look back out again. The wind was too strong and cold to be out for any length of time.

"This is impossible. We're just gonna hafta sit here for a while and wait for it to die down before we can go any farther," Blake stated as he rolled up his window. He tugged on Ryley's coat. Ryley popped his head back inside and put up his window. "Forget it, Rye. We're gonna sit and wait."

"This sucks," Ryley grumbled. "It was supposed to be nice all weekend."

We weren't idling for more than a minute when I could see Blake was getting antsy. "Screw this," he said and shifted into first.

"Can you see any better?" I asked.

"Nope."

"So you're what? Going by memory?"

"Memory and luck."

Blake gradually negotiated his way around the first turn. It straightened out, and we were parallel to the main road. There would be another corner that turned to the left and then a straightaway to the house.

"Ever happen to count the time to go from corner to corner?" Blake asked.

"Umm, no. And besides, we're going a lot slower. It wouldn't matter."

"It could be figured out if you take the average speed versus the distance travelled."

"This is starting to sound like a math question," Shane noted.

"Stop," I said suddenly.

Without asking for an explanation, Blake applied the brakes. The Bronco slid through some snow-covered muck and came to a stop. "What is it?"

"Turn hard left here," I instructed.

"We can't be at the corner already," Blake said.

"Yeah, I think we are."

Blake glanced out his window. "Wish I could see that house or something to be sure."

"Trust me."

Blake sighed. "Well, I hope you learn how to do body work, cuz if I put this thing in the ditch, it isn't my fault."

"Are you sure about this, Caleb?" Shane asked me.

"Yeah. I think we're almost off the road right now."

"How can you tell?"

I shrugged. "I can't."

"Well, here goes nothing," Blake said and turned the wheel hard left. He gave the truck some gas, and it spun free of the mud and moved.

"Straighten it out now," I said a few seconds later. Blake did as I told him to do, and the little Ford drove down the last strip of the road. We could just make out the house as the trees at either side of the road stopped and we entered the cul-de-sac.

"Good work, Caleb," Ryley said.

"Yeah. That was pretty incredible," Blake agreed.

We got out of the Bronco and ran up to the front door, the wind going through our coats and chilling us to the core. Blake had to take his bottle of lock deicer from his pocket and spray the front door before he could get his key in the slot. With some effort, he was able to open the door, and we rushed inside. After taking our coats and boots off, we went into the living room, and I got a nice fire going. Blake made hot chocolate in the kitchen and brought it to us. We sat drinking our steaming beverages as the flames danced over the logs in front of us.

The phone rang, and Blake jogged to the kitchen to get it. When he came back to the living room, he said, "That was Mom. She just heard a weather report that this storm is supposed to last until sometime tomorrow. It's actually supposed to get worse overnight."

"Worse?" Shane asked.

"Apparently. Anyway, I told her the roads are the pits and that it isn't a good idea to test them. She's gonna wait until Dad gets off work, and they'll figure out what they're gonna do."

"They should stay at the motel," Shane said. "I'll call my mom, but I know she'll let them have a room for free for the night."

"Oh wow, that'd be great, Shane," Blake said.

"Just let me call my mom, and then you can call yours."

"Thanks."

Shane called home, and then Blake called our mother back at the drugstore. She was very appreciative and was going to call Dad and tell him to meet her at the motel. We asked her to promise to call us when they were both there safely. She agreed and suggested we fill the tubs with water in case the power went out.

After he got off the phone, Blake cooked some macaroni and cheese he made from scratch for our lunch. I was covering gooey noodles with ketchup when we heard a loud bang at the front of the house.

"What the hell was that?" Blake asked no one in particular as we all shot up out of our seats.

"Probably just a shutter that came loose in the wind," Ryley said.

"We'd better check it out," I said.

We all went into the living room, where the fire was still blazing. I added another log for good measure and joined the guys at the window. We could barely see a thing, let alone anything causing the noise.

"Almost sounded like it came from the barn," Shane suggested.

I peered out the side window and could just make out that the side door of the barn was open and snow was beginning to accumulate inside.

"Shit. I gotta go out there and close that," I grumbled, going to the foyer to put on my hat, coat, gloves, and boots.

"I'm coming with you," Shane said and put on his own outerwear. The two of us went out the front door and trudged through the heavy snow over to the side of the barn.

"We should probably check inside first!" Shane yelled over the noise of the wind.

"Right!"

We went inside and looked around the barn. The air was frigid, but there was no wind.

"Wanna check the loft?" Shane asked me.

"Yeah. Guess we should. You go first."

Shane laughed. "So in case there's anything up there, I get to be the one who has to see it first, right?"

"Umm, well, there's that, but I also get to check out your ass this way."

Shane smirked. "Naughty boy."

"Hey, not my fault you wore my favourite pair of your jeans today." They were Guess, dark blue, faded from wear in all the right places, and fit him very nicely.

He shook his head, smiling, and grabbed the rung over his head. After he got to the top, I started on my way up. When we were both in the loft, we examined it carefully.

"Toby? You in here?" I asked the barn.

We heard nothing other than the wind licking at the walls.

"See anything?" Shane asked.

"Nope. You?"

"Zilch."

"Guess maybe this was just one of those things that happens, huh?"

"Yeah. Guess it happens to people with ghosts, too."

I chuckled. "Come on, let's go back inside where it's warm."

"I could make it warm here for you," Shane said slyly.

"I'm too cold to get horny, so don't even try," I mused.

"Aww, c'mon. Not even a little?" He walked over to me and brushed one of my hairs back along the side of my head, lightly touching my ear as his finger went by it.

"You know that drives me crazy."

Shane smiled mischievously, and I couldn't resist him. I kissed him, and he unzipped his coat, pulled me close, and wrapped his coat around the two of us. "Well, hello there," he said with a smile as our noses were just an inch apart. The door banged hard again and made us both jump.

"We should get back," Shane said.

"Yeah."

"Think maybe we can convince Ryley to sleep in another room tonight?"

"We can always just lock him out when he goes to brush his teeth," I giggled.

"That might work."

We went down to the floor and left the barn, securely closing the door before running back to the house and the warmth of the fire.

We had a leisurely paced day after the barn-door incident, just lazing around watching movies and playing games together. Mom called when she arrived at the motel safe and sound and called once again when Dad got there. It had taken my father fifteen minutes to drive from the warehouse to the motel, when it normally would have taken him two. He said that the roads were terrible and it was too cold for the salt to have any effect. They still had power, as did we, but with the way the lights dimmed and flickered, we all knew it was only a matter of time before it went out. Out on Wakefield Road, the phone lines were likely to go down as well.

I kept stoking the fire to ensure at least one room of the house would be warm if the power failed. The door leading to the hall and the one into the dining room were kept shut to trap the heat in the main room. In a short time, we'd be very glad we had planned ahead.

We were sitting in the kitchen eating the chicken stir-fry with basmati rice that Blake had made when the house went dark. It's always the quiet that freaks me out more than the dark. The hums and whirs and ticks of all the appliances stopping instantly makes you realize that you never truly live in silence. Even with the power out, the battery-operated clock on the kitchen wall continued to count out the seconds. *Tick, tick, tick.*

I went over to the junk drawer and pulled out a book of matches, striking one and walking over to the ever-present candle in the centre of the kitchen table.

"Candlelight dinner for four. How romantic." Shane chuckled.

"Did we ever put those surge protectors on the TV, computer, and stuff?" Blake asked me.

"Yup. Done."

"Good."

"Afraid of losing all that downloaded porn?" Ryley teased.

"It's nothing to joke about. It took me hours to get all those pictures," Blake shot back.

"God bless the Internet," Ryley laughed.

Without thinking, I turned on the tap to rinse my plate off. I shook my head as nothing came out of the faucet, and then I put the plate in its proper slot inside the dishwasher.

"Guess we won't be having any dessert tonight," Blake mumbled.

"Got any marshmallows?" Shane wanted to know.

"Oh, hey. Good plan," Blake said, snapping fingers on both hands and pointing at Shane. He went to the pantry and grabbed a four-hundred-gram bag of Fireside marshmallows.

"Got anything long enough to roast them with?" Shane asked.

"We could use my dick—it's plenty long, but it's sensitive and I don't want to burn it," Ryley said, trying to keep a straight face.

"Better let us use it, man—might be the warmest place it ever gets put," Shane snickered.

"Burn!" Blake laughed and high-fived Shane.

"You're just jealous it'll never be in you," Ryley laughed.

"Why would I want a cocktail wienie when I've got kielbasa over there," Shane asked, motioning toward me.

I blushed.

"What's this, then? Have we something to tell?" Ryley asked, intrigued. "Caleb's getting awfully red."

"Screw off," I laughed and threw my balled-up napkin at him.

We carried on for a while like that. It was so good to be relaxed and able to joke around. I'm not sure why it is we guys never seem to find an end to how amusing penis jokes and mother jokes are, but we never do.

As the evening wore on and we'd finished the entire bag of marshmallows (roasting them on the metal skewers from our camping supplies), we found ourselves talking more about Toby and our experiences of the last six months.

"I wish I coulda met him," Shane said.

"What would you say to him if you did?" Ryley asked.

"I'd thank him for saving my life and let him know that, because of him, I'm here today—with the three best friends a guy could ever have. And ..." Shane twisted his hands together, "this might sound stupid, but I'd ask him if he, I dunno, if maybe he could say hi to my dad for me."

I put a hand over Shane's and squeezed. He gave me a soft smile in the firelight.

"How 'bout you, Rye? What would you say to him?" Blake asked.

"I'm not sure. I guess I'd just say how bad I feel for how he had to go through all that shit, and I'd thank him for everything he's done for all of us," Ryley replied.

"I tell you what I'd say to him," Blake offered. "I'd tell him how grateful I am that he chose us to talk to and that it's been the most important thing in my life. Cuz of all this, I've figured out what I want to do for a career. I wanna be a social worker for troubled teens so I can help kids like Toby, like all of us. Get people to talk. Ya know?"

"You'd be amazing at that," Shane said.

"Yeah. That's awesome, Blake," Ryley confirmed.

"Whattaya think, bud?" Blake asked me, his voice having gone from enthused to concerned.

"I can't think of anything you're better suited for. You've already helped me so much, I can just imagine how much you're gonna help a lotta other kids."

"Think Mom and Dad will approve?"

"Approve? I think they'll be thrilled."

"Yeah, you guys are so lucky. Your folks seem like the kinda people that as long as you do your best, try your hardest, and are passionate about it—then you know they're gonna support you all the way, whether it's what they envisioned for you or not," Ryley said. "My parents expect me to wanna be a lawyer or something. Business, at the very least."

"What do you wanna do?" Shane asked.

"No idea. Probably some sorta trade. I love working at carpentry and stuff. I thought at one time I'd like to be an architect, but I'd rather build the building than design it. My folks'll have a field day with me doing blue-collar work. It's gonna suck."

"A good carpenter can make a lotta money. And they're always in demand," Blake said. "'Sides, it's your life. Gotta be happy in your work, or else it's just a job."

"True enough. I guess I'll cross that bridge when I come to it."

"Hell, you'll build the bridge," I joked.

"So, you think we'll ever get to talk to Toby?" Shane asked me.

"I wish I knew. I sure hope so. There's so much more I want to ask him. I think it all depends on Wendell somehow."

"I can't understand why he doesn't come back here. I mean, he knows the truth now. If it were me, I'd be back in a flash," Ryley stated.

"I'm not so sure," Blake said. "Some people need to leave the past behind. We can't say for sure what we'd do in Wendell's place. He's wrestling with a lot of different emotions right now. Maybe it's just all too much for him. And his sister just passed away, as well. He's going through a lot. Imagine being his age and dealing with everything we told him, as well as losing your last living sibling. It can't be easy."

"That's true, but still, I know, no matter what, I'd give anything for just one more minute with my father. If I even had an inkling of hope that that were possible, I'd do whatever it took to see it out for myself," Shane stated.

"Shane, may I ask you something … and you don't hafta answer or if you think I'm an asshole for asking, I'm sorry, okay?"

"Sure, Rye. Go ahead."

"I was wondering … were you there, when your dad died?"

Shane sighed heavily and nodded as he hugged his knees to his chest. "He'd been sick for so long, in that hospital for weeks and weeks and then home again. Then back. It had all gotten almost like routine, and I guess I didn't fully appreciate the gravity of it all at the time. I knew he was dying, but we'd known that for almost two years; and even though he kept getting worse, when you're with someone twenty-four-seven, you don't really notice it so much. But that last time we took him to the hospital, I shoulda seen it. Thinking back, he was so sick I shoulda been able to tell he wasn't ever coming home again. But I was ten and he was my dad, and no matter what anyone said, I knew that my dad was going to live, cuz what God would take a father away from his kid like that?

"Anyway, we were down in his room for hours and hours every day. My mother never left his bedside, and since it was summer, I was there all the time too. We tried to make him smile by playing games or telling jokes. I'd draw for him. He …" Shane put a hand up for a second to catch himself from losing it. His voice was much shakier as he went on. "He had his entire room covered with pictures I had done, and he'd always point them out to the nurses and doctors when they came in. Sick as he was, he was still encouraging me." Shane's lip trembled, and I resisted the urge to hold him. I wanted him to finish his story, to unload it all.

"It was on a Wednesday night, the twenty-fourth of July. The town festival, that they used to have until two or three years ago, was on, and the motel was booked solid. Even with the extra people to help out, Mom had to be there to look after things. It was one of the rare times she wasn't at the hospital and the only time I was there by myself. We were watching a baseball game on the little TV in his room. I was getting sleepy, so Dad told me I could lie down with him on the bed for a bit if I wanted to take a nap. I lay down next to him on that hospital bed and rested my head on his chest. I could hear his heartbeat, but it was so weak …" Shane wiped at his eyes. "My eyelids got heavier and heavier, and I heard my father trying to softly sing as he patted my head. His voice was thin, but I could make out the words. He was singing 'Take Me Out to the Ball Game.' The last thing I saw was Chipper Jones coming up to bat as my father sang the last line of the song. Then I fell asleep.

"When I woke up, it was the middle of the night, and I had to pee. I was very careful not to wake my dad, cuz he was a light sleeper. When I came back to the bed, I bumped the table, and a metal tray fell to the floor making an awful crash—but Dad didn't move." Shane's body shook. "I looked at him carefully, and I knew something was wrong. I kept saying, 'Dad, Dad, Daddy,' and he just lay there. I put my little hand in his big one and … he was so cold. I didn't call for a nurse or anything. I just curled back up with him and wrapped my arms around him, and I told him how much I loved him."

Shane wept openly, and I quickly went over and held him.

"Jesus Christ," Ryley whispered, wiping a tear away.

The wind blasted gust after gust of snow across the fields and around the house. Shane would later tell us that he'd never told another person about what had happened that night. When the nurse came in at dawn, she'd found Shane still holding his father. Shane pretended to wake up when she came in the room and made an excuse to leave before she could say anything. He left the room and ran down the hall, calling his mother from the pay phone in the lobby. When she got to the hospital, he met her in the parking lot and told her that his father was gone. He never told her that he'd held his father for three hours after he had passed.

We didn't talk too much after we got in our sleeping bags (Shane and I zipped ours together for added warmth). We had piled the fire high so we'd be kept warm as we slept, but I knew that Blake would wake himself periodically to add another log or two throughout the night. It didn't take any of us long to get to sleep. It had been an exhausting day.

When the sunlight entered the room in the morning, it woke me from my slumber. The others were still resting peacefully, and the fire was still going, although the last log was three quarters burned. I checked my watch and saw that it was just a few minutes before seven. Outside, the wind was almost nonexistent and the storm appeared to be over, but I imagined the roads were still treacherous. I got up and placed another log on the fire before going to the washroom. The house was frigid beyond the living room. I checked the thermometer outside the kitchen window before going back to the warmth of the fire. The mercury was fixed at nine degrees below zero.

I returned to the living room and snuggled back into the sleeping bag with Shane. He partially woke up and cuddled with me, sticking one of his legs between mine, the coarse dark hairs of his shin tickling my calf.

"You're so nice and warm," I whispered. "Power's still out. It's freezing."

He grunted contentedly and went back to sleep. I drifted off again too, not getting up until sometime after eight when Blake dropped the fireplace tongs against the hearth.

"Sorry, fellas," he apologized when he saw the three of us wake up and glare at him.

———

The last day of school before Christmas break was the first day I experienced any kind of discrimination firsthand. Word had slowly gotten around that Shane and I were gay, but up to that point, no one had said or done anything directly to us that was negative. Most people just didn't really care—which is perfect. We had a few people tell us how cool we were, and I even had one kid from the junior high follow me into the washroom one day at lunch and, checking to make sure no one else was around first, tell me he hoped he could be as brave as me someday. We would have talked more, but some other guys came in and he bolted.

I was gathering my things at my locker at the end of classes on that final day before break when some kids (three guys and two girls) I didn't really know strolled by my locker. One of the guys, putting on a show (to impress?), said, "Hey, fag. You know you wanna come over here and suck my dick."

I closed my locker door and responded, "No, I don't eat pussy."

Shocked by my response, he put his hands on his hips and glared at me. "What did you say to me?"

"You mean you can't hear *and* you're an asshole? Life just isn't fair sometimes, is it?"

"Man, you are askin' for it."

"For what? I'm standing here minding my own business and you come along and throw hate at me, and I'm the one who's asking for it? Fuck you."

I turned and headed up the stairs at the end of the hall. I heard some rumbling of voices behind me and someone running up the steps as I made my way out the side door.

I was in the student parking area on my way to the Bronco when I heard the kid yell, "Get back here, you little faggot."

Blake was in the Bronco, and he got out, slamming his door. He was about to speak when someone else yelled.

"Hey, Allensbee!" a voice boomed from over by the rough-kids' section.

The kid following me stopped and stared. Tim Weller calmly walked over to him. "Come with me for a second," he instructed.

I was at the Bronco with Blake, waiting to see how things would play out. Tim escorted the Allensbee guy over to where we stood. Allensbee looked hopeful he had a comrade-in-arms.

"Hey, Caleb," Tim greeted me.

"Hey, Tim. How's the car working?"

"Fine, thanks. Makes a bit of a clunk on corners, though."

"Probably a ball joint. Possibly a bearing. Want me to check it out for ya sometime?"

"Thanks, that'd be cool," Tim replied. "Now, on to business. I believe Steve here has something he'd like to say to you, don'tcha Steve?"

"Man, what the hell? You're sticking up for this douche bag? Don'tcha know this guy's a fag?"

"I don't need to stick up for Caleb. Kid's got bigger balls than anybody I know." Tim smirked at me, remembering what I'd said months before. "And he might be gay, but he ain't no fag." Tim grabbed Steve's collar and pulled it tightly, choking off the guy's air supply. "Now, I want you to apologize to him and to promise him—and me—that you ain't gonna bother him or his boy, Shane, or anybody else for that matter, cuz if you do … well, let's just say it won't be in the best interest of your health. Understand?" Tim let go of Steve's collar and pushed him forward so he was within inches of me.

"I'm waiting," I said forcefully, glaring at Steve.

"Ah. Look … what I said before … I'm sorry, all right?"

"No. It's not all right. Where the hell do you come off talking to me like that? Huh? What have I ever done to you?"

"Nothing, man. I just heard … you know."

"What? That I'm gay. So what? That gives you the right to spew your hate at me?"

"Um. No. I mean. God. You just surprised me when you talked back."

"Oh, so I shoulda just taken it, felt bad about myself, and walked away so you could pick on me every day for the rest of the year?"

Steve hung his head and stared at his boots. "Um. No. I guess not."

"I might not look like much to you, but I'm somebody you'd be better off having as a friend than an enemy. So," I said, putting out my hand, "would you like to try again at making your first impression?"

Steve looked at my hand and then up to my eyes. He took a deep breath and let it out slowly. He took my hand and shook it. "I'm really sorry," he said. That time I believed him.

"Apology accepted."

Our hands parted, and he gave me a weak smile.

"Everybody cool?" Tim asked.

I nodded. "Yep. Good here."

Steve nodded as well. "Yeah." He sighed again and ran a hand through his hair as he turned to go.

"Have a good Christmas, Steve," I said as he walked away.

He turned around and replied, "Umm. Yeah. You too," and went back to his friends, who all had stunned, silenced expressions on their faces.

"Thanks, Tim," I said.

"Don't sweat it, dude. You didn't need me anyway. You're one tough little shit."

"No kidding, huh?" Blake confirmed.

"Want me to look at the car?"

"Nah, man. It can wait. You have a good Christmas."

"Thanks. You too."

"Count on it."

Tim moseyed back over to his car, and Blake and I got in the Bronco. I didn't have any more run-ins with Steve, or anyone else for that matter, after that. Steve and I never became friends, but he'd acknowledge me in the halls with a "hey." Sometimes the small victories are just as satisfying as the big ones anyway.

Chapter Twenty~Five

Our first Christmas in Wakefield House was one to remember. The house was decorated throughout the main floor, with our big fir tree taking up more than its fair share of the living room. As you drove down to the cul-de-sac, you could see it standing cheerily near the window, its colourful decorations and white lights twinkling. There was a wreath with a red bow on our front door, as well as on the barn over the double doors at the front. Dad had put in spotlights to show off the fronts of the buildings, and everything felt cozy, warm, and wonderful.

On Christmas Eve, Shane came over to spend the evening with us. He was going with his mother to spend the afternoon the next day with his uncle's family, like he had told me before, so we exchanged our gifts that night. I had gone online and ordered a baseball jersey (a black Buster Posey # 28 with the World Series Champions patch) to complement Shane's Giants hat and placed it under the tree next to Blake's gift for Alicia, who was also coming over for the evening after the church service Blake was attending with her.

They arrived home shortly after eight, and we all sat down in the living room to enjoy coffee and nibble from a large assortment of sweets. Shane and I were on the sofa; my brother and Alicia were on the love seat.

"Guess that leaves the chairs for the old married couple," Dad said with a chuckle as he sat down in the recliner. "Your mother will be up fussing the whole time anyway. You know her." Dad smiled as he spoke. As predicted, Mom would spend most of the evening running back and forth to the kitchen.

We had a really nice evening together, playing some games and chatting. My father, in one of the best moods I've ever seen him in, even spiked my coffee with mint chocolate Bailey's, giving me a wink and a *don't-tell-your-mother* smile. As it got later, my mother decided it was time for presents, and she handed one to Shane and another to Alicia, saying "It's just something small" to each of them.

Shane unwrapped his present and discovered a large hardcover book on famous artists and a gift card for HMV. Alicia was given a gift card for Chapters and a book about ancient Egypt (I hadn't known until then that she was fascinated by ancient cultures and was strongly considering getting into archaeology). They both thanked my parents, and my mother made an excuse to go to the kitchen, calling for my father when she got there. I knew she was giving us some space so we could exchange our presents privately.

Shane handed me my present, and I gave him his. He watched me open mine first. He gave me a Miles Austin (my favourite player in the NFL, the Dallas Cowboys wide receiver, who is not only a great athlete, but also an absolute Adonis) gem-mint 10 rookie card and a subscription to *Motor Trend* magazine. I gave him a big hug and a kiss.

"Oh, that's so cute," I heard Alicia say from the other side of the room, causing me, of course, to blush.

Shane was beaming, pleased I liked the gift so much.

"Okay, your turn," I said.

He unwrapped his present and smirked. "Wow. This is perfect," he said, putting the jersey on immediately. "I love it."

Alicia and Blake exchanged their presents, and afterward Blake called out, "It's safe to come back in now!" to our parents.

Mom scurried in, and we proudly displayed our presents for her.

Midnight came quickly, and we got ready to take Alicia and Shane back home. Blake and Alicia went ahead of us to the car. Shane and I were just about to go out the door when Shane said, "Oh, hey, wait a sec. I almost forgot." He took another present from the bag he'd put his things in and said, "This is for your parents."

My father had already gone up to bed, but my mother was still in the kitchen. "Mom, can you come here for a sec?" I called down the hall. We already had our boots on, and we didn't want to traipse through the house in them.

Mom came down the hall, smiling. "What is it, hon?"

"I wanted to give you this," Shane said, handing her the nicely wrapped parcel.

"Oh, why thank you, Shane. May I open it now?"

"If you'd like."

Mom carefully slid her finger under the paper and popped the tape up so as not to rip the pretty design. She gently laid the paper on the floor and opened the box it had covered. Folding back the tissue, she found the gift. A hand went to her mouth. She set the box on the small table next to the pile of car keys and removed a framed picture. "Oh, Shane ... it's ..." but Mom didn't finish her sentence. Still holding the picture, she wrapped her arms around my boyfriend and hugged him. "Thank you so much." She gave him a kiss on the cheek and wiped at her eye as she gazed at the gift.

Shane, bashfully, asked, "You remember what I told you about what I draw?"

Mom nodded. "What you find beautiful," she whispered tearfully as she met Shane's eyes.

Still not having seen the picture, I asked, "May I see?"

Mom handed me the frame. I expected to see a picture of our house or perhaps even the family. Instead, I found something that surprised me. It was a drawing of me, done in graphite, sitting on the cement floor of the garage in front of the Bronco, in my jeans and St. Louis ball cap. You could see the bumper behind my back. One of my knees was drawn up, my greasy hand resting on it, clutching a can of Coke. A wrench sat on the ground to my right side. I looked happy without smiling.

I smirked at Shane, impressed and touched at the same time.

Blake honked the horn of the Focus as I handed the picture back to my mother.

"You don't know how much this means to me," Mom said to Shane.

He grinned. "I'm glad you like it."

"I love it."

His grin grew wider. "Thanks for everything, Karen. Merry Christmas."

"Merry Christmas to you, and to your mother. Please send her my best."

"I will. Good night," he replied as he opened the door.

"Night."

"Back in a bit," I said to my mother.

"Okay. Drive safe."

We joined Alicia and Blake in the car and drove into town.

A lot happened in the weeks following Christmas. It was almost like we all made New Year's resolutions to have our best year yet—to be more confident and have more fun. Hunter asked out Heather Markus (who said yes), and Moira started seeing Blake's teammate, Aaron (who we had thought was conceited but was actually really cool once we got to know him).

The first dance of the year was for Valentine's Day. It was going to be awkward, but Shane and I wanted to get the first one since being open about our relationship out of the way. We discussed strategy with our friends—who were all supportive and protective. As Drew put it, "You dis one of us, you dis all of us—and there are a lot of us now." And he was right. Our group had grown exponentially. When we got together for Ryley's sixteenth birthday party, there were twenty-eight of us.

When Shane and I had our first slow dance together, our friends provided a bubble for us, with us dancing in the centre of their circle. As the evening wore on, it seemed it was unnecessary to continue such a formation, as we hadn't heard anyone being rude or giving us a hard time in any way. So we let down our guards and continued having fun, getting to be more relaxed. Shane and I danced with our friends as well as each other, and we were having a great time, our sense of relief adding to our fun.

There must have been a conversation going on across the room that wasn't as favourable, as we heard a loud "Screw you guys!" and watched as Blake stormed across the gym floor to join my group. He sat down next to me on the bench.

"You okay?" I asked.

"I'm great, bud."

"You look pissed."

"Disappointed is more like it."

"Oh." I felt guilty even though I had done nothing wrong. I knew Blake was upset with some of his teammates, and I figured it was about me. "Guess I was kinda naïve to think no one would have a problem with us."

Blake shook his head. "Nah, man. You expected it. You and your friends even prepared for it … and you still came out here and were yourself. I can't tell you how much I admire that."

"Thanks."

A guy I recognized from the hockey team walked across the gym floor and over to where we sat. He had a determined look on his face.

"Blake, I heard what those assholes were saying, and I want to thank you for speaking up. I should have said something myself."

"Don't sweat it, Corey."

Corey nodded and looked at me. "Caleb …"

"Yeah?"

"Wanna dance?"

I shot a surprised glance at Blake, but he was already smiling. In that one instant, I understood what had happened.

"Sure," I said, smiling myself.

Corey, the popular and handsome left wing on the high school hockey team, had asked me to dance. As we walked out to the centre of the gym together, I could feel the eyes of all the students on us. I sensed the unease on Corey's face. I took his strong hand in mine and said, "Fuck 'em all."

He laughed nervously, and we began to dance to the medium tempo music. When the song ended, Corey said, "Thanks. That was nice."

"Yeah. You're a good dancer. Must be all that practice you get on the ice, huh?"

He chuckled and let out a sigh of relief. "Well, there's that, and, um, I didn't want to let down my hot counterpart."

I blushed. When a good-looking jock tells you that you're hot, what else can you do?

"I'd better get back to Shane. He might get jealous," I said jokingly (but also a bit seriously).

"You mind if I ask him to dance? Just one dance. I promise."

"Go for it."

"Cool. Thanks, Caleb. You know, if you two weren't an item, I'd definitely be asking you out."

Before I could say anything else, Corey was gone. Shane's eyes found mine, as if surprised and wondering if I was okay with his dancing with Corey. I smiled and nodded.

It was pretty flattering that Corey found me attractive, and Laura pumped me for details when I sat back down on the bench. I looked out on the dance floor and watched Shane dance with him. I couldn't take my eyes off Shane. I liked being flirted with, but it reminded me of how much I love my boyfriend.

When the Mariana's Trench song ended, Shane came back over to the bench next to me and Corey performed his bravest act of the night—he walked back over to his teammates and sat on the bench with them. We kept our eyes on him for a while, making sure he was okay. They all seemed to be talking, and the expression on Corey's face was one of relief. He smiled over at me and flashed a discreet thumbs-up.

That night seemed to mark a change in our school. Other kids would come out that spring, too. A guy in grade nine, a girl in grade eleven, and another guy in grade twelve. I wondered about that kid from the washroom from time to time. He saw me in the hall once and smiled at me. I said, "Hey, bud," to him and returned the smile. Hopefully, sometime he'd be out too.

The month of February was frigidly cold, but there was very little snowfall. The snow that was down, however, stayed down. Blake and I did some cross-country skiing when we got the chance. We'd go over the meadow and to the edge of the forest. We'd listen carefully as we trekked along, but neither of us heard anything other than nature.

On one of our ventures, I asked, "What do you think's happened? We haven't heard anything from Toby since before Christmas."

"I'm guessing we're at a stalemate. Toby knows there's no more we can do. It's up to Wendell."

"But you'd think he woulda tried to push us to get Wendell out here, wouldn't ya?"

"Who's to say?"

Our skis slid along the crunchy white snow covering the meadow. We could see the ruts of our previous journeys as we made our circles around the perimeter of the forest.

"I miss him," I admitted.

"Yeah. I do, too."

Shane's birthday was next on the list of my friends' sixteenth celebrations. Hunter, Laura, and Adria all already had their beginner's licences, and Drew was days away from having his full licence. Ryley was going that week to get his test done. Poor Moira had failed her first attempt and was waiting a while before going again. Since she was seeing Aaron on a regular basis, he was driving her everywhere anyway. I'm sure *she just hated* being seen with him in his nicely done-up Jeep Cherokee (complete with the four-litre engine and sport package. It was older, but it was in great shape).

I would be the last to turn sixteen in our group, if you didn't count Heather—which at that point, you probably should count, as she was with us all the time. Shane's big day was only a week away, and I was stumped for a present idea. My other friends were a lot easier to buy for—gift cards always worked. My boyfriend, that was much more challenging. I wanted to get him something special, but I didn't have much money. Blake was nice enough to lend me a bit, but I'd have to be creative.

I was rummaging around in my closet when I was struck with inspiration—literally. I was getting a pair of jeans from one of the milk crates and caused the crate to slide out of place. I shoved it back forcefully, and it caused Toby's box to fall off the shelf and hit me on the head. I swore and rubbed my head as I picked the box up. I opened it for the first time in a while and realized I had never given one of the photographs to Shane.

I figured I could afford to buy a nice frame for it—either silver or black would look best—and give him that along with the watch I had already picked out. I couldn't wait until I could start working so I'd have a few bucks in my pocket. The manager at Ryley's store had said I might be able to work there for the summer, which was great, but I really hoped to get a job at the Petro-Canada station—pumping gas to start with, and maybe getting to move into the service area and do the basics like tire and oil changes. I'd put my name in and made a point of talking to the manager. I was hopeful.

As I took the photo that Constance had originally given me over to my bed, I heard something I hadn't in quite some time.

Caleb

I glanced out my window but saw nothing. The wind picked up, and there were no other sounds.

On Shane's birthday, I gave him a rather slick new watch with all sorts of features on it, from compass to phases of the moon, in front of our friends and saved the photograph for when we were alone.

Blake was on his way to pick me up when I gave Shane his second present.

"More? Caleb, the watch is wicked, and more than enough," he said as he took the present from my hands.

"This one didn't cost me much. I swear."

He cocked an eyebrow and unwrapped the box. "Oh, hey. That's great," he stated, sounding pleased.

"I had forgotten all about it till the other day."

"Thanks. I'm really glad to have it." He gave me a kiss and flipped out the stand on the back of the frame, resting it on his bedside table.

"It was strange. When I took the picture outta the box, I heard Toby call out for Caleb."

"Really? It's been a long time since you've heard anything. Right?"

"Yeah. Since before Christmas."

"Wonder why you heard him now? You think it was cuz of the photo?"

I shrugged. "I dunno. I guess."

Shane gave me a naughty-looking smirk. "Wanna make out till your brother gets here?"

"I dunno. I guess," I repeated.

"Brat," he said, pulling me to him.

All too soon, I heard the Bronco pulling into the parking lot. Shane watched me put my things together to leave.

"Hey, it's pretty cold out there tonight. You should take my hoodie," he said, offering me his favourite hooded sweatshirt (a dark blue colour with the words Old Navy in gold across the chest) by taking it off and handing it to me.

"Aww, thanks, but I can't take that. It's your favourite."

"That's why I want you to have it."

I grinned and put down my bag of things, pulling the sweatshirt over my head. It was a little big for me, but I didn't care. It was Shane's and I was wearing it. I was happy.

"I'll give it back tomorrow, okay?"

"No—I want you to keep it."

I held the collar up to my nose and sniffed, inhaling Shane's scent. I smiled as I let the fabric fall away from my face.

"Thanks."

Shane nodded and leaned in to kiss me once more.

"Welcome."

"Happy birthday." I put on my jacket and added, "See ya tomorrow?"

"You bet."

I stepped into the frigid night and turned to wave to Shane before getting in the truck with Blake and heading for home.

On my birthday, everyone got together at my place. My parents kept their distance, merely being a presence but not a nuisance, until shortly before five. They called me out to the kitchen and told me that, since I was older they didn't want to get me a bunch of little gifts, instead deciding to get me one larger present. I wasn't sure what they were driving at until, along with Blake, they walked me out to the barn. I opened the door and snapped on the lights. What I saw I couldn't believe.

"No way!" I screamed out.

"I think he likes it," my father said to my mother.

"Are you shitting me right now?"

"Whoa, language, Caleb," Mom said, trying to sound stern but obviously pleased with my reaction.

"Sorry, but … really … no joking?"

There, in the centre of the floor, stood a 1989 Mustang LX fastback.

"Now, I gotta tell ya, Caleb, it's gonna need a lotta work before it's roadworthy, but I've done my research and the car came from a very reputable source. The original engine is still in it—I made sure it was the five-litre, cuz I know how you feel about the ones with four or six cylinders; and there's no rust—that was the clincher for me. It's been sitting in a garage for years and it was well undercoated, but I also know it's probably not what you ever pictured your dream car would look like. I hope you're not too disappointed," Dad said.

"Disappointed? Oh my God, Dad. This rocks! I can't wait to work on this. If I put everything I have into it, I might have it done in time for my senior prom. Man, that would be sweet. Can't you just picture it: all done up with a fresh coat of metallic paint—deep purple, like a grape Popsicle, and offset rims, sparkling silver. I'll put a hood scoop on it, a Saleen body kit, and louvers on the rear window." To most people, it would have looked like a faded, cream-coloured money pit. To me, it was countless weekends and afternoons of pleasure to look forward to.

I ran over to my parents and hugged them both. "You guys are amazing parents. I am so fortunate …" I found myself choked up, so I stopped talking.

I was on such a high that I couldn't even feel my feet touching the ground. My parents made me promise not to brag to my friends (who were still inside watching a movie), but they knew I wouldn't have anyway. I felt rather guilty at accepting such a gift, but I was told it had only cost a few hundred dollars more than Blake's volleyball camp, and that wasn't even a birthday present. I felt better after learning that.

"Your brother chipped in, too," Dad told me.

"You did?" I asked him.

"Yeah, man. I figure this car will be the one that you use to show off your mad skills. You'll be opening up your own shop before you know it," he told me, ruffling my hair.

"Caleb's Custom Cars," I said under my breath.

When the party was over and everyone else had gone home, I went upstairs to get ready for bed.

It was almost one o'clock as I went to use the bathroom before calling it a night. Blake's door was open, and he called out to me.

"Hey, Caleb. Come here for a sec."

"Sup?"

"Shane wanted me to give you this." He held out an envelope for me.

"What is it?"

"I dunno, bud. Why don't you open it?"

I tore the seal of the envelope and removed a card. Shane had already given me a card with my present (a leather-bound journal with a pen set, engraved with my initials), so I was unsure why I was getting another. The front of the card was a generic 'Happy Birthday,' with a picture of a Ferrari on it. Inside the card, I read the bland message that came with the card, and then read Shane's note on the opposite side:

Caleb, you know how much I love you, and there is nothing in this world that can ever change that. I could write the words a million times or say them over and over for eternity—but it still wouldn't be enough. I can think of only one thing that I can give you that will be special enough for you. I know it'll be late when you read this, but I hope you'll go out to the barn and see what I've left for you. Lots of love, Shane xoxo.

"What's it say?"

"It's kinda private," I replied.

"Ah. Okay."

"Thanks for giving it to me. And for the car ... I mean, how did you keep that a secret?"

"That was rough. I had to duck outta school the other day and help

Dad get it out here and in the barn. Toughest part was keeping you from going out there for a few days."

"You mean it's been out there ..."

"Since Friday."

"No way."

Blake laughed. "Seriously."

"You guys rock."

"Hey, it's your sixteenth. You deserve it."

"Thanks so much. For everything."

"No prob. Have a good night, bud."

"Yeah. You too."

I tried not to make any noise as I crept out the back door of the house. For April, it was a relatively mild night, and I left my jacket open as I went to the barn. I opened the door slowly and stepped inside, shutting it behind me—making sure it latched so it wouldn't blow open and crash against the building.

I looked around the barn, trying to see if there was anything wrapped up or another note for me to find. I checked over the car, making sure to lock it before gingerly closing the door. I heard a faint scratching noise from the loft. I considered for a moment that there were mice in the barn or that Toby was signalling me. I took the first rung of the ladder to the loft in my hands and climbed up. As I peered over the opening at the top, I could scarcely see a thing. I pulled myself up onto the floor and stood, trying to find the source of the noise.

A light snapped on, and I raised my hand to shield my eyes. The light went down to shine on the floor, and I could see a figure walking toward me.

"Hey you," Shane said softly.

"Shane? What's going on?"

"Blake give you your card?"

"Yeah."

"Didn't you figure it out?"

It all suddenly became very clear.

"I think I just did," I replied, leaning in to meet his kiss.

He led me over to the end of the loft, where he'd laid out blankets, pillows, and some candles. He lit the candles with a long, plastic, barbecue lighter and turned to face me.

"Is this all right?" he asked me timidly.

I smiled at him. "It's perfect."

He gently placed a hand on the side of my face. "I love you, Caleb."

"I love you, too, Shane."

He took my hand in his, and we lay down on the blankets together.

Chapter Twenty-Six

After having the best birthday of my life—surpassing any preconceived notions of what a sweet sixteen could be—I found myself sitting opposite Blake the next morning at the breakfast table. I couldn't wipe this stupid smile off my face, and Blake, who could always see right through me, waited for Mom to go get something from the fridge before mouthing the words, "Did you?" I smiled even wider and nodded. Blake flashed me a thumbs-up from the side of his bowl, and we continued to eat our cereal as Mom joined us at the table. I filled him in with the information I was willing to share as we walked up the road to meet the bus later that morning, including how Shane had gently woken me up with a kiss before walking home at dawn.

One day toward the end of the month, due to high winds and blowing snow, school was cancelled partway through the morning. It would turn out to be the last snowstorm of the year. Shane and Ryley decided to come home with Blake and me (they forged permission slips from their parents during computer class so they could go on the bus), and we returned to an empty house, both my parents never fortunate enough in their lines of work to get storm days.

The walk from the bus to our house was bitterly cold and tricky underfoot. The road was a glare of ice, as the snow had turned to freezing rain and ice pellets. Upon entry into the house, we discovered the power was out. As we had done before, we closed off the living room and built a nice fire in the fireplace. We raided the pantry and played *Hearts* while we snacked. Blake was able to shoot the moon in the first round, and his luck continued as he slaughtered us in the first game. We were in the middle of game three when we heard a knock at the door.

We all exchanged a look of uncertainty. Who on earth would be knocking on our door during an ice storm?

"Maybe it's some really committed Jehovah's Witnesses," Ryley joked.

Blake laughed as he got up to answer the door. He snapped back the dead bolt and opened the front door.

"Good morning," Wendell Hildebrand said, his face drawn but attempting a smile.

"Wendell … it's good to see you again," Blake said. "Please, come in."

Wendell stepped inside the foyer, and Blake closed the door. Our unexpected visitor seemed transfixed as his gaze scanned over the house, taking in the sight he hadn't seen since the early 1940s.

"Join us in the living room, where it's warm," Blake motioned.

Wendell took off his boots (they were a sort of rubber boot that zippered over his shoes) and followed Blake into the living room.

"I'd offer you a coffee or something, but the power is out," Blake said.

"That's fine. Fine." Wendell looked around the room. "Place feels the same, except it's brighter. New windows and lightening of the stain on that wood has made a world of difference. Did your family do all this work?" he asked Blake.

"Some of it. Most was done by previous owners."

Wendell nodded. "They did a nice job."

"I, umm, I didn't hear a car pull up. How'd you manage to get here in this weather?" Shane asked. "Aren't the roads terrible?"

"Indeed they are, but I was able to make it all the way to the first corner on this road before my car went in the ditch."

"Oh my God. Are you okay?" Ryley asked.

"Yes, I'm quite all right, thank you. I was going very slowly and I don't think I even did much damage to the car, but it's stuck all the same. I walked the rest of the way. Rather felt like old times, walking this road again."

"Why today, of all days? In this weather?" Blake inquired.

"I honestly couldn't say. I merely awoke this morning after having some very peculiar dreams, and I felt this overwhelming compulsion to come here." Wendell shifted in the rocker, where he'd chosen to sit. "I must confess I've done a great deal of soul-searching since that night we talked at the shore. I'd lie in bed at night and I could see and hear the events of the past, but they were clearer—much clearer than before. I'm very grateful that the letter I wrote way back then never fell into hands as naïve as those that penned it. I'm ashamed of how I condemned Tavis for Toby's death. I let my emotions speak for me, I'm afraid."

"It wasn't done intentionally. You were devastated," Blake said.

" That is true, but it's no excuse." Wendell looked upon each of our faces in sequence. "You boys have been through a great deal. I know."

"I think I speak for all of us when I say we'd do anything to help Toby," Shane said.

"Yes. I believe you would. But … I wonder, would you be willing to do something for me?"

"What would that be?" Blake asked nicely.

Wendell sighed and folded his hands. "I wonder if you'd accompany me into the woods."

We all held our breath in disbelief. Did he really just say that?

"Umm, yes. Yes, of course," Blake replied. "But why the change of heart?"

"I've been having this dream lately. Well, not really a dream, more like a vision. I have it both when I sleep and when I'm awake. I see this hand reaching out to me from the darkness, but I don't take it, I simply follow it. It leads me through a maze of trees and hedges until I reach a babbling brook. When I look into the water, I see these flowers, like iridescent roses. I notice they're pinned in place below the surface. I kneel down and put my hand in the clear, cool water to pick one of them up, and when I bring it to the surface, it instantly dies in my hand. I have this image run through my mind once or twice a day. What do you make of it?"

No one knew what to say, and Wendell didn't really need us to tell him, anyway. He looked about the room nostalgically. "If you don't mind, I should very much like to walk around the house a bit before we go."

"Please, feel free," I said.

"I shan't be long."

Wendell got up from his seat and immediately made his way to the stairs, taking his time to climb them, holding the banister for support.

We waited in the living room, not talking at all, each of us lost in his own thoughts, for twenty minutes or more. When Wendell came back down the stairs, he didn't rejoin us in the living room. He stood in the hall and said, "Okay. It's time to go now."

We went to the foyer and put on our outerwear, dressing warmly. The freezing rain had stopped and the sun was out, but it was chilly. At first, Blake and Ryley stood on either side of Wendell, in case he felt he might slip on the path; but Wendell was surprisingly sure-footed, and I noticed how the toes of his boots had spikes on them for traction. He had come prepared and led the way.

Wendell stopped before we went over the stream. Without turning to face us, he asked, "What will I see?"

"I don't know," I answered honestly.

"I can't bear the thought of seeing Toby suffer."

"I don't think you'll see anything like that," Shane said. "I think Toby just needs to see you."

Wendell took a deep breath. "Fair enough." He stepped over the narrow part of the stream and entered the threshold to the woods. The snow in the forest wasn't as deep or covered in as much ice, the trees taking the brunt of the pellets on themselves. The woods were mostly silent, other than our crunching feet, a light breeze, and the occasional bird flying about in the distance.

We made our way to the clearing, stopping at the top of the slope down to the waterfall. Blake led the group down, Wendell using my brother's shoulder for leverage on the descent. At the base of the oak tree, we stopped, and Ryley swept away snow from the engraving so Wendell could see it.

Wendell traced the letters with his finger, removing his glove, despite the temperature, to get a true feel of them. "I remember the night Toby carved this. I had given him a jackknife for his birthday. It had a …"

"A real marble handle," I finished.

Wendell looked at me.

"That was with Toby's treasures," I let him know.

Wendell smiled. "This was our sanctuary. Our safe haven from the world. We'd come here whenever we could get away. We'd arrange to meet late at night. I had a path that I used through the woods that came out behind my father's barn. It was a long walk, but it was worth it. On hot summer nights, we'd lie out here and watch the stars together. When I think of it now, it seems like only yesterday—but at the same time, so very long ago." Wendell stared off into the distance as he spoke.

We continued down the slope to the clearing, where Wendell went directly to the waterfall, which was frozen in place like a giant icicle. He peered at the frozen water of the stream by his feet. There was a rustling sound in the distance.

"What was that?" Wendell asked no one in particular.

Before anyone had a chance to respond, we heard a familiar voice.

Caleb

"Did one of you say that?" Wendell asked us, spinning around to face us.

"No," I replied.

"That's not funny. It's cruel. This is all some sort of cruel joke, isn't it?" He sounded truly frightened.

"Wendell, I can assure you, this is no joke," Blake insisted.

"Then who said that? Who called my name?"

"I think you know who it was," Shane said.

Shane motioned with his head for Wendell to turn and focus on the spruce trees behind him.

"You haven't forgotten my voice, have you?" Toby asked. He stood just in front of the path between the trees, grinning at us with that boyish smile of his.

Wendell slowly turned around to face the same direction as the rest of us. Tears spilled from his eyes when they fell on Toby. "Dear Lord," he whimpered. "This can't be happening."

Toby walked over to him and gazed into Wendell's eyes. "But it *is* happening, Caleb."

"B-b-but how? Why?"

"I don't know how. All I know is that I've been waiting to see you so I can tell you how much I love you. I always have, and I always will." Toby reached a hand up to Wendell's face and wiped a tear from his cheek. "You're still the most beautiful boy on earth," he said sweetly.

Wendell shook his head. "I've lost so much time."

"We don't lose time any more than we lose the people we love. Time goes on forever. It just changes location."

"What do you mean?" Wendell asked, confused.

"I can't explain it any better than that. All I know is that I have to go soon."

"No. No, please. You can't go; I can't lose you again," Wendell cried, stumbling back and sitting on the log.

"I don't have a choice, Caleb. I'm sorry."

The wind picked up, and a chill went through the clearing before everything became silent again. With the new silence, there also came a warm amber glow, diminishing the cold. The ice melted, and the waterfall splashed into the brook. Everything in the clearing became fresh and green, like it was a late spring day.

Toby walked over to us and said, "I can never thank you boys enough for what you've done for me. I don't believe a guy could ever hope to have better friends."

"Toby?" Ryley said, stepping over to him. "I just wanna, I wanna thank you for helping us all out, ya know, and for bringing us all together. I'll never forget you." He put his arms around Toby, and they hugged.

"It's a privilege to call you my friend," Toby told him.

"Toby … I don't know how I can ever thank you enough for what you've given us," Blake said. "You've made all of us better people, and because of you, I know that I want to go on and help more kids, so what happened to you doesn't happen again."

"That means a great deal to me, Blake," Toby said. "You're going to be a wonderful role model for many kids, especially your own."

Blake gave Toby a hug, and Toby whispered something in Blake's ear. Blake chuckled and patted Toby on the back.

"Toby ... I gotta ask you something," Shane said nervously.

Toby strolled over and stood in front of Shane. "Ask me anything."

"Um ... I don't know where you're going now, but if you see my father, would you tell him his son misses him?"

"Oh, Shane, he knows how much you miss him. He misses you, too."

Shane looked at Toby with big, wet eyes. "You've seen him?"

Toby nodded. "Yes. He's very proud of you. He wants you to be proud of yourself, too. Why else would he ask me to hold you that night?"

Shane couldn't speak for a moment. "You ... you mean ...?"

"Uh-huh."

Tears ran down Shane's face. He embraced Toby, wrapping his arms around him and resting his head on his shoulder. "You're an angel, aren't you?"

Toby's boyish grin returned. "I'm just a kid like you."

Shane shook his head. "You are so much more than that."

When their embrace ended, he placed a kiss on Toby's cheek and stepped back, wiping his eyes.

Toby stepped over toward me. "I can't tell you how glad I am that our paths crossed, Caleb."

I nodded, barely able to speak. "Me too."

"Your bravery inspires me."

"My bravery? It's you who've given me the strength and courage to be myself. I wish more than anything that you didn't have to go."

"Aww, Caleb, that's sweet, but as I said before, if you love somebody, they never really go away. I'll always be with you, and you with me."

"I do love you, Toby."

"So do I," Shane said.

"Me too," Ryley added.

"Love doesn't seem like a big enough word," Blake said.

"It's the biggest word we have," Toby replied. "I love you all, too. We'll meet again someday, but not for a very long time."

"I'm going to miss you so much, Toby," I whispered, my voice giving out. I pulled Toby to me and held him with all my might. I looked into his eyes, finding a deep glow of absolute beauty, and kissed him softly on the cheek. "Good-bye, Toby."

"Good-bye, Caleb."

Toby walked over to Wendell, who had been silently sitting on the log as we said our good-byes. He looked forlornly at Toby, his time being so short with him.

Toby reached out his hand, offering it to Wendell. "Would you like to come with me?"

Wendell raised his eyes to the boy he'd lost so long ago. "I'm not the boy you once knew, Toby. I'm an old man. You don't really want me to come with you."

"Caleb, to me you look the same as the last time I saw you. You'll always look that way to me. If you come with me now, you'll see for yourself. But that isn't what matters. What matters is that you know you're the one I love, regardless of what you look like. If you come with me, you'll see everyone as I do. You'll see the beauty of their souls."

"But what about the people who don't have beautiful souls?"

Toby shook his head. "You don't have to worry about seeing anything like that."

"Am I really allowed to come?" he asked for reassurance.

"Yes," Toby said warmly. "There is nothing to fear."

Wendell reached out his hand and placed it in Toby's. They walked over to the spruce trees together and turned to face us one last time. Having heard and seen everything that had occurred, we didn't ask any questions. We smiled at them, each of us with fresh tears in his eyes.

"Good-bye, boys. Thank you for all you've done," Wendell said.

I nodded. "It was an honour," I replied.

"Are you ready?" Toby asked his Caleb.

"Yes."

"I love you, Caleb."

"I love you, too, Toby."

They smiled at each other and clutched their hands firmly together. Before our eyes, Wendell went from being an old man to looking as he did when he was sixteen. It happened so gradually, we didn't even realize what we were witnessing until it was accomplished. We watched as the two boys pushed their way between the spruce trees. We listened to hear the sound of voices or footsteps on the snow, but all we heard were the spruce branches waving back into their normal position. Then, silence. We stood, unmoving, as this amazing energy washed over us and, as quickly as it came, disappeared. When it was gone, we knew our friends were too.

None of us spoke or moved, each of us absorbing what had happened. After a few minutes, the silence was broken, but not by any of us. A brilliant stag sauntered through the clearing and drank from the waterfall. His white tail flickered a moment as he saw us, but he didn't rush away. He lapped at the cool waters and then slowly pushed through the trees. I went over to the log and sat down, soon followed by the others. We stayed, listening to the peacefulness of the woods, as everything gradually froze over once more.

Chapter Twenty-Seven

When my father came home after work, he asked if we knew there was a car off the road around the corner. We told him, quite truthfully, that we hadn't seen anything when we came home. To be on the safe side, my father reported it to the police.

When Blake and I returned to our house from taking Ryley and Shane back to their homes, we went out to the barn to attach the plow to the Bronco. As we finished, a police car came down the road and parked in our driveway. Blake and I both knew what that meant. We locked up the garage and got our stories straight before going inside the house.

"Boys, could you come in here, please," my mother called as we took off our boots.

We stepped in to the living room, where an RCMP officer was seated across from my mother. Mom got up when we came in.

"Guys, this is Constable Peterson. He's here about the car your dad found off the road."

Blake and I both shook the constable's hand.

"Have a seat, fellas," he said. "I need to ask you a few questions."

Blake and I sat across from the officer on the sofa. Mom sat on the arm of the couch next to me.

"The car your father reported is owned by a man named Wendell Hildebrand. Your mother tells me you know him."

"Yes, sir. He's Constance Durant's brother," I said.

"And who is Constance Durant?"

"She's the elderly woman we used to visit at Golden Meadows. She passed away last autumn. We met Mr. Hildebrand at the home," Blake said. (We had both agreed to not refer to Wendell by his first name, as it might arouse suspicions.)

"Did you speak to him?"

"Yes, actually, a while later, he invited us to visit him at a friend's house in Angler's Cove," I answered.

"And what did you talk about?"

"Local history, mostly. He grew up down the road a ways from here and had all sorts of stories. He fought in the war, too. I talked to him a lot about that because I was going to do a research paper on World War II for Canadian history," I explained.

"When you last spoke to him, did he seem at all, how do I say this sensitively … senile to you boys? Did he confuse easily?"

"No. He was very sharp. He could remember everything about the war and growing up here," I replied.

"Sometimes older people remember the past well, but the present can be difficult to understand. You sense anything like that at all?"

"No, sir," Blake answered.

"Hmm. Do you have any idea why he would be coming out here?" the officer asked.

"Well, we did tell him to drop by and visit us anytime—though we wouldn't expect him out in weather like this," Blake said.

"No, it does seem strange." The officer shook his head. "We're gonna hafta form a search party and scour the surrounding area. He may have injured himself when he put his car in the ditch and gone looking for help. Mix the bad weather with perhaps being disoriented, chances are, he got lost."

"Is there anything we can do to help?" I inquired.

"Yes. If you could check your property thoroughly for any signs of him, that would be a help, but don't put yourself at any risk and never go searching alone. Stay in pairs and let someone know where you are at all times. Dress warmly and take some supplies with you—flashlights, water, and so on. If you do see anything, let us know right away. We'll be asking the community to assist in finding him. It's already been a few hours and it's bitterly cold, so time is of the essence."

Blake and I exchanged a look that the constable mistook for despair. "Don't lose hope though, guys. Mr. Hildebrand may be somewhere safe. We've been making announcements on the radio for anyone with information to call. He could be on his way back home, for all we know. But if he is out there, we need to find him before the elements prove to be too much."

The officer stood to leave. "Just remember, if you do go searching, be prepared and be careful."

"Yes, sir. We will," I confirmed.

"Thanks for your time."

Mom showed Constable Peterson to the door. As soon as the RCMP's Crown Victoria was out of sight, we made a beeline for the forest, telling Mom before we left. We grabbed our backpack and supplies from previous ventures and wasted no time getting to the clearing and past the spruce trees. After that point, we slowed down.

"Do you think we'll find his body?" I asked.

"I dunno, bud. But if there's a body to find, it should be us who find it."

"Yeah. I don't want a bunch of strangers roaming around back here."

"Me neither."

"I have a feeling I know where Wendell's body is."

"Down below?"

"Yeah."

We trudged down the hill to the wild rosebushes, getting up to our waists in snow at times. When we reached the thicket of thorny bushes, we dug away at the snow so we could slide underneath to where Toby was buried at the centre. As we suspected, Wendell's body was there. The remains were that of an old man, but the smile frozen on his face was young. There was a warm amber glow around us.

"What do we do now?" I asked Blake.

"We've got to make a decision," Blake stated.

I looked at him, already knowing what that decision would entail, but not sure which option was best. He read my thoughts and nodded.

"I know … I'm not sure either."

I took off my cap and ran a hand through my hair. I took a deep breath.

"Okay. We move him. I don't want the cops digging around and take a chance that they might disturb Toby. Let's put him up someplace random—way off the path."

"Good call," Blake agreed. He inhaled loudly through his mouth. "You ready for this?"

"Let's just do what we have to do."

I slid out from under the bushes and pulled the feet of the body as Blake pushed on the shoulders. When we were both on the same side of the bushes, we each took an end, and I led the way, using the same path Toby had shown me months before. Wendell's body was much lighter than I had anticipated, but I didn't comment on it and neither did Blake. We found a location a hundred metres or so from the top of the waterfall and put Wendell's frozen body down. The woods were quiet and deep around us. And then the weather changed. Suddenly the sky opened up, and it began to pour. The rain came down so intensely that, within minutes, all our tracks in the snow were gone. By the time we got home, there would be no trace of where we, or Wendell, had been.

When we returned to the house, it was nearly eight o'clock. Dad was putting on his winter coat when we came in the back door.

"Guys, I was just getting ready to come help you," Dad said.

"No need, Dad. We found him," Blake stated sombrely.

"You did?" Dad asked, shocked. "Is he …?"

"Yeah. Could you please call Constable Peterson? We can take him right to the body."

"Oh God," Mom gasped. "The poor man."

"Are you guys okay?" Dad wanted to know.

"We're fine," I replied. "A little shaken up, but fine." Water teemed from our jackets and caps.

"Okay. I'm gonna call the RCMP. You boys get some warm soup or something in you. I'm afraid it's going to be a long night," Dad said.

Dad went to the phone and called the police as Blake poured us each a cup of coffee. In less than two hours, we were back in the woods, shining our lights on the body of Wendell Hildebrand.

There was little in the way of an investigation. A small article appeared in the provincial section of the newspaper a few days later about Wendell's body being found. It was presumed he had died of exposure after becoming disoriented in the woods.

It was nearing the end of May, and the first full year we'd spent at Wakefield House, when I received a letter in the mail. I opened the envelope to read a letter from the desk of Gregory R. Lesterman, attorney for the late Wendell Hildebrand. The letter was to inform me that I had been designated as responsible for the proper distribution of Mr. Hildebrand's ashes, his mortal remains being temporarily housed at the Stapeton Funeral Home. I was to contact Thomas Archibald, the funeral home's proprietor, for further information.

I called the funeral home and spoke to Mr. Archibald. I could come by anytime to collect the urn and discuss further details with him. I thanked him for the information and hung up the phone. Blake took me into town that evening.

"What about a headstone?" Blake asked Mr. Archibald.

"The only thing Mr. Hildebrand specified was that his ashes were to be held in a vessel made from English oak. There was nothing about a headstone, but if you would like to purchase one, I can show you a wide variety of different options."

"I don't think we can afford anything like that," I said.

"One can always be purchased at a later date, if it's more financially viable."

"Good to know," Blake said.

"If you have questions at any time, please feel free to contact me."

"Thanks. We appreciate it," I told him.

We left the funeral home with the wooden box containing Wendell's ashes. We stopped to pick up Shane and Ryley on the way back to the house.

The four of us took Wendell's ashes to the ring of roses and buried them to the right of where Toby's body lay.

"I was thinking, guys, what if we all went together to buy some sort of marker for them?" Blake suggested.

"Good plan," Ryley agreed.

"Yeah. I've got an idea for it, too," Shane said and told us his thoughts.

"That's perfect. I'll call Mr. Archibald tomorrow and see what something like that will cost," I told the group.

We returned home, our plan set.

That evening, I went with Shane to his place for the night. I picked up the photo I had given him while I lay on his bed and waited for him to come back from brushing his teeth. I put on my glasses to see it more clearly, and I felt my breath catch and my eyes grow wide.

"What's up?" Shane asked as he entered the room.

"Look," I insisted, handing him the photo. "Notice anything different?"

Shane squinted at the picture. "Holy shit."

You could faintly see a reflection in the truck's rear window. The two boys were holding hands.

The first week of summer vacation, the four of us made one last trip together to the roses to set the grave marker. The marker we purchased wasn't very expensive, as it wasn't very big and had no words engraved on it. We had a brass plate engraved that we attached to the monument. It said all that we needed it to say, and I think both Toby and Wendell would have been very happy with it. Blake levelled the small area with a trowel, and Ryley placed a single oak leaf on the ground where Shane and I brought the marker to rest. We stood back, and we each silently recalled the events that led us to that moment.

The rough-edged, small, grey wedge of stone we had purchased sat on the ground at the front of the roses. It simply read:

> ┌───┐
> │ Toby Everett & Caleb Hildebrand   │
> │   Together Forever   │
> └───┘

Shane stared at the marker, and I could tell he was replaying the events of the last year on its granite surface.

Ryley motioned to Blake and said to me, "We're gonna head back. We'll see you at the house, okay?"

"Okay," I replied. "We'll be along in a while."

Blake looked up at the trees and felt the warm breeze on his face. "It's a beautiful day. Take your time."

I smiled at my brother. In typical Blake fashion, he smirked, casually put his right hand in the pocket of his jeans, leaving his thumb exposed, and followed Ryley up the hill toward the path.

"I just can't leave yet ... okay?" Shane asked me softly, his eyes glassy.

"Sure." I put an arm around his waist and gently squeezed him.

The leaves of the forest rustled, and the birds sang above us. Some of the first roses were budding, and there was the faintest fragrance of them in the air. A few bumblebees buzzed about us.

"We'll come back, won't we?"

"Of course, we will."

I kissed my index and middle fingers and reached down, touching the stone with them.

I turned my gaze to Shane and smiled. "Okay?"

Shane nodded and repeated my action, kissing his fingers and then touching the stone. "Yeah."

We walked by the orange shoelace, which had greatly faded, and pushed through the branches of spruce. We felt the spray of the waterfall as we passed, and the warm sun of the clearing shone down on us as we went by the fallen tree.

As we began our ascent to the upper path, I stopped at the base of the old oak tree. I rubbed the initials in the weathered wood.

"They'll always be here," Shane said with a thoughtful smile.

"Yeah," I agreed. I took the marble-handled jackknife from the pocket of my cargo shorts and began to cut into the bark. When I had finished, I turned to Shane and added, "And now, so will we."

We kissed in front of the tree trunk that now displays four sets of initials and two hearts, before joining hands and heading for home.

Made in the USA
Lexington, KY
28 December 2015